WRITE
TO DIE

ALSO BY CHARLES ROSENBERG

Death on a High Floor

Long Knives

Paris Ransom

WRITE

TO DIE

CHARLES
ROSENBERG

THOMAS & MERCER

Published by Thomas & Mercer, Seattle

www.apub.com

Amazon, the Amazon logo, and Thomas & Mercer are trademarks of Amazon.com, Inc., or its affiliates.

ISBN-13: 9781503937611
ISBN-10: 1503937615

Cover design by Dan Stiles

Printed in the United States of America

For Sally Anne, the best wife anyone could ever hope to have.

Chapter 1

SUNDAY

The story began when his phone rang.

He struggled out of a deep Sunday morning sleep, fumbled the phone to his ear, got out "Hello" and heard a deep voice say, "Rory, Joe Stanton. I need to see you."

"Joe, I just saw you on Friday."

"Well, so what? I need you again. My office. Five o'clock."

Rory wanted to say, "It's Sunday, and I have plans." But he knew he had no real choice. Joe's studio, TheSun/TheMoon/TheStars, was his firm's largest client. Joe was the general counsel—the guy who distributed all of the litigation work on which Rory's law firm feasted. But even as he stifled his real thoughts and said, "Okay, see you there," he realized Stanton had already hung up.

***

Rory had been on the studio lot so frequently in the past few years that they had finally caved and given him a drive-on pass, something unheard of for outside lawyers. He flashed it at the guard gate—the security camera would later document that he drove through at 5:06 p.m.—and made his way, via the fake streets used to film cityscapes, to the oddly named Executive Office Structure. There were a few other cars around, but not many, and Rory amused himself by sliding into the slot reserved for the studio head.

Joe's office was on the top floor, and Rory took the steps up, the better to add a little more exercise to his day. His bad knee always did better going up than down. It had surprised him that the entry door into the stairwell was unlocked and annoyed him that he was out of breath by the time he got to the top.

The door to Joe's assistant's office was wide open, and nobody was at the desk—amazing in itself because when Joe was in the office, an assistant was always there, too, day or night. The door to Joe's own office was to the right of the assistant's desk. It was closed.

Rory knocked. When there was no answer, he knocked again, louder, eased the door open and peeked around the edge. Joe was sitting in his leather chair, behind his over-large black granite desk, his body tilted slightly to the left. An ugly black-and-blue bruise spanned his neck from ear to ear, and his swollen tongue protruded from his mouth. Blood clotted in his hair.

What went through Rory's head was remarkably rational, considering that his heart rate had accelerated to twice normal speed. *If I go in there, I'll get my fingerprints and probably my DNA all over everything. And the guy's clearly dead, so I can't help him.*

He closed the door, but not all the way, called 911 on his cell, calmly reported the body and its location and waited. While he waited there in the assistant's office, the door to Joe's office swung entirely open again on its own. He wanted to turn away, but he had the odd feeling it was somehow disrespectful to the body to do that. So he just stared at it until suddenly a breeze, or something, slammed the door shut again.

The 911 call had apparently alerted studio security, as well as the city's emergency system, because within a few minutes a studio cop showed up, out of breath from running up the steps. Rory pointed to the door and tried to say, "Dead," but all that came out was a croak. He tried again and got the word out.

"Anyone else in there?"

"Don't think so, but I'm not sure. I opened the door, but then it closed again on its own. The wind, maybe."

The guard motioned him away, drew his gun, flattened himself to the wall beside the door and, while turning the doorknob with his spare hand, kicked the door wide open. Crouching slightly and holding the gun straight out in front of him, he cleared first the open doorway and then, moving inside, the space to each side of the door. Rory thought it a brave thing. If somebody had been inside with a gun or a knife, the guard could've bought the farm.

"The room's clear," the man said. Then, as if he had not yet really focused on the corpse in the chair, he added, "Oh my God."

Rory heard the sirens as the police and paramedics arrived, and he watched LAPD uniforms stream out of the stairway, consult the studio guard and go through the same routine of clearing the room, guns drawn. Within ten minutes, there were six more people, including men and women wearing white coats with the LAPD insignia stitched above the pockets. Suddenly, yellow crime scene tape was everywhere.

Rory heard the studio guard on his walkie-talkie, telling the front gate, "Don't let any media in here . . . No, nobody, even if they've got a pass . . . They'll be coming soon; they've probably already heard about it on the police scanner. And post somebody on the walk-in gate on the back lot."

A Detective Johnson, according to his nameplate, a big African American guy who was actually taller than Rory's own six foot five, and maybe heavier, too, emerged from Joe's office wearing white bootees and latex gloves. He peeled the gloves off and took out a small notebook. "You the guy who found him?"

"Yeah."

"The other detectives will want to talk to you later. I'll get the basics from you now."

It didn't take long. Rory answered that he didn't know if Joe had any enemies, in part because he didn't know the victim very well.

"Any idea why he wanted to meet with you?"

Rory shrugged. "I'm an outside entertainment lawyer representing the studio in a big copyright case. There's a court hearing going on about it right now. Maybe he wanted to talk about that. But he didn't say. Just said he wanted to see me today."

"I see."

"So, Detective," Rory said, "is there any way he could have . . . choked himself, somehow? Is that possible?"

"Not unless you can strangle yourself and make the rope disappear afterward."

"No sign of it?"

He shook his head. "It was good you didn't go in there. A lot of people would have. How did you have the smarts not to?"

"A long time ago, I was a deputy DA. You learn stuff in that job."

"And now you're—what did you say? An entertainment lawyer?" Without waiting for Rory to confirm, he rolled on: "Hey, have you heard this one?"

Here we go, Rory thought. Even in the middle of a gruesome crime scene.

"What's the difference between a dead lawyer and a dead armadillo in the road, Counselor?"

"I don't know. What?"

"No skid marks in front of the lawyer." He guffawed at his own joke.

Rory had been thinking up good responses to lawyer jokes for years. Maybe this wasn't the time to try one out, but then again, maybe it was.

"That's funny, Detective, but what about this one? How many clients does it take to screw in a lightbulb?"

"Uh, I dunno."

"Well, no one knows, because clients always call their lawyers to come over and help."

"Huh?"

"It's a client joke."

"I gotta think about that one."

"Yes. Do that. May I go now?"

"Yes."

"You have my card. If any of the other detectives need to talk to me, please tell 'em to give me a call."

"I expect they will." He paused. "Say, do lawyers often tell each other client jokes?"

"Nope, but they should."

Rory left Detective Johnson, walked back to his car in the parking lot and opened the door. Then he turned around and threw up on the asphalt, getting some on his pants. When he felt like it wasn't going to happen again, he drove home, cleaned up and tried to eat something. But he wasn't hungry. Then he tried to sleep but found it hard. He finally got up, rummaged in his medicine cabinet and found a bottle of Valium that an old girlfriend had left behind. He took one and fell into a troubled sleep.

Chapter 2

MONDAY MORNING
FEDERAL COURT—CIVIL DOCKET
Broom v. TheSun/TheMoon/TheStars

Xavier X. Cabraal, the oldest federal district court judge in Los Angeles, perched in his chair beneath the Great Seal of the United States. Well-liked and already into the late stages of avuncularity, he cast his rheumy eyes down upon attorney Kathryn Thistle, who was sitting at the plaintiff's table. Kathryn was thin, somewhere in that not-yet-middle-aged place between thirty-five and forty, with a pageboy haircut bleached to a bright platinum.

"Ms. Thistle, I've read your very well-written motion papers, listened to your eloquent arguments and carefully considered what you have had to say on behalf of your client. But, although I haven't fully made up my mind as yet, I'm strongly inclined to deny your motion to enjoin the defendant studio, TheSun/TheMoon/TheStars, from distributing its new movie, *Extorted*."

Scrunched uncomfortably into his much-too-small chair at the defense table, Rory was surprised Judge Cabraal had decided to move directly into his views on the case. He'd half expected him to begin the hearing by mentioning the death of Joe Stanton and offering his condolences to the studio and Joe's friends and colleagues. After all, Joe had been in his courtroom only a few days before. Perhaps the judge thought it awkward in the midst of such a hard-fought case. But it hardly mattered. They were gonna win, which was the best memorial possible for poor Joe.

"May I ask your reasoning, Your Honor?" Kathryn said.

"Assuming a final review of the papers already submitted doesn't change my mind, my written opinion, which I'll draft tonight and file tomorrow, will say that although there may be similarities between the script your client, Mary Broom, allegedly wrote—of which we have at this point only a detailed outline, by the way— and the studio's shooting script for the movie, they are not similar enough to suggest that the studio stole the script. So you will almost certainly not win a copyright infringement suit at trial. As you well know, if I can't conclude that you are likely to win at trial, I can't properly issue an injunction."

"With all due respect, Your Honor—" Kathryn began, rising from the table, clearly agitated.

"Please let me finish, Counsel. Even if an argument can be made that the scripts are more similar than I believe them to be, there is still the fact that, other than your client's bald statement that she submitted the finished script to the studio years ago, there is no corroborating evidence—no cover letter, no receipt, no e-mail, no nothing. And, in fact, no actual copy of the script she says she wrote, just the so-called detailed outline, which in my view isn't very detailed."

"Saying you can't find a written record of something doesn't mean it didn't happen, Your Honor."

"True. But both the studio head and the film's writer-director have flat-out denied in sworn declarations that they ever received or saw your client's script or the outline of it. So there's no proof whatever that either one of them had access to Ms. Broom's script. And how you steal something without getting access to it is a mystery to me."

Rory wasn't the least bit surprised. Kathryn's case had been weak from the start. He wasn't sure why she'd even bothered to bring it.

Meanwhile, half the reporters had left the courtroom so they could tweet the result of the hearing. Rory suspected they were gonna miss the best part, because Kathryn had her fists clenched and had moved to the lectern between his table and hers, directly facing the court.

"Your Honor, permission to speak freely?"

"Well, Counsel, in my experience, you always speak freely, with or without permission, so go ahead."

"Your Honor, the expert whose declaration we filed states that he has never seen two film plots and sets of characters that were so similar unless they were simply two different drafts of the same script. He concludes that the studio's script, which the studio admits was written only two years ago, could only have been copied from my client Mary Broom's earlier detailed outline."

"Yes, Counsel, but I'd have been astounded if your expert had said anything else. Let's face it: sad as it is, experts are paid to say what the lawyers who hire them want them to say. And the studio submitted a declaration by its own expert, who said just the opposite. Plus, to me—and I'm the decider on the similarity issue for the moment—the not-so-detailed outline and the script seem quite different."

Kathryn was quiet for a moment, as if trying to decide if she really wanted to say what she was thinking of saying. She took a deep breath. "Your Honor, candidly, you only think they're different because every judge in this courthouse regards the studios as the home team. No studio has ever lost an infringement case brought by a nobody. And probably never will."

Rory cringed. Kathryn had only last year been sanctioned by the state bar for telling a reporter for the *LA Times* that a certain state judge lacked the smarts needed to peel carrots. She later claimed that the comment was off the record (and had told Rory privately that what she had actually said was that there might as well have been a carrot sitting on the bench). But the state bar didn't care what record the comment was on or off and publically reproved her. It also made her attend twenty hours of continuing legal education ethics training—a fate worse than death, in Rory's view.

Cabraal stared at Kathryn for a few seconds, then burst into laughter.

"Counsel, as I said, it's late in the day, plus this injunction hearing has been hard fought, and we're all tired. Especially a certain eighty-five-year-old judge. Would you like to apologize?"

"I'm sorry, Your Honor. It's just that—"

"Apology accepted."

"But—"

"Stop while you're ahead, Ms. Thistle." He took a sip from a large glass of what he always claimed was Coca-Cola, kept handy on the bench.

Rory looked over at Thistle to see if she would retreat or march forward into danger.

"Thank you, Your Honor," she said.

"Mr. Calburton, since Ms. Thistle has spoken at length, do you have anything you want to add?"

Rory had a lot he wanted to add. Which included leaping up and raining down scorn on Kathryn and her client. He had a well-deserved reputation around the courthouse for an acid tongue. But back when he was a baby lawyer, an early mentor, who had reminded him very much of Yoda, had taught him that if opposing counsel is busy digging himself a deep hole, there ain't no need to grab a shovel and help. So Rory locked his hands behind his head, leaned back in his chair, channeled Yoda and just said, "No, Your Honor. Nothing at all to add."

"In that case I will have the last word," Cabraal said. "And it is this, Ms. Thistle. If you were actually to look into the record of the judges of this court instead of getting your information from TQEN or TMZ or wherever you get it, I think you'd find that they have bent over backward to deal evenhandedly with the powerful and ordinary citizens alike."

"I respectfully disagree," Kathryn said.

"At the risk of continuing this dialogue when I claim to have ended it, Ms. Thistle, do you honestly believe that the plaintiff here, Mary Broom, is a nobody?"

"Yes, when put up against a billion-dollar studio."

"As I recall, she used to be one of the most famous actors on the planet, at least until she disappeared herself to Nepal."

"It was India, Your Honor, and she didn't 'disappear herself.' And she apologizes for not being present today. She's out of the country."

"Well, there's no requirement, of course, that she be here for this type of hearing, in which we take witness testimony only by written declaration. But wherever she was before she filed her lawsuit, and whatever she was doing there, Ms. Broom apparently failed to notice until little over a month ago that 'her' script had been stolen—despite all the publicity the movie has received while it was in production. Which is just one more factor that makes it difficult to enjoin the release of a film on which the studio has spent over a hundred million dollars and which is scheduled to be released late next week. The premiere is in just a few days, I believe."

"Are you going, Your Honor?" she asked.

"You're really pushing it, Counsel." He stood up. "I am not going. I am going back to my chambers, and we're adjourned. I'll send out a written ruling on the motion tomorrow, Wednesday at the latest."

The judge started to move off the bench, then, stopping next to the small door that led to his chambers, turned suddenly and addressed Rory. "Mr. Calburton, I want to offer my condolences to you and your firm for the untimely and tragic death of Joe Stanton. I recall when he was first called to the bar of this court, and he will be missed."

"Thank you, Your Honor," Rory said. He wanted to say something further, but the judge had already disappeared into his chambers. *Why had the judge waited 'til the end to say anything?* He had no clue.

Rory got up and followed Kathryn toward the back of the court-room. He wanted to grab her before she was surrounded by the gaggle of reporters outside. He caught up to her just as she went through the courtroom doors and motioned toward the attorneys' lounge down the hall, where reporters couldn't follow.

Chapter 3

She followed him into the room, and as the distance between them closed, it became apparent just how much Rory, at six foot five, towered over her.

"Let's sit down," she said. "You may be a gentle giant, but you're still a giant."

"I like to stand."

She rolled her eyes. "Fine. So, tell me, Rory, to what do I owe the honor of this *tête-à-chest*? You want to tell me how sorry you are that I lost today?"

"You deserved to lose. What I want to talk about is settling the case."

She cocked her head. "Now, that's interesting. I'm about to lose this injunction hearing, and you're making me a settlement offer. That must mean if we pursue this thing further into discovery, we'll find something that might cause old Double-X to change his mind."

"Trust me, there's not even a crumb of adverse evidence to be found."

"Why is your client so hot to settle, then? Is it because someone bumped off that consummate asshole, Joe Stanton? AKA Mr. Never Settle?"

"Joe's death has absolutely nothing to do with it. Anyway, what do you care why we want to settle?"

"Like I just said, if you're hot to settle, you must be hiding something."

"Well, I'd call us lukewarm to settle. At best. And only because we've got a brand-new studio head. Whatever happened with the script didn't happen on his watch, and he wants the launch of *Extorted* to be flawless and without controversy. That means getting your lawsuit settled, so long as it doesn't cost too much and can be finished up quickly. He's told legal to *get it done*."

"What about you, Rory?"

"Personally? I'd rather not settle at all. Because taking Mary Broom apart on the witness stand—and showing she's the liar I think she is— would burnish my reputation."

"And the acting general counsel?"

It was tempting to tell her the real reason: that the acting general counsel wanted to settle quickly and on the cheap to suck up to his new boss, the better to position himself for Joe's job permanently. It was also tempting to just tell Kathryn the reasons why didn't matter. But he'd found over the years that candor tended to grease the wheels of settlement.

Instead he said, "Fred Service, the acting GC, knows your reputation for prolonging litigation and generating lots of publicity for it along the way. So he knows that even if you lose this injunction hearing—which you're gonna—you still have a shot at getting it to trial, maybe even in front of a jury. That means lots of expense, lots of headaches. Plus, the marketing department is on his ass. They've been shelling it out for this movie, and your lawsuit is distracting from the campaign. Oh, and it's pricey to keep fighting your baseless motions, and Fred assumes those motions will keep on keeping on."

"Because I have a reputation for never giving up 'til the last dog dies?"

"Or the last carrot is crunched."

She smiled. "That was one of my better moments. But you know, my case isn't quite as thin as you believe."

"Oh?"

"You'll see in the next little while. But, hey, I don't want to keep my press waiting, so hurry up and say what you want to say about settlement."

"Bottom line, if this thing can be settled real quick, the studio would be willing to fork over a modest sum—say two hundred fifty thousand dollars—to be rid of the controversy and stop spending money on my law firm."

"The amount's a joke. It would have to be a lot, lot higher. Closer to five million. But what Mary wants, on top of the dollars, is to get back in the game by writing and directing a film, and acting in it, too. The full trifecta."

Rory reared his head back in what he hoped would communicate his astonishment at the demand. "You're saying the number has to be large enough for her to finance production of her own film?" He laughed. "You're talking tens of millions for the kind of film an actress like her would agree to be in."

"You're not understanding. What we want is for the studio to use its own money to finance the film, with Mary as the producer-director. Plus guarantee wide-release distribution and a substantial marketing budget."

Rory closed his eyes and shook his head rapidly back and forth, as if trying to clear it. "That's ridiculous, Kathryn, and you've been around this town and this industry long enough to know it. No movie studio in its right mind is gonna turn the direction and production of a motion picture—released under its name—over to a woman who's never produced or directed one before, or even written a produced script. They'd be better off just giving her a bag of money and being rid of her."

"Ha! You're making a mistake, Rory. Agreeing to our demand would be like Mary paying the studio."

Rory smiled. "This I gotta hear."

"Given her reputation, that film, even with only a twenty-million-dollar budget—we're not asking them to finance a blockbuster—will have boffo box office and make the studio a ton of money. And we still want the five million in cash, of course."

Rory laughed. "Mary Broom is hardly Marilyn Monroe in the public memory, Kathryn. More like Fatty Arbuckle maybe."

"Who's that?"

"Look it up." He was pleased to find something Kathryn didn't know. Maybe he'd send her a copy of a Fatty Arbuckle biography if he could dig one up.

"Well," she said, "in any case, your settlement offer sounds fishy to me. Who, exactly, is authorizing this? I don't want to get caught saying yes for, say, twenty million for the film finance plus five million in cash, to you and this Fred person, only to find later, when we try to nail down the nitty-gritty details, the new studio head isn't really on board."

Rory thought for a moment about what to say. Settlement negotiations were an intricate dance, as much about body language as dollar numbers. When he'd dissed Kathryn's outrageous demand that the studio finance a movie, she had, as he read it, gone back to wanting cash, but at a stupidly high number. An out-of-reach demand like that often meant the other side really didn't want to settle. But watching her react, his gut told him there was interest here. He'd find out.

"Kathryn, do you wanna talk numbers, or shall I just walk away?"

"I need to talk to Mary."

So they *were* interested. But he didn't want to give her any hints, at least right now, that he'd budge off his two hundred fifty thousand offer.

He and Fred had come up with that number as a nuisance settlement, but one carefully calculated to result in a contingent fee for Kathryn in the range of seventy-five thousand to a hundred thousand dollars. That, they thought, would interest her when it looked like her case was going down the tubes.

He chose his words carefully. "Well, Kathryn, take our two hundred fifty thousand offer to your client. If she accepts, I can assure you that the studio head will be on board if we reach a deal that Fred and I both like. And we both like that number."

"Rory, if Joe Stanton were still around—I detested him, but he was at least a man of his word—I'd assume we could reach a deal right now—for a great deal more money, though. I have more trouble with your word and the word of this Fred guy—someone I've never even met. All of which reminds me, rumor has it that you discovered Joe's body. Is that true?"

"I did, but the police told me not to discuss the details." Rory was happy enough to obey, since thinking about it still made him nauseous. He didn't know if he'd ever get the image of Joe dead in his desk chair out of his head.

"I see," Kathryn said. "Well, back to the settlement. Raise your number, Rory."

"I'm not bidding against myself. Make us a specific counteroffer. Personally it'll be fine with me if you don't. I'll enjoy crushing you in this lawsuit."

"I'll talk to my client and think about it."

"Don't think too long. The offer's open only until Wednesday, which ain't far away."

"There's something you should think about, too, Rory."

"What?"

"Yesterday, Mary Broom found a copy of the actual script she wrote and submitted to the studio, not just the detailed outline. It's got Alex

Toltec's handwriting all over it, with suggested changes. So chew on that."

Rory tried hard not to reveal his shock. Alex Toltec had directed *Extorted*. More important, Alex swore to him, not two weeks ago, that he had never seen or even heard about any script or outline written by Mary Broom. He insisted that he had written the entire initial draft entirely by himself. The declaration Rory had drafted for him and submitted to the court said exactly that. Rory had pushed aside any suspicions he might have had—*should* have had, really—when Alex told him he no longer had a copy of his initial draft. That's what you got trusting witnesses you didn't know from Adam.

"Earth to Rory," Kathryn said. "You haven't responded to what I just told you."

"Yeah. I was just thinking how it can't be true. Because we're talking about a supposed script Mary couldn't find at all during the proceedings in front of Judge Cabraal, right?"

"Correct. But now she has."

"Call me skeptical. Fork it over, and if we think it's real—and that it was actually submitted to someone at the studio *before* Alex wrote the script—maybe it will change the settlement numbers."

"I will give it to you as soon as I have it authenticated. It's with an expert now. I should have his report back soon."

"What about a cover letter or e-mail from Mary that went with the script when she supposedly sent it to the studio? Or something back from the studio, like a submission agreement?"

"She's still looking for those, but it's hardly needed, because we're going to prove that it was Alex Toltec who brought the draft script to the studio." She got up, walked to the door and turned around before opening it. "See you at Joe's funeral, Rory."

"You're going? I thought it was by invitation only."

"Gladys and I went to the same college. Twenty-five years apart, but our reunions are always on the same weekend. We met at one of them years ago and became friends."

As Rory watched her leave, he realized he really did want to crush her. The question was whether this supposed business of Alex Toltec and Mary Broom's script was gonna screw it up. If even a little bit of what Kathryn had said was true, the studio could win the injunction hearing and lose the case at trial. Well, that was the wrong way to put it. *He* could lose the case. And look like a fool for having submitted a false witness declaration. Or worse, look like he caused a witness to lie to the court. He needed to go out to Malibu and interview Alex again.

Chapter 4

On the way back to the office, Rory called Alex's cell phone. He left a message: *Please call, urgent.* He left the same message on the home phone. He had a bad feeling about it.

He wasn't feeling great about the settlement discussion, either. He had tried to argue Fred—who'd been on the job for less than a full day—out of making any offer at all. No court was going to enjoin a major motion picture shortly before its scheduled wide release, and for sure not one in Los Angeles. Kathryn Thistle no doubt knew that, too, which would make her highly suspicious of any settlement offer by the studio. Which was exactly what happened.

But Fred had called him right before he left for court and insisted he offer the two fifty. Like a good soldier, Rory had carried out his orders, wrongheaded though they were.

Unfortunately, Kathryn Thistle, despite the mouth on her, was one of the most strategic lawyers in town. She had immediately smelled a rat, which might have been okay, except for the fact that there might actually be one, and it wasn't the Alex Toltec thing.

He shrugged. What was done was done.

The supposedly newly discovered script with Alex's handwriting on it, though, seemed too convenient. Perhaps he should stop worrying about it until he talked to Alex again. On the other hand, he was a worrier. Which, he supposed, was one of the things that had made him a successful litigator and earned him his partnership.

He'd just turned over his car to the valet in the motor court of his firm's high-rise office tower in Century City—the drive from downtown had taken him less than thirty minutes—when he found himself face-to-face with the firm's seventy-five-year-old founder, a man who knew everyone in Hollywood and had been Rory's (mostly unwanted) mentor from the day he'd arrived as an impressively uncredentialed kid, with two years' experience trying sordid criminal cases, who didn't know a movie deal from a blooper reel.

Hal Harold had apparently come down to the motor court lobby to wait for him.

"Rory, congratulations on your win!"

"Thanks, Mr. Harold, although it wasn't much of an earned run. It was so easy I hardly had to open my mouth."

"Nonsense, son. You always underestimate your own skill at this game."

"Maybe."

By then they were in the elevator, heading up to the thirtieth floor. They rode in silence, both aware of the camera in the cab. As soon as they exited into the firm's own lobby, Harold turned to him and said, "Did you pitch settlement?"

"You already knew about that?"

"Sure, the acting GC called me about it early this morning. Fred whatever-his-name-is."

"Fred Service."

"Yes, that guy."

Rory found himself annoyed that Fred had called his boss without even telling him about it. But he pushed it aside.

"Yeah, I pitched it. And just as I feared, Kathryn Thistle instantly saw it as a sign of weakness and thinks there must be something out there to be found."

"Do you think she knows?"

"How could she? We hardly know ourselves."

"That file has to be somewhere, Rory."

"If there ever was one."

"I'm sure there was. Joe Stanton was sixty years old. Not the kind of guy to keep his files electronically. But either way, we'll be better off if someone shredded it or deleted it or whatever. Unless, of course, what was in it is helpful to us."

"You know I'm kinda tired. I'm still a bit flipped out about finding Joe's body. I'd like to go to my office and crash for an hour. If it's okay, Mr. Harold, maybe we can talk later."

"Absolutely. Terrible thing, Joe." He shook his head somberly. "And, Rory, you're a partner now, so it's okay to call me Hal."

"That'll take getting used to after calling you Mr. Harold for eight years."

Hal slapped him on the back. "You'll get used to it. And thanks again for the hard work on the case. Much appreciated."

When Rory entered his office, a young woman was standing there, looking at his law school diploma, which hung on the wall just inside the door. She wasn't just pretty but beautiful—high cheekbones, lovely nose, alabaster skin and the figure of a model back when models were allowed to have hips and breasts. Her eyes were green and wide, without a trace of makeup around them, and the thick hair cascading to the middle of her back was the color of spun gold. His first reaction was that she must be a young actress who had somehow gotten past the firm's heavy lobby security.

He felt himself starting to stare and, feeling embarrassed, looked away and said to the far wall, "Who the hell are you?" When he looked back on it, he attributed his rudeness—not usually his MO—to his discomfort at the impact her mere appearance had on him.

She seemed not to notice his discomfiture and said, "Oh, hi, Mr. Calburton. I'm your new associate, Sarah Gold." She stuck out a nicely manicured hand for him to shake, giving him no choice but to look her directly in the eye and meet her proffered hand with his own.

"Rory Calburton. Nice to meet you."

Her handshake was firm, but not overly so, and certainly not the limp-wristed kind he had half expected.

"It's my first day here," Sarah said, releasing his hand. "Mr. Harold told me to come down to your office and take a seat, that you were on your way back from court. But, uh, there was nowhere to sit except your desk chair"—she made a sweeping motion with that same nicely manicured hand to take in an office otherwise devoid of furniture—"and sitting in your personal chair seemed, uh, not appropriate."

"Oh, sorry about that. I just got made partner. The promotion comes with a new, bigger office and fancier furniture. It's supposed to come later today. And you can call me Rory, by the way. The only person around here who's known as mister is Mr. Harold. At least for associates."

"An odd tribal custom."

"Huh?"

"Oh, apologies—I majored in cultural anthropology, so I'm always looking at things through that lens."

"You'll find a lot of odd things to study here."

"I'm sure."

He smiled. "Let's go down the hall to the small conference room, where there's more than one chair."

Once they got there, Rory said, "I saw you on the list of new associates, but I just recently came back from a six-month sabbatical, so I wasn't here when you interviewed. So I don't know anything about you."

"Where did you go on sabbatical?"

"I went to a camp in Arizona where they teach you to drive race cars, and then I went to a boxing camp. And it turns out that boxing with a bum knee isn't such a great idea. So, last but not least, I went to a place in the sun to let my bruises heal."

"Wow. You sound competitive."

"Only on the outside, Sarah. Inside I'm a cream puff, but I have to do all this macho stuff to keep the cream from leaking out."

She smiled. "That's a very awkward image."

"I suppose," he said. "I failed Metaphors 101. Anyway, please tell me about yourself."

"Just free-associate?"

"Uh-huh."

"Well, I grew up in Manhattan, I went to Bob Jones University and then—"

"The Christian school?"

"Yes."

Rory knew he was now on treacherous ground, given all of the firm's policies about discrimination, not to mention state and federal law, but he plunged ahead. "So you're religious?"

"I'd say that at this point in my life—I just turned thirty—I'm spiritual. And still somewhat culturally conservative."

"Okay." He had no idea what all that meant but decided he'd best change the topic.

Before he had the chance, though, she said, "Mr. Calburton—I mean, Rory—you really don't need to worry about any of that."

"What makes you think I'm worried?"

She smiled a broad smile, showing perfect teeth. "You furrowed your brow when I said I'd gone to Bob Jones."

"Sorry. It's just that it's . . ."

"Unusual around here?"

"Something like that."

"I think you'll find me unusual in a number of ways. Good ways, I hope."

Rory decided to steer back to more traditional interview questions. "And after college, what?"

"I went to law school at Georgetown."

He paused, wondering if he should really ask. But then he went for it. "You didn't get into Harvard or Yale?"

"I did. But I was interested in government, and I decided DC was the place to be for that."

"Well, we do have a government here in California, that's for sure. But it's not like the one they've got in Washington, so you may be disappointed."

She gave a small shrug. "Toward the end of law school, I lost interest in government. I'm much more interested now in entertainment law."

Rory smiled. "A lot of law students think entertainment law is interesting. But it can be dull, believe me. So, what'd ya do after law school?"

"I clerked for Judge Raymond Fisher on the ninth circuit and then for the Chief Justice."

"Of the United States?"

"Yes, that one."

"Quite a glittery resume."

"Yes, I suppose it is, but I know I have to earn my way here like everyone else."

"Glad to hear it." As he said it, he thought how enormously pompous he sounded. Maybe to hide the fact that he found this woman enormously attractive. "But in any case, you're a prize for the firm, obviously. You must have had a lot of offers."

"I did, but I decided I wanted to go to an entertainment litigation firm. This one has a reputation for being the best in the city, and I got good vibes when I was here interviewing."

"Good. Well, I'm working on an interesting case right now, and I've already got one associate working with me, but if it goes forward to trial, I'll need some more help. So let me tell you about it."

"May I ask you about yourself first?" she said.

"Just free-associate?"

She laughed. "Fair is fair, so yes. And maybe you'll have to look at me when you talk about yourself, like when we shook hands."

"I'm sorry. It's just that . . ."

"It's not the first time I've had this problem. Men, well, not just men, but women, too, some of them just stare, which is uncomfortable. But some, like you, look away, and I don't like that, either. I'm just a normal human being, you know."

"Alright," he said, looking directly at her. "I grew up in LA, on the west side. Went to a snotty private high school and then to college at Pomona."

"Where you played football?"

"How did you know?"

"Well, you're very tall, but . . . uh, I wonder if I really want to say this."

"Oh, go ahead."

"Not that graceful when you move. So I'm guessing football."

"You'd be right. I was a star until I wrecked my right knee in a way that's been difficult to fix, which may account for the lack of grace. I was benched at the end of my sophomore year, and then I dropped out and never finished college anywhere."

"Is that why you went to a law school I've never heard of? I was looking at your diploma on the wall."

"Yeah. The Chester A. Arthur School of Law. You didn't need a college degree to get in. It's up in Sylmar, near Magic Mountain. The students and alums call it Chet."

"Did you, uh, like Chet?"

"Not as much as I would have liked going to Georgetown." Despite his success at The Harold Firm, he still had a bit of a chip on his shoulder about where he had gone to law school. Not to mention how he'd gotten hired at The Harold Firm.

"I'm sorry," she said. "I didn't mean to . . ."

"It's more my problem than yours, Sarah."

Just then his cell rang, and he glanced at it. "It's the receptionist, so let me see why she's trying to track me down." He put the phone to his ear. "Yeah? Okay, I'm in Conference Room Two. Please put him through to the phone in here. It's got better reception."

When he hung up, he nodded at the phone on the conference table. "That's going to be the Chief Judge of the US district court. Can't think of any good news he might be calling with."

The phone rang a couple of seconds later. "Yes, sir, good afternoon." He paused. "Oh my God, I'm so sorry to hear that. I know you were close. My condolences and those of our firm." He listened again. "With all due respect, sir, can't you assign it to yourself?"

There followed a much longer pause as Rory listened again. "I see. Alright we'll be there at eight a.m. tomorrow. And, again, I am so sorry to hear this news." He slammed the phone back into its cradle. "Shit."

"What happened?"

"Judge Cabraal, who was about to rule in our favor in the preliminary injunction hearing in the Broom case earlier today? He tripped in his chambers, right in front of his clerk, and hit his head on the desk. He was DOA at the hospital."

"Before putting anything in writing?"

"Yup."

"Can't the Chief Judge simply read the transcript and enter the order?"

"In a sane world, yes. But, unfortunately, Judge Cabraal didn't actually rule. He only said he was *leaning toward* denying the plaintiff's motion."

"Bummer."

"It is. So instead the presiding judge is assigning the case to a new judge. A very new judge."

"Who?"

"Nicola Franklin."

"Is that a problem?"

"Well, she was sworn in as a federal judge only two weeks ago, and before that she was one of the city's most prominent personal injury lawyers, which means she knows zippo about entertainment and copyright."

"Won't she be able to get up to speed on it? Most people appointed to the federal bench are smart."

"Yeah, but there are other problems."

"Which are?"

He heaved a sigh. "A few years ago, she ran unsuccessfully for a state court judgeship that opened up. And I contributed a healthy sum to one of her opponents, who won."

"That doesn't sound good."

"Nope, it's not."

"What was the other problem?"

"We don't do personal injury cases around here, but a few years ago I represented a friend who was a defendant in a PI case where he didn't have insurance. And I said something rather unkind to her in a settlement conference."

"What was it?"

"I think I'll decline to remember. It's embarrassing. Anyway, change of topic. Have you already taken and passed the California bar?"

"Yes. And I'm admitted."

"Maybe I can send you to argue the Broom matter."

"I, uh, don't have much courtroom experience."

"Sarah, you gotta start somewhere."

"You're not serious."

"I think I might be. Let's go back to my office, and I'll give you some of the materials and the password for the online files so you can get acquainted with the case."

"What about the associate you mentioned who's already working on it? Wouldn't he be better suited for this?"

"He just left for a safari in South Africa. His first vacation in five years. Won't be back for three weeks. I let him go because I thought this case was about to go into a slow period for a month or two."

She looked at him, stricken. "Okay, well, I guess if I have to do it, I will."

Rory leaned back in his chair and laughed uproariously. "I *am* just kidding, Sarah."

"Thank goodness. Is the other associate really in South Africa?"

"That part is true."

"Okay."

"Sarah, I'm genuinely sorry." He shook his head. "I can't seem to help playing practical jokes, and some of them can get a little mean. It's a way to let off steam, and today I'm more than a bit stressed out."

"May I ask why?"

"Because yesterday the general counsel of the defendant company in the case—our biggest studio client—was murdered."

"Oh my God, that's terrible."

"What made it worse was that I found the body. I went there for a late afternoon meeting and found him dead in his desk chair."

Sarah leaned toward him. "I'm so sorry. That must have been enormously stressful. Have you seen someone to talk about it?"

"You mean like a therapist?"

"Yes, or a close friend."

Rory thought about it for a moment before responding. "Well, no. It didn't occur to me that I needed to. I had a big hearing this morning, so I prepared for it and went to court." He considered telling her about throwing up and about his difficulty going to sleep that night, but decided against it. It wasn't the kind of thing he shared with people. Instead, he said, "Life doesn't stop just because you find someone dead."

Rory found he was looking down at the conference table.

Sarah started to move her hand toward him, as if she were thinking of taking his hand to comfort him, but then seemed to think better of it and withdrew. "Rory, life may not stop for the world because you find someone dead, but, trust me, it stops for you until you deal with it."

"You sound like you have experience."

"Not exactly, but close enough to know you need to find someone to talk with about it."

"Maybe you're right."

"Were you close to him?"

"No. In fact, I didn't much like him. He was kind of . . . I hate to speak ill of the dead. Let's just say he wasn't a nice person."

"Oh."

"Let's go back to the case for a moment. Just to be clear, you don't have to study up on it big-time right now. Just skim the papers so you'll have some context, and come along to the hearing. It will be educational for you."

"Alright, I will. But please consider finding someone to talk to."

"I'll think about it."

***

After Sarah left, Rory walked back to his office and called Hal Harold, who answered on the first ring. Which was odd, because usually his secretary picked up.

"Hi, Mr. Harold, I'd like to drop by your office. I need to bring you up to date on something."

"Hmm. I'm kind of busy with someone here who's working on something right in my office. Why don't I come by yours instead?"

"That would be fine, Mr. Harold."

"Okay, I'll be there shortly. And please, call me Hal."

As Hal stepped through Rory's doorway a few minutes later, Rory thought he saw a man in a police uniform, gunbelt and all, moving down the hallway.

"Hi," Rory said. "Was that a cop?"

"Yeah. LAPD. I was just talking with him. They think poor Joe Stanton was murdered in some kind of private feud, so they're investigating."

"Don't they usually send detectives to do that? That guy was wearing a uniform."

"I don't really know."

"What did he want to know?"

"They're interviewing Joe's close friends to find out if he had any enemies."

"How could anyone that dumb have enemies?"

"He wasn't dumb, Rory."

"Sorry. Well, did he have any enemies?"

"None that I can think of. Although his marital situation was maybe a little complicated."

"Should I ask?"

There was a pause as Hal seemed to think about it for a moment. "No," he said at last. "The guy's dead, so it's best left unspoken."

"But you did tell the police about it."

"Sure. Anyway, what's on your mind?"

"Well, Mr. Harold—excuse me, *Hal*—there's some bad news."

"What?"

"Double-X fell, hit his head and died. The Chief Judge is giving the case to Nicola Franklin."

"I'm very sorry to hear that about Judge Cabraal. I didn't know him well, but he always seemed a fine human being. But Jesus, Rory, did we hedge our bets with Judge Franklin?"

"What do you mean?"

"I mean when she was running for that state court judgeship several years ago, did we contribute to both her and her opponent?"

"I have no idea. I was just an associate back then. I did what I was told, which was to contribute to her opponent. The max permitted."

"Alright, alright, I'll need to check into it. But maybe we need to think about replacing you on the case, at least for now."

"I'm thinking of sending Sarah Gold."

"Really?"

"No, not really. I'm joking."

"That might actually be a good idea. She doesn't know anything yet. So it would be easier for her to avoid talking about something she doesn't know about."

"Sooner or later it's gonna surface."

"Sure, but not 'til after the movie opens and is well on its way to a two-hundred-million-dollar-plus box office."

"Hal, why don't you go yourself?"

"Mind if I smoke a cigar?"

"Suit yourself. I mean it's against the rules. But hey, who am I to tell you not to?"

"Right, who are you?" He laughed and pulled a cigar and a silver lighter from his coat pocket. He flicked the little wheel on the lighter and rotated the cigar in the resulting flame, drawing on it 'til the tip glowed red. Then he looked up at the ceiling and exhaled a fat stream of smoke.

"Rory, to answer your question. Why don't I go myself? I haven't been in a courtroom in more than forty years. My job is to know every studio head, big-deal producer, hot director, great casting director and major actor in town. Your job is to go to court for those people when it's needed."

"So you've told me now at least once each year for the eight years I've been here."

"And so I will continue to remind you—and others—until I'm carried out of here in a box."

Rory suppressed a smile as he pictured himself as one of the pallbearers. "Well, Hal, let's hope that's not too soon. But it reminds me, I assume you're going to Joe Stanton's funeral tomorrow?"

"Of course. In fact, I'm the main eulogist."

"What time is it happening?"

"At ten a.m. See you there."

Chapter 5

TUESDAY MORNING

The funeral was in the big Methodist church on Wilshire Boulevard, just a couple of miles down the road from the firm's offices in Century City. Rory was intentionally late, hoping that the event would be mostly over by the time he got there. He stood briefly and scanned the crowd for Kathryn Thistle, but failed to spot her. Finally, he slipped into an empty pew in the back just as the minister was finishing his eulogy and Hal was walking toward the lectern to speak.

Hal looked down at the flower-covered coffin in front of him and said, "My friends, all of us who knew Joe Stanton during his almost twenty-five years as general counsel at TSTMTS—the longest anyone has ever served in that role—knew his dedication to his job, his reverence for his sainted mother before she passed from this earth and the affection he showered during his too-brief lifetime on his numerous nieces and nephews." He nodded at the young men and women in the front row of pews.

Rory felt someone slide into the pew beside him. It was Sarah.

"Why are you here?" he asked. As soon as he said it, he realized it sounded abrupt.

She seemed not to notice, leaned over close and whispered, "Mr. Harold suggested I come. He said it would be educational for me because all of Hollywood would be here."

"Okay. Although the funeral's been held on such short notice that a lot less than all of Hollywood is here. But you may see a few bigwigs."

"Why is it being held so quickly?"

"I heard someone say the church is closing for renovations tomorrow, and Joe's widow wanted it to be here at their longtime church and not in some temporary place."

He turned his attention back to the lectern, where Hal was saying, "We all know of Joe's love of Shakespeare—he was a great supporter of Shakespeare in the Park *and* The Bard for High School—as well as his famous and fabulous collection of the early folios. But not many of you know, as I do, that his favorite play was *Julius Caesar*. And just as Caesar was taken from the Romans by a brutal killing, so, too, has Joe been taken from us. Although we do not yet know who did the deed, I'm sure we will soon enough." He nodded to the chief of police, who was seated in the second row.

Then he continued. "Today I thought it appropriate to modify Mark Antony's words from the play a bit and say, 'We come today not only to bury Joe Stanton, but to praise him.'"

Sarah leaned over again. "Whom do you suspect?"

"No one. I'm a lawyer, not a detective."

"But aren't you at least curious?"

"Not really. Like I told you before, I didn't like him. He was kind of a schmuck."

She nodded off to their right. "You see those three cops over there? Do you think they're here looking for the killer?"

"I couldn't tell you."

A narrow-faced woman in the row in front of them turned halfway around. "Shh!"

Sarah looked past the woman and asked Rory, "Who's the woman in the front row who's sobbing so hard we can hear her back here?"

"The one in a black veil?"

"Yes."

"That's Gladys, the widow."

The blade-faced woman who'd shushed them turned fully around and said, "Would you please shut up?"

"Let's get out of here," Rory said. "You can meet all of Hollywood later."

Sarah's apartment was in Westwood, not many blocks from the church. She had walked, so they took Rory's car back and ended up at a Starbucks not far from where she lived. Once seated with coffee, Sarah said, "So, Joe Stanton was a schmuck, huh? Yesterday, I thought you were about to say that he was an asshole."

"He was both."

"But finding his dead body upset you anyway? You weren't happy to find him dead?" She grinned.

"No, have you ever found a dead body?"

She blinked. "Uh, no."

"And just so you know, Sarah, the police have told me I am not a suspect."

"I wasn't suggesting you were. But I'm curious. What made him such a bad person?"

"Why didn't I like him? Well, did you see *The Godfather*?"

"Every educated person has seen it."

He laughed. "I don't know about that. But do you recall the lawyer in that film, the consigliere?"

"Sure. Tom Hagan."

"Very good. Well, Joe was like a consigliere to the studio, but even more powerful than Hagan. And longer lived. He was there for twenty-five years, through six different studio heads. So he knew a lot of secrets about a lot of people, and he wasn't above using them to the studio's advantage. And to his own."

Sarah's eyes had lit up. "What kind of secrets? And did any affect you? Is that why you didn't like him?"

"Let's leave that discussion for another day. Did you have a chance to look at the injunction papers? Anything I can clarify?"

"I looked mostly at the fact sections, not the endless discussions of the law. And some of the facts are, well, strange."

"For example?"

"One of the basic questions in the case is whether the studio has any record of receiving a script from Mary Broom, right?"

"Right. And we said we don't."

"I saw that. But the key declaration, from the studio's head of business affairs, says only that she found no record of a script having been submitted."

"So?"

"Well, logically, I'd think that a declaration like that would detail what she did to search: to whom she spoke, what electronic records she queried and so forth. It doesn't say any of that. It just says she didn't find anything."

"And this troubles you?"

"Sure. For all I know, she found nothing because she looked only in her top desk drawer."

Rory was impressed at her insight. A lot of young lawyers, taught in law school to focus on the law, would tend to pass over odd fact patterns. He looked around and saw there were people sitting within earshot. "Let's take a walk around the block."

They walked, and Rory talked. "Sarah, you're perceptive. But here's the deal. I wrote the declaration about the search, and the head of business affairs signed it. She's not sophisticated about this stuff, and she had no problem signing it because it's true that she found nothing."

"Did you ask her what kind of investigation she did?"

"Uh-uh."

"Why not?"

"I didn't want the studio pinned down at that point."

"I'm confused."

"It has to do with the funeral we just walked out of."

Sarah blinked at him. "Now I'm really confused."

"The Friday before Joe Stanton died, I met with him about the case, and he told me he had done a quiet investigation of the supposed script submission and had found 'some interesting things.' He said he still had a little work to do on the file over the weekend, but he'd have his assistant personally bring it to me on Monday."

"Was that unusual, the personal delivery by his assistant?"

"Very. Normally, he would have had it scanned and e-mailed to me. Or if it was that sensitive, he would have had it messengered. In fact, I assumed he asked me to come in on Sunday to pick up that file."

"Did you tell the police that?"

"I told them I didn't know why he wanted to see me because he never said. I saw no point in speculating about it."

"Doesn't somebody in his department have the file?"

"No one seems to even know about it, and his assistant, Sylvie Virtin, has disappeared. I tried to find her yesterday after the hearing, but no one at the studio seemed to know where she was or how to reach her."

"Was she his assistant or his secretary?"

"Assistant. No one in Hollywood calls them secretaries anymore."

"Are the police looking for her?"

He stopped and looked down at her. "Why are you asking me for all these details?"

She raised her eyebrows in surprise. "Because you asked me to work on the case. I'm just trying to find out what's going on."

"Okay, I'm sorry. I'm just still a little on edge, I guess." They walked on. After taking a moment to gather his thoughts, he said, "I got in touch with the police yesterday. And they are looking for her. They told me she's not a target or a suspect, just a witness. But they also said she's not been home since early Monday morning. She apparently left not long after I found Joe's body."

"Which was when, exactly?"

"A little after five on Sunday."

"Do you know Sylvie well?"

He thought about it for a second. "I've seen her a lot over the years, but I can't say I really know her."

"Have you ever been to her house?"

"Once. I went to a dinner party she had. She was trying to fix me up with a friend of hers. Didn't work out."

"Why don't you go to her house and look around yourself? I bet that's where the file is."

"I'm still not a detective."

"Perhaps I'll go, if you give me the address."

"Now you're a PI?"

"Yes, I actually am. I started in college as a way to make some extra money. Found a training program not far from school, and then I really got rolling making money during law school. Lots of money."

"That college let you do that?"

"They didn't know about it. I got it done during vacations, school breaks and weekends when I was off visiting my parents."

"Your schools were in South Carolina and DC, right?"

"Yes. I ultimately got licensed in both jurisdictions. Then when I came out here for my ninth circuit clerkship, I managed to get waived into a California license and also wangled a California concealed-carry permit. It was a hat trick to get it done, but I did."

Rory considered the possibility that she was putting him on. "Seriously?"

"You're kind of shocked, aren't you?"

"More surprised. I mean it's tough to imagine someone so young being truly effective at that."

"Rory, a beautiful woman—and I know I'm beautiful, at least for this brief moment in time—can pretty much go anywhere and talk to anyone if it needs to be done in person, especially if you can feign being vulnerable. Being young can make it even more effective. And hey, I'm smart, too, you know? Plus the Internet—the main tool of the trade—doesn't care who you are."

"Weren't you afraid?"

"Like I said, I have a concealed-carry permit."

"Do you actually carry a gun?"

She stopped and looked around to see if there were people near them. Seeing no one, she turned toward him and hiked up her skirt. "Sometimes."

What he saw was a small silver handgun in a shiny black holster strapped to her very pretty thigh.

He stared at it. "Wow." His mouth had gone a little dry.

She dropped her skirt and laughed. "You can stare at that part of me, huh? No problem?"

His face turned red, and he said, "That's really unfair, Sarah. Any guy would enjoy looking at that." He tried to recover by turning back to practicalities. "Is having a gun truly helpful to a PI?"

"It's a psychological crutch, really. If someone were pointing a gun at me, I couldn't get mine out of that awkward holster in time to do much about it."

"What about when the someone else doesn't have a gun?"

"I might well have the advantage."

"Did you wear that to the office yesterday?"

"No, of course not. I tend to wear it when I'm going to be in a large crowd, like the funeral today, or when I think the situation is threatening for some other reason."

"I see. Well, in any case, time to get back to work."

"Yes, but a favor, Rory. I still have a few things to take care of with my apartment—a few errands to run and so forth. Can I take the afternoon off?"

"Sure. There's not a lot to do at the moment in any case. Be at the firm tomorrow morning by seven, and I'll take you with me to 'the hearing before the new judge."

"I'll be there."

"Sarah?"

"Yes?"

"Don't go to Sylvie's house."

"I can hardly do that, since you haven't told me where she lives."

Chapter 6

Sarah had, in fact, already finished furnishing her tiny apartment in Westwood the weekend before, and she had no errands to do. What she had in mind instead was a small adventure, something that could be finished in the remaining part of the day and wouldn't expose her to any danger. Well, okay, that wouldn't expose her to too much danger. Because the truth was that she had been an adventure junkie since the night of her twelfth birthday, when she had first climbed out of her bedroom window and not come back 'til first light, her parents none the wiser. Back then, the only danger had been the risk of getting caught. But over the years, she had found that a little more danger than that was needed to generate the proper frisson.

The obvious thing to do was to find Joseph Stanton's assistant, Sylvie Virtin, or, failing that, to at least find the file she had so clearly taken with her. And if Sarah found the file, she'd certainly have helped Rory's case out.

Rory had uttered the woman's name—Sylvie Virtin—but had said nothing about where she lived. A few minutes online had solved that problem—Sylvie lived in a neighborhood not far from LAX—and Sarah had then quickly surveilled the property on Google Street View and Google Earth. Fortunately, Sylvie's residence was not an apartment but a stand-alone house on a street where the neighboring houses were not close by. And there were a lot of trees. Best of all, it was within walking distance of a bus stop.

Before leaving, she used her iPad to look up Sylvie's Facebook account, which was, surprisingly, public—totally open to anyone to look at. A collection of photos showed her to be a slim woman, probably somewhere in her sixties, once likely stunning, who had allowed her hair to go mostly gray and her face to wrinkle with no obvious attempts to roll back its age. One picture showed her standing between Joseph Stanton—who was tagged by name in the photo—and a famous actor, but other than that there was no hint she worked anywhere near the movie business. She had only fifty Facebook friends, which suggested she wasn't exactly a power user. The "work and education" line said, simply, "secretary." Sarah tried to figure out her exact age, but Sylvie had avoided giving her high school graduation date or revealing anything else that would nail down how old she was.

The pictures and timeline on the Facebook account also suggested that Sylvie was without husband or children but had nieces and nephews on the East Coast. One niece in particular looked as if she might do for what Sarah had in mind.

She checked online and saw the police still hadn't located Sylvie. Which meant, as far as Sarah was concerned, that she had either fled or died. In either case, she wasn't likely to be at home.

By the time the bus got Sarah to Sylvie's, it was midafternoon. She walked to the house, which was a one-story stucco bungalow with a red tile roof. The green lawn and flower beds visible on Google Street View had been ripped out, no doubt in response to the California drought, and replanted with a collection of succulents. A large lemon tree still stood to the left of a small set of concrete steps that led to the solid wood front door.

She was about to walk up the steps when she noticed a short Asian woman and a tall, bald, bearded Caucasian man coming toward her on the sidewalk, pushing a stroller with a baby aboard. He was wearing mirrored sunglasses and an open-collar green shirt. They were deep in conversation and seemed not to notice her.

Sarah took out her cell phone and pretended to check it while she waited for them to pass by. As they did, she caught a glimpse of the baby. She couldn't see it all that well because it was swaddled in a blanket, but it looked odd. In fact, she could have sworn it was a doll, but she didn't want to stare and call attention to herself. Why would adults be walking a doll in a stroller? Well, this was Los Angeles.

She waited until the couple was out of sight, looked around to make sure no one else was nearby, marched up the steps and rang the bell. She heard it chime inside, but no one came. After a while, she knocked loudly but still got no response. She turned the doorknob, using her coat sleeve to keep from putting her fingerprints on it, but it was locked.

A concrete walkway led around the side, and she followed it to the back of the house. She walked up the steps to the back door, which had a small, uncurtained window. She peered in and saw an orderly kitchen with bare counters and no signs of disturbance. Again using her coat sleeve, she tried the doorknob. It turned, and she pushed the door open. She stood there on the threshold, asking herself the same question she'd had every time she'd done something risky since childhood: Why am I doing this?

She had by now learned the technical answer, of course. She had what the shrinks called ICD—impulse control disorder. Yet the label didn't explain what the underlying cause was. She only knew that she got off on the thrill.

This time, though, the stakes were higher than usual. Entering a house without the permission of the owner, even if the door was unlocked, was a crime if you entered with the intent to steal something or commit some other felony. But even if she could wiggle out of a felony charge by proving she didn't intend to steal anything, going inside would still be at least a misdemeanor criminal trespass. And that was the kind of misdemeanor that would put not only her license to practice law at risk but her private investigator license as well.

She went in anyway.

Inside, the house was what she expected. The kitchen had been redone sometime in the 1970s—you could tell from the yellow Formica counters and the avocado-green appliances. The living room and an adjoining small dining room featured heavy oak furniture in a vaguely Mexican style. The walls were adorned with bullfight posters, and there was a tall oak bookcase in the living room, perhaps three feet wide, every shelf completely stuffed with books.

When she walked into the bedroom, the double bed—not queen-size, she noted—was neatly made, with a red bedspread pulled all the way up over the pillows. A nightstand and a small lamp stood to one side. A blond dresser stood against one wall, with a louver-doored closet across the room from it.

She took a pair of plastic surgical gloves out of her briefcase—she had carried a briefcase instead of a purse, so that she might look more like a professional, as though coming to call on a client—and skinned them on. She stood there and considered the possibilities. She had taken a course in PI school called, "Where Do People Hide Things?" Americans, the instructor had remarked, were amazingly predictable. The most likely hiding place for things other than drugs, he had said, was almost always in the bedroom, mostly likely in an underwear or sock drawer.

She carefully opened each drawer on the blond dresser and went through them, one by one.

The first drawer held Sylvie's underwear, which was, she noticed, rather plain—white bras and panties, plus a couple of pairs of stockings shoved in the back that looked as if they'd not been worn in years. To one side there were also a dozen or so pairs of socks in various muted colors. But there was nothing else there, so Sylvie, if she had hidden anything, was not predictable.

Sarah had brought a small camera with her, and she methodically photographed what was in the drawer before she closed it. It was another thing she had learned to do in PI school—although the photos had never proved to be of any use. Still, she did it.

The second drawer held blue, green and red sweaters, mostly cashmere, the third, carefully folded blouses, all of them white and conservative. Neither drawer yielded anything of interest.

The fourth drawer looked more promising. It was filled with paper. Rifling through it, she found a 1982 high school diploma from University High in West Los Angeles, and a 1986 bachelor of arts diploma from Occidental College in Eagle Rock. So Sylvie was a local girl. More interesting was a playbill from 1985 showing her in a leading role in a local playhouse production of *Oklahoma!*. A girl with showbiz dreams, apparently. But amid all of the other papers, which were mainly photos, family mementos and old utility bills, there was nothing related to the studio or the movie.

She crouched down and looked under each drawer, under the dresser itself and then under the bed. Nothing.

Hearing what sounded like a creak in a floorboard, Sarah stood stock-still and listened. After a minute, having heard nothing further, she continued her search. The closet contained a rack of business-appropriate suits, all on wooden hangers, followed by more casual clothes on wire hangers, plus three garment bags, zippered closed. She opened each, but found only clothes suitable for visiting a much colder climate than Los Angeles. There was nothing stashed in the bottoms of the bags.

More interesting were the suitcases. There were two matching blue roller bags, one very large, one quite small. Between them was a space that could have held a third, medium-size bag. Sure enough, a depression in the carpeting outlined where the middle bag had been, presumably recently. So Sylvie had apparently had time to pack before she left, which probably ruled out violence in her disappearance.

She heard the creak again and stopped and listened again, but it didn't repeat. Just the cooling of the house as the outside temperature began to drop. She went quickly through the two suitcases and again found nothing. Then she patted down the bedspread and pillows to be sure nothing bulky was hidden inside or under them.

In the kitchen she checked in the oven, refrigerator and freezer—the last another place her instructor had said modern Americans often stashed secret things. She looked quickly in the kitchen drawers and cabinets, of which there were many. She also checked the bathroom, including under the lid of the toilet, but again found nothing. She skipped the toilet bowl, where people sometimes hid bags of drugs suspended on a string into the pipe, because she wasn't looking for drugs.

She went back into the living room and scanned the bookshelves. Inside a book, the instructor had said, was a very, very favorite place for small, secret papers. But was the file she was looking for small? She had pictured it, in her mind's eye, as lodged in a manila folder. And in any case, there were hundreds of books.

She looked carefully at the bookshelves. They were dusty, but she noticed a relatively dust-free spot in front of a single book on the second shelf, a hardback copy of a novel called *Pleasures and Days*, a work of Proust's she'd never heard of. She pulled it off the shelf, and it immediately fell open to a 5″ × 8″ photo lodged between the pages. It showed a much younger Sylvie sitting side by side with Joseph Stanton on poolside chaise lounges with an expansive lanai and palm trees behind them. They were drinking what looked to be martinis and grinning broadly at the camera. They were both stark naked.

She turned the photo over. On the back, in blue ink, someone had written, "Soon, together always." It was signed, "Love, Joe," with the *o* in Joe turned into a smiley face and with a small goatee sketched under the *e*. She dropped it into her jacket pocket and reshelved the book.

"Oh, how dumb of me!" She said it out loud and immediately pulled the book back off the shelf. All this time, she had been searching for a physical file, but it had finally dawned on her that—duh—even for someone as old as Joe Stanton, a file could just as easily be stashed on a flash drive. She should have focused on that possibility to start with.

She peered into the empty space where the book had been but saw nothing. She reached into the hole and fished behind the other books on the shelf with her fingertips. To the right she felt something and pulled it out. It was indeed a flash drive, and it said "64 Gigabytes" on the side. She held it up to the light to see if she could make out an identifying mark of some kind. There was nothing.

"I'll take that," a deep voice said as a hand reached out and deftly lifted the flash drive from her fingers.

She whirled around to face a middle-aged man who held the flash drive up in front of her, as if taunting her to try to get it back. Which she was actually considering until she looked more carefully at him. He was perhaps five foot ten, his head shaved completely bald, and his chin sported a salt-and-pepper goatee. He was wearing combat boots, shorts and a red wifebeater T-shirt, which showed off intimidatingly buff upper arms, no doubt capable of beating almost anyone but most certainly her. She'd never get her gun out in time.

"I think," he said, "I'm going to need a no-bullshit explanation of what you're doing here."

Chapter 7

Instead of responding to the man's demand, Sarah just stood there and stared at him. Experience had taught her that investigations were filled with one-on-one confrontations and that strategic silences could prove useful. They not only put most people off balance, but, more importantly, they gave you time to think. Which she sorely needed, because she couldn't, in the instant, come up with any good options.

One, which she seriously considered, was to turn on her heel and leave. It had the benefit of disclosing nothing and just might protect her identity, particularly if Wifebeater Man chose not to follow her or call the police. On the downside, he would get to keep the flash drive she'd just found, and it might also give him an excuse to try to detain her, and then she might be tempted to use her gun, and then it would all go to hell. A second option was to bluff, something she'd proved good at in the past and had come prepared for.

After five or ten seconds ticked by, and it became clear that the man was not himself going to break the silence, she said, "I think the better question, sir, is what are you doing here?"

"What I'm doing here is trying to find out why you're trespassing on a property that I own."

"I don't know who owns it, but Sylvie Virtin lives here, and her niece in New York has hired me to try to find her. She's gone missing, you see. I'm a private investigator."

Now the stare was his. Finally, he said, "That's a lot of horse manure. Sylvie isn't missing; she's on an extended vacation. Her boss died, and she felt she needed to take some time off."

"Tell you what, sir. Tell me where she went on vacation and give me the contact information. If it checks out, I'll let her niece know, and that will be the end of this."

"I'll give some thought to that, but in the meantime, let's see some proof that you're actually a PI who represents Sylvie's niece. Otherwise, I'm going to call the police."

"No problem." She heaved her briefcase onto a nearby table, clicked open the locks and pulled out a crisply folded letter, which she handed to him. She'd noticed that when she'd opened the briefcase, he'd made no effort to protect himself against the possibility that she had a gun stashed in there. Men just couldn't seem to get used to the idea that a woman, too, could go armed, especially a PI.

Still holding the flash drive in one hand, he took the letter from her with the other and read it.

When he'd finished, he said, "I have no idea if Sylvie really has a niece named Miriam Kelter or, even if she does, that the niece wrote this letter to you. This could be a total fake."

"Look the niece up online if you like," she said. She hoped he wouldn't, because while she'd put an accurate address on the letter when she'd forged it, she'd very carefully avoided adding the niece's listed phone number to it.

He stood there for a moment, clearly pondering how to end the confrontation.

She waited. Most people disliked conflict, and if no one insulted or humiliated them, they would normally try to find a way out. The important thing for her was not to be the one who de-escalated.

Finally, he said, "Why don't you just go, okay? And we'll forget about it."

"No, because as far as I'm concerned, and as far as her niece is concerned, Sylvie is still missing. And that thumb drive you're holding may hold the clue."

"Listen, girlie, here's the deal. I'm keeping the thumb drive. I assume Sylvie will want it when she returns. You're free to go if you go now. Otherwise I call the cops."

It seemed like a deal she couldn't really turn down without using her gun, which seemed a poor idea. The utility of guns, she had found over time, was limited unless you wanted to shoot someone or hold them until the police came.

"Fine, I'm going. But you need to call the cops and tell them you have that thumb drive. Because if something has happened to Sylvie, that thing's a clue, and you're obstructing justice by holding on to it."

As she said it, she knew it was largely nonsense. Prosecutors could make almost anything into an obstruction of justice, but the threat she had just uttered seemed a stretch.

She walked to the door, casually opened it, snatched the phone out of her pocket, spun around and snapped a picture of him. "Ciao, asshole."

And then she just ran.

About a block from her bus stop, she slowed down to a walk and glanced behind her. The guy didn't appear to have followed her. A block later, she sat down on a bench to await the bus. As she sat there, she noticed the couple with the baby stroller walking by across the street. They were once again deep in conversation and seemed not to notice her.

Chapter 8

WEDNESDAY MORNING—7:00 A.M.

Rory had been awake much of Tuesday night, worrying. He had won the preliminary injunction motion before Judge Cabraal without any difficulty, which was hardly surprising. A summer intern could have won it. What troubled him now was the possibility that the new judge might refuse to sign the order and would permit substantial early discovery and that Kathryn would somehow sniff out the fact that the late GC had created some kind of file on the case. And who knew what was in it? Maybe nothing. Maybe a lot.

And the new judge was, well, new. New judges had been known to charge into cases like they were the first judicial officers God had ever put on earth, not to mention that she might remember Rory had supported her opponent in the state judicial election.

He had finally gotten up, dressed and gone into the office. He was at his desk by six a.m. There wasn't a lot to do to prepare for the hearing; after all, he had worried about it all night long. Instead, he continued to catch up on the hundreds of e-mails he had received and ignored while on sabbatical. Most of them were of no interest. Then he spotted one dated just a few weeks earlier, attaching the press release the firm had issued announcing the imminent arrival of Sarah Gold, recently a law clerk to the Chief Justice.

What interested him most were the career dates. If she had told him the truth about her age—thirty—and if her graduation dates from college and law school on the press release were correct, then there was a two-year gap on her resume between college and law school.

Just a few minutes later, Sarah stepped into his office.

"You're here early," he said.

"I am an early bird. I didn't expect to find you in, though. I was going to leave you a note."

"Saying?"

"Saying I had something you need to see."

"Which is what?"

She pulled the picture of Joe Stanton and Sylvie out of her pocket and dropped it in front of him. "This."

He picked it up and looked at it. "Wow, they were a lot younger. Where did you—"

"I'll tell you in a minute. But is that your only reaction? That they were a lot younger?"

"No, but I'm not surprised. Affairs are even more common in Hollywood than in other businesses. And at least she was single."

"And he was married to Gladys, the weeping woman in black."

"Yep. But he rarely talked about her, at least to me. So maybe it was a marriage of convenience."

"I found something else, too."

"Before you show me anything else, where did you get that picture?"

"At Sylvie's house."

"I thought I told you not to go there."

"I'm not going to bill for it. I went on my own hook, using my PI license."

Rory rolled his eyes. "Please. That doesn't make it any better. If you'd been caught, the firm would have been in trouble."

"Do you want to know about the other thing I found there or not?"

"Show me."

"I'll tell you."

When she had finished, Rory just sat there and looked at her. He had done some crazy things in his own lawyer youth, but nothing like what Sarah had just described.

"You haven't said anything, Rory."

"What the hell were you thinking?"

"I was thinking that, logically, if there was a file and it's now missing, Sylvie took it and probably hid it in her house."

He knew he should report her to the firm's executive committee. Well, first to Hal Harold, and then let them all deal with it. On the other hand, his attitude about life had revolved around the idea that what's done is done. It was how he had felt when the only law school he could get into was the distinctly down-market Chet. He had done that to himself through sloth and indifference, so he had decided to make the best of it, and it had worked out. More or less. He could deal with this, too, and avoid being a chickenshit and reporting her. This time. But before they finished today, he needed to make damned sure she didn't do it again. That could wait a few minutes, though.

"Rory, are you still there?"

"Oh, sorry, I was just thinking about my own misspent youth."

"You're hardly old. Or you don't look old."

"I'll be forty in a couple of weeks."

"Ten years older than I am."

"A decade can be a century sometimes." This was an opportunity to find out what Sarah had done during the missing two years on her resume, but he needed to deal with the issue at hand first. "So the guy who took the flash drive from you still has it."

"Yes."

"Any idea who he is? Neighbor? Security guard?"

"No idea, but I have his picture." She clicked the photo up on her cell and handed it to him.

"Shit."

"What?"

"That's Joe Stanton's brother, Peter."

"How do you know?"

"Met him at a couple of parties that the GC threw."

She looked puzzled. "But he doesn't look like a GC's brother; he looks like a thug."

"He kinda is. He and Joe inherited a small amount of money when their parents were killed in a plane crash. Joe invested his in real estate. Peter had always liked cars, so he bought an auto repair shop. Which is a tough business. Lots of physical labor, lots of confrontations with irate customers, lots of cash transactions."

"That wouldn't explain the biceps."

"He's also a workout freak."

"Good thing he didn't chase me, then."

Rory laughed. "He was in an auto accident a few years ago and broke both legs in multiple places. He limps badly, and he certainly can't run. So when you ran, you made the right decision."

"How do you know all this?"

He smiled. "Peter got drunk at one of Joe's parties and told me his life story. People like to do that with me, for some reason."

"Was he at the funeral?"

"I'm not sure. I couldn't see all of the people in the front rows, which is where he would have been."

"If he was in the front row, he probably didn't see me."

"Probably not."

"You know," she said, "the fact that that mafia guy—because that's what you're really telling me he is—is the GC's brother and he's hanging around Sylvie's house means she's dead."

"I don't see the logic."

"Rory, are you a betting man?"

"Sometimes."

"I'll put money on Sylvie being dead. Name the stakes."

He smiled. "What outrageous amount are we paying you?"

"One sixty. Plus I got a hundred-K signing bonus for coming here from my Supreme Court clerkship. So let's say twenty grand. That's real money."

He was tempted. Sorely. But it was absolutely crazy to be betting an associate that kind of money, especially about whether someone was dead. It would just encourage her to do more nutty things to prove she was right.

"That's too much money. How about a great bottle of French red? Winner picks the year and the vintage."

"I don't drink."

"Ah, okay. How about dinner at a restaurant of the winner's choice?"

"Where?"

"Anywhere in California, loser to pay transportation if it's out of LA."

"Okay, deal." She got out of her chair and put her hand out. They shook on it.

"And please forward a copy of the picture you took of Peter to me. Mark it 'Attorney Work Product.'"

"Okay. Will do." She turned as if to leave.

"Don't go yet, Sarah."

She turned back and faced him.

"We've just had a lot of fun with the bet and all that, but I have something serious to say."

"Okay."

"What you did in breaking into that house was highly unprofessional, not to mention potentially criminal, and if it got known, it could seriously damage the firm."

Instead of looking directly at him, she hung her head slightly. But only slightly, he noticed. "I'm really sorry, Rory," she said, looking up. "I'm afraid I had my PI brain working and not my lawyer brain."

"Okay. I'll be blunt: I want you to cut out this fucking PI stuff."

"I get it, Rory. Although the profanity wasn't necessary."

He ignored her protest and went on. "Will you promise that you will not, under any circumstances, do any more PI-type investigation on this case? Or any other case the firm is handling? If you promise those things, we'll just write this off as a learning experience, and although I think I need to alert Hal, I won't tell anyone else in the firm."

"I promise."

"You had your right hand behind your back."

"I was scratching an itch."

He stared at her for a couple of seconds and said, "Let's hope that's what you were really doing. Because crossed fingers don't work with me."

As she left, he realized he had forgotten to ask her about the two-year resume gap. He was very curious. A PI who had a concealed-carry permit? How much, he wondered, did the firm really know about its prized Supreme Court clerk? And what else might there be to know?

Chapter 9

WEDNESDAY MORNING—8:oo A.M.
FEDERAL COURT—CIVIL DOCKET
Broom v. TheSun/TheMoon/TheStars

At 8:oo a.m. sharp, Judge Franklin emerged from a doorway behind the bench and walked toward the judge's chair. She was a portly woman with shoulder-length red hair parted down the middle and a distinctly crooked nose. Rumor had it that she had worked her way through law school as a stand-up comic, although Rory, in his few encounters with her before she became a judge, had never found her particularly witty.

The judge's clerk intoned, "All rise!" and Rory and Sarah stood up. Rory noticed that there were perhaps twenty other people seated in the courtroom, which meant the judge had a heavy calendar. They could be there all morning.

"I am going to hear the *Broom v. TheSun/TheMoon/TheStars* matter first."

Rory breathed a sigh of relief. Usually, when a judge put a matter first on the calendar, it meant that it wasn't going to take very long. It had to mean that she was just gonna sign whatever order Double-X had prepared. He headed for counsel table, trailed by Sarah, and, as he arrived there, said, "Good morning, Your Honor. Rory Calburton and Sarah Gold for defendant TheSun/TheMoon/TheStars."

"Kathryn Thistle for plaintiff Mary Broom, Your Honor."

Rory started to sit, as did Sarah and Kathryn.

"Counsel, there's no need to take a seat. This isn't going to take very long."

That meant, Rory thought, that Franklin would quickly reaffirm Judge Cabraal's leanings and rule in his favor, and they'd be out of there in a few minutes. Then he'd go get something to eat. He had skipped breakfast, and he was starving. He'd take Sarah with him and—finally—find out about the two-year gap. He had all kinds of imaginings about it.

Kathryn must also have thought she was about to lose, because she quickly said, "Your Honor, I would like the chance to reargue our injunction motion."

"I think that would be premature at this point, Ms. Thistle, since I've not yet had the chance to review the injunction papers. I'm going to ask my clerk to consult with you both about dates, and we'll set a rehearing of the matter in about a week."

Rory felt his heart sink. "Your Honor, may I be heard on the issue of delay?"

"Of course, Mr. Calburton. But let me guess. You plan to urge me to sign the order that Judge Cabraal drafted before his unfortunate fall."

"Yes, Your Honor. You've read my mind."

"Well, unfortunately, there is no such draft order, or at least no one can find it. His clerk is unaware of its having been dictated or written down. And as you know, Judge Cabraal passed away, so we can't ask him where it is."

As she was speaking, Rory was thinking how to escape the situation, which promised to screw everything up. "Your Honor, wouldn't it be possible for you to just read the transcript of the hearing we completed?

Judge Cabraal indicated his reasoning and the result—denial of the motion—during the hearing. If there's an issue of cost, my client would be happy to pay for an expedited transcript."

"I've thought about that approach, Mr. Calburton, but I'm just not comfortable ruling on such an important matter based on a hearing transcript. I'm afraid I'll have to read the injunction papers filed by both sides and probably hear limited reargument. But I hope I can plow through the papers quickly and we can get this over soon."

"Your Honor, with all due respect, my client has a film opening in wide release in a matter of days, and plaintiff is trying to enjoin the opening. This will be hanging over the whole thing."

Judge Franklin looked down at him. "Candidly, I don't see the problem, Counsel. Obviously, there will be no injunction in place right now, so the film can open without a problem. And if I later decide a preliminary injunction is warranted, I'm very unlikely to shut down a movie that has already opened around the country. If that happens—unlikely, given Judge Cabraal's tentative ruling—I'll have to come up with some other appropriate remedy."

What Rory wanted to say to her was that her approach was totally at odds with the way federal judges, even new ones, behaved. They felt the power running through their veins and were inclined to use it. If Judge Franklin later decided there were grounds to enjoin the film, she wouldn't likely let it continue to be shown just because it had already opened. No matter what she said now.

Instead, he said, "Your Honor, I think having this hanging over the film is likely to be damaging. Uncertainty is bad for films. It unnerves distributors and audiences, too."

"Many things hang over films, Mr. Calburton. Like bad reviews and bad box office."

"This film has had good early reviews, Your Honor, and no box office yet, since it hasn't opened."

She shrugged. "Perhaps your studio client will figure out how to take advantage of the situation. Or perhaps"—she smiled a Cheshire cat smile—"if you're really worried about uncertainty, this would be a good time for the parties to talk settlement, eh?"

He could hardly contain himself from bursting out with a "Yes!" and seeming too eager. Instead, he said, "It's perhaps a little early, but settlement might be worth talking about, if Ms. Thistle's client is amenable."

Kathryn popped out of her chair. "My client isn't in court today, Your Honor, but I know she shares my view that it's *much* too early. Judge Cabraal permitted only very limited discovery prior to the injunction hearing. We'd need to take several depositions before we'd be able to evaluate whether we want to talk settlement."

"Whom do you want to depose, Counsel?"

"At a very minimum, the director, who supposedly wrote the script, several producers, the head of business affairs at the time the film was green-lighted and the lead actor."

"An actor? What could he possibly know?"

"We have reason to believe that he knows exactly what the studio is hiding."

Now Rory was on his feet. "We're not hiding anything, Your Honor."

The judge looked down at them. "Counsel, let's not quarrel. Here's what we're going to do. I will set the reargument of the motion for preliminary injunction for sometime next week. In the meantime, I will permit the plaintiff to take two depositions, for four hours each. Which two do you want, Ms. Thistle?"

"In that case, we'll skip the lead actor and take the director and the head of business affairs."

"Those people may not be easily available on short notice, Your Honor," Rory said.

"Counsel, if your client is really nervous about uncertainty, it can reduce that risk by finding them and making them available."

"Alright, Your Honor."

"Is there anyone you want to depose, Mr. Calburton?"

That put Rory on the spot. On the one hand, he wanted to take Mary Broom's depo. But the actress was said to be reclusive, and his best bet was that she wouldn't want her depo taken, ever. So if he waited, and they were close to settlement but not yet quite there, threatening to take it right then could be the thing that pushed the settlement to completion.

"No, Your Honor," he said. "At some point we'll certainly want to take Ms. Broom, but I think it's a little premature right now."

Sarah poked him and handed him her iPhone. He glanced quickly at the screen. It showed a breaking news alert from the *Los Angeles Times*.

Looking up, Rory said, "Your Honor, I'm afraid we won't be able to produce the director, Alex Toltec, for a deposition."

"Why not?"

"According to the *LA Times* website, he's dead."

Chapter 10

"I need to check that out myself," Judge Franklin said. They all watched as she tapped on her keyboard, presumably pulling up the *LA Times* website. She stared at her screen for a moment and did what any good judge does when in a quandary.

"Counsel, we're going to take a fifteen-minute recess while I consider this development. Please be sure to be back here on time." She was already standing and walking toward the private door behind the bench as she said it.

Not two seconds after the judge left the room, Kathryn Thistle strode over to Rory's table and said, "Did you kill him?"

"No, did you?"

"Why would I kill him?"

"To keep him from putting the lie to your case."

"To the contrary—"

"Kathryn, before you bang on, let me introduce our newest associate, Sarah Gold. Sarah, meet Kathryn; Kathryn, meet Sarah."

"Pleased to meet you, Kathryn," Sarah said, standing up and extending her hand.

"And pleased to meet you, too, Sarah," Kathryn responded, reaching out to shake it. "I read your firm's press release announcing your arrival. Looks like you recently spent time in high places. Welcome to the rough-and-tumble low place where lawyers duke it out with witnesses instead of briefs."

"I was embarrassed by that press release," Sarah said. "And I certainly plan to earn my stripes here in the rough-and-tumble."

"Good. So, Rory, returning to my question, I didn't mean did you personally kill him. I assume you would have had some underling do it."

"Kathryn, let's talk about what the judge wants us to talk about—settlement."

She ignored that and said, "Did you, Rory?"

"Did I what?"

"Have some underling kill him."

He drew back half a step. "Oh my God, you're serious. Like I said, I'd much rather have him alive."

"I doubt it. Because your studio client is clearly hiding something. I can smell it. It's something that would break this case wide open. And I think famous director Alex Toltec was the one person with the secret. Now that he's gone, you think your secret's safe. That's why you want to settle."

"Kathryn," Sarah interjected, "I'm brand-new to this case. I know almost nothing about it. Why do you think the studio is hiding something?"

"Well, good question. I've tried to explain it to Rory, but he refuses to see the logic of our position. You're probably smarter, so let me explain it to you."

Rory winced at the remark, as his Chet inferiority complex rose up once again. He pushed it aside and focused on how easily Sarah had slipped into the role of ingénue, eager to learn from Kathryn. And how well it seemed to be working—in part, of course, because Kathryn loved to hear herself talk, and in Sarah she had a brand-new audience.

He wondered if Kathryn might be more guarded if she knew that Sarah sometimes carried a gun.

"Sarah, have you ever seen *Terror in Santa Monica*?" Kathryn asked.

"Sure, when I was maybe twelve. Against my parents' wishes."

"That movie was directed by none other than Alex Toltec. Did it scare you?"

"Out of my seat."

"It was a horror movie, right? But Alex Toltec only directed it. He got no screen-writing credit."

"Are you suggesting he got cheated out of his writing credit?" Sarah asked.

"God no. I'm suggesting he got no credit because he didn't write a word of it. And he didn't write it because he's not a writer. And not only didn't he get a writing credit on that one, he didn't get one on any of the six god-awful sequels that followed, all of which he directed, including the execrable, but highly profitable, *Terror in Torrance*."

"Okay," Sarah said. "So he's not a writer. What does that have to do with this case?"

Sarah had read the file on the case, so she had to know exactly what Kathryn's argument was. She was playing the role of the wide-eyed innocent to perfection.

Kathryn was responding. ". . . and so the claim of your studio client is that Toltec not only directed *Extorted* but wrote it."

"Why couldn't he have written it?"

"Because it's totally out of his genre, for one thing. Even if he had wanted to try his hand at writing for the first time, he would logically have tried to write one in the genre in which he achieved both fame and wealth. Horror. Not presidential sexual high jinks."

Rory intervened. "Kathryn, lots of first-time screenwriters have written brilliant first scripts."

"Alex Toltec couldn't possibly have written a polished, brilliant, Oscar-worthy script his first time out. Not after spending the twenty years before that directing guys in lizard suits."

"Why do you think Mary Broom, who has no history as a screenwriter, could have written a polished, brilliant script first time out, huh?"

"That's different. For a whole lot of reasons that will come to light."

Rory sighed. "In any case, it's too bad Alex is dead, because he could explain to you how he came to write this script. Something he'd tell you—which he reminded me when I interviewed him—is that he *did* write a bunch of scripts. Early in his career he wrote like ten of them for straight-to-video B movies. So maybe they weren't Oscar bait, but he put in the time learning the craft, even if he moved away from it later."

"You interviewed him? Now that he's dead, I think we have a right to see your notes of that interview—"

"All rise!"

Everyone stood as Judge Franklin returned and took her seat on the bench.

"Counsel, I have good news and bad news. The good news is Mr. Toltec isn't dead. The bad news is that he was severely injured in a small plane crash, is in a coma and apparently won't be in any shape to give a deposition for some time."

"We're obviously very sorry to hear that," Rory said.

"Your Honor," Kathryn said, "if we can't take Mr. Toltec's deposition right now, we want to take the studio's head of business affairs'. All we've got now is a declaration that says nothing. And when Mr. Toltec recovers sufficiently, we want to take his depo, too, in his hospital room if necessary."

The judge stared at her for a moment. Rory hoped she was thinking what he was thinking—that it was hard to believe that Kathryn had not uttered a single word of regret about the plane crash and was already thinking of deposing Toltec from his sickbed.

"Counsel, I'm not today going to order any kind of deposition for Mr. Toltec. We'll wait to see how he does and let his doctors be the judge of when he's ready to testify."

"Thank you, Your Honor," Kathryn said.

Rory tried to figure out a way to capitalize on Kathryn's lack of sensitivity, but he couldn't come up with one. So he just said, "We'll make the head of business affairs available, Your Honor, and we'll all"—he turned and looked at Kathryn—"hope Alex recovers quickly."

"Is there anything else, Counsel?" the judge asked.

"Just one more thing," Kathryn said. "In the past couple of weeks, prior to the first injunction hearing, we had trouble arranging for the depositions we wanted to take."

"It's hard to get people on short notice," Rory said.

"Precisely. Your Honor, I'd like to be able to come back here tomorrow if we're unable to arrange things to our satisfaction and ask the court to order the people we want to appear for their depositions."

"As you know, Counsel, federal judges don't usually get into that level of detail on discovery. I can send you to the magistrate judge for that. *If* it happens."

"This is an unusual case, Your Honor," Kathryn said.

"Well, some things about it are unusual, I can see that. But I'll tell you what. I have a better idea. One that will avoid all of these problems."

Rory tried to suppress a smile. If his instincts were right this time, the judge was sufficiently irritated with Kathryn that she was gonna reverse course and simply approve what Judge Cabraal had originally done without bothering with a new hearing.

"Here's what we're going to do," the judge said. "We'll skip all the discovery for now and have a preliminary injunction proceeding with live witnesses. That way, each witness can take the witness stand"—she pointed to the empty chair in the railed-in witness box beside her—"and say what they have to say. And you can cross-examine them right here to your heart's content."

"But, Your Honor—" Rory said.

"Don't 'but, Your Honor' me, Counsel."

Kathryn was on her feet, too, with her mouth open.

Judge Franklin looked at her sharply. "And not you, either, Ms. Thistle. This is the perfect solution. You can each line up your witnesses and bring them here, and if you need to call witnesses who are beholden to the other side, you can work it out between you. If not, you can just subpoena them to appear, and I'll enforce those subpoenas."

"Your Honor," Kathryn said, "for me that will be like groping in the dark. I really need to depose—"

"I don't think so, Counsel. I think you can put on an effective case, perhaps even a winning one, by just calling your own witnesses. But in any case, that's the way we're going to do it. It will save everyone a lot of time and"—Rory thought he saw her actually roll her eyes—"will save a lot of discovery disputes, too. Not to mention a lot of paper."

"When will this be scheduled?" Rory asked.

"The clerk will call you to confirm the date, but I'm thinking probably this coming Monday. That will give you plenty of time to get ready. And since you already argued the matter in the prior hearing, that should be more than sufficient."

The clerk, who had been sitting silently, looked up and said, "You do have that entire day free, Your Honor."

"Good. Then Monday it is. At eight a.m." She looked down at her calendar. "Oh, I see that I have a personal matter in the morning. Let's start instead on Monday at two p.m. You can exchange witness lists by end of the business day tomorrow."

"Your Honor," Rory said, "I assume we are still free to go forward with the premiere tonight."

"Yes, you are. Have fun at the after-party, Mr. Calburton."

"I'm going, too, Your Honor!" Kathryn said.

"Well, perhaps the two of you can belt back a few, go off to a corner and settle this thing."

As they turned to leave, Judge Franklin was saying, "Next I'll hear the trademark matter of *Churros, Inc. v. Chu Ro, Inc.* . . ."

Rory was surprised to see Hal Harold sitting in the very back row of the courtroom. He got up and followed Rory and Sarah out into the hall. "Great job, Rory. Having a live witness hearing will help us enormously. Thistle's never going to be able to prove her case with her own witnesses alone, and I assume she won't find any of ours."

"Excuse me," Sarah said. "You're not suggesting we're going to hide people?"

"Of course not. It's just that Alex has had an unfortunate accident, and I suspect he's the only one who's got any real information. As for the head of business affairs, I think she just left on vacation or something."

"That sounds suspicious," Sarah said.

"Sarah, we're about to get in an elevator," he said. "We never discuss cases in elevators, even if they're empty. We'll continue when we get out."

They stood in silence as the elevator descended, then exited and walked quickly to the door out to the street.

The first thing that caught Rory's eye was a full TQEN camera crew, fronted by its chief correspondent, Dana Barbour. The second thing he noticed was six police cars and a dozen LAPD cops deployed on the sidewalk.

One of them stepped up to them and said, "Mr. Harold, you're under arrest. You others, please move aside. Mr. Harold, please move your feet apart and hold your arms out to your sides, palms down."

Harold complied without protest.

"What am I being arrested for, if I might ask?"

"The murder of Joseph Stanton. Now please point your thumbs toward the ground."

As he did so, the arresting officer grabbed the middle two fingers of Harold's right hand, forced his arm slightly upward, snapped a cuff on the right wrist and pushed his now-cuffed right hand into the small of his back. Then he reached over and forced Harold's left hand behind his back and cuffed it, too. The whole thing took maybe five seconds.

Sarah looked over at Rory. "Good technique."

"Shit, Sarah. Did you know this was about to happen?"

"No, not at all. I was just admiring the way he did it."

Rory noticed that his hands were shaking from the adrenaline rush of the unfolding event, but Sarah's were steady.

Despite the fact that the cameras were running, or maybe, as he reflected on it later, because they were running, Rory stepped forward. "I'm Mr. Harold's attorney, Rory Calburton. I demand to know what this is all about."

"He's not my attorney, Officer," said Harold, who seemed to be taking the whole thing in stride. "No offense, Rory, but call Quentin Zavallo and tell him I've been arrested. He'll know what to do. Where are you taking me, Officer?"

"Parker Center."

Rory watched as the cop put a protective hand on top of Hal's head and forced him into the police car. Then Rory turned to the TQEN reporter. "Who tipped you off to this, Dana?"

"No one. We just got lucky."

"Bullshit. When will this air?"

"My guess is the producer will want to break into our normal programming with it."

"Will you leave out the part about, 'He's not my attorney, Officer'?"

"That's up to my producer."

"Will you ask your producer to leave it out?"

She smiled a broad, local-news smile, all white teeth and red lipstick. "What do I get in exchange?"

Rory stood there for a few seconds, thinking. What would a hot anchor for a slime network like TQEN possibly want? A vacation with him to a tropical island? Then it dawned on him.

"Dana, is your camera still running?"

She glanced over her shoulder at the cameraman. "No."

"Okay, then. How about I take you to the premiere tonight as my date?"

She looked him up and down as if considering whether he were worthy of escorting her somewhere and said, "You mean not in the roped-off press area, but as an actual person going to the movie and the party?"

"Precisely."

"It's a deal," she said. "And I'll see what I can do about persuading my producer to skip airing that really very juicy piece of video in which you're made to look foolish." She flashed him a sexy smile and walked back toward the TQEN truck.

As he watched her go, Rory wondered how he was gonna accomplish what he had just promised. Because the truth was that lawyers didn't have a lot of clout at studios, and it was through Hal that he had achieved his own ticket. He'd have to spend a year's worth of favors to get it done.

Sarah poked him in the side. "Earth to Rory. Where are you?"

"Oh, sorry, just thinking about something."

"Well, I overheard everything, so I can guess what you were thinking about. I'm just curious why you're so sensitive about what Mr. Harold said."

"One second. I need to call Quentin Zavallo."

After he'd finished, Sarah said, "You were about to tell me why you're sensitive about the whole 'not my lawyer' thing."

"It's like this. When I became a partner three months ago, right before I went on sabbatical, the firm threw a big party for me. And sent out all kinds of announcements. And arranged an interview for me with the *Daily Journal*. They made a big deal about my becoming a partner."

"What's the *Daily Journal*?"

"Wow, you really are new here. It's one of our local legal newspapers."

"That all sounds good."

"It is. But to have Hal Harold—the founder of the firm that bears his name—tell me in front of God and everyone that I'm not his lawyer sounds like he lacks confidence in his new partner."

"Does he?"

"If he did, they wouldn't have made me a partner. But on the other hand, the press release failed to mention where I went to law school."

"You think they were embarrassed by it?"

"I do."

"Why didn't you just tell them you were pissed that they left your law school out of the press release?"

"It's not that simple, Sarah. If you go to an unaccredited law school, it follows you around like Banquo's ghost."

"Who?"

"It's a literary allusion. Shakespeare."

"Literature has never been my strong suit."

"TDB."

"Too damn bad?"

"Yep."

"Anyway, what's a jock like you doing quoting Shakespeare?"

"Before I dropped out, I sat through a course we called No Fear Shakespeare. There were a lot of football players in it and, uh, a lot of girls who liked guys who worked out."

Sarah rolled her eyes. "Alright, I get the picture."

"I bet you do."

"Rory, you know how in military movies someone is always saying to a higher officer, 'Permission to speak candidly, sir'?"

"Yep, I've seen that."

"Well, even though we are only getting to know each other, may I speak candidly?"

Rory's first reaction was to say no. This woman was getting beneath his psychological armor—which usually did a pretty good job of keeping everyone out—and he wasn't really sure he wanted to give Sarah permission to keep asking questions. But in the end he said, "Sure. I like candor."

"You're a tremendous success," she said. "You're a partner in one of the country's best entertainment litigation firms. The firm's press release may have failed to mention your law school, but I read the profile on you that *American Lawyer* ran. It's like they couldn't find anyone to say anything bad about you. The superlatives are almost nauseating."

"So?"

"So get over the law school thing. No one cares except you, Rory."

"I think you'll see as you spend more time here that that's not quite true. But that's not the core of the problem."

"What is?"

"Are you, like, a psychologist or something?"

"No, although I do have some experience in working with people under stress. But I just think you need to open up."

"Sarah, this is ridiculous. For one thing, I'm your boss. Plus I hardly know you, and for all I know next year you'll skip out, go to work for one of our competitors and spread whatever I tell you all over town."

She paused, as if considering how to counter his suspicions, and finally said, "No, I won't. You can trust me. So risk it."

He asked himself if he could trust her. And the answer was no, not really, especially not after her adventures at Sylvie's house.

"Not right now," he said.

"Okay, fine. Anyway, moving on, can I have a ride back with you?"

"Sure, but how did you get here?"

"I took the bus."

"Seriously?"

"Yes. I took the bus in DC all the time. Why not here?"

"Um, it's just not done by, um, people like us."

"People like us?"

"That was an awkward way to put it, I suppose."

"I'll say."

By then they had reached the open-air parking lot across from the courthouse.

"Hop in," Rory said.

"Wow," she said. "This is not the car you drove me back to Westwood in yesterday."

"Nope, that was a rental. This one was being serviced yesterday."

"So today it's a Tesla Model S. Not bad."

"Partners in our firm make a lot."

She smiled. "That's why I came."

As they accelerated onto the Santa Monica Freeway, heading west, Sarah said, "Can you see the red car that's behind us? I think it's a Honda."

"Yes. Why?"

"I can't see it very well out of the side mirror, but you can probably see it perfectly."

"Yes. And so?"

"What does the driver look like?"

"He's got a shaved head, a beard, and is wearing mirrored sunglasses. Open shirt, green. Why?"

"It's probably just a coincidence, but when I visited Sylvie's house, a man and a woman were pushing a baby stroller down the sidewalk in front of the house, and I saw them again at the bus stop. The guy had a beard and a shaved head and was wearing mirrored sunglasses and a green shirt."

"Well, there's no one in the passenger seat. I think you're paranoid. There are thousands of guys with shaved-bald heads in Los Angeles, and mirrored shades and green shirts abound, as do beards."

"Okay, you're probably right."

"Let's see if Hal's arrest is on the news yet," Rory said. "They have a lot of local news on the half hour." He punched the button for KNX, the local all-news AM radio station.

As the sound came up, the KNX anchor, Tony Simms, was in the midst of his report, saying:

"... *prominent entertainment attorney, is charged with the murder of movie executive Joe Stanton. Stanton was found dead last Sunday in his studio office. Elizabeth Sabato is at Parker Center. Elizabeth?*"

"*Tony, Hal Harold was expected to be moved from here to the Men's Central Jail, but we're told he's already posted bond and been released. His attorney, Quentin Zavallo, has scheduled a news conference at his office in Beverly Hills this afternoon. We'll be there live.*"

"*Thanks, Elizabeth—*"

Rory reached over and turned it off.

"He's already out? Wow!" Sarah said.

"Not that surprising, really. There's a bail schedule. Bail for murder one is one million dollars. If you have it, you get out. I guess Hal has it, and that was that."

"Zavallo sounds very effective. Do you know him?"

"Talked to him on the phone once or twice. That's why I had his number. But don't really know him."

"To return to the earlier topic, Rory, perhaps I'm out of line because I really just met you, but again, I think you need to learn to deal better with the whole where-I-went-to-law-school problem. I'd like to help you with that. And I think I can. If you're willing to be helped."

Rory concentrated on driving. Eventually, just to fill the empty air, he said, "There's a lot of traffic today."

"Yes, there is," she said. "But I can tell from your affect that you're not really thinking about the traffic. You're thinking that I'm out of line."

"A bit, yeah."

"I'm sorry. I really like to help people, and sometimes, I know, I offer when help isn't wanted. Or at least not from me. Or—"

He cut her off. "It's okay, Sarah. I know you mean well. And, truth be told, I could probably use some counseling about all that." Then he thought carefully about what he was about to say, realizing that it crossed a line, but said it anyway. "Maybe we can go out for a drink sometime and talk about it."

"Except I don't drink."

He laughed. "That is a problem. Anyway, I don't think I'm ready for it yet. Maybe someday." And as he said it, he reminded himself that it was a particularly bad idea to get into all this with her when he'd been on the verge of trying to get her fired.

"Okay," she said. "We'll work our way there. Going out for a drink could be fun, even if I don't drink."

"One other thing before we leave the topic. I'm not making up this stuff about where you go to school. And it's a problem you're never gonna have. You went to Yale and clerked on the Supreme Court, so everyone will always assume you're brilliant."

She sighed. "Everyone always thinks I went to one of the Ivies. But as I told you, I went to Georgetown, not Yale. And maybe people would be suspicious of me if they looked closely enough."

"The two-year gap in your resume?"

Sarah didn't immediately respond. He glanced over at her and saw that she was staring straight ahead. Finally, she said, "What gap?"

"Between college and law school. There's nothing about that period on your resume."

She laughed. "What in your fondest dreams do you think I did during those two mysterious years?"

"I don't dream much, Sarah."

"Well, you must think it was nefarious in some way, or you wouldn't be so evasive about what you imagine I was doing."

"I wasn't imagining anything at all."

"I'm half tempted not to tell you, just to drive you crazy. But whatever; I worked as a waitress at a bar in DC called Another Bird in the Hand."

"Sounds kind of sexist."

"That was maybe the intent. But in fact the owner was an ornithologist. He traveled the world collecting bird samples. There were stuffed birds sitting on branches all over the bar."

"So not sleazy at all?"

"I wouldn't go that far."

"Why do you hide it?"

"I don't. I just told you, didn't I?"

"It's not on your resume."

"Why on earth would it be? If I'd been a paralegal, I'd have put it down. But a cocktail waitress?"

"People *do* list their postcollege jobs. But okay, I'll drop it."

She turned her head and looked behind them. "That red Honda is still with us."

"We're on the Santa Monica Freeway. If he's going the same place we are, there's no reason for him not to be behind us."

"What exit would you normally take?"

"National, probably."

"Why don't you get off at the exit before that?"

"Okay."

They took the Robertson exit, and Sarah glanced behind her again. "Still with us."

"What do you want me to do?"

"See that gas station over there?" She pointed. "Stop there and get some gas."

"This is an electric car, Sarah."

"Oh, right. Well, stop and appear to be putting air in your tires."

He pulled in, and she said, "The car sped on by."

"Probably on his way to wherever he's going."

"Maybe. Let's wait here a few minutes."

They sat and waited, but the red Honda didn't show up again.

"Can I resume my trip to the office?" Rory asked.

"Yes. And now let me ask you something, Mr. Nosey-About-My-Postcollege-Jobs."

"What?"

"Are you really taking that girl to the premiere?"

"She's a woman."

"Where I come from, anyone who wears that much lipstick is a girl."

"I see. Well, assuming she keeps my embarrassing moment with Hal Harold off the news, yes, I am taking her. Are you jealous?"

"No, I don't want to date you, but I would love to go to the premiere."

"I can get you in, I think."

"To the after-party, too?"

"I think so. Just don't bug me when I'm with Miss Lipstick. I want to find out what she knows about this thing with Harold being arrested for murder."

"Oh, so your interest in her is purely professional?"

"Yep."

"What's the proper dress for one of these things?"

"As little as you're comfortable wearing."

Chapter 11

Sarah sat at her desk and surfed some Oscar after-party images. Even though tonight's event wasn't the Academy Awards, some of the attire might be similar. She was mildly shocked at what she saw on the women. No backs, no sides, marginal fronts and very, very high heels.

She called a friend who was about her size and led a wilder-by-far life than she did. Her friend said yes, she could loan Sarah something that might work. A text with a photo came minutes later. Sarah tilted her head and looked at it on her screen. She'd never worn anything like it before, but then, she'd never lived in LA before. DC had been much more a little black dress kind of place. At least for her. And her college had been something else entirely.

As she was contemplating how she'd look in it, and whether her workout routine would show to advantage, Rory gave a perfunctory knock on her open office door, waited there, and asked, "May I come in?"

She looked at him filling up the doorway—he really was good-looking—and understood why his No Fear Shakespeare class had been filled with girls.

"Of course."

He walked in and said, "Time to get to work on the hearing."

She laughed. "Still days away."

"Given that there are gonna be live witnesses, it's just like a trial. We need to give it intense preparation starting now, or we'll get killed. You can be sure Kathryn's office will be working on it day and night."

"Well, you know, Rory, I took a couple trial practice courses, including the advanced course, but I've never done any kind of actual trial before."

"How did you do in those courses?"

"I won the prize for best cross-examination in the advanced course."

"What about the nonadvanced course?"

"I won the prize in that one, too," she said.

"You also took a copyright course, right?"

"No, nothing at all related to intellectual property. I was planning on being an environmental lawyer."

"What about when you were clerking on the Supreme Court?"

"We had a couple copyright cases on the court when I was there, but they weren't about this kind of thing. I'm great at legal research, obviously. So tell me what you want researched."

"Nothing at this point. I already know what the law is."

He moved to the whiteboard on the wall—Hal Harold insisted everyone have one in their office—and picked up a marker. "It's really pretty simple. Here are the four things she's got to prove to win." He quickly scrawled them on the board:

1. *Mary Broom wrote her script before Alex Toltec wrote his.*
2. *T got access to B's script.*
3. *T copied it.*
4. *His script ended up substantially similar to hers.*

"How's Kathryn going to prove all of that?" Sarah asked.

"She'll put Mary on the stand to testify she wrote it and when. And how Alex supposedly got access to it."

"Like how?"

Rory took the marker and wrote "STOLE IT" next to the second point.

"Stole it? Like broke into her house or something?"

"Mary was vague about the details in the sworn declaration she filed for the prelim before Judge Cabraal. She just said Alex stole it, without any detail. Which is probably why they lost the motion."

"But what if the script Alex wrote is so similar to Mary's that it could only have been copied? Even though no one knows how that happened?"

"If the two scripts are amazingly similar, and one was clearly written before the other, courts will assume the newer one was copied and not be too worried about proof of access."

"But Judge Cabraal didn't buy it, did he? Because he was about to deny the injunction."

"Right. He thought the whole thing was too flaky. But now they're getting a second crack at this thing, and my guess is that Mary Broom will have a lot more to say about how Alex supposedly stole the script. How he got access."

"So we need to get ready for that."

"Yes."

"How?"

Rory leaned back against the whiteboard, tossed the marker high into the air and caught it crisply at his waist as it fell. "Damned if I know." Then he laughed. "Since we don't get to take her deposition, we'll be questioning her cold."

"And trying to make the best of it?"

"Yeah. It will be like on television. We'll question her aggressively and hope she confesses on the witness stand."

"Have you ever done that before?"

"No. Not even close. You only question witnesses in civil trials these days after they've turned over all their documents and had their depositions taken under oath."

"So trial testimony without discovery doesn't seem to me the best way to get at the truth of what happened."

"It's not."

"Why is the judge doing it this way, then?"

"She wants both sides to be afraid and settle the case."

"And you want to."

"More than anything, now that Alex can't testify and we know there's a file out there somewhere that may be damaging, even though we can't find it."

"Well, what do you want me to do if there's no legal research to be done?"

"Find out everything you can about Mary Broom. Especially what she's been doing the last ten years, since she more or less disappeared."

"Sounds kind of fun."

"And, Sarah?"

"Yes?"

"The assignment only includes using lawful means."

"Roger that. But one more thing."

"What?"

"Did you get me into the party?"

"I got you into the movie. It's at the TCL Chinese Theater. Your name will be on a list. All you'll need is your driver's license."

"But not the party."

"No, I couldn't swing it. I pulled in a bunch of favors just to get you into the film. But it was too late for the party. Sorry."

"I'll live with it."

"I know you're disappointed. But if you stay at this firm, we represent enough studios, actors, directors and producers that you'll soon be sick of going to these parties and will look for excuses not to go."

"I really wanted to go to this one. I wonder if you tried hard enough."

"Sarah?"

"Yes?"

"Enjoy the movie."

Chapter 12

WEDNESDAY—LATE MORNING
DOWNTOWN LOS ANGELES
THE DOWNUNDER

Rory and Lester Lovejoy had gone to law school together. Lester, who had been an LAPD cop even back then, had attended Chet's night program. He and Rory met during their second year when Rory, as a lark—he had no intention at the time of doing any criminal law—had taken Advanced Criminal Procedure, which was taught only in the evening. They'd had almost nothing in common: Lester was only five foot six, weighed one hundred twenty pounds on a good day and had grown up in a trailer park. Rory's parents had been, if not truly rich, at least quite well off. Despite their differences, they'd hit it off immediately. They had stayed beer buddies ever since, attending each other's birthday parties and promotion parties (Rory had gone to the shindig celebrating Lester's promotion to detective) and spent assorted nights out on the town together.

Rory had never asked a favor of Lester before, but now he needed one. He made the call.

Lester was working robbery-homicide downtown and suggested they meet at a place near Parker Center. Rory really didn't want to drive back downtown, but he didn't want to miss seeing Lester. He also had the classic Los Angeles problem in mind.

"Too hard to park near Parker Center," he said. "How about the DownUnder? They now have valet parking."

"That's a lawyer hangout."

"I'm a lawyer, Lester, ya know?"

"Alright, since I wear a suit these days, I'm willing. I can walk there in maybe twenty minutes. It will be good for me."

"How about eleven thirty, before the lunch crowd gathers?"

"See you there, my friend."

Rory puttered around in his office for a while, then called for his car and drove back downtown.

The DownUnder was set below ground, reached by a small set of concrete steps. Rory looked around, but didn't see Lester. He slipped into a booth for two and waited. A few minutes later Lester sauntered in, looked around, spotted him and slid into the other side of the booth.

"Whoa!" Lester said. "What happened to the old Mexican bar with the weird gangster theme and the red plastic booths?"

"New owners gutted the place a couple years ago. You don't like the chrome and leather look?"

"No. What about the food?"

"It's now something called light French lunch fare. Just your kind of thing, Lester."

A waitress whose name tag said "Madge" appeared and handed each of them a menu. "Drinks, gentlemen?"

They both asked for water only and studied the menu.

"Rory, what are pommes frites?"

"French fries."

"What's a croque monsieur?"

"Ham and cheese sandwich on buttered toast is close enough."

"Sounds tasty but hardly light."

They made small talk for a while until the waitress returned.

"I'll have fries and the croque," Lester said. "It's appropriate for my line of work."

The waitress looked perplexed. "Huh?"

"I'm a homicide detective. I investigate when people croak."

She rolled her eyes and turned to Rory. "And what will you have, sir?"

"I'll have the salad niçoise."

"Let me guess. You're a tuna fisherman?"

"Very funny." He smiled.

"Your food will be right up." She left.

"So," Lester said, "we've done a lot of stuff together over the years, but I don't think you've ever before called me up and asked me to lunch on a weekday. Is this about your boss?"

"In part."

"What's the other part?"

"It's about who killed Joe Stanton."

"We think Hal Harold did. So there's both parts answered."

It was, Rory thought, classic Lester—a flip answer containing just a hint of real information. But he knew if he pressed he could probably find out more.

"What's your evidence against Hal?"

"Hal? You always used to call him Mr. Harold."

"I'm a partner now."

"Wow. Rank hath its privilege."

"Sometimes."

"Are you a member of Mr. Harold's defense team, Rory?"

"No."

"Why should I tell you anything?"

"You know something, then."

"I do. I'm one of the investigating detectives. But not the lead."

Madge reappeared and put their plates down in front of them. "Enjoy."

"Wow, that was fast," Rory said.

"Only the best service for the city's finest."

When she was gone, Rory said, "I'll tell you why I need to know what you know."

"Hit me with it. But before you do, am I supposed to put anything on this croque?" He pointed at it. "Ketchup? Mustard?"

"Nope, you eat it just as it is."

He took a large bite. "It's good. Anyway, you were explaining."

"Yes. You see, I'm working on a civil case in which Joe Stanton was my link to important facts—secrets, let's call them—which apparently only he knew. Now that he's dead, he can't tell me about them. Or testify if I needed him to."

Lester pulled out a small paper notebook and wrote something in it.

"That info interests you, Lester?"

"Maybe. But while you're right that dead men can't testify, they can tell tales in other ways."

"Uh-huh. Anyway, if Hal Harold murdered Joe Stanton, it's gonna make my copyright case a lot more complicated."

"Because someone will argue that your law firm was trying to get rid of a witness who knew things that would have been bad for your case?"

Rory tried to put on his best horrified look. "Is that what you really think happened?"

"No." Lester picked up a fry, bit into it, then picked up another, dumped some ketchup on the plate, dipped another fry in it and chowed it down. "Help yourself to the fries, my friend. They're light, they're French and they're tasty."

"Is that your way of saying you're not gonna help me out? I've never asked a favor of you before."

"The problem is that I'm going to have to tell my colleagues that I gave you the information you want, and they're going to ask what I got in return. That's just the way it works."

"Maybe I do have something for you, Lester."

"I'm all ears."

"Have you talked to Joe's brother, Peter?"

"Not personally, but someone on our team has. Why?"

"I have reason to believe he was snooping around the home of Joe's missing assistant, Sylvie Virtin."

"And you think that makes this a brother-icide?"

"Is that what you cops call it when guys kill their brothers?"

"Nah, I just made it up. Sounds good, though, huh? All that law training sharpened me right up."

"Well, whatever it's called, you don't think that's worth investigating?"

"Maybe. But on the other hand, Sylvie is no longer missing. Peter gave us a phone number where she could be reached, and we called her and confirmed that she's okay. Turns out she's visiting friends in Washington, DC. Her boss's death really upset her, and she wanted to get away and try to make sense of it."

They sat for a moment and ate their food, neither one of them saying anything. Finally, Rory said, "Do I get something in exchange now?"

"Sure. The evidence against Mr. Harold—Hal, to you—is that he was the last person to see Joe Stanton alive, or at least that's what we currently think. It could be very wrong, though, just to be on the up-and-up with you."

"Is that it? That's like half of nothing."

"No. There was a spot of Hal's blood on Joe Stanton's office rug, and we have a security camera clip that shows Mr. Harold driving very fast out of the studio, looking red faced and disheveled."

"Have you seen the clip yourself?"

"No."

"Well, Hal often looks that way. Did he leave right after the time of the murder?"

"Soon enough after to be very suspicious."

"So you know the exact time of the murder?"

"Exact, no."

"What's Hal's motive?"

"Only he knows that—for the moment."

"Sounds like a weak spot in your case."

"There are lots of murderers rotting in prison who will take their motives to the grave."

Madge reappeared. "Dessert, gentlemen?"

"No, I don't think so," Lester said. "That croque was great, though."

"Thanks. What about you, Tuna?"

Rory laughed. "Nope. Just the check please."

She pulled the check out of her apron pocket and set it on the table. "There you go."

After she left, Rory said, "Has it occurred to you, Lester, now that I've told you about Peter snooping around Sylvie's house, that maybe he gave you a fake phone number and the person you guys spoke to wasn't Sylvie?"

"We took some precautions about that."

"Like what?"

"That's a bridge too far, to tell you that. You got anything else, Rory?"

"One thing. I have reason to believe that Peter has a flash drive he found hidden in Sylvie's house."

"Which you know how?"

"I can't really say. Maybe you can get a warrant and look for it."

"What class did we meet in, back in law school?"

"Advanced Criminal Procedure."

"Jeez, Rory, you must not have paid close attention. You want me to go to a judge and say, 'An unnamed friend believes Peter Stanton has a flash drive that belongs to someone who's not a suspect, and even though it hasn't been reported missing, it's somewhere in his house and contains something of interest, but we don't know what. We'd like to just go look around for it. Can I have a warrant?' Give me a break."

"I thought maybe—"

"There's no maybe. I'd be asking for a general warrant. The founders of the republic had such a bad time with those that they wrote into the Constitution that we can't do that. You need probable cause, and you have to particularly describe the place to be searched, and the persons or things to be seized. Fourth Amendment. Check it out."

"What can I say? I've been a civil lawyer far too long now," Rory said. "I've forgotten all of that stuff." He reached for the check. "Let me buy you lunch."

Lester shot his hand out and snatched it up. "No can do. LAPD regs."

"Okay. Let's just split the bill on our credit cards, then."

When the card receipts came back a few minutes later, Lester turned his customer's copy over, presumably intending to write down the business purpose of the lunch, and laughed out loud.

"What's so funny?"

"Madge wrote something on the back of my credit card slip."

"What?"

"Colonel Mustard in the library with a knife."

Rory grinned. "Nice. But hey, listen, are you gonna investigate Peter Stanton? I *know* he was snooping around Sylvie's house last weekend."

"I'll give it some thought." Lester started to get up.

Rory stood up, too, and faced him across the table. "I need you to do more than give it some thought. You're a clever guy. Figure out a way to get ahold of the thumb drive Peter Stanton found in Sylvie's house."

"What do you think is on that thumb drive?"

"The reason Sylvie Virtin was killed."

"The one who was alive when we talked to her?"

"You talked to a fake, Lester."

"Like I told you, we took precautions to make sure we were talking to the real person."

"Are you a betting man?"

"You know I am."

"Okay, I'll bet you Sylvie Virtin is dead."

"What are the stakes?"

"Loser buys dinner at a restaurant of the winner's choice anywhere in California. Loser pays travel costs, too." With that, Rory had hedged his bet. If Sylvie turned out to be alive, he'd have to pay Lester, but Sarah would have to pay him.

Lester wasn't taking that bet, though. "I don't bet for pussy stakes. Why don't we make it five thousand dollars and the *winner* buys dinner?"

Rory paused for a few seconds. "Ha! You haven't changed a bit. It's a deal. But, uh, where are you getting that kind of dough?"

"Started a really profitable pool-cleaning business a couple of years ago."

Rory wasn't sure if Lester was telling the truth or not but decided not to press it. "So we have a bet, then?"

"Yes. And I'll see what I can do about a warrant—or something—without landing myself in a disciplinary proceeding."

"Great. By the way, Lester, when are you guys gonna release the autopsy report about exactly how Joe died?"

"Later today, so I might as well tell you what I think you already know. He was hit over the head with a blunt object and then garroted to death with a piece of rope."

"Fits what I saw when I opened the door."

"You know it's weird you found the body, Rory."

"Yeah, I know."

"That reminds me, though. Have you heard that the entire security camera system in the studio's Executive Office Structure had been broken for at least a week before the murder? It's why we don't know for sure who killed him."

"No, I hadn't heard that."

"Any idea why they wouldn't have fixed it right away?"

"Not specifically, but you have to understand, Lester. Studio security might imagine that someone could try to off a movie star, or a famous director or well-known producer, or even, at the outer limit of possibility, a writer. But they probably don't think much about murder in the EOS. It's filled with suits. My guess is that no one in security could imagine that anyone would want to kill a suit. So they didn't get around to fixing it right away."

"Suits," Lester said with a smile. "That's what the uniforms call detectives."

"Exactly. When was the last time someone shot a detective, Lester?"

"It happens, but not all that often."

* * *

No sooner had Rory stepped back into his office than the phone rang. It was the receptionist. "There's someone calling for you named Madge. She says you had lunch with her today."

"That's sort of true. Put her through."

"Hi, Tuna. Remember me?"

"Yep. How did you locate me?"

"Your name was on your credit card slip. I looked you up on the state bar website, which lists your law firm and its phone number."

"Oh. Of course. Well, what can I do for you, Madge?"

"I wanted to let you know that I think someone is following you."

"Do tell."

"Not long after you and your friend arrived, a tall guy with a shaved head, wearing mirrored sunglasses, came in and took a table that was more or less around the corner from yours. He could see you, but you couldn't see him. He ordered only an espresso and a croissant. When you got up to leave, he slapped a twenty down on the table and followed you out. He didn't eat the croissant, and he didn't come back for his change."

"How do you know he wasn't following my cop friend?"

"Maybe he was. But I don't call cops up. So I'm calling you. You can tell him if you want to."

"Well, thanks. I will definitely look into it."

"You're welcome. Do you want me to send you a photo I took of the guy?"

"You took a photo of a guy minding his own business in your restaurant?"

"If he was minding his own business, I'm an armadillo. Do you want the photo or not, Tuna?"

That meant giving her either his e-mail or his cell number. What the hell; he gave her his number. "Thanks, Madge, I'll look for the photo via text. Let me know if you see the guy again, huh?"

"Will do."

He was about to say something else, but realized that the call had been terminated. A moment later, the photo arrived.

He looked at it, sat and thought about it for a while. The guy looked a lot like the guy in the red Honda. He needed to tell Sarah about it, but that could wait.

Chapter 13

WEDNESDAY EVENING

While Sarah had found the hoopla around the premiere of *Extorted*—spotlights in the sky, the red carpet leading into the theater, ushers to take you to your seat and the big tent with canapés and champagne—exciting, the movie, beyond the blessed absence of ads and previews before it started, had left her well south of wowed.

On emerging from the theater, she pulled out her phone, gave the film a bad rating on both Metacritic and Rotten Tomatoes and posted a review:

> *[Spoiler alert] Sitting president roomed in college w/ two other guys. Had homosexual affair with one, who later died of AIDS. 3rd roommate, knew about it, returned to his African country. Now head of state there. Has been extorting president for years for small things, now needs large military assistance package worth billions. President up for reelection, running on family values. If he refuses, all will be revealed. President*

invites leader to DC for formal visit, makes plans to have him assassinated. President and wife are gunned down instead, Grinning VP, now the pres, embraces African leader. Bad acting, stupid, predictable plot, cheap CGI. Too long.

That made her feel much better about having been denied an invite to the party. She'd been careful, though. Instead of posting under Sarahhot, her usual *nom de movie* (as she called it), she'd put the review up under a new pseudonym less likely to get her caught: *Criticfromtheheartland.*

As she was heading back to the parking lot, she spotted the buses that were to take people to the after-party, leaned in through the doors of one and said to the driver, "Hey, I'm driving to the party, but I've forgotten the address."

The driver smiled at her and said, "Lady, I can't give you the address unless you show me your invite to the party."

"Please?"

"No can do. I could lose my job."

A dapper man wearing a tux, who was getting on the bus, said, "If you'll have a drink with me at the party, I'll give you the address."

"Okay."

He gave her the address and said, "My name is John Esparza. What's yours?"

"Sarah Gold."

"Okay, see you there, Sarah. But you're not going like that, are you?" He gestured at her spangle-covered white jeans and red peasant blouse.

"No, I'm planning to change into something a good deal more, well, fun."

"I'll look forward to seeing that."

***

Rory arrived early at the party, hoping to catch Hal Harold, who, he knew, liked to get there early and leave early. Assuming, of course, that he chose to come at all, under the circumstances. Rory was standing by the bar, scanning the door, when he felt a tap on his shoulder. He turned, and there was Hal.

"Hey, Hal, I was watching the door for you. How did you get in without my seeing you?"

"Sneaked in through the kitchen. There are too many media types out front. I know they're waiting for the celebs, but given my situation I didn't want to give them the opportunity to pounce on me, too."

"Yeah, for once you're the subject of attention instead of your clients."

Hal nodded. "I appear to have lost my anonymity. I'll have to get used to that until this ridiculous murder thing blows over."

"What evidence have they got against you?"

"How about a drink, Rory?" Without waiting for an answer, he turned to the bartender. "Two extradry Grey Goose martinis, one with olives, one with a twist." They stood in silence while the bartender made the drinks and set them down on the polished wood counter without spilling a drop. Hal handed the one with the olives to Rory, picked up the other and raised his glass. "To the end of this murder nonsense."

They clinked glasses, and Hal took a large swallow of his martini.

Rory said, "Yes, to that. And now, as I was asking, what have they got against you?"

"Nothing, so far as I know. This is all about the DA having it in for me for reasons that go back a long way."

"A small bird told me that they found a spot of your blood in Joe's office."

Hal took another sizable swallow of his martini. "Where'd you hear that?"

"A source."

"Who was the source?"

"I'd rather not say, Hal."

"I thought we were law partners."

"We are, but I'm not your lawyer on this, remember? Quentin Zavallo is representing you."

"Do you know him?"

"Not really."

"He's around here somewhere. He's wearing one of those stupid purple shirts he always wears. If you see him, introduce yourself."

"So what was a spot of your blood doing in Joe's office?"

Hal put the martini to his lips and finished it off. "Do you know the funny thing about blood?"

"No, enlighten me."

"Once it's dry, it's hard to tell how old it is."

Rory took a small sip of his own martini. "Why was your blood *ever* in Joe's office?"

"Cut my hand in there."

"How and when?"

"Do you want another, Rory?"

"Not yet."

Hal turned back to the bartender. "Another of the same." He turned back to Rory. "You need to learn to take advantage of these open bars. But where were we?"

"You were about to tell me how and when you cut your hand in Joe's office."

"You know, I wasn't born yesterday, son. Your source is probably a cop. And right now, the cops don't know how or when I cut my hand. I prefer to leave it that way for now and not take the risk that you're a police spy."

"I'm not."

"So you say."

"My source told me another thing, Hal."

"Hit me with it."

"He said that on top of the blood evidence, they've also got a security video clip of you looking red faced and disheveled as you drove off the studio lot, not long after the murder."

"Bullshit. They don't even know exactly when the murder took place. Besides, I've always looked disheveled. My kindergarten teacher sent a note home to my mother complaining about it." He laughed, the raucous laugh of someone getting drunk in a hurry.

Hal finished off the martini and asked the bartender for a third. Then he said, "Whoa! Look at that," and pointed to the middle of the room.

Rory looked and saw a beautiful blonde talking to a man who appeared to be in his late fifties but was wearing a purple shirt better suited to someone a good deal younger. The woman had her back to Rory and was swathed in a tight black dress, her back bare from the waist to a thin black strap around her neck.

"That's our new associate, is it not?" Hal said. "She certainly cleans up nice."

"What the hell is Sarah doing here?"

"You didn't get her an invite?"

"Nope. I tried, but couldn't get it done."

"Maybe she persuaded someone else with more clout. She's a go-getter, I hear."

"Who'd you hear that from?"

"Just when we checked her out before we hired her."

Rory drank down what remained of his martini in two gulps. "Hey, that was great. Bartender? Hit me with another."

"That's more like the Rory I know and love," Hal said.

"So, Hal, how carefully did you investigate Sarah before we hired her?"

"Just the usual. Among other things, she'd already been vetted for the Supreme Court clerkship, so I didn't think we needed to do a lot. Why?"

"Did you check out the two-year gap on her resume between college and law school?"

"I did ask her about it. She said she worked as a waitress or something to save up some money for law school."

"Yeah. She told me the same thing. Funny thing is, the place she says she worked—a bar called Another Bird in the Hand—doesn't exist. Or at least I can't find it."

"Maybe it closed."

"Yeah, maybe, but it should have left some trace on the web."

"I'm sure there's an explanation. Anyway, I see your refill is here." He turned to the bar and handed Rory the new martini. "Drink up."

"Thanks."

"In the meantime, I'm going to go circulate. In the short run, my current notoriety should make people even more interested in the firm, and it'll generate future business in the long run."

"Unless you go to jail."

"Trust me, I'm not going to jail."

Rory watched Hal wander into the crowd, which was growing thicker, and launched himself, martini in hand, toward Sarah and the purple-shirted man he assumed was Quentin Zavallo.

Chapter 14

When Rory approached, Sarah was deep in conversation with the man. Rory stood politely to the side and waited for one of them to acknowledge him. Finally, the man in the purple shirt looked over at him.

"Hi," Rory said, addressing him. "I'm Rory Calburton. I assume you're Quentin Zavallo. Hal Harold suggested I come over and introduce myself. Apologies for interrupting."

"Nice to meet you, Rory. No apology needed. Hal has mentioned you to me, quite favorably I might add. And I saw your partnership announcement. Congratulations."

"Thanks."

"I assume you know Sarah Gold here, since you're in the same firm."

"I do. We're working together on a case." Rory took another swallow from his martini and turned to Sarah. "How the hell did you get in?"

"Oh, you didn't have an invite?" Quentin said.

"No, I didn't. I used my wiles, you might say."

"Were your wiles assisted by that dress?" Rory asked.

"Do you like it?"

"It's not appropriate for a lawyer from our firm, frankly."

"What, you don't like the slit up the side to my waist, or the lack of a back?"

"More the two smallish swatches of material covering your, uh, upper body. Held on in a way I don't quite get."

"You like?"

"No."

"Well, you're the one who suggested I wear, if I recall your exact words, 'as little as you're comfortable wearing.' And I'm quite comfortable, thank you."

"Maybe we should take this conversation in a different direction," Quentin said.

"Yes," Sarah said. "Quentin and I were just discussing the fact that Joe Stanton's brother, Peter, may have a flash drive that will shed light on who murdered Joe."

"Did you tell him how you got that information, Sarah?"

"No, I like to protect my sources, Rory."

Quentin laughed. "I don't need to know the source. Unfortunately, there's very little discovery in a criminal proceeding at this stage, at least for the defense, so we can't subpoena something like that from Peter right now. But I'm going to send an investigator out to talk to him."

"Ask Peter about his past relationship with Sylvie Virtin," Sarah said. "Something's going on there. And I think Sylvie's dead, by the way."

"She called me just this afternoon," Quentin said. "To give me some information that she thought might help exonerate Hal."

"How do you know it was really her?" Rory asked.

"She seemed to know a lot of details about Joe, Peter, Hal and other things that an imposter wouldn't know."

"Unless someone briefed her," Sarah said. "Did she tell you where she was?"

"Yes, near DC."

"Why don't you ask her for her address and send someone to talk to her, too?" Rory said.

"Not a bad idea. I think we'll do that."

"I have to go follow up on my wiles," Sarah said. "I owe someone a visit for getting me in here."

"Can I get you a drink first?" Rory asked.

"I don't drink. As you well know." She turned to Quentin. "Another leftover from my past."

"What past are you referring to?" he asked.

"It's not really important," Sarah said. "By the way, Rory, where's your date?"

"Dana? She's out front doing her TQEN duties. But she'll be in soon. I got her name on the invite list."

"Hers, but not mine," Sarah said.

"It's different if you're bringing a date. And by the time I'd gotten her in here and gotten you into the movie, I was out of favors to cash."

"I see."

Rory decided to ignore Sarah's icy stare and move on. "Here comes Dana now," he said. "Do you guys want to meet her?"

"Maybe later," Sarah said.

"I already know her," Quentin said. "And I don't want to renew the acquaintanceship right now. See you guys around."

"Bye," Sarah said.

Thirty seconds later, Dana walked up to him. She was wearing a short red skirt and an ecru blouse with a gold chain necklace. "Did the two people you were talking to just flee because they saw me coming?"

"Kind of."

"One was Quentin Zavallo, right?"

"Yeah."

"We've always had a good relationship. Wonder why he fled."

"Maybe he didn't want to talk about the Hal Harold case."

"Could be. Who was the tall blonde in the nothing black dress?"

"Associate in our firm, Sarah Gold. Working on a civil case with me. She was at the courthouse today. Guess you missed seeing her."

"Which case? The stolen script thing?"

"It wasn't stolen."

"You know, I might know a little something about that."

"Do tell."

"What are you drinking?"

"Grey Goose martini."

"Take me to the bar, order me a double, and we'll talk."

They stood at the bar, drinking. Rory ordered a third martini, and Dana got to work on her double.

"Okay, Dana. What do you know?"

"I know two things."

"Which are?"

"What have you got to trade?"

He sighed. "So I'm learning that in your world, I gotta pay for information."

"Economists would say it's an efficient system."

"Okay, do you know who Sylvie Virtin is?" Rory said.

"Yes."

"I think she's dead."

"Really. Now that's something I'd like to hear about. Tell me what you know."

He did, and she listened, got out her cell and took some notes.

"Alright, Dana, what do I get in exchange?"

"The plane crash Alex Toltec was in?"

"Uh-huh."

"The engine on his plane apparently ran out of oil. Because the oil filter was screwed up somehow."

"Broken or jimmied?"

"The National Transportation Safety Board is working on that. We have a source there, so we hope to know as soon as they know."

"How good a source?"

"Well, actually, let's say we know someone who knows someone at the NTSB."

"So not so good a source. What's the second piece of information?"

She looked around the room. "Why don't you take me around and introduce me to everyone you know here? Not just the celebs; I know a lot of them already. The backroom people are a lot more valuable to me."

"And then I'll get the second piece of information?"

"Let's see how the evening goes, Rory."

Chapter 15

THURSDAY MORNING

Rory awoke with a splitting headache. The bright sunlight streaming into the room wasn't helping. He started to get up to close the drapes before realizing he was naked and there was a naked female leg draped across his. It wasn't exactly a movie-star-quality leg, but it was a very nice leg nonetheless. When he followed the leg upward, across an equally naked body, he saw a peacefully sleeping Dana, her hair spilled out across his pillow. Then it all came back to him.

After a few minutes, she opened her eyes and stared at him for a moment, clearly trying to put together where she was. "Oh, jeez," she said. "Please don't tell anyone I went to a Hollywood party and went home with a lawyer."

"If you won't tell anyone I brought a reporter from TQEN home with me. A lot of our clients would never speak to me again."

"We didn't drive here, did we?"

He pushed himself up on an elbow. "No, we grabbed an Uber." He fell back down onto the mattress.

"Is this the beginning of something special or just a one-nighter?" she asked.

"We had a good time, and the sex was great."

"It was."

"So that's a start."

They lay there for a few moments more, in that awkwardness that sometimes occurs between people who've been intimate for the first time with no real history behind them.

"Dana, I hate to ask this, but . . ."

"You want to know what the second piece of information is."

"Yes."

She sat up. "Do you like what you see?"

"I do."

"Well, let's do it again, and see what it's like in daylight now that we've gotten to know each other, and maybe I'll tell you."

An hour later, after they'd both fallen asleep again, he woke and asked, "What time is it?"

"I don't know."

He reached over to the nightstand and picked up his cell. "Shit, it's already nine."

"Works for me. I don't have to be in today until three."

"Thank God I don't have any appointments this morning."

"You still want to know the second piece of information?"

"Yeah."

"So unromantic, Rory."

"Just fucking tell me."

"Mary Broom and Alex Toltec had an affair."

"Seriously? Our firm has a file of research on each of them, and there's not a thing about their even knowing each other."

"Maybe they met at a party." She giggled. "Which reminds me. Did you use protection last night? I know you did this morning, but . . ."

He looked on the floor beside the bed. "Looks like I did. When was the affair?"

"At least ten years ago, maybe much longer. That's all we know at the moment. We're working on it."

His cell rang. He picked it up and touched "Answer."

"Why aren't you here, Rory? Did you go home with her last night?"

"None of your business, Sarah."

"I saw the two of you stagger out together."

It was loud enough that Dana could clearly hear both sides of the conversation. She reached over and grabbed the phone from his hand. "Eat your heart out, dear." She touched "End" and said, "What's your relationship with her?"

"Don't have one, except a professional one."

"You weren't attracted by the dress? Or the lack of most of it?"

"She looked good in it, but I don't trawl in the law firm pond. Been there eight years, and it hasn't happened yet and won't. But hey, you sound jealous."

"Maybe. You're quite a large hunk of guy, and I like that."

"Do you remember what we talked about last night?"

"Kierkegaard, I think."

"You wouldn't know Kierkegaard if you ran into him in the park."

"Well, he's dead, so he'd probably have a lot of dirt hanging off of him, making him hard to recognize. But I majored in philosophy. I'm not just a pretty face with a camera trained on it."

"I hear you. We'll see where this goes. But in the meantime, I have what is effectively a trial to prepare for that starts on Monday. I need to get to work."

"Will it be open to the public?"

"Of course."

"Maybe I'll come."

Chapter 16

Rory made it into the firm by ten.

Sarah reported to him on her factual research on Mary Broom. The long and short of it was that Broom had once been one of the planet's most famous actors, and then, ten years earlier, at what seemed the height of her career, she had quit and moved to India to follow a guru in the mountains north of New Delhi. Six weeks ago she had reappeared out of nowhere, hired Kathryn Thistle and held a well-publicized, mobbed press conference in front of the *LA Times* building, attended, it seemed, by all the world's media.

"Do you want to see any clips from the press conference?" Sarah asked.

"No. No need right now."

"Okay. Well, after that she marched down the street to the federal courthouse—followed by the press as if she were the Pied Piper—and personally filed her lawsuit, claiming that she alone wrote the script for *Extorted* and seeking to enjoin its release. But of course you know all about that."

"That's it?"

"No, there's more. I decided to examine what's been written about her in the press in India. I started with the English-language papers there, like the *Times of India*, and I also checked out a couple of the Hindi papers."

"Do you speak Hindi?"

"No. I started out using Google Translate, but that wasn't working for me. So I called on my alumni network, found someone who spoke Hindi and got him to translate a couple of the articles that looked interesting based on the rough Google translations."

Rory had to admit that he was impressed. "What did you find?"

"There's some secret surrounding Mary Broom and the ashram she's been living in these last ten years."

"Like what?"

"I'm not sure. But the ashram was a pretty open place before she got there. You could go and visit, or just spend a weekend. Or take tours even. And they were actively seeking new acolytes, if that's the right word. Shortly after Mary Broom arrived, the tours got canceled, they stopped taking new people and it became a very hard place to get information about. Oh, and they built a new facility. Kind of like a new dorm, with serious security."

"Maybe it's just because they had a famous person there. Why do you think there's gotta be some secret on top of that?"

"I don't know. I can't put my finger on it. But there's something there, and I'm sure it has to do with more than just a famous person showing up."

"Well, it's interesting, but I don't think that's anything I can use to cross-examine her. I can't say, 'Ms. Broom, please tell us the secret of your ashram.'"

Sarah laughed. "No, probably not."

"Keep after it. Maybe you'll figure it out, and maybe it will turn out to be something we can use."

"I will."

"I need to go on getting ready for the hearing on Monday. Plus I've got to catch up on a few other things. I also want you to see what you can find out about Alex Toltec."

"Okay, on my way to do that."

Not long after Sarah left, Hal walked into his office, sat down without invitation in one of the newly arrived guest chairs, as was his wont, and said without so much as a hello, "Did you go home from the party with that—with Ms. Barbour?"

"No, she came home with me. And you were about to call her a slut, huh?"

"Maybe."

"You're what, seventy-five?"

"Close enough."

"Hal, maybe in your day, women who went home with men were sluts, but these days, women with healthy sexual appetites are simply called normal human beings."

"If you say so." He picked up a minibasketball that was sitting on Rory's desk, tossed it in the air and caught it.

"Why do you care who I go to bed with, Hal?"

"She's already gone on the air to report that I've been charged with murder. Hinting that I'm guilty as hell. And my arrest wasn't even hours old."

"It's her job."

Hal threw the ball against the wall and caught it on the rebound.

"Hey," Rory said, "you're gonna mess up my wall. I just got this office, and it just got painted."

"Hey, Rory?" Hal said. "In effect, I own this office, and every other office in this place, so live with it."

"So true."

"Don't you think it's unethical to shack up with a woman who's already started pummeling me on TV?"

"Maybe if I were on your trial team, but as you yourself said, I'm not your lawyer."

Hal sighed. "I shouldn't have said that. I was, as you might imagine, quite shocked at being arrested. I apologize."

Rory considered whether to respond with the words of apology Hal was clearly looking for. But he wasn't quite ready to do that, so he used the old politician's trick and responded instead to a different part of Hal's statement. "Yeah, I can understand you were upset. I visited the jails back when I was a deputy DA, and they're not great places, even if you were just in a holding cell for a few minutes before you got released."

"True enough. But I hope you can see my point about Dana Barbour."

"It's Barbour. And here's the way it is, Hal. It's been hard for me to find a woman I really like, and I'm not getting any younger. I'm not giving her up because you perceive some imaginary ethical conflict on a case in which the firm isn't even counsel."

"Not the answer I was hoping for. Particularly after only one night together." Hal threw the ball against the wall again, much harder this time, and caught it on the rebound. It left an even larger spot.

"Hal, I'm feeling like we haven't gotten to the real reason you dropped by. I assume you didn't come in here just to gripe about my sex life."

"You're right." Hal sat up and squeezed the ball between his hands. "Here's the question. Do you know anything else about my case other than what you told me at the party?"

"About the blood spot and your looking disheveled?"

"Right."

"No, not a thing." He paused. "Well, come to think of it, that's not exactly true."

"Tell me."

"Joe Stanton's brother, Peter, was inside Sylvie Virtin's house and, uh, found a flash drive hidden there that might—and I emphasize the word *might*—contain a file related to the script-theft case against the studio."

"Which could be related to my case, how? I don't see the connection."

"Not sure. Maybe someone killed Joe to prevent that file from seeing the light of day. But if someone else killed him, you're off the hook."

"Or maybe it was me that wanted to keep the file from seeing the light of day."

"Why would you want to keep it hidden?"

Hal picked up the basketball again and took a shot at the small basket Rory had hung on the wall. An air ball. "Shit. I was never any good at basketball."

"To repeat, why would you care about a stolen file?"

"I don't think I necessarily would."

"Okay."

"Rory, when you said Peter was inside Sylvie's house, you hesitated slightly. Is there something you're not telling me?"

"Caught." Rory got up from behind his desk, scooped the basketball up off the floor and shot it toward the rim. It had a beautiful arc and swished through the net.

"You were a lot closer to the basket."

"No, I'm just a better athlete."

"In my time—"

"Yeah, yeah. Anyway, what I didn't tell you was that Sarah was at Sylvie's house and found the flash drive hidden behind some books. Peter surprised her there and grabbed it from her."

Hal gave his head a small shake. "What was Sarah doing at Sylvie's house?"

"In effect, she broke in to look around. Well, 'broke in' is too strong. The back door was unlocked."

Hal smiled. "That girl is a go-getter."

"You're not upset?"

"No, as long as she wasn't caught." He grinned. "But you must be upset, or you wouldn't have bothered to tell me about it."

"Yeah, I am. It could damage the firm big time if she gets caught doing something like that."

Hal put his hand on Rory's shoulder and squeezed ever so slightly. From his football days, Rory recognized that he was about to be coached.

"Son," Hal said, "you're a partner now. That means not only managing cases, but nurturing people. So think about Sarah as someone with a lot of talent who needs to be nurtured into the great lawyer she'll eventually be. Not many people get a chance to do that with a Supreme Court law clerk."

"That's good advice, I guess. It was just that what she did was outrageous."

Hal took his hand off of Rory's shoulder. "Well, what did you do to vent your outrage?"

"I told her to cut it the fuck out, that she's not a PI anymore."

"Well, that's a start, but swearing at people isn't really recommended as the best way to mentor."

"Yeah, I guess that's right. I'll think on how to, uh, mold her." Even as he said it, he realized that, with Sarah in particular, the comment could be misinterpreted.

But if Hal picked up on that, he didn't remark on it. He just said, "Was there anything else I need to know?"

"Yeah. She found a photo in the house that's of possible interest."

"Oh?"

Rory reached into his desk drawer, took out the photo and handed it to Hal.

Hal peered at it for a moment, a look of nostalgia passing across his face. "Oh, look how young Sylvie and Joe are there," Hal said. "I guess we all were once."

"You knew about their affair?"

"Everyone knew about it. Except his wife, of course."

"How do you know she didn't know?"

"Gladys lives in her twenty-thousand-square-foot house in Palos Verdes that Joe bought her, supervises her staff of five, rides her horses and drives her Bentley to Saks in Newport Beach."

"So?"

"She was too busy to know, and even if she did know, I doubt she would have cared as long as it wasn't in the *LA Times* and her lifestyle marched right on."

"I didn't know GCs made the kind of money to support that kind of lifestyle."

"They don't. Joe made a lot of smart real estate investments about thirty years ago, and they paid off."

"So you don't think Gladys killed him."

"No." Hal picked up the basketball again. "What if we had a contest, Rory? Best of nine."

"Just for the fun of it?"

"No. There have to be stakes. No one in this firm ever plays a game unless there are stakes."

"What did you have in mind?"

"Want to put your Tesla up?"

Rory laughed. "No, we'll have to find something more interesting."

Hal's cell phone rang. He plucked it out of his breast pocket, put it to his ear and listened for at least a minute. His face turned ashen. "Alright."

"What's going on?" Rory asked.

"That was Quentin Zavallo. The DA is going to ask a judge to revoke my bail and put me back in jail."

"Oh my God, why?"

"I'm accused of trying to intimidate a witness."

"Who?"

"They won't say. I have to appear immediately in department twenty-two in the Criminal Courts Building. Quentin is picking me up."

"Do you want me to come?"

"Yes, and bring Sarah. I'll meet you there."

Chapter 17

THURSDAY AFTERNOON
LOS ANGELES COUNTY SUPERIOR COURT—CRIMINAL
DIVISION
People v. Harold

Rory and Sarah got downtown in record time and parked across from the metal and glass high-rise formally known as the Clara Shortridge Foltz Criminal Justice Center but usually referred to by lawyers as the Criminal Courts Building, which had been its name until 2002. As they approached the metal detector at the entrance, Rory said, "Sarah, I'm guessing you don't have the card that gets you through security more quickly?"

"No. It's in the mail, they say. But it hasn't come yet."

"Alright. You'll have to go through the normal, slow way, then, with everyone else." He glanced at the line, which snaked around the corner. "Sorry the line's so long. You can catch up with me."

"Okay."

Rory got through the metal detector in under a minute and was in front of the courtroom on the fifth floor minutes after that. When he walked inside, passing through the two sets of double doors into the courtroom itself, the judge was not yet on the bench, and the spectator seats were starting to fill, mainly with members of the media—some of whom were sitting in the jury box, and many of whom he recognized from his last brush with a celebrity trial. He also noticed Gladys Stanton sitting in the front row, dressed all in black.

He took a seat near the door, looked around and saw that J. T. Trucker, the chief deputy DA—a man who gave frequent interviews to the media but rarely tried cases—was already seated at the prosecutor's table next to the jury box. Hal Harold and Quentin Zavallo were at the other table. Zavallo's shirt was white instead of purple, but his tie was a bright shade of green with large red dots.

Hal turned around, saw Rory and gave a quick wave.

"All rise!" the clerk intoned, and everyone stood as the judge walked to her chair. Rory remarked to himself that this was a very formal courtroom. Most superior court judges had long ago dispensed with the all-rise stuff.

The judge was Tassy Gilmore, who'd recently been profiled on the front page of the *Daily Journal* on the occasion of her twenty-fifth year on the bench. According to the profile, she was a no-nonsense judge (had any judicial profile, Rory wondered, ever described one of their honors as a nonsense judge?) who ran a tight ship but had a wry sense of humor when it pleased her to display it.

Judge Gilmore was tall and slim almost to the point of being bony, with her hair cut short. The last time Rory had seen her, when he was a deputy DA, her hair had been blonde. Now it was mostly gray. Her most distinctive feature back then had been her bloodred nail polish. That had not changed.

"Well," Judge Gilmore said, looking down at Trucker. "To what do I owe your sudden appearance in my courtroom, Mr. Trucker? I thought you mainly stayed up on the high floors of this building, running the

DA's office. I can't recall the last time I saw you down here slumming amid the people and doing trial work."

Trucker smiled a not particularly human smile—more like the rictus Rory had seen on pictures of corpses—and said, "Your Honor, I'm here because of the importance of this matter to the People. The defendant, Mr. Harold, as I believe Your Honor is aware, is out on bail, but we have today discovered that he has been trying to corrupt key evidence."

"And you want him admonished—told he's a bad boy, don't do it again? Or what?"

"No, we request that his bail be revoked and that he be remanded to custody."

"That's a fairly serious request, particularly about a longtime member of the bar with, so far as I know, a sterling reputation and deep community ties. And who has posted a million-dollar bail. What are the alleged facts?"

"There's nothing alleged about them, Your Honor. One of the key pieces of evidence against Mr. Harold is that a drop of his blood was found in the victim's office, between the victim's desk and the office door."

"And he went at it with some spot remover? An 'Out, damned spot' sort of thing?"

Trucker, clearly not used to being gently made fun of by a judge, smiled a tight smile. "Not hardly. Mr. Harold's defense counsel"—he gestured at Zavallo—"has informed us that Mr. Harold's defense is that he cut his hand while in the victim's office at an earlier date, that that's how the blood got on the carpet and that there is a witness to that event."

"Why would defense counsel tell you that as opposed to just springing it on you at the preliminary hearing and making you all look like—well, look bad? There's little that Mr. Zavallo enjoys more, as I recall." She smiled down at Zavallo, who beamed.

"He told us because he wants us to drop the case, although he was cagey about the identity of the supposed witness."

"Okay. Go on."

"We've been able, through independent investigation, to learn the identity of that supposed witness, and we have interviewed him."

"Out of curiosity, was the defense aware you were interviewing him?"

"Not so far as I know."

"So what's the problem? Both sides are permitted to interview anyone who will talk to them."

"When we interviewed the witness—an interview, I might add, that he agreed to only reluctantly, since he'd prefer not to be publicly identified with this matter—he said he had absolutely no recollection of the hand-cutting incident Mr. Harold's counsel has told us about."

"And?"

"We learned today that Mr. Harold went to see the witness late yesterday evening and, after learning that he had no recollection of the episode, pressured him to change his mind."

Quentin Zavallo was suddenly on his feet. "This is absolutely, totally, completely false, Your Honor."

"And utterly false, too, Mr. Zavallo?"

"Yes, please add that to the list, Your Honor."

"Alright. Well, you'll get your chance at this, Mr. Zavallo. Mr. Trucker, how do you propose to prove this very serious allegation to the court?"

"By calling the witness to testify."

"Which will disclose his identity."

"Not if you close the courtroom to the public."

Rory was stunned at the request. With the exception of juvenile matters, American courtrooms were almost always open. The only exceptions he could think of were certain national security matters.

Judge Gilmore clearly had the same shocked reaction. She actually reared back in her chair.

"I can tell you right now, Mr. Trucker, I'm not going to do that. I've never closed my courtroom, and I'm not about to start. And certainly not for this."

"In that case, Your Honor, we will simply have to call the witness, and the People will have to live with the consequences of his being identified before a preliminary hearing or a trial."

Rory smiled to himself. Whenever a prosecutor referred to himself as the People, Rory always wanted to look around to see if there was a large crowd jostling to get into the courtroom. Of course, when he'd been a deputy DA, he'd always used the same phrase himself. It sounded so much better than saying "the prosecution."

"What consequences to the People?" Judge Gilmore asked.

"He'll be besieged by media."

"The wages of living in an open, democratic society, Mr. Trucker. Do you want to identify him now, or have him just walk through the courtroom doors, like on *Perry Mason*?"

"No, we'll identify him. He's waiting out in the hall." He nodded to the young woman who was sitting next to him. She got up and headed through the courtroom doors and out into the hall, presumably to fetch the witness.

"The People call Peter Stanton," Trucker said.

"Shit," Rory muttered, loudly enough to cause the man next to him to turn and stare. Rory jumped up and pushed through the first of the swinging double doors that led to the hallway just as Peter Stanton came through the outer set of doors, almost bumping into him. Peter gave him an odd look, which he ignored. He had to find Sarah before she walked into the courtroom and Peter got a look at her.

Chapter 18

Rory looked up and down the hallway but didn't see Sarah. Seconds later, she stepped out of an elevator about fifty feet down the hall. Rory sprinted to meet her. "Peter Stanton is in the courtroom about to testify." He pushed the "Down" button on the elevator bank. "You need to get out of here."

"Rory, I don't see a big downside in his identifying me."

As she said it an elevator arrived with a ding. "Get in."

She did, and he got in with her and pushed the button for the ground floor. No one else was in the cab with them. "Rory, honestly, even if he—"

He pointed to the camera in the corner of the elevator. "I have no idea who has access to that tape."

They stepped out into the courthouse elevator lobby. "Sarah, it may be the case that he'll eventually figure out who you are no matter what we do. But for now, I don't need that complication in our case. And I don't think Hal needs it in his."

"Even if Peter identifies me, I'm in a position to nail him for sneaking around Sylvie's house and taking that flash drive."

"As I recall, you were the one who was sneaking around the house. He just happened to catch you."

"That's one way to look at it. But he's got that flash drive, and I'm betting he doesn't want anyone finding out that he does."

"Be that as it may, I don't want you in that courtroom."

"It's a public courtroom."

For a moment, he could only stare at her, and this time it was unrelated to her beauty. "Hey, Sarah?"

"What?"

"I don't know quite how to get this through your head, but you're a member of our law firm, not an independent agent who can simply do as you please. You need to learn to be a team player."

"Alright, chief. I'll go back to the firm like a good girl." She smiled.

"I don't think that was a genuine smile."

"You'll never know. I'm good at faking it."

"Whatever, get out of here. I need to get back to the courtroom."

He watched her until she'd actually walked out the door to the street. Then he hightailed it back to the courtroom.

When he walked back in, Peter Stanton was on the witness stand, in the midst of testifying.

"And after I told Hal—for the second time—that I had no recollection whatsoever of his having cut his finger in Joe's office while I was there, he got up out of his chair, shook his finger in my face and said, 'You're fucking lying.' And then he closed his fist, and I thought he was about to punch me."

Trucker, who was doing the questioning while standing up at his table, asked, "What, if anything, did you say in response?"

"I told him I felt like he was threatening me and to get out of my face."

"Did he say anything in response to that?"

"Yes. He said, 'I'm not threatening you, but I'm in a very threatened situation myself. I need your help.'"

"Did you respond to that?"

"Yes. I asked how I could help, and he said, 'By remembering the event as I remember it, because that's the way it happened.'"

"Mr. Stanton, did the event in fact happen the way he said it did?"

"No, not at all. I never saw Hal cut his finger in my brother's office. Or anywhere else for that matter."

"Did he finally leave?"

"Yes, and slammed the door hard as he did so."

"And to be clear, you said earlier that this was at your house?"

"Yes."

"And that he arrived late at night without letting you know he was coming?"

"Right. It was around eleven o'clock, and he announced himself by pounding on the door."

"I have no further questions."

This didn't sound like the Hal Harold Rory had known for the last eight years. He'd never seen Hal get physically in anyone's face, even in heated situations. And in recent years, Hal usually went to bed at eight o'clock.

Judge Gilmore looked to Zavallo and said, "Your witness, Mr. Zavallo."

Zavallo stood and said, "Mr. Stanton, did Hal actually threaten you in any way?"

Rory noted Zavallo's use of "Hal" rather than "Mr. Harold." It was great tradecraft as a way to make Hal seem less threatening.

"I felt threatened by Hal."

Perfect, Rory thought. Peter had bought into using Hal's first name.

"That wasn't my question. I asked if Hal actually threatened you."

"I felt threatened by Hal's body language and by his shaking his finger at me and closing his fist."

"Are you married, Mr. Stanton?"

"Yes."

"Has your wife ever shaken her finger at you?"

A titter went around the courtroom.

"Yes."

"Did you feel threatened?"

"No, but my wife is only five foot two and a hundred pounds on a good day, so it's rather different." He gestured to Hal as if to point out to everyone that Hal looked large and in charge. "And she never waved a closed fist at me."

"Mr. Stanton, you still haven't answered my question. Did he threaten you verbally?"

"No, I guess not. But like I said, I certainly felt threatened."

"With regard to your claim that Hal closed his fist, did he at any time move it toward you?"

"No."

"Did he actually shake his fist?"

Peter paused, as if trying to recall the image into his own mind. "No."

"Did you ask him to leave at any point?"

"No."

"So he left of his own accord."

"Yes."

"Are you and Hal friends?"

"More like acquaintances."

"Is there bad blood between you?"

"Objection," Trucker said, not bothering to get up from his table. "Ambiguous and uncertain."

"Overruled. You may answer, Mr. Stanton."

If Peter Stanton were smart, Rory thought, he'd take a cue from his lawyer's objection, even though it was overruled, and say he didn't understand the question.

"I'm not sure what you mean, Mr. Zavallo," Peter said.

"I'll withdraw the question and make it more specific. Have you and Mr. Harold had heated arguments in the past?"

"We've argued, yes. But I wouldn't call the arguments heated."

"What were the arguments about?"

"Objection, Your Honor," Trucker said. "The witness's past history with the defendant is irrelevant as to whether the defendant showed up at his apartment late at night and tried to get him to change his testimony—to suborn perjury. And if they had a hostile relationship, that would make the late-night visit even more threatening."

"Why don't you gentlemen approach the bench?" Judge Gilmore said.

Zavallo, Trucker and Hal Harold all rose from their seats.

"No, not you, Mr. Harold," she said. "You're playing a different role this time. I only want to talk to your lawyer." Hal sat back down.

As the two lawyers reached the bench, the court reporter picked up her stenotype and moved closer. Judge Gilmore leaned down and said, "What were the arguments about, Mr. Zavallo?"

"Will the transcript of this bench conference be released, Your Honor?" Zavallo asked.

"I'll seal it for now. We'll have to see, as the matter proceeds, if it stays sealed. I'll give it every consideration, but that's all I can promise."

"Okay," Zavallo said. "Mr. Stanton's brother, Joe, had been having an affair, over a long period of time, with his assistant, Sylvie Virtin. Mr. Harold is a close friend of Mr. Stanton's wife, Gladys, and he took her side in the whole thing. He and Peter Stanton argued about it a lot."

"What has that got to do with Peter Stanton, if it was his brother, Joe, who was having the affair?"

"Peter routinely lent Joe and Sylvie his guesthouse as a place to meet."

"I see," Judge Gilmore said. "Is that it?"

"Not fully," Trucker said. "We've looked into this a bit, because Peter Stanton is obviously going to be an important witness. It seems that Sylvie had an affair, at one time or another, with both brothers."

Judge Gilmore raised her eyebrows. "Well, here in Sodom and Gomorrah on the Pacific, I suppose nothing surprises. Was this simultaneous?"

"No," Trucker said. "Not to our understanding."

Judge Gilmore seemed to ponder the situation for a moment. Finally, she said, "I don't think we need to get into all of this right now. It doesn't really shine a bright light on the question whether the defendant was trying to change a witness's mind through threat or coercion. Let's go back on the public record."

The court reporter went back to her position, and the lawyers returned to their respective tables.

"The objection is sustained. Please move on to your next question, Mr. Zavallo."

"I have only a couple more," Zavallo said. "Mr. Stanton, how old are you?"

"Sixty."

"Are you sometimes forgetful?"

"I think everyone is a little bit at this age."

"Uh-huh. Well, did you recently visit a neurologist because you were concerned about memory loss?"

"Objection," Trucker said. "Invades the witness's privacy. Also irrelevant. Even if, like all of us, the witness might occasionally forget where he put the sugar, he clearly remembers Mr. Harold's late-night visit quite well."

"I will permit the witness to answer the question," the judge said. "But I don't think it's worth plumbing the details at this point."

"I'll break the question into two parts," Zavallo said. "Sir, did you recently visit a neurologist?"

"Yes."

"And was it because you were concerned about memory loss?"

"Yes."

"Your Honor, I need to ask the first follow-up question just to preserve my record."

"Go ahead."

"Mr. Stanton, did the neurologist diagnose you as having any kind of memory problem?"

"Objection. Hearsay, no foundation and privacy."

"Sustained. At least for now. Please move to your next topic, Mr. Zavallo."

He shrugged. "That's all I've got for the moment, Your Honor."

To Rory, the shrug said it all. Zavallo was probably gonna lose, and he knew it.

To Rory's surprise, Judge Gilmore said, "I have a question for the witness." It was rare for judges to question witnesses, and Rory couldn't recall this judge ever doing that when he'd been before her years ago.

She turned her head toward the witness. "Mr. Stanton, I can't help but notice that you have rather well-worked-out upper arms."

"Yes, Your Honor, I'm a bodybuilder."

"And how old are you?"

"Fifty-eight."

"Well, I've not yet decided if the relevant question here is whether you had reason to be afraid of Mr. Harold or if the question is whether Mr. Harold intended you to be afraid. Maybe both are relevant. But either way, why would you, given the age difference between you and Mr. Harold and your own physique, be afraid of Mr. Harold unless he was armed? And there's no evidence he was."

She leaned toward him—a witness in the witness box is only a few feet from the judge—and waited for the answer.

"Your Honor," Stanton said, "I used to race cars. About ten years ago I was in a bad auto accident on an Indy track. My right leg and hip were broken in several places. I can still walk, but only slowly, and I certainly can't run."

"Did your inability to run affect your interaction with Mr. Harold on the night in question?" the judge asked.

"Yes, it did. Rationally or not, that kind of situation puts me in greater fear of people who I perceive as threatening."

"Greater fear as compared to whom, Mr. Stanton?"

"Greater as compared to the person I was before the accident. Back then, I could have run away or have better defended myself if we came to blows."

"Did Mr. Harold know of your disability?"

"Objection," Zavallo said. "Calls for speculation."

It was interesting, Rory thought, to see a lawyer object to a judge's question, but he supposed Zavallo felt he had to do it.

"If he knows," Trucker said, "it's not speculation."

"Gentlemen," the judge said, "I'm a little rusty at this, so let me revise my question. Mr. Stanton, do you know if Mr. Harold was aware of your disability?"

"Yes, Your Honor. We had discussed it many times."

"Thank you, sir. I have no further questions." She looked away from Stanton and said, "Do either of you attorneys have further questions for the witness?"

"No, Your Honor," they both said, almost in unison.

Rory was a bit surprised Zavallo didn't want to try to repair the damage on recross—if it turned out to be damage—but perhaps he feared he'd only make it worse. He was also surprised Trucker hadn't brought up the disability on direct. Maybe he didn't know about it.

"Okay. Mr. Trucker," the judge said, "do you have any other witnesses?"

"No."

"What about you, Mr. Zavallo?"

"Your Honor, I'd put Mr. Harold on the stand right now to put the lie to the testimony you just heard. But if I do that, and this case goes to trial, the DA is no doubt going to claim that Mr. Harold, by testifying today, has waived his Fifth Amendment right not to testify and can be forced to testify at trial. And if that doesn't work, the DA will instead try to read Mr. Harold's testimony today directly to the trial jury and somehow wiggle it into something incriminating. That would also violate my client's precious Fifth Amendment right not to testify against himself."

"I can see your concerns, Counsel."

Zavallo turned toward Trucker. "Mr. Trucker, if Mr. Harold testifies, will you agree not to argue that he's waived any Fifth Amendment rights and agree not to introduce any of his testimony here in the trial of this matter, either directly or otherwise?"

Trucker didn't hesitate. "No. I won't agree to either of those things."

Zavallo looked at Hal, seated to his left, and made a gesture with his hands universally read as "What do you want to do?"

Hal shook his head in the negative.

"Mr. Harold is not going to testify today. And I don't have any other witnesses."

"Very well. We're going to take a very short break. Please return in exactly ten minutes. When we come back, we will have *brief* argument, gentlemen, and then I will rule from the bench."

Rory walked up to counsel table, where Zavallo and Hal were huddled, talking. Zavallo waved Rory into the huddle. "What do you think?" he asked.

"Incredibly weak evidence for putting someone in jail," Rory said. "If he were a guy off the street, maybe. But a respected member of the bar? I don't think so."

Hal chimed in. "I didn't shake my finger at him. I raised it to emphasize a point. This is all bullshit. I should have testified."

"Testifying would have been a bad idea," Zavallo said.

"I could have told the judge that even though Peter can't run fast, he could have beaten the shit out of me if he'd wanted to."

Zavallo ignored Hal's comment. "In any case, I agree with Rory. They haven't put on the kind of evidence it would take to put you in jail. The stuff about your closing your fist is laughable. What I wonder is why they're bothering to put on this dog and pony show. They must realize they're going to lose."

"So the question is, what's really going on?" Rory said.

"Well, whatever it is must somehow involve the judge, or they wouldn't have found this excuse to haul all of us down to her courtroom."

"We're no doubt gonna find out very shortly," Rory said.

Chapter 19

At the ten-minute mark, the judge was back on the bench. "We'll have argument now," she said. "Mr. Trucker, please keep it short."

Trucker moved to the lectern between the two tables. "Your Honor, I think the matter is crystal clear. Mr. Harold went to Mr. Stanton's house and threatened him. Even though no actual words of threat may have been uttered, the physicality that the witness has described, together with the unannounced visit and its timing late at night, are enough in and of themselves to make anyone feel threatened. And with that threat came a specific request to Mr. Stanton to 'change his mind'"—he raised his hands and put air quotes around the phrase—"about something he felt certain of. The 'or else' was well understood. And we now know, thanks to Your Honor's perceptive question, that Mr. Stanton cannot move quickly, and so had additional reason to be afraid."

What a suck-up, Rory thought.

Trucker paused, as if considering whether he had any more evidence to cite before reaching his conclusion.

"The People have many witnesses to put on in this case, and we will inevitably need to disclose their names, in advance, to defendant's counsel. The People believe those witnesses will not be safe from harm or intimidation unless Mr. Harold is incarcerated while this case proceeds. The People request that Mr. Harold's bail be revoked and that he be remanded to custody. If Your Honor has any questions, I'll be glad to answer them."

"I don't have any questions. Mr. Zavallo, your argument?"

"Your Honor, all that the People have proved here is that two longtime friends had a sharp exchange about their respective memories. There was no testimony that Hal Harold actually threatened Mr. Stanton or used threatening words while he was at Peter Stanton's house, and Hal left of his own accord."

Judge Gilmore looked skeptical. "But there were, according to Mr. Stanton, physical actions that he felt were threatening, were there not? And they included a clenched fist."

"Well, so Mr. Stanton says. But I'd also point out that, with a history of arguments between them, the witness has reason to want to sandbag Mr. Harold by exaggerating or even lying about this episode."

"Except there's no evidence of a history of Mr. Stanton trying to sandbag Mr. Harold other than your raw contention that it's so. All Mr. Stanton said was that they had argued in the past."

"I think it's a contention well worth considering, given the context."

"You don't contend, do you, Mr. Zavallo, that the visit didn't take place? Or that Mr. Harold didn't show up at Mr. Stanton's home late in the evening with no notice?"

"No, but if Mr. Harold were to testify, he'd explain that he called multiple times that day, seeking a meeting, and Mr. Stanton told him to blow off."

Rory thought about what Zavallo had just done. It was clearly improper to tell the judge what Hal would say if he testified when Zavallo had just said Hal wasn't gonna. But lawyers always lived for another day, and maybe he just wanted to let the judge know a different side to the story.

"Mr. Zavallo, you could have asked Mr. Stanton about those calls you just mentioned, but you chose not to. Or you could have put Mr. Harold on the stand and asked him. But you chose not to do that, either. I don't know whether to sanction you for, in effect, testifying by making those comments just now, or to just admire your gall. But since I'm in a good mood, I'm just going to say please don't do it again. The court reporter will strike from the record Mr. Zavallo's last comment about multiple calls."

Rory wondered why Zavallo hadn't asked Stanton about the calls. It was not likely a rookie mistake. He'd ask Zavallo if he got the chance.

"Is there anything else, Mr. Zavallo?" the judge said.

"Two points, Your Honor. First, I think what this is really about is the prosecution wanting to make it more difficult for me to prepare Mr. Harold's defense. We all know that it's a lot harder if your client is in jail."

"Not so," Trucker said.

Zavallo ignored him. "Second, I'd like to make the point that there is nothing in the law, so far as I know, that precludes a defendant—one, I'd point out, who is facing a possible life sentence if convicted—from interviewing witnesses in order to find out what they are going to say or, indeed, from suggesting to them that their memory is faulty. That is not suborning anything. It is preparing a defense."

The judge wrinkled her nose. "Which is, Mr. Zavallo, work normally carried out by lawyers, or, better yet, investigators, so as to avoid the very problem we're dealing with here. The line between intimidation and inquiry."

"Thank you, Your Honor," Zavallo said.

If Rory ever retired from being a lawyer, he might write an article called "How to Say 'Thank You, Your Honor' and Have Everyone Understand That You Just Said 'Screw You.'"

"I can rule on this matter now without further argument or research," Judge Gilmore said. "I find that the evidence that Mr. Harold attempted to intimidate a witness is persuasive. And that the People's argument that he should be incarcerated for the duration of the matter as a way to protect other witnesses is also persuasive. Mr. Harold's bail is revoked, and he is ordered to custody. The bail amount of one million dollars is ordered returned to Mr. Harold forthwith."

Rory was shocked. The evidence seemed weak. What the hell was going on? And they had just told Hal not to worry.

Zavallo had to be shocked, too, but he was trying to deal with it as best he could. "Your Honor," he said, "I think in the case of Mr. Harold, a respected member of the bar, that a stern warning would suffice, and I will represent to the court, as an officer of the court, that it won't happen again. I think jail is, with all due respect, not needed to correct the problem the court perceives."

"Mr. Zavallo, I believe that I would revoke the bail of any defendant who behaved toward a witness as Mr. Harold did here. But his behavior is particularly troubling *because* he's a lawyer and should have understood the gravity of what he was doing. His behavior seems to me an unfortunate harbinger of bad things to come if he is left free."

She looked down at Hal. "Mr. Harold, I truly regret having to return you to custody. But you've been a member of the bar of this court for what, fifty years?"

"Fifty-one," Hal said.

"Fine. For fifty-one years, and you should have known better."

Hal did not respond, and the bailiff, who was nearly as wide as he was tall, moved to handcuff him, assisted by two other men in uniform. No one messed with the bailiff, who was affectionately known around the courthouse as the Jolly Green Giant and was famous for shooting a witness who was trying to flee Judge Gilmore's courtroom.

"One moment," Judge Gilmore said. "Mr. Zavallo, I notice that the preliminary hearing in this matter is set well down the pike—almost two months from now. With Mr. Harold in custody, he is entitled by law to a prelim within ten days if he wants it."

"The prosecution is ready and raring to go," Trucker said. "Our evidence is strong. So any time the defense is ready, we're ready."

"My calendar's clear on Monday," the judge said.

Rory saw Trucker blanch ever so slightly at this. From his own experience, he knew prosecutors assumed defendants always wanted to go later rather than sooner. Now the judge was calling Trucker's bluff about just how ready the prosecution really was.

"Mr. Zavallo, what's your pleasure?" the judge asked. "If Monday is too soon, we can do it later."

Zavallo walked over to Hal and whispered something in his ear. Hal nodded, and Zavallo looked up at the judge. "We want a preliminary hearing as soon as possible. Monday will be just fine."

The judge had been looking at a paper calendar on her desk. "Consider it done. Mr. Trucker, how long do you think it will take you to put on the People's evidence?"

"It's a straightforward case. I think we can easily show probable cause that Mr. Harold murdered Joe Stanton with only two days of testimony."

"Alright, I'll reserve four days on my calendar. Two days for you. Two days for the defense, if they need any days at all. I'm of course aware that defendants sometimes put on no witnesses in a prelim. We're adjourned."

Rory watched as everyone began to scatter and the bailiffs escorted Hal out the side door of the courtroom reserved for prisoners and security personnel. Then he headed out himself. As he entered the vestibule between the two sets of doors that led to the hallway, he caught sight of a woman ahead of him in the crowd who reminded him of Sarah, except that she had somewhat darker skin and brown hair. She was wearing large sunglasses and a big, floppy straw hat. When he got out into the hallway, he looked for her, but she was gone. He was almost sure it was Sarah. If it was, it meant that she had gone rogue on him again, despite his warning. Or maybe she'd never really agreed to change her behavior.

But one way or another, it would mean she couldn't control herself, and it was time to fire her. Or get her fired, since he didn't think he had the authority to do it all on his own.

As he was getting into the elevator, his cell beeped with the arrival of a text. It was from Sarah:

```
Bet Sylvie knows all answers. See you at
office
```

Ignoring the bit about Sylvie, Rory texted back:

```
how did u get to office
```

```
uber
```

```
lunch w friend kosher burrito dwntwn.
join us?
```

```
nt
```

He shrugged. Sarah was indeed a strange duck. He headed out to Kosher Burrito to meet with Lester, who had texted him, got something for you.

Chapter 20

THURSDAY AFTERNOON

The Uber car arrived within minutes, and Sarah climbed in. She gave the driver the address of the firm's office and settled back to check her e-mail. She heard a faint ringing and realized it was her second cell phone, which was buried deep in her purse. She dug it out and managed, just, to answer before the caller hung up, but she didn't get a chance to glance at the caller ID before the conversation began.

"Hello . . . This is Sarah. Oh, hi!"

She listened for a while and said, "I see, and I understand. I just don't know if I can arrange to come right now."

She listened some more and, finally, said, "I see. Well, maybe I can do it if I rearrange some other things. I'll get back to you, okay?"

Maybe Rory would let her go.

***

Kosher Burrito was not, of course, the original stand, which, long before Rory was born, had been a popular place across from City Hall where lawyers scarfed down greasy lunches. The original had been plowed under in the early 2000s to make way for the Caltrans building. Years later someone had bought the name and opened a new place just a few blocks away. It served an offering akin to the original burrito—pastrami, chili, cheddar cheese, onions, pickles and mustard, all wrapped in a thin flour tortilla. Rory had become a devotee of the new place during a long trial he had done nearby early in his career.

Lester was already there, sipping a Coke directly from the can.

"I already ordered two," Lester said as Rory slid into the small green leather booth on the other side of the red Formica table. "But I held the pickles on yours. I get that right?"

"You did."

"You used to eat this stuff all the time. Didn't it wreck your sleep?"

"Never bothered me."

"And you didn't pack on the pounds?"

"I did, some, but I'm so big that no one noticed."

"Oh. Not true for us small folks. That's why I never came back here after the couple of times you insisted we try it."

"So what's up, Lester?"

"Well, I couldn't figure out an excuse to serve a search warrant on Peter Stanton to search his house. But we don't need a warrant to have someone followed."

"You followed him?"

"Not personally, but I had someone else do it."

"Weren't you asked why?"

"No, I'm high enough up the food chain now that I can pretty much do what I want within regs. Especially on a murder investigation."

The waitress appeared, plopped a plastic plate in front of each of them and dropped their burritos, each wrapped in wax paper, onto the plates.

"You want anything to drink?" she asked, looking at Rory.

"Just water, no ice," Rory said.

"We don't got no ice anyway, honey. This ain't the Ritz. So no problem."

"I guess Peter went somewhere interesting," Rory said. "Or we wouldn't be here."

"Right you are."

"Gonna tell me?"

"Sure. In a minute." Lester took a big bite out of his burrito, which promptly dripped all over his hands. He wiped the mess up with a napkin. "God, this thing is impossible to eat. You need tools." He spotted the waitress. "Could we trouble you for knives and forks?"

"Sorry, honey, the management don't supply them."

Rory laughed. "Eating these things is an art, Lester. The way to do it is you just let your hands get messy and keep cleaning them up with napkins." He pointed to the napkin holder. "The management does supply those."

"Thanks."

"Okay, now tell me where Peter Stanton went."

"To a copy center out in Riverside. Maybe an hour's drive from his house. My man saw him give a flash drive to a clerk there. Stanton came back an hour later, after eating lunch nearby, and picked up the flash drive and a thick eight by eleven manila envelope, which looked to my guy like it had a thick sheaf of papers inside."

"A script?"

"Hold on." Lester had a backpack with him, sitting on the seat beside him. He fished inside and handed Rory a thick sheaf of papers. "We think this is what was in the envelope and, most likely, what was on the flash drive."

Rory thumbed through the pages. It was indeed a script. *"Extortion,"* he said, closing it and reading the title. "Slightly different, but close."

"You see the handwritten notes here and there?"

Rory nodded. "How did you manage to get it out of the envelope without Peter realizing it was gone?"

"We didn't. It's a copy."

"Alright. How did you manage to copy it without Stanton knowing?"

"My guy—buffed out, crew cut, in uniform—goes up to the clerk, an eighteen-year-old kid, flashes his LAPD ID and tells the kid he's working on a murder investigation, and he needs to see what was on that flash drive."

"And?"

"Kid says, 'Well, the machine he used to copy what was on the flash drive saves the file until it's wiped.' That's the way they've set it up in case the customer comes back and wants a second copy. They wipe all the files the next morning."

"So he gave your guy a copy?"

"Something like that, after making sure the guy was willing to pay for it. You owe me a little over ten bucks."

"This wasn't, I take it, a FedEx store?"

"No, they would never have done it. It was some fly-by-night place that offers cheaper rates than the big guys."

"Was that legal, Lester?"

"If you just ask someone for something, and they give it to you, is that illegal?"

"Not if you're a private citizen, but maybe if you're a police department . . ."

"Sounds like a law school exam, huh?"

"Well, thanks for bending the rules—if you did."

"If I did, you're welcome."

"Hey, Lester, I want to show you a photo." He brought up the photo Madge had sent him on his cell phone. "You know this guy?"

Lester paused, looked at it more closely and said, "I don't think so. Why?"

"I think he may have been following me. Or maybe following one of my colleagues."

"Any idea why?"

"None."

"You want to send me a copy, and I'll ask around?"

Rory hesitated. Did he really want the photo floating around? After all, Madge had taken it surreptitiously, and all it showed was a guy having coffee in a public place. On the other hand, there seemed to be evidence that he wasn't just any guy. "Why not?" he said, and forwarded the photo to Lester. "Let me know if you turn up anything."

"Now I want to show you something else," Lester said. He swiped his cell phone a few times and handed it to Rory. "Watch this video. It's only a few seconds long."

Rory watched the video unfold. It was an incredibly blurry clip of someone walking away from what might be a fence. Or might not.

"Do you know who the person in the video is?" Lester asked.

"Well, where is it?"

"I'd rather you see first if you can ID the person."

Rory peered at it, then reran it several times. "The best I can tell, it's a woman, from the body shape, wearing a hat. But that's about all I can say." He handed the cell back to Lester. "Now will you tell me where it is?"

"Sure. It's the back gate into the studio lot. The gate, which is really just a big wooden door, has a keypad to unlock it."

"The video is from the security camera?"

"Yes."

"Why is it so blurry?"

Lester laughed out loud. "Someone sprayed foam of some kind on the lens. But not quite enough to block the image entirely."

"Who has the key code to the gate?"

Lester laughed again. "More or less everybody. The code hasn't been changed in ten years. Even an old woman who sells cookies on the lot to help her granddaughter pay for college has it."

"Sounds like a giant security hole."

"The former studio head, the guy who just left, insisted it be there. You could ask him why. I have my guesses, but they have nothing to do with this case."

"And the clip was taken when?"

"The time clock on the lens is broken, but it recycles every day at 12:01 a.m. So the best we can say is that it's from the day Joe Stanton was killed, and it's the only image of anyone coming through the back gate that Sunday."

"Who do you think it is?"

Lester shrugged. "We have no clue. The mystery woman, we call her."

"Is she coming in or going out?"

"We think she's going out, but we can't be sure."

"What time did that happen?"

"Like I said, time clock's broken. Stuck at 12:01 a.m."

"So all we know is that whoever went out—if that's the direction they were going—went out after midnight on the day Joe was killed?"

"Correct." Lester nodded at Rory's basket. "You haven't touched your burrito, there."

"Oh, I'm gonna get a box and take it back to the office. Really need a knife and fork." He laughed uproariously.

"You're an asshole, my friend."

Chapter 21

Rory found Sarah busy at her desk when he walked into her office.

"Hey, Sarah, did you hang around the courthouse after I sent you away to keep you out of Peter Stanton's sight?"

"No, of course not. I'm not a moron. I walked to a café at least ten blocks from there and did some work, and then I did a spot of shopping and took Uber back here, like I texted you. Why?"

"I could have sworn I saw you there when the hearing broke up."

"There are a lot of people who look like me. My father used to joke that I was Standard Issue WASP, Model Two."

"What's Model One?"

"The male version."

He laughed.

"Rory, while I was at the café, I did a lot of thinking."

"And?"

"There's got to be a connection between our case and the murder case against Hal."

"Why do you think that?"

"Well, Sylvie was apparently one of the last people to see Joe Stanton alive, and she's also the person who knows where the missing file on our case is, or at least we think she does."

Rory was pretty sure, despite Sarah's denying it, that she had been in the courtroom. So she had just lied to him. Did he want to share with her that Lester had given him a script with Alex Toltec's handwriting? And that, if authentic, it probably came from the so-called missing file and would screw up his whole case? No.

"Sarah," he said, "for all I know, there is no file and never was."

"You don't want to find it, do you?"

"Let me put it this way. If we find the file, the federal rules require me to turn it over to Kathryn, and my gut tells me that whatever's in it wouldn't be helpful. But, you know, it's a funny thing. If I don't got it, well, I don't gotta turn it over."

"Aren't you required to look for it if you think it exists?"

"Yeah, but I'm not required to move heaven and earth to find it."

"Have you moved anything, Rory?"

He smiled. "I've asked the police where Sylvie is, and yesterday I asked the acting GC to look for the file. He called me earlier today to say he can't find any such thing, or any record of it. I said, 'Hey, keep on lookin'.' I don't know what else I can do."

"Well, I think we should move heaven and earth to find it, because if that file shows—somehow—that Alex Toltec wrote the script from scratch, with no connection to Mary Broom, then we win our case." She paused and bit her lower lip in what Rory interpreted as a sign of regret. "But I know that doesn't help poor Mr. Harold win his murder case."

"Now he's back to being Mr. Harold?"

"It's the way I was raised. If you had asked me to call you Mr. Calburton, I would have been happy to do so. Right now I only seem to do it when I'm irritated at you."

"You are—"

"I know. An odd duck."

"Let's change the topic, Model Two. I want you to take charge of an expert who may examine a questioned document for us."

"What document?"

Rory answered carefully, because he didn't want Sarah to know that there might be two copies of the same document—the one Kathryn had told him about and the one Lester had just given him. He felt bad about the deception, but he needed to protect his case from this madwoman. Still, maybe he could make use of her talents and have her work on something where she couldn't do any harm.

"Kathryn told me that Mary Broom miraculously found a paper copy of the script she supposedly wrote and submitted to the studio— the one she couldn't find before. And that she's gonna produce it in court tomorrow. And get this: it supposedly has Alex Toltec's handwriting on it, suggesting changes he wanted."

"Do we have it yet?"

"No, she says she's having it examined by an expert. Once she's done with that, we'll get it and have our own expert take a look at it. He'll examine the paper and the ink for authenticity—especially age."

"Sounds like fun."

He tossed a thick white booklet on her desk, Velo-bound at the spine with a red plastic strip. "This is the transcript of the exam and cross-exam of a questioned documents examiner I used in a trial last year. His name's Carmen Egerdahl. I called him on the way back, and he's available. You'll find his contact info on the firm's intranet."

"Okay."

"Before you call him, read that transcript I just gave you. It will teach you a lot about how documents are examined for authenticity and how those experts are examined and cross-examined."

"Will do."

"And, Sarah, I'm gonna let you cross-examine Kathryn's expert, if she has one, and put on our own expert in the hearing if we need one."

"Wow! That's super."

"Well, in truth, I'm taking a big risk. But I can't do this whole thing myself, and the litigation department manager is refusing to give me any senior associates to help. And, of course, I'll be looking over your shoulder."

"I appreciate your confidence in me." She paused. "Such as it is."

Rory ignored what she had just said. "I'll check back with you tomorrow on how it's going," he said. "And you should expect it will take more than a day. We work on weekends around here."

"You don't seem pissed that Kathryn is withholding the script from you."

"In court on Monday afternoon, when we resume, I'm gonna seem very pissed." He smiled. "Wait and see."

"Rory, I need to ask you something."

"What?"

"Will it be a problem if I talk with Egerdahl and work on this while I'm out of town tomorrow and this weekend?"

"I think I need to sit down," Rory said, easing himself into one of the much-too-small guest chairs. "You just started work this week, and you want to go on a personal trip when there's important work that needs to be done in the next three days?"

"It's a special circumstance. My mother, who lives in DC—well, actually in a Virginia suburb—suffers from high anxiety. She called earlier and wants me to come see her. She sounded really, really stressed. And I can only see her doctor if I'm there on Friday."

"I see."

"She just moved to a new place—something I advised against, by the way—and it's apparently not working out very well."

"And so?"

"I have to go see her. Basically, she's a little whacked-out."

"The son of a duck quacks."

"What?"

"An old Japanese saying that's the equivalent of 'the apple doesn't fall far from the tree.'"

"You think I'm whacked?"

"I didn't say that. Anyway, what do you propose?"

"I can take a red-eye tonight, spend Friday, Saturday and Sunday there and take a late evening flight back on Sunday. I can contact Egerdahl today by phone and work with him via e-mail and Skype while I'm away. And I'll be here at the crack of dawn Monday morning with everything done. I promise."

"I guess I don't have much choice but to say okay."

"Thanks, Rory. I really appreciate it. So does my mom."

"One thing."

"What?"

"When you work with Egerdahl, phone is fine. E-mail is not."

"Why not?"

"Because if he's a testifying expert, everything in his file is available to the other side. So we don't want him to have much of a file. And absolutely no reports from him, draft or otherwise."

"Got it, chief."

After Rory left, Sarah picked up the phone and called a number in Northern Virginia.

Chapter 22

FRIDAY MORNING
CHANTILLY, VIRGINIA

Sarah loathed red-eye flights, but sometimes there was no choice. She grabbed a 10:40 p.m. flight out of LAX and was at Dulles by six thirty Friday morning. She brought two changes of clothes, a toothbrush and some makeup, all packed into a small backpack.

She was in her rental car by 7:00 a.m. and on her way to see the woman she had called. Fortunately, she lived in Chantilly, Virginia, which was only about seven or eight miles south of Dulles, away from Washington. Otherwise, she would have been stuck in the hideous traffic into the city, which she saw in the opposite lane as she sped along.

The house was a large two-story brick colonial set back fifty or sixty feet from the curb and surrounded by green lawns and oak trees with bare branches. Sarah walked up the brick sidewalk, thin leather briefcase in hand, and thumped the large brass knocker. After less than a minute, a short, thin woman with short brown hair cut into bangs opened the door. A gold locket hung from a gold chain around her neck. Sarah knew from her recent research that Sylvie was only forty-eight, although she had looked a good deal older in her Facebook photos and did now, in person, too. Stress, maybe?

"Hello," Sarah said. "I'm Sarah Carter, the woman who sent you the letter."

"The forwarded letter about my inheritance."

"Yes. And just to confirm, you are?"

"Sylvie Virtin."

"Perfect. I can only deal with you directly, as I'm sure you can understand."

"Yes, of course. Please come in. I've been expecting you."

She led Sarah to a sitting area in the living room, which was furnished with a large-armed sofa in a muted floral pattern and two matching wing chairs. A round, beveled-glass-topped table with its wooden edge and legs done in antique gold leaf sat in the middle.

"Would you like coffee, Ms. Carter?" Sylvie asked.

"Yes, please."

"I'll be right back. I'm afraid I don't have any help today."

While she was gone, Sarah looked around the room. She recognized the furniture, from her own childhood, as Ethan Allen–brand colonial furniture, or at least an excellent copy of it. It was a style favored by those in Virginia who thought of themselves as being of a certain class. Sarah had always found it amusing, since Ethan Allen was a hero of the American Revolution from Vermont. The rest of the room was bare except for wall-to-wall beige carpeting—not at all favored by the colonially minded. And there was no art on the walls, just an unadorned brick fireplace at one end of the room.

Sylvie returned minutes later with a ceramic pot of coffee, dainty cups and cream and sugar, all on a large silver platter.

"Well, Sarah, I must say I'm rather surprised by this inheritance. Remind me—how much is it, and who is it from?"

"It's five hundred thousand dollars. That's before our ten percent fee is deducted, so it would be a net of four hundred fifty thousand to you, free of federal estate tax, since it's an inheritance and the total estate is below five million. Are you currently a resident of Virginia?"

"Yes."

"Then it will also be free of state inheritance tax."

"That's great! I can certainly use the money. But again, though, who is it from?"

"The way it works is that you need to sign paperwork acknowledging our fee before I can identify the actual person from whom you have inherited, although I can tell you that he's a third cousin of yours, twice removed, who died without a will and without close heirs. We traced you as the sole living heir when the estate was about to be escheated to the state in which he died. That's our business model."

Sarah snapped open her briefcase, took out a two-page document and handed it to Sylvie. The tiny red light in the inner corner of the case indicated that the recorder was functioning. "Please take all the time you need to read the document."

Sylvie read through it and looked up. "This looks fair. I'm thrilled to get the money, and your company has certainly earned its fee." She took a pen that Sarah proffered to her, then signed and handed the document back to Sarah.

"Is that it?"

"No, I have to do a routine identification, but I'm sure that won't be a problem."

"What's involved in that?"

"Well, it's a bit old-fashioned, but first I have to see if you look like the photo I have of Sylvie Virtin." Sarah pulled a glossy 8″ × 10″ photo out of the briefcase and held it up in front of her, looking from the woman's face to the picture. "Yep, it's an exact match."

"Of course it is. What else?"

"I have to take your fingerprints." Sarah pulled a small ink pad out of the briefcase, along with two fingerprint cards, one for each hand, and put the ink pad and the cards down on the coffee table.

"Why?"

"Because we have your fingerprints from when you were fingerprinted when you temped for the US government during a college summer, and we want to match them. Since you look like Sylvie, I'm sure you will check out as Sylvie, but we have to be certain."

"Who else could I be?"

"No one, I assume. But we had a very bad experience several years ago when we gave the inheritance funds to the wrong person and then got sued by the right person, so we can't be too careful."

"I see."

"Please give me your right hand first, and I will get the print cards scanned and faxed back to our office right away. It will only take maybe ten minutes to match them—we have an arrangement with the LAPD to do that—and then I can give you this check." She reached into the briefcase again and held up a large-format check on which the name Sylvie Virtin and the amount of $450,000 could clearly be seen.

"I don't want to give you my fingerprints."

"Why ever not?" Sarah tried to work up a look of astonishment. "I've been doing this for five years, and I've never had anyone decline before."

"I just don't."

"Is it because you're not Sylvie?"

"I *am* Sylvie. What the hell is this about?"

"Are you sure you're not Clara Virtin?"

The woman paused for a long moment. "How do you know about Clara?"

"I looked up your high school yearbook. They're all online now, you know. Two Virtins graduated that year from University High. Clara and Sylvie, who look to me to be identical twins. But identical twins don't have identical fingerprints."

"I didn't let you print me, remember?"

"Your prints are all over the piece of paper you just signed."

"Get out of my house."

"Is Sylvie dead, Clara?"

Chapter 23

"No, of course she's not dead."

"Why should I trust you on that, Clara?"

"Well, why should I trust *you*, or give you any information at all, Sarah Carter? If that's really even your name. After all, you ran a scam on me to get me to meet with you."

"Actually, I ran a scam on Sylvie."

"Whatever, I've said what I have to say to you. Now get out. And get out right now."

"As you wish." Sarah put the document Clara had signed into her briefcase, along with the ink pad and the fingerprint cards, snapped it closed and started to get up.

"Give me that document with my signature back."

"No, it will be a good sample of your handwriting if we need it."

"Give it back, or I'll call the police."

"Oh, I doubt you're going to call the police . . . Clara-not-Sylvie."

"Why do you need that document at all?" Clara shouted at her as Sarah walked toward the front door.

Sarah couldn't immediately think of a good answer, so she tried a Hail Mary pass. "To help the police prosecute an obstruction of justice case against you. You see, I'm actually a PI helping the police investigate the murder of Joe Stanton. I can show you my ID if you like."

"I have nothing to do with any of that. Nothing."

"You probably don't. But Sylvie might, and the police wanted to talk to her. Instead, I believe they ended up talking to you."

"I told them the truth as Sylvie explained it to me."

"Clara, I believe you," she said, reaching for the front doorknob, "but the fact is that the police thought they were talking to Sylvie. You impersonated her, and that's obstruction of justice. It's no different than if you'd taken evidence and buried it in your backyard. The penalty for obstruction, if you're convicted, is ten years. Maybe seven, if you don't have a prior record." Sarah actually had no idea what the penalty was, but the high numbers sounded good.

"Alright, alright," Clara said. "Let's sit back down and see if we can start over here."

They walked back to the sitting area. Sarah set her briefcase on the table and opened it again.

"Okay, Clara, why don't you tell me what this is all about, okay? And I'm recording it, just so you know." She pointed at the briefcase.

"Okay, but I don't know much. And before I tell you, how will that help with the obstruction case?"

"I have a lot of influence with the detectives I'm working with. If you tell me everything you know—and it turns out to be truthful, of course—I'm sure they'll go easy on you and decide to forget about the obstruction charge they could otherwise bring."

Clara eyed her for a long moment. "You know, before I tell you anything, I need to be sure you are who you say you are. Do you have ID with you?"

"Sure." Sarah dug into her purse, extracted her wallet and pulled out her California private investigator ID. "Here you go."

Clara took it and read aloud. "State of California Bureau of Security and Investigative Services. Private Investigator. Sarah Carter." She peered at the photo on the card. "You look way young in this photo."

"I was younger back then. Getting older. It happens to all of us."

"In the photo, you look like you're in grade school.'"

"I've always looked young for my age."

Clara looked up from the ID card and studied Sarah's face. "Okay, I guess you're legit." She handed the card back.

"Now tell me what's going on."

"Alright. Sylvie called me and told me that she was going to get out of LA because she was flipped out at Joe Stanton's death. She came here, to this town, because our grandparents lived here when we were kids, and we used to visit here a lot. Although it was mostly horse country back then."

"Go on."

"She called me and asked me to join her here, so I did. We stayed in a hotel for one night, and then Sylvie rented this place for one year, furnished." She looked around. "Well, sort of furnished."

"Where do you live normally?"

"In New York City."

"Where is Sylvie now?"

"I don't know. She left right after this place was rented, and she left me instructions to call a particular detective at the LAPD who had been trying to reach her, pretend to be her and tell him that I was fine."

"And you did."

"Yes. And I used Sylvie's regular cell phone, which she left behind for me to use."

"Who was the detective?"

"Detective Lester Lovejoy."

"Didn't Lovejoy ask you anything about the murder?"

"Not much. You see I—well, Sylvie—didn't discover his body or anything. It was a Sunday, and Sylvie never worked weekends. So all

I got asked was whether I knew of any enemies that Joe had. I didn't and said so."

"Did you call Sylvie and ask her if Joe had any enemies?"

"No, in part because I don't know where to reach her. She calls me, and when she does, she uses a phone with a blocked number."

"I see."

"Do you mind if I warm up the coffee? There's a microwave in the kitchen," Clara said as she pointed to the carafe on the table.

"No problem. But no offense, I think I'll follow you into the kitchen."

"Sure."

Clara put the carafe in the microwave, and they both stood there for a moment and watched the turntable inside go around. Sarah used the time to think of what else she really wanted to know, not that Clara, assuming she was telling the truth, was likely to know much.

"Clara, did Sylvie and Joe have an affair?"

"Oh, yes, for many years running. It's been over for at least a year though. Why?"

"Maybe Joe's wife was the killer."

"Gladys?" She smiled and took the carafe out of the microwave. "You want some, too?"

"No thanks. Talk to me about Gladys. Isn't she a potential killer out of jealousy?"

Clara paused a moment, seeming to think it over, and said, finally, "I can't see why. She was aware of the affair for years, didn't complain about it while it was going on so far as I know and is richer than Croesus. Why would she kill him now, with the affair over?"

"Do you know if Joe had any life insurance?"

"Sylvie told me he had a policy for fifteen million dollars, with Gladys as the sole beneficiary."

"Again, doesn't that make Gladys a potential killer?"

She shrugged. "If Gladys were poor, maybe. But not in her circumstance. She'll probably just use the money for charity or something. She couldn't possibly need it in her personal life."

"Couldn't the desire to be a big deal on a charity board be a motive?"

She laughed out loud. "Kill someone in order to be on the board of the LA Philharmonic? Sounds more like a movie than real life."

Clara started to pour coffee into a cup she took down from the cupboard. Her hand shook, and she spilled some on the counter.

"Are you nervous?" Sarah asked.

"No. I have Parkinson's."

"Oh, I'm so sorry."

"No problem."

"Does Sylvie have it, too?"

"Not that I know of. Identical twins don't always have identical diseases."

Sarah realized her medical faux pas had thrown her off the track of her questioning. She had two areas left, the last one perhaps the most delicate.

"Again, Clara, I'm sorry for being so insensitive. But if you can put up with me for a few more minutes, I'd appreciate it."

"Sure. You sure you don't want some coffee?"

"Maybe I will take some. But let me pour." She reached for the carafe.

"No. I need to get used to this disability." She took another cup down, reached for the carafe and poured again, spilling still more.

"Can I wipe it up?" Sarah asked.

"No, I'll do that, too." She took a sponge and sopped up the spill. "What's your next question?"

"How did Sylvie's affair with Joe Stanton end?"

"He dumped her, but she was pretty calm about it. Went on working for him, so that should tell you something."

"They didn't argue?"

"Not during the breakup, so far as I know. They had some stormy times a few years before that. She even called the cops on him once, when he slapped her."

"What happened to that?"

"She refused to press charges, and the whole thing was dropped."

They both stood there and sipped their respective cups of coffee, Clara's hand shaking each time she brought the cup to her lips. Eventually, Clara said, "You're thinking Sylvie killed Joe?"

Sarah hadn't seriously considered it, but since Clara had suggested it, maybe she knew something Sarah didn't. Perhaps it was best to play along.

Sarah took a long sip of her coffee and looked at Clara over the rim of her cup. "Or perhaps Sylvie hired someone to do it," she said.

"Why would Sylvie want to kill Joe?" Clara said.

"I don't know, Clara. You brought up the idea. So I thought you might know what Sylvie's motive could be if she is the killer. Do you?"

"No."

"How long are you going to keep up the charade of being Sylvie?"

"For as long as she wants me to. She's paying me to do it."

"Oh. Do you need the money?"

"Yes. Sylvie went to Hollywood and did well there. Mostly because she invested with Joe, I think. I went to New York to write plays."

"That's not gone so well?"

"I've had a few produced, off-off-Broadway. But I'm still living in a six-story walk-up with two other girls." She paused. "Well, I guess we're all old enough now that I should say two other women." She laughed.

"Were you going to keep the money from the inheritance even though it was meant for Sylvie?"

"You bet I was. We set up a joint bank account here, and it would have been easy to do and easy to hide it from her."

Sarah stared at Clara for a moment. "You know, you've been standing there, tapping your foot, for a long time now. Is there something else you want to tell me?"

Clara looked over at the briefcase and made a motion indicating, "Please close that." Sarah did.

"Despite what I just said, you should look at Sylvie as a serious suspect."

"Why?"

"Joe had promised her that when he retired in a couple of years, they would travel the world together, married or unmarried, Gladys or no Gladys. When he broke it off a year ago, that all went away. She was calm on the outside, but my sister is a vindictive bitch when she's crossed, and I wouldn't put it past her."

Sarah blinked. Clara suddenly calling her sister a bitch? Where did that come from? But she had the sense that now was not the time to drill down on that.

"I may want to talk to you again, Clara."

"You have my number. Just one thing, though."

"What?"

"How do you know I'm not actually Sylvie? Most people, even those who know us well, can't tell us apart."

"The two of you look different now," Sarah said.

"How?"

"I'm not planning to tell you."

"Now you really do need to get the fuck out."

Chapter 24

Sarah left the house and walked to her car. The traffic toward DC was, she thought, likely still heavy, so she drove to a Dunkin' Donuts, ate two doughnuts, drank more coffee and called Egerdahl, the expert on questioned documents. They talked for well over an hour. She bought a third doughnut, this one with a jelly center. As she was about to put it in her mouth, she remembered that there was something she'd neglected to ask Clara. She punched in the number; Clara answered on the first ring.

"What d'ya want now, Sarah?"

"In Sylvie's house, someone found a flash drive hidden behind a set of books in the living room. Then Peter Stanton took it."

"Peter's a piece of work."

"What do you mean?"

"He was always hitting Joe up for money. Then he'd blow it and come back and ask for more. Joe was always a chump and gave it to him."

"Was Peter the beneficiary of a life insurance policy on Joe?"

"I have no idea. Lissen, I really need to be—"

Sarah realized Clara was getting drunk. Which couldn't be good with Parkinson's.

"Clara, I need to know if you know what was so secret on the flash drive that it needed to be hidden."

There was dead silence on the line for a long time.

"Are you still there, Clara?"

"Uh-huh. Tryin'a think what would be secret that Sylvie'd hide it like that."

"Or that Peter would want to steal it?"

"That, too. But can't think of anything."

"I'm surprised you don't know. I assumed you two, as identical twins, would be super close."

"Kinda, but I live in New York, and she lived in Los Angeles. We didn't know ever' single thing about each other."

"Why did you use the past tense—'lived' in Los Angeles, and 'didn't' know each thing about each other? Is she dead?"

"You gotta get over this dead stuff. She's not dead. Iss juss she doesn't live in LA now. She left. Past tense. *Lived* in LA."

"I'm not convinced, Clara."

"This's getting old."

"When you talk to her, will you ask her what's on the flash drive?"

"Sure." Whereupon Clara ended the call.

Sarah devoured the third doughnut and drove on toward DC to visit some old friends who were officed not all that far from Chantilly. They could take her to lunch, which she badly needed.

After lunch she drove to her mother's place in Arlington and spent an hour with her. Her mother hadn't been expecting her but had seemed pleased to see her nonetheless. She declined her mother's invitation to stay overnight and lied about needing to go back to LA that evening. She checked into a cheap motel and spent the rest of the day Friday, and most of Saturday and Sunday, trying to find out if someone in Washington was having her followed. The answer seemed to be no, but it wasn't 100 percent. You could try to shut your past away in a box, but you couldn't guarantee the box would remain shut. Someone was always lifting the lid. And that was particularly true, it seemed, if you'd gone to work for certain government agencies.

In her spare time, she followed up with Egerdahl on the phone about some additional aspects of dating paper and ink and promised to get him an exemplar of Alex Toltec's handwriting so he could compare it to the writing on the script. She made a note to herself to see if someone at the studio had a sample.

She caught a 5:00 p.m. flight on Sunday evening from Dulles back to LA. There was Wi-Fi on the plane, and she spent most of the flight studying up further on issues involved with questioned documents. Her particular focus was on how to get a questioned-document examiner qualified to testify in their proceeding. Federal courts were very picky about what was acceptable science and what was inadmissible "junk" science.

As the plane descended for a landing, it was already dark out, and Sarah watched the lights of the city spread out below her as far as the eye could see until they faded into the dark of the mountains to the north and ended sharply at the inky black of the ocean to the west. Minutes later, as the plane touched down with a slight bump and reversed its engines with a roar, she wondered how much she was going to tell Rory, and how she was going to explain the way she had learned it. She also wondered if she was going to cop to her brand-new therapist in LA that she had done something she wasn't supposed to do. Again.

***

MONDAY MORNING
LOS ANGELES

When Sarah walked into Rory's office for their seven o'clock meeting, he was already at his desk, cradling the small basketball in his hand and tossing it up and down.

"Hi, Sarah."

"Hi, Rory. Did you miss me?"

"Not so much, truth be told."

"Oh? Well, then, how's Dana?"

"She. Is. Just. Fine. Thanks for asking."

"Any more inside info from her?"

"Not yet." He raised the basketball head high and shot. Swish. Sarah scooped it up off the floor and moved to the far corner of the room.

"From the desk, that's an easy shot," she said. She launched the ball toward the net, and watched it swish through.

"I bet you can't do that again," Rory said.

She did it again. "Satisfied now that it wasn't a fluke, Mr. Calburton?"

"I guess so. Have to say, I'm impressed. Girls usually can't hit them like that."

"You need to watch more women's basketball, Mr. Calburton. And anyway, I'm not just any girl," she said and sank into one of the guest chairs.

"So I'm finding out. Anyway, how's your mother?"

"Calmer."

"And how was the trip in general? Were you able to talk to the questioned-documents expert while you were on the road?"

"Yes. But according to him we're going to have a tough time putting definitive dates on either the paper or the ink. So if Mary Broom testifies that it got printed at a particular time or the handwriting got laid down at a particular time, it won't be easy for us to use an expert to rebut whatever she says."

"Why not?"

"Because unless paper is really old, it's hard to age date, except by paper type. But the kinds of paper available ten years ago are pretty much the same kinds available today. So unless she was dumb enough to print it recently and use a type of paper that wasn't available ten or fifteen years ago, we're out of luck on that front."

"Doesn't paper oxidize over time—get yellowed?"

"He says sometimes, but the rate of yellowing depends on the type of paper, storage temperature, ambient light to which the paper is routinely exposed, whether it's in an airtight container, how tightly a stack of paper is bound, etc. So something a month old can look and test years old, and vice versa, depending."

"What about the inked writing on the script?"

"He says it's not that hard to detect ink a few days old versus a year old, but beyond that it's very difficult unless, like the paper, the ink is really old, of a type no longer produced, or laid down by a type of writing instrument no longer used."

"Like what?"

"Like a quill or one of those old, scratchy-style fountain pens."

"So we're probably out of luck on that argument."

"Probably. But hey, I also talked to Sylvie Virtin."

"What?"

"Yes. You remember the police said she called from DC?"

"Uh-huh."

"Well, I had some spare time, not to mention the need to get away from my mother for a while, so, using some computer databases, I tracked her down in Northern Virginia and went and knocked on her door."

"So where is she?"

"In Chantilly. Except the person who's really there is her identical twin sister, Clara. She's the one who called the police to say she was okay, pretending to be Sylvie. Sylvie is somewhere else at the moment."

"What did this Clara person have to say?"

Sarah recounted the interview in detail and finished by saying, "So I learned quite a bit."

"Well, what you learned were things that might be helpful to Hal in defending the murder charge. In particular, that other people may have had motives to murder Joe, too. I'll pass that on to his lawyers."

"I can do that. They might as well hear it directly from me."

"Okay. But keep in mind we're not Hal's lawyers, and, unfortunately, you didn't really learn much that's helpful to our copyright case. And we still don't even know where Sylvie is. Nor whether Joe Stanton for sure prepared a file on Mary Broom's case against the studio, and, if so, where it is."

"You're right."

"While you were gone, I had some luck, though." He smiled a wide smile.

"Tell me!"

Rory reached into his desk drawer, pulled out the script copy that Lester had given him and handed it to her. She paged through it.

"This has lots of handwriting on it."

"Yep."

"Where did you get it?"

He told her and then said, "And so now we know what was on that flash drive."

"Have you read it?"

"Yes. I'd describe it, in terms of plot and character, as far away from Mary Broom's so-called detailed outline and much closer to the shooting script for the movie. But there's no writer's name on the cover page, and the notes, assuming they're Alex's, could as easily be directed to himself as to anyone else."

"So it doesn't really resolve anything about who wrote the script."

"No."

Sarah rose, picked up the ball, turned her left side toward the basket so that she could see it when she twisted her head, and flipped the ball toward the hoop from behind her back. It fell neatly through the hoop. She scooped it up off the floor and tossed it to Rory. "Here, you try it."

Rory remained fixed in his desk chair. "Not a chance. I yield to your superior athletic skill, at least in this very narrow area."

"Ha!"

"It's too bad I can't set up a mini–football field in my office."

"Double ha!"

"Sarah, are you, like, feeling superenergized, or doing speed or what?"

"No, I'm trying to think how to tell you nicely that you have no feel for technology."

"What do you mean?"

"That flash drive Peter stole could hold sixty-four gigabytes. That's more than enough to hold the entire *Encyclopedia Britannica*, a thousand photos and a couple of movies. So all we know is that Peter decided to download one single thing from the flash drive and have it printed. We still have no idea what else might be on it."

"On the other hand, Joe may just have grabbed the nearest flash drive, and that may be the only thing on it."

"True. I need to get to my office," Sarah said, starting to head for the door.

"Don't leave just yet. Because we have something else to discuss."

She said nothing for many seconds, just looked at him coolly, though it was clear to Rory that she had some inkling of what was about to come down. "Okay," she said at last. "What?"

"We have to have a come-to-Jesus meeting about your trip to Virginia."

"I'm sure I know a lot more about that than you do, but what do you mean?"

"Look me in the eye, and tell me you hadn't already planned to see Sylvie when you came in here and told me that cock-and-bull story about your mother."

She paused again and sucked in her lower lip. "Okay, it's true I was already planning to see Sylvie, but I did also see my mother."

"But seeing her was just an excuse, right?"

"Kinda, yes."

"What do you think I should do about an associate who not only lies to me but puts the firm at risk? And while you're at it, why don't you tell me how you actually found Sylvie?"

She didn't say anything immediately, but Rory could almost see the gears turning, and she came back at him with an argument.

"I don't think I put the firm at risk. What I did was perfectly legal—it's called spoofing someone by pretending to be someone or something you're not. In this case, I pretended to be someone who had discovered an inheritance she was due. It's an old tried-and-true PI trick."

Rory sat and stared at her. "And you think that's legal, even for a PI?"

"Yes, if you're not extorting them for money or something of value, it's okay."

"Accepting that for the moment—and I'm not sure you're right—don't you think it's up to me to decide what does and does not put the firm at risk?"

"Do you mind if I sit down? Standing here in front of you like this while I'm being dressed down makes me feel like a private facing a general."

"Sarah, I doubt you've ever felt like a private. But go ahead and take a seat." He gestured at the guest chairs.

She sat down and said, "Well, okay, maybe you're right, but I'd also argue that the two big things I've done that were perhaps risk producing have worked out well and produced valuable information for the firm."

"I can see you're someday gonna make a great lawyer. You have an answer for everything. Except my question."

"I've forgotten it."

"What do you think I ought to do about an associate who lies to me?"

"Fire me?"

"If I could, I would—"

She smiled a broad smile. "But you can't, right?"

"What makes you think that?"

"Well, this firm's a professional corporation. Its bylaws are on the firm's internal website. I read them, including the most recent revision. Hal Harold isn't the managing partner anymore, but he's still the CEO, and only he can fire an associate. And I'll bet that's not what he wants to be bothered with right now, huh?"

"I think he could be bothered with it, but I've come up with a better solution. At least for controlling your risk taking, although it won't fix the fact that you're whacked. For that you'll need a therapist."

"Rory, I'm not whacked," she said, but then suddenly her composure crumbled, and she started to cry. Which had the weird effect of making her look even more beautiful. Rory had to resist the temptation to wipe away her tears.

"I'm sorry," she said. "Starting a new job, and not getting along so well with you, and Mr. Harold ending up being charged with murder and ending up in jail, it's a bit too much for me. I better go."

Rory sighed.

"I'll tell you what, Sarah. Let me tell you my better solution." He took a Kleenex out of a box in his desk drawer and handed it to her. "I'll not talk to Hal about this right now on two conditions."

"Which are?"

"First, you promise me that in the future you won't do anything that puts the firm at risk in any way, or that might have even a hint of being illegal or unethical, without talking to me about it first."

"Okay, I can and will do that. What's the second?"

Rory paused. Was he really gonna do this? It sounded like something out of a movie. On the other hand, it might just work, so why not?

"My second condition," he said, "is that before you leave today, you give me your letter of resignation, addressed to the managing partner, dated today and effective in thirty days."

"Really?"

"Yes, really."

"I don't know, I mean—well, wait. What are you going to do with it?"

"Put it in my desk drawer, and if everything works out over the next month, I'll tear it up. If it doesn't, I'll send it to the managing partner, and you'll be gone. Easy-peasy."

"Do you see that as the only way?"

"No, you could quit right now." As he said it, he realized that the powers that be would be furious if she quit. They'd see it as him firing her. But he needed to do what he needed to do.

"Okay, I'll do it," she said. "But don't you want to know what's wrong with me?"

"I already know what's wrong with you. You can't tell the truth, and you're addicted to doing crazy, inappropriate things."

"No, I have a medical condition."

Rory was immediately on alert. "Medical condition" often meant that federal and state law would require the firm to make reasonable accommodation for the condition. But what could possibly be reasonable accommodation for compulsive lying and risk taking? And it wasn't like she was working as a barista. She was a lawyer in a high-profile firm.

"Alright, Sarah, I suppose I need to hear what's wrong with you if you want to tell me, although part of me thinks I should just send you to HR and let them deal with it. And please be aware that you are not required to tell me."

"I have something called impulse control disorder—ICD."

"Never heard of it. Is that something you just made up?"

"No, it's a recognized psychological disorder. It's got five stages: first I feel an impulse to do something, then tension where I try to figure out whether to do it or not—"

Rory's laughter interrupted her. "Seems to me you always just do it, whatever it is."

"Um, no, there are things I haven't done that I really, really wanted to do. But to finish, if I do the thing I want to do, I get pleasure from it, and then sometimes I feel guilty, but sometimes not."

They were both quiet for a moment until, finally, Rory said, "Are there drugs you can take for your problem?"

"Yes, but they don't work very well, and the religious background I come from frowns on putting that kind of thing in your body."

He sighed. "Okay, I'm certainly not gonna tell you to take drugs. But here's what I don't get. How did you survive two prestigious judicial clerkships? Neither Judge Fisher on the ninth circuit nor the Chief Justice strike me as wild and crazy guys who'd put up with this kind of crap."

"I developed alternatives. I'd go out and do crazy things not related to the clerkship that kind of let off the steam. A safety valve."

"What's an example?"

"Oh, like putting fake animal tracks on a friend's ceiling while she was out."

"So what's wrong with doing that here in Los Angeles?"

"Well, I used to have special friends I could count on to do, uh, 'out there' things with me. But one is back in DC, and the one who was here in LA during my clerkship has moved away. I haven't had time to find someone new."

She looked at him, and Rory knew what she was thinking.

"Count me out," he said. "And count out anybody else in this law firm."

"Okay, we probably wouldn't work very well together on that level anyway. You have no sense of adventure."

"Fortunately. But whatever, you need to find a way to manage your problem without bringing it here. And if you can't or won't, then I will find a way to get you gone. *Capiche?*"

"I didn't know you were Italian."

"I just want to be sure you get it."

"I do."

"Good. Now you can go."

As Sarah rose, she said, "You know, when you're angry, you don't have any difficulty looking at me."

He couldn't help but smile. "Just go, Sarah."

She had not yet left when Rory's phone rang, and he picked it up.

"Hi, Rory," the voice on the phone said. "It's Hal."

"I thought you were in jail."

"I am. But they have phones here, surprising as that is."

"Right, of course. Hey, Sarah's in my office, so let me tell her I've got to talk to you." He pointed to the door, and Sarah finally headed toward it.

"No, she can stay. Put on the speakerphone so she can hear, too." Rory waved Sarah back, and she sat back down.

"Okay, Hal, the speaker's on. What's up?"

"As you know, the first day of my preliminary hearing is today."

"Yes, at eight a.m., according to the calendar."

"I'd like you to come down and observe."

"Why?"

"It will just feel good to have someone from the firm there. A show of support, if you will."

"And a show to the media that the firm's behind you?"

"That, too."

"I'd love to do it, but we have our preliminary injunction hearing with live witnesses today at two. So we're kind of busy."

"I think we're pretty much done with everything we need to do for that," Sarah said.

Rory raised his eyebrows and shot her a look. "In fact, Hal, Sarah's never been involved in one of these hearings before, so she doesn't, to put it bluntly, know what she's talking about."

"There you guys go again," Hal said and laughed. "Rory, I'm asking you as a special favor to come."

Rory paused and said, "Okay. But it's already past seven, and with rush hour traffic and all, there's no way I'll be there by eight."

"That's okay. I'm sure there will be a bunch of preliminaries, and if you leave right away, you can probably get there before the testimony starts."

"I'd like to come too," Sarah said. "I can be a big support for you, Mr. Harold. Especially if there's a lot of legal research to be done. I mean if your defense counsel needs some help."

"Good idea," Hal said.

Rory threw his arms up in the air. "Oh what the hell, why not? It's your law firm, Hal."

"Thanks, Rory. I really appreciate it."

After Hal hung up, Rory looked at Sarah and said, "Okay, let's pack up what we need for our own hearing. Fortunately, we don't have to go first, so there's not much to take at this point. I'll get the letter from you when we get back."

"Did you send them a list of our witnesses, as Judge Franklin ordered?"

"Yeah. We've only got one right now, the head of business affairs. There were two others I wanted, but one is dead, and the other's in the hospital."

"Who did they list?"

"Mary Broom; Julia Chen, who's our head of business affairs; Alex Toltec, who's unconscious; Gladys Stanton and an expert."

"Gladys? That's an odd one. Why do you think they want to call her?"

He shrugged. "No idea. But we can speculate about it later. We need to go. Did you finally get your courthouse entry pass in the mail?"

"Yes."

"Good."

"Hey, aren't you worried Peter Stanton might be there again and see me?"

"Not so much anymore. Why don't you just disguise yourself with your big, floppy straw hat?"

"I don't have a hat like that."

Rory tilted his head and looked at her. "I thought you were gonna stop lying to me."

She smiled. "I'll go get the hat."

"I wasn't serious about bringing the hat. I am serious about truthfulness. Let's go get my car and head down to the courthouse. If Zavallo lives up to his reputation, sparks will be flying."

Chapter 25

MONDAY MORNING
LOS ANGELES COUNTY SUPERIOR COURT—CRIMINAL
DIVISION
People v. Harold

When Rory and Sarah got to the courtroom and took seats in the back row, Judge Gilmore was already on the bench. Trucker was at the prosecution table, and Zavallo was at the defense table, with Hal beside him. Two sheriff's deputies stood nearby, ready, Rory supposed, to tackle the seventy-five-year-old accused killer should he get out of hand or try to escape.

"Now that we've completed the preliminaries, are the People ready to proceed with the first witness?" Judge Gilmore asked.

"Yes, Your Honor," Trucker said. "But before I do that, I want to alert the court that we've entered into an agreement with defense counsel that witnesses may make reference to the criminalist's report, the autopsy report and the blood-analysis report without any hearsay objections being raised by defendant. And that those reports may be admitted into evidence, for purposes of this hearing only, without the reports' authors necessarily having to testify. We both believe it will save time."

"It's nice to see cooperation, Counsel. It's rare in these courts these days. Mr. Zavallo, are you in agreement?"

"Yes, Your Honor. We have no quarrel with the reports. We do, however, plan to show that someone other than Mr. Harold shed the blood and caused the gruesome injuries detailed in those reports."

"So, Mr. Zavallo, your defense is going to be what they call on TV plan B? Blame someone else?"

"It's not a plan, Your Honor. It's simply the truth that someone else killed Joe Stanton."

Trucker, who had resumed his seat, didn't even bother to get up to respond. "We'll let the evidence we have speak for itself," he said. "And it's overwhelming."

"Alright, I guess I'll be enlightened as we go along," the judge said. "Mr. Trucker, let's now finally get started."

"The People call Roberto Gonzalez."

Gonzalez, a short, stocky man in his midthirties, with jet-black hair parted down the middle, rose from a seat in the audience, walked to the witness stand with a self-confident stride and took his seat. He lowered the microphone to match his height and looked expectantly at Trucker.

"What is your profession, Mr. Gonzalez?" Trucker asked.

"I'm a criminalist, employed by the Los Angeles Police Department."

"And where do you work?"

"At the state-of-the-art facilities of the Hertzberg-Davis Forensic Science Center, which undertakes forensic investigations for both the LAPD and the LA County Sheriff's Department."

Rory rolled his eyes at Gonzalez's blatant advertisement for the science center. Then he remembered that a lot of press people were watching from the jury box. He hoped they hadn't noticed his eye roll. It was the kind of thing reporters loved to write about. When he looked over at them, he found Dana looking back at him.

"Mr. Gonzalez, did you conduct a forensic investigation of victim Joseph Stanton's office?" Trucker asked.

"Yes."

"Could you please tell us what you found?"

"Yes, there were what appeared to me, based on my experience, to be small amounts of what was likely blood on the desk, on the desk chair, on the clothing worn by the body in the chair and on the carpeting nearby. And there was also what appeared to be probable blood on the body itself, including the neck, face and hands. And also matted on the victim's hair."

"Did you find anything else that you considered to be of forensic significance?"

"On those same surfaces, I found nonblood tissue that appeared to me, based on my experience, likely to be human tissue."

Rory wondered, as Gonzalez droned on, if human flesh looked different on a rug than flesh from dogs or cats. No attached fur on the human stuff?

"Mr. Gonzalez, did you sample any of the blood or other material?"

"After the scene was photographed, I took multiple samples of the probable blood from the desk, the chair, the clothing, the body and the carpeting; placed numbered markers on the places I'd taken the samples from; bagged the samples and labeled each bag. The room was then photographed again to show the numbered markers."

"Have you reviewed the blood-analysis report performed by the lab on your samples?"

"Yes."

"Your Honor, we'd like to have the blood-analysis report marked as People's Exhibit 1 and, by stipulation between the parties, entered into evidence," Trucker said. He passed a copy to the clerk for the judge to see. "Defense counsel already has a copy."

"Any objection, Mr. Zavallo?"

"No, Your Honor."

"Alright, People's Exhibit 1 will be received in evidence."

"Thank you, Your Honor." Trucker turned back to the witness and elicited from him that, based on DNA analysis, all of the spots collected were human blood and that all of the blood on or near Stanton's desk belonged—no surprise—to Stanton himself. He then led the witness to a perhaps more important finding—a single brown spot on the rug near the office's exit door.

The whole thing took a tedious ten minutes. Sarah poked Rory and whispered, "This is boring."

Rory whispered back, "Welcome to real-life trials."

Trucker was taking Gonzalez through his steps in cutting out the piece of carpet by the door and testing the rest of the carpet for human blood by spraying it with luminol.

"How, Mr. Gonzalez," Trucker continued, "does luminol indicate the presence of blood?"

"Luminol is chemiluminescent. That means that if you spray a sample with it, take the sample into a dark room and shine a bright light on it, it will briefly glow blue as it binds with iron molecules in the hemoglobin in blood. However, it can sometimes give off false positives. Bleach will also cause it to glow, for example."

"Other than the blood and fleshy material, which you marked and bagged, Mr. Gonzalez, did you come upon any other kind of material of interest to you?"

Rory had been drifting a bit, slouched back in his chair. Based on his years in the DA's office, he knew pretty much all he needed to know about luminol, and the other questions and answers had so far gone pretty much as expected. But the question just asked caused him to sit bolt upright. What else could Gonzalez have found worth collecting?

Gonzalez was responding. "Yes, I found, down on the floor under the chair, a stringy piece of material perhaps two inches long that looked to me like it might be part of a piece of braided rope."

"Were you able to determine what type of material it was made of?"

"It looked like plastic rope of some type."

Zavallo rocketed from his seat. "Objection, Your Honor! I have read all of the reports that the prosecution has shared with us, including this witness's written report, which has not yet been introduced in evidence, and there's not a single mention of this item. None. I move the last two questions and answers be struck from the record."

Trucker, who had been questioning the witness while sitting down, rose, too, and said, "Our apologies to both counsel and the court. This item, which was marked by Mr. Gonzalez as Item 42, was somehow misplaced and so didn't get into Mr. Gonzalez's report, and Mr. Zavallo is correct that we haven't yet offered it in evidence."

"I continue to object," Zavallo said. "I request that there be no further questions to this witness on this subject by Mr. Trucker until the witness has prepared a supplement to his written report. And he—or someone—should address the question of chain of custody. Exactly where has Item 42 been hiding? Who had custody of it until today, and where is it now?"

Judge Gilmore turned back to Trucker. "What's your response, Mr. Prosecutor?"

"Your Honor, I have no objection to delaying more questions on this subject until Mr. Gonzalez has had time to prepare an addendum to his report."

"Very well. Mr. Zavallo, do you have anything further to add?"

"Yes. You know, when I was young, I worked on a project that added sandbags to a Mississippi River dike, so I know very well the sound a sandbag makes when it slaps down. That's what I'm hearing here, except the sandbag is slamming down on Mr. Harold. If this alleged piece of rope wasn't in Mr. Gonzalez's report, and the evidence was lost, how is it that Mr. Trucker knew to ask the witness about it just now?"

Rory didn't imagine for one moment that the piece of rope—obviously part of the one used to strangle Joe Stanton—had been lost.

Originally, Trucker must have assumed that he wouldn't need it to meet the easy standard of proof in a prelim and planned to save the fragment for trial. Why in hell did he all of a sudden need it now? Rory assumed the judge had the same question, but that was not what she was saying out loud.

"Well," Judge Gilmore said, "I guess we've reached the end of cooperation. For now, I'm going to order that the last two questions and answers be struck and that no further questions be directed to the witness by the prosecution about the rope fragment, if that's what it is, until a supplemental report has been prepared."

"Your Honor," Zavallo said, "if I may, will you also order the DA's office to prepare a sworn report on how the evidence became lost and then found?"

"Yes, Counsel, I will add that to the order. And if I'm not satisfied with the answers, I reserve the right to hold a separate hearing into how that occurred. Now, Mr. Trucker, do you have any further direct examination of this witness?"

"Please give me a moment, Your Honor," Trucker said, consulting a notebook on the table in front of him.

Sarah leaned over and said to Rory, "The piece is obviously part of the murder weapon. Why did they skip it earlier and suddenly focus on it now?"

"I don't know, and Zavallo doesn't know," Rory said. "And that's the problem Zavallo's got. No one suddenly adds a piece of evidence for nothing, and he's got to be worried he's about to be skunked somehow."

Trucker looked up from his notebook. "Just one more question, Mr. Gonzalez. Based on your reading of the blood-analysis report, which we earlier introduced into evidence as Exhibit 1, whose blood was on the spot by the door, on that piece of carpet you cut out?"

"Based on comparison with a reference vial of blood taken from Mr. Harold, and referencing the blood-analysis report, the blood on the carpet came from Mr. Harold."

"Thank you, Your Honor. I have no further questions."

"Mr. Zavallo, your witness," Judge Gilmore said.

"Your Honor, I could use a brief break," Zavallo said.

"Of course. Let's take ten."

Zavallo got up and started to head toward the back of the courtroom. Hal started to follow him, but one of the sheriff's deputies held out his hand and stopped him.

"I'm sorry, Mr. Harold, but you are in custody," Judge Gilmore said. "If you want to talk to your counsel, the deputies will be glad to arrange that in one of the secure rooms."

"Sorry, Your Honor," Hal said, and sat back down.

Rory followed Zavallo out of the courtroom, and Sarah trailed after them. Zavallo headed down to the end of the corridor and pushed open the door to the men's room, turning slightly toward Rory just before the door closed after him, clearly expecting Rory to come in behind him. Rory started to when Sarah said, "Hey, if you're going in there, I'm going with you. I don't plan to be cut out of whatever conversation you guys are about to have."

Rory stopped short and said, "Jeez, okay, I really don't need to go. Let's wait for him to come back out, then we can all talk."

"This place should have gender-neutral restrooms," Sarah said.

"When you get to be the presiding judge, you can work on it."

"I will. Count on it. But I don't think we're going to have to wait that long for modern times to come to this courthouse."

Zavallo emerged from the men's room, looked at the two of them and said to Rory, "I thought you were coming in so we could talk."

Rory tilted his head at Sarah. "She wants to talk, too."

"Not a surprise, I suppose," Zavallo said. "Let's just chat here. There's no one around."

"Okay."

"Rory, what did you make of the surprise question and answer about the rope fragment?" Zavallo asked.

"I don't think the fragment was lost," Rory said. "It just wasn't important until now. So the question is, why has it suddenly become important?"

"Excellent observation," Zavallo said. "You're as smart as Hal said you are."

"Thanks."

"I have a thought," Sarah said. "Right now, all they have on Mr. Harold is a spot of blood, and I assume you're going to try to prove it got there some other way."

"Correct."

"And the only other thing they've got is the really weak piece that Mr. Harold supposedly looked disheveled when he drove off the studio lot."

"Right," Zavallo said. "And even taken together, those don't add up to probable cause."

"Exactly," Sarah said. "So it must mean that they now have something that will connect that piece of rope to Mr. Harold. Something they didn't have before."

"Makes good sense," Rory said. "The question is: What is it?"

"We just have to try to figure it out," Sarah said.

"Well, whatever it is, they were supposed to have turned it over to us," Zavallo said. "But if they follow their usual pattern, they're going to produce it later and say, 'Oh, so sorry, we forgot,' or 'we just found it,' or whatever. So we're going to have to dig for it. Let's go back in, and I'll give it a try."

"I have an idea," Sarah said. "Try asking him where it is right now."

"That's very smart," Zavallo said. "Where did you go to law school, Sarah?"

"Georgetown."

"Ah, excellent place. What about you, Rory?"

"I went to Chet."

An expression passed over Zavallo's face as if he had just heard someone fart. And then he recovered. "Ah, yes, interesting place. Why on earth did a smart fellow like you go there?"

At least he was candid. "Couldn't get in anywhere else."

"Surprising, that. Well, in any case let's get back in. I have a cross-examination to conduct."

Chapter 26

Gonzalez was back in the witness box.

"Good morning, Mr. Gonzalez," Zavallo said.

"Good morning."

"Did you read the autopsy report, Mr. Gonzalez?"

"Yes."

"What did it say was the cause of Mr. Stanton's death?"

"Objection," Trucker said. "The autopsy report itself is the best evidence of what it said. It's also beyond the scope of my direct."

"Your Honor, that's true," Zavallo said. "But this is much more efficient. And having agreed with the prosecution that witnesses could testify about the contents of the reports without having hearsay objections raised, it's pretty annoying to have them now throw the best-evidence objection in my face. And the scope of cross is permitted to be very broad."

"The objection is overruled."

"Restating the question, Mr. Gonzalez. What did the autopsy report say was the cause of Mr. Stanton's death?"

"Asphyxiation secondary to head trauma by blunt object and strangulation by ligature."

"In other words, Mr. Stanton was hit over the head and then stran-gled from behind with a ligature of some kind?"

"Objection. Calls for a medical conclusion."

"Overruled."

"I'm not a medical doctor, but that's my lay understanding of the report's conclusions."

"Have you processed crime scenes before that involved death by ligature strangulation?"

"Yes. Maybe four or five times."

"In your expert opinion, are they messy deaths?"

"I'm not sure I understand your question."

"In your experience, do deaths by ligature strangulation normally create a lot of blood and tissue that sloughs off the rope?"

"I don't know about a lot, but some, certainly."

"Have you processed crime scenes involving head trauma caused by a blunt instrument?"

"Yes."

"Are they bloody?"

"Sometimes very. Although if the victim was already dead when his head was hit, less so."

"So the blood of the victim and the tissue you identified could well have come from both the head wound and the ligature wound?"

"Yes, that's certainly plausible."

"Did you measure Joe Stanton's office when you processed the crime scene there?"

"Yes."

"How large is it?"

"I'd have to look at my notes to recall exactly, but I'd say it's about twenty-five by twenty."

"So approximately five hundred square feet?"

"Yes."

"Is it carpeted throughout?"

"Yes."

"What color is the carpet?"

"Sort of a dark brown."

"And its texture is nubby?"

"Yes."

"Was it hard to find the blood spot by the door that the lab report ultimately identified as Mr. Harold's blood?"

"It could have been hard to find. By chance, I just happened to notice it."

"And you cut that piece of carpeting out, right?"

"Yes."

"And took it back to the lab for it to be analyzed?"

"Yes."

"You didn't do the analysis yourself, did you?"

"No."

"Besides blood that turned out to be from Mr. Harold, did you find any other blood on the carpeting?"

"Yes."

"And were you able to identify the person or persons from whom that blood came?"

"Yes. Almost all of it was the blood of the victim, Joseph Stanton."

"Almost all of it? Does that mean that you collected blood that was ultimately found to match persons other than Mr. Stanton and Mr. Harold?"

"Yes. There was a single spot about halfway between the desk and the door that tested positive for blood but remains unidentified as to source."

"Was that spot—let me call it the mystery blood spot—larger than the spot identified as Mr. Harold's blood?"

"Objection," Trucker said. "Calling it the mystery spot suggests something not in evidence, namely that it is a mystery."

"Overruled," Judge Gilmore said. "You may answer."

"Maybe two or three times the size of the spot from Mr. Harold."

"So the Harold spot, let's call it, might have been from a single drop of blood?"

"I don't think a blood drop is an exact enough unit of measure to say."

"Okay, would it be fair to say that the mystery spot, which was two to three times as large as the Harold spot, came from two to three times as much blood as the Harold spot?"

"That would be a fair assumption."

"Did you request that the DNA from the mystery blood spot be compared to DNA data in the FBI's DNA database?"

"Yes, but there were no matches."

"What about the state of California's DNA database?"

"Yes, and again, no hits."

"What about the LAPD's DNA database?"

"Again, no hits."

"Did you request that the DNA from the mystery blood spot be compared to the DNA of all other people who work at the studio?"

"Yes, but the blood-analysis report says that it wasn't felt practical to gather blood samples from every studio employee, since there are thousands. So they took reference samples from everyone whose name was on the guest register for Mr. Stanton's office that day and the three days beforehand and from those who worked on the same floor."

"Because they felt that people are usually murdered only by people who work on their own floor?"

"Objection, Your Honor. Argumentative."

"Sustained. That was funny, Mr. Zavallo, but you know, this is not really the place for funny."

"Oh, I'm sorry, Your Honor, I've unwittingly violated that unwritten local court rule about humor in courtrooms."

"Which rule is that, Mr. Zavallo?"

"Humor shall be initiated only by the court."

The judge quirked her lips but said nothing in response other than, "Please resume your questioning." Rory wondered whether the judge and Zavallo knew each other, and, if so, how intimately.

Zavallo resumed. "Mr. Gonzalez, do you know if any effort was made to take DNA samples from employees who used to work on Mr. Stanton's floor?"

"I don't know."

"Or former employees who might have had a grudge against Mr. Stanton?"

"I don't know."

"I notice, Mr. Gonzalez, that you used the passive tense in your original answer about whether all studio employees were tested. 'It wasn't felt practical,' you said. Do you know *who* actually thought it wasn't practical?"

"No, I don't."

"Did all of the studio employees from whom they sought to take blood samples cooperate?"

"So far as I know, yes."

"But no matches to the mystery blood spot were found?"

"No."

"Mr. Gonzalez, did you test the entire five hundred square feet of dark brown nubby carpet for indications of possible blood?"

"No."

"Why not?"

Gonzalez hesitated. "Well, it's just not very practical."

"Is it just that it costs too much for all that luminol to spray the whole thing?"

"Uh, I don't know how much luminol costs, so I'm not sure."

"Oh right, you're a city employee, so cost doesn't matter much."

"Objection, Your Honor, he's harassing the witness."

"Sustained. Cut it out, Mr. Zavallo."

Zavallo pressed his palms together and bowed his head slightly as if praying for forgiveness. "Sorry, Your Honor." Turning back to the witness, he said, "Mr. Gonzalez, let me ask it this way: you could have sprayed the whole carpet with luminol, right?"

"Yes."

"Why didn't you?"

"With a dark brown carpet, it's hard to identify by eye what looks like a bloodstain. And since luminol also glows blue when it comes in contact with bleach and certain other old cleaning solvents, among other things that might be on the rug, testing a five-hundred-square-foot rug is likely to yield dozens or even hundreds of false positives."

"How would you test all those spots?"

"You'd have to test every spot that glowed blue under luminol, using more sophisticated tests that can positively identify human blood. So, as a practical matter, you'd have to remove the entire rug and take it back to the lab."

"And the LAPD doesn't ordinarily make that kind of effort?"

"The FBI does, but we normally don't."

"To go back to not testing the entire rug for a moment, is it possible that the rug has bloodstains from still other people that didn't get identified?"

"It's . . . possible, I suppose."

"One final question, Mr. Gonzalez. The Harold blood spot, did someone tell you where to look for that particular spot?"

"Yes, come to think of it. My supervisor, Mr. Agape, suggested I search there."

"Did he say why?"

"No, but I'd suspect that—"

"Your answer is 'No,' is that correct?"

"Yes."

"I have no further questions at the moment, Your Honor, but we reserve the right to recall this witness during our own case."

Sarah poked Rory and whispered, "Zavallo didn't dig for the why of the rope piece."

Rory shrugged. "Maybe he couldn't figure out where to start."

"Mr. Trucker," the judge was saying, "do you have any redirect?"

"Yes, Your Honor. One question."

"Go ahead."

"Mr. Gonzalez, before Mr. Zavallo cut you off, you were about to say why you suspected your supervisor suggested you look by the door. Please tell us why."

"Because someone fleeing a crime scene has to go through the door to get out of the room, so if they're injured and dripping blood, the pathway to the door is a logical place to look."

"I have nothing further, Your Honor."

"Recross, Mr. Zavallo?"

"Yes. Mr. Gonzalez, did your supervisor actually say to you that you should look by the door because it was a logical place to look?"

"No."

"He just said, 'Look over there,' right?"

"Correct."

"Your Honor, I realize I do have one more question," Zavallo said. "With apologies to the court and Mr. Trucker, may I be permitted to ask it out of order?"

"I have no objection," Trucker said.

"Go ahead, Mr. Zavallo."

"Mr. Gonzalez, when did you last personally see the small rope fragment—if that's what it is—about which Mr. Trucker asked you earlier?"

"This morning, before I left to come here."

There was a small stir in the courtroom. Rory didn't know exactly where Zavallo was going, but wherever it was, he liked it.

"Why did you look at it before you came here?"

"Mr. Trucker asked me to."

The stir in the courtroom was larger this time. Rory noticed that Judge Gilmore, who had been relaxed into her chair, had sat forward and was watching the witness carefully.

"Did he say why he wanted you to look at it?"

"Just to see if it was still in the forensic-evidence room."

"And it was?"

"Yes."

"Did he say why he wanted to know if it was still in the forensic-evidence room?"

"No. Not exactly."

Rory looked over to Trucker to see if he was displaying any concern about the direction of the questions, but he looked nonchalant.

"Not exactly?"

"Well, he was carrying a list of items of evidence gathered at the crime scene and checking to see if all of them were still there."

"Carrying a list of items? So does that mean he came personally to your facility to ask you about it?"

"Yes."

"Was that unusual?"

He paused, then said, "A bit."

"When was the last time he came to you?"

"Maybe two years ago."

"Did he have anything else with him this time?"

"Not that I noticed."

"Did Mr. Trucker say anything at all as to why he was interested in the small rope fragment?"

"No."

"Even if he didn't say right then, do you know why he was interested?"

"Objection," Trucker said. "No foundation and calls for speculation."

"Overruled. You can answer."

"No, I don't know why he was interested."

"I have no further questions."

"Mr. Trucker, redirect?"

Rory looked at Trucker sitting there, clearly thinking whether to let it be or try to repair the impression there was some skulduggery at work. In the end, he let it go. "No further questions."

"Mr. Trucker, please call your next witness," Judge Gilmore said.

Rory leaned over and whispered to Sarah, "Zavallo seems to have this well in hand. We need to grab lunch and get ready for our own hearing. So let's go."

"Mr. Harold said he wanted us here."

"I know. But we've got an obligation to the client in the other case."

Chapter 27

They walked out of the courthouse and crossed the street to Grand Park, which swept from City Hall on their left to the Music Center on their right, blocks away at the top of the hill.

"It's a pretty view," Sarah said.

"Yes, in an LA kind of way, it is," Rory said. "Let's talk about our case for a moment, and then we'll think about lunch."

"Sounds good. But we need to sit and talk somewhere we can't be overheard. Let's sit on that bench over there." She pointed to a steel bench about ten feet away.

Once they had sat down, Sarah looked around and said, "Okay, this seems safe, because we're screened by those trees in front of us."

"Screened from what? I mean, who do you think might be listening, and how would they do it?"

She turned and pointed to the top of the Criminal Courts Building, now behind them. "If that bald guy sat up there with a certain kind of parabolic microphone, he could hear everything we're saying."

"Why would anyone want to bother? Our case doesn't exactly involve national security."

"Was I followed or not, Rory?"

"That's true. You were. And I forgot to tell you—it just skipped my mind somehow amid all the craziness—that I might have been, too." He pulled out his cell phone and clicked up the photo Madge had sent him. "This guy was in the restaurant the other day when I had lunch with a cop friend."

"Shit," Sarah said. "I think that's the same guy who was at Sylvie's house when I was there. Does he look like the guy in the red Honda?"

"Pretty much, yes."

Rory's cell phone rang, and he answered.

"Hi, Quentin. What can I do for you?"

He listened for a moment and said, "Uh-huh. Sure. Can do. Tomorrow morning works if it's really early, because Sarah and I will probably have to be in court for our civil case by eight." He listened again for a few seconds and then said good-bye.

"What was that about?" Sarah asked.

"I'll tell you in a minute. But first, back to the guy who was following me." He held up his cell again, with the guy's picture displayed. "Are you sure this is the guy who saw you at Sylvie's house?"

She peered at it. "Yes."

"Why would he want to follow me, too?"

"I don't know."

"Don't lie to me, okay?"

"I'm not. I swear. I just really don't know what's going on. When I find out, I will tell you. I promise."

"Okay."

"What did Zavallo want?"

"They're at a break in the trial. He and Hal want to meet me tomorrow before their hearing starts to talk strategy in the case."

"You're getting sucked into this criminal case. Is that really what you want?"

Rory smiled a big smile. "It's not being 'sucked in' when all they're doing is consulting me for my profound wisdom."

"You have a huge grin on your face. A Duchenne smile."

"What?"

"It's a broad smile that indicates true happiness. Uses muscles both below the mouth and above, including around the eyes. Very hard to fake. Named for the nineteenth-century French neurologist who discovered how it works."

"Some people smile with only the bottom of their mouths?"

"Uh-huh, like flight attendants."

"Well, aren't we full of information? Where did you learn all that?"

"I minored in neuroscience as an undergrad." Sarah twisted around again and peered up at the top of the courthouse. "Let's get up and walk. I thought I saw the glint of the sun on a lens up there."

Rory rolled his eyes. "You know, I'm not used to hanging out with paranoids."

"You think the guy who followed you to the restaurant was a figment of my imagination?"

"Fair point, although nobody's been up on top of a building yet. But, okay, fine. Where do you want to go?"

"You pick."

"Let's walk down Spring Street toward downtown."

As they walked, Rory said, "I'm nervous about our hearing this afternoon."

"Why?"

"You know, sometimes when people get a second bite at the apple, they do better. Especially when they tasted your defense with their first bite. And Kathryn certainly learned a lot on that first round in front of Judge Cabraal, even though there were only sworn declarations and no live witnesses."

"In other words, she's had time to regroup and gather more evidence."

"Yes, or make it up."

"Not much you can do about it."

"As you'll learn with time in the trenches, Sarah, there often *is* something you can do about a problem if you think on it hard enough. But in this case I'm most worried about Mary Broom as a witness, and I haven't yet come up with a plan."

"Why are you worried?"

"Maybe she really did spend ten years in an ashram, but she's still a world-famous actress. In the first hearing, she only got to say something in writing. Here she'll be acting live, and acting can be persuasive."

"Not much you can do about that, either." She glanced over at the entryway to a nearby building. "Did you see a bald guy dart in there?"

"No. Sarah, maybe you should go live in a city where all the guys are either young or wear toupees."

She stopped walking abruptly and fixed him with a stare. "You shouldn't make fun of the attention I pay to things going on around me. The world is a much more dangerous place than you imagine. And I'd think that guy spying on you in the restaurant should make that manifest to you."

Just as she finished speaking, a rock the size of a softball crashed down on the sidewalk in front of them and shattered into three pieces. The biggest chunk hit Rory in the leg as Sarah jumped out of the way of another.

"Go, go!" She shoved him hard toward the entrance to the building next to them, which had an overhang. Once they were in the doorway, Sarah said, "Are you okay?"

He rolled up his right pant leg to the knee, and they both looked at it. "I'll be OK. It's just a small bruise."

"It doesn't look as if it broke the skin."

"No, I don't think it did. Let's just let it go. Probably just a weird coincidence of some kind."

"Or someone was trying to kill us. If that rock had hit either one of us on the head, we'd probably be dead."

"Why would anyone want to kill us?"

"Good question. I'm going inside to try to find the security guard. Keep an eye on that rock. We don't want anyone messing with the evidence."

He stood for a few minutes, rubbing his shin and looking at the shattered rock. Sarah was right. It could easily have killed one of them.

After a few minutes, she returned with, as luck would have it, a tall, nearly bald man wearing mirrored sunglasses and said, "This gentleman reports they've been having some problems lately with kids sneaking up to rooftops in this area and dropping things off the edge."

The man introduced himself as George Rutherford, the building's chief of security. He reached out and shook hands with Rory. "I'm deeply sorry about this. Unfortunately, this has been happening often in this neighborhood of late, and the culprits have figured out how to escape quickly, so no one's ever been able to find them, even though we search the building after it happens."

"It's not a big deal, Mr. Rutherford," Rory said. "I'm a little shaken up, but I'm okay."

"Your colleague tells me your leg was hit by a piece of the rock. We can supply a car to take you to an ER if you want to have it checked out."

"Thanks, I appreciate the offer, but no need. I'm fine. And we have to get back to court very soon."

"Mr. Rutherford, are you going to call the police on this one?" Sarah asked.

"One of my assistants has already made the call."

"Good. Please don't handle the rocks in the meantime, and please ask the police to try to take some latent prints from the fragments."

"From stones?" Rutherford said.

"There are some new techniques—using the chemical ninhydrin or sometimes superglue, depending on the type of rock—that can work. Especially if the thrower had sweaty or oily hands."

"Really?"

"Yes, really. I'm sure the LAPD crime lab will be familiar with the newest techniques. But if they need some consult on that, here's my contact info." She handed him a business card.

He looked at it and said, "You're a lawyer?"

"Yes, but I had a prior life as a PI, so I know about some of these things."

"Oh, I see."

"Hey, Sarah, we need to get going," Rory said.

"Yes. Indeed. Thanks for your assistance, Mr. Rutherford."

On their way back, Sarah said, "That was freaky."

"Oh, it'll be okay. It doesn't even hurt."

"No, I mean Rutherford. Tall, reflective sunglasses, completely shaved head."

"Sarah, your paranoia is on the march again. Yeah, he's pretty bald, but he had a small fringe around the edges, just cut really short."

"Are you sure?"

"Yeah, I'm sure."

"A rock coming down on us is not a sign of paranoia."

"Assuming it was aimed at us. And there's no evidence of that."

They walked down to Little Tokyo for lunch and ordered sushi—salmon sushi and tuna roll for Rory, fugu for Sarah.

"You know, Sarah, that's puffer fish. If it's not done right, it will kill you."

"I'm aware. But life is full of risks, Rory. As we just saw."

"I read somewhere that learning to prepare it right—taking out the poisonous liver and other organs—takes a three-year apprenticeship."

"Do you want to ask the sushi chef if he's had the proper training? He's standing right over there." She pointed across the sushi bar.

"Nope. You're the one who's gonna eat it. But frankly, it might go better for you if you just let people toss rocks at you from rooftops."

"That's quite different. Rocks don't taste good."

"What's in that fish that kills people?" he asked. "Do you know?"

"It's a potent neurotoxin called tetrodotoxin. I learned about it . . ."

"When you were minoring in neurology."

"No, it was when I spent some time in Japan, in Kyoto. In restaurants like this, it's almost always prepared properly."

The food came quickly. Rory ate his salmon sushi and tuna roll. Sarah ate the fugu. As they walked out and headed for the federal court building, Rory said, "You seem alright."

"It takes several hours to get sick and die. If I fall over, you'll know what to tell the EMTs, although there's no real treatment."

Rory laughed. "I'll keep that in mind. But let's talk about this afternoon's hearing. I'm counting on you to be my Internet eyes and ears."

"Meaning?"

"To do any factual research or legal research I need done during the hearing."

"Sounds easy. I'll be sitting right there beside you."

"Yes, but here's the problem. The local rules of the federal court and this judge's own courtroom rules prohibit us from using the Internet while we're in the courtroom. So if I want something researched, you'll need to leave and go down the hall to the attorneys' lounge."

"Okay. No problem."

Chapter 28

MONDAY AFTERNOON
FEDERAL COURT—CIVIL DOCKET
Broom v. TheSun/TheMoon/TheStars

"All rise! This United States district court is now in session."

The judge crossed the bench and took her seat. Rory could have sworn that the last time he'd seen her, her red hair had been parted in the middle. Now it was parted on the right. Her nose was still distinctly crooked.

"Ms. Thistle," she said, "are you ready for the plaintiff?"

"Yes, Your Honor."

"Mr. Calburton, are you ready for the defendant?"

"Yes, Your Honor," Rory said. "And I will be accompanied today by my colleague, Sarah Gold."

"Welcome, Ms. Gold."

"Thank you, Your Honor. And if I may, I have a request."

"Yes?"

"The local rules ban the use of the Internet inside these courtrooms. But because of the short notice for this hearing, I still have some final research to do while I am assisting Mr. Calburton." She shrugged and grinned the grin of the powerless subordinate.

"And so?"

"The rules give you the power to suspend that ban in your court-room, and I wondered if you might be willing to do so today only so that I might continue my research."

Judge Franklin stared at her for a moment, clearly uncertain, from the expression on her face, whether to take umbrage at the request or admire the audacity of it. Rory thought he saw her nose twitch slightly.

"It's an unusual request, Ms. Gold, but under the circumstances, I'll grant it. All counsel are permitted during this hearing to access the Internet from the courtroom, but only on notebook computers, not on cell phones. And absolutely no texts, phone calls, photos, or video recordings. Nor may you watch videos on your computer."

"Thank you, Your Honor."

Judge Franklin looked out into the ranks of spectators. "The full Internet ban inside the courtroom still applies to all spectators, and"—she turned toward the jury box, where she had made room for the press—"most especially to members of the media.

"Alright, Ms. Thistle, now that we're done with Ms. Gold's side trip, please call your first witness."

"Your Honor, might I first direct a few remarks to the court, in order to put this matter in context?"

"No, you might not. We'll have argument, if needed, later. Let's get on with it."

"Very well. The plaintiff calls Mary Broom."

In the audience, where the public had been seated, there was a slight murmur as Mary Broom—in a demure ankle-length maroon dress, belted at the waist, and a simple gold mandala necklace—rose from a seat in the back row, strolled to the front of the courtroom, and took her seat in the witness box. She had a large Louis Vuitton bag slung over her shoulder and set it on the floor beside her as she sat down. Reporters in the jury box strained to get a good look.

Rory noted that although Broom was covered from neck to toe, she had nonetheless chosen a tight-fitting dress that emphasized her thin waist and her shapely breasts. It was as if she were saying, "Still here, guys"—a reminder that although she had won two Academy awards and was once considered one of the most serious actresses of her generation, she had famously posed in a nothing bikini for *GQ*, and her poster had adorned many a dorm room. Including his own.

While the witness was being sworn in, Rory leaned over to Sarah and whispered, "Talk to me first before you do that kind of thing again."

"At least I didn't lie to you."

"That's not the point. Bottom line, you don't want to get a reputation in this courthouse for being a whiner."

Sarah raised her eyebrows. "Oh, you're educating me. I appreciate it. But I'm on the trail of something. You'll like it."

"A new rule, Sarah. We seem to keep needing them. In the future, clear it with me if you want to do anything out of the ordinary in a courtroom."

Meanwhile, Kathryn was posing her first question to Mary Broom.

"Ms. Broom, what is your profession?"

"I am a follower of the spiritual teacher Amrit Ram."

"Is that a profession?"

"It is a life, and I suppose it is therefore the nearest correct answer to the Western concept of profession."

"When did you become a follower of Amrit Ram?"

"I first encountered him twelve years ago when I was shooting a film in India, but I did not enter his ashram and become a formal follower until ten years ago."

"Prior to entering the ashram, did you have another profession?"

"Yes, I was an actor."

"Of any particular kind?"

"I acted in films, on TV, and on the stage in both the United States and Britain."

"Were you famous?"

Rory considered objecting that the question was improperly ambiguous without a definition of fame, but decided that the objection would seem ludicrous. Mary Broom was famous by anyone's definition.

"In the Western concept of fame, yes."

"Throughout the world?"

"Yes."

Judge Franklin interrupted. "Counsel, is there much more of this? Ms. Broom's probably more famous than the president. There's no jury to impress. Can we move on?"

"Yes, of course, Your Honor. Ms. Broom, did you have any other profession before joining the ashram?"

"Yes, I was a writer."

"Were you a published writer?"

"No."

Kathryn had, as lawyers liked to say, pulled the sting. Instead of waiting for Rory to extract the same damaging answer from Broom in cross-examination, Kathryn had solicited the answer herself. Some people thought it was a good tactic because it got the problem out of the way early. Others, and Rory agreed with them, thought pulling the sting called even more attention to the problem. Amazingly, someone had written an entire book on the subject.

"What form did your writing take?" Kathryn asked.

"I wrote short stories, novels and screenplays for both film and television."

"How many, would you say?"

"I'm not sure of the exact count. Three novels for sure. Maybe four TV pilots and five screenplays."

"Did you show them to anyone?"

"No. With one exception, not ever."

"Why not?"

"I was afraid. Beneath the persona of the world-famous actress, there was a fearful little girl who didn't want to expose herself to ridicule."

"Please elaborate."

Rory had finally had enough. He rose.

"Objection, Your Honor. The question calls for an improper narrative. And it's also irrelevant. Although we may all"—he gestured to the assembled press in the jury box—"like to know more about how people who are famous feel about their fame, these questions have zero to do with the issue here: whether Ms. Broom, against all common sense, and despite her obvious talents in front of a camera, wrote the screenplay for *Extorted* after, before that, doing nothing like it at all."

"The objection is sustained."

Rory was starting to sit down when the judge said, "You can go on standing for a moment, Mr. Calburton. A word of caution, save the speechifying for outside. Saying just 'Objection, calls for a narrative,' is generally enough."

"I'm sorry, Your Honor. With no jury present, I thought some elaboration would be helpful to the court."

"Really, Mr. Calburton, let's face it. You were trying to be helpful to our reporter friends over there"—she motioned toward the jury box—"not to the court."

"I won't do it again."

"Good, let's get back to questions and answers."

Out of the corner of his eye, Rory noticed that Mary Broom was carefully watching the back and forth between him and the judge, turning her head from side to side to follow the action, almost as if she were taking it all in for a film in which she might be asked to play a lawyer. It had the effect of making her lustrously black shoulder-length hair swirl gently around her head.

Kathryn conspicuously consulted her notes as if looking for the next line of questioning and asked, "Ms. Broom, when did you start writing the script for *Extorted*?"

"On March fifteenth, fifteen years ago."

"How do you know that?"

"Until recently, I wasn't certain of it. But then I recalled that I kept a diary at the time and that I had noted in that diary the day I began the script. Ten years ago, when I left for India—intending, finally, to stay there—I entrusted the diary to my then agent for safekeeping."

"And who was that?"

"Heather Prim."

"What happened after you recalled that she had your diary?"

"I called her up, went over to her house, where she had the diary secured in a wall safe, and I sat in her home office and read it."

"What did it say about the date you started the script?"

Rory was on his feet again. "Objection! Leading, and, also, testimony by this witness about what the diary says is rank hearsay. It's also not the best evidence, because they could just bring in the diary, and we could all read it. I move that the answer about the date be struck."

"This isn't hearsay, Your Honor," Kathryn said. "If I'm permitted to ask a few more questions, it will be obvious that I'm asking the witness what the diary says about the date only in order to show that her recollection has been refreshed by reading it. That makes the diary present recollection refreshed, which is not hearsay."

"I continue my objections," Rory said. "And I add that if the diary is being used to refresh the witness's recollection, I'm absolutely entitled to see it."

"Overruled for now. Go ahead with your questions, Ms. Thistle. Let's see where this is going."

"Before you consulted your diary, Ms. Broom, did you have any recollection at all of when you started writing the script for *Extorted*?"

"Yes."

"Why, then, did you need to consult the diary?"

She sat up straighter, put her finger to her chin in a pose Rory recognized from a poster for one of her Oscar-winning movies and said, "Because I recalled that I wrote a note to myself in that diary the very day I began the script. I needed to look at the date on that diary page to refresh my memory on the exact date."

"Did you recall, before you looked at it, what topic you were writing about on that diary page?"

"Yes. Very specifically. I just needed the exact date."

"Your Honor," Kathryn said, "I think we have now established that this is present recollection refreshed, which isn't hearsay because we're not seeking to admit the diary itself. Ms. Broom's testimony as to the date should, therefore, be admitted."

"Your Honor," Rory interjected, "before you rule on the admissibility of Ms. Broom's testimony about the date, can I take the witness on voir dire first?"

"You want to ask her questions now, in the middle of Ms. Thistle's direct examination, before your cross?"

"Yes. I want to use out-of-order questioning to show that this testimony shouldn't be admitted under any kind of theory."

Kathryn looked agitated. "Your Honor, I strenuously object. The purpose of permitting voir dire by opposing counsel in the middle of direct testimony is to keep a jury from being polluted with information that shouldn't come in. But there's no jury here."

"It can also save the court's time, Ms. Thistle," Judge Franklin said. "And by the way, in my courtroom, strenuously objecting is treated no differently than just plain objecting without festooning the objection with an adverb. In any case, overruled. Go ahead with your voir dire, Mr. Calburton. Ask your questions."

Kathryn retreated to her table as Rory strode to the lectern. He knew what he was about to do was risky. He was gonna ask a question he didn't know the answer to in advance—an approach that would let the witness screw him with a bad answer. His gut said go for it.

"Ms. Broom, what else did the diary page say—the page with the date on it?"

"Objection," Kathryn said. "Now *that* calls for hearsay."

"The sauce principle applies here, Your Honor," Rory said.

Judge Franklin wrinkled her nose. "I don't think I'm familiar with that, Mr. Calburton."

"What's sauce for the goose is sauce for the gander," Rory said. "Or in this case, if what the diary says isn't hearsay for Ms. Thistle's purposes, then I don't see how it can be hearsay for ours."

The judge laughed. "Your objection is overruled, Ms. Thistle. Please continue, Mr. Calburton."

"I'll repeat the question," Rory said. "What else does that diary page say?"

"I'd rather not answer that."

"Well, I'm afraid you have to answer," Rory said.

She paused. "I prefer not to, Mr. Calburton."

Rory could see in the tilt of her chin and hear in the tone of her voice the haughty attitude of a global star who had once upon a time been walled off by teams of agents, managers and publicists and responded only to those questions she wanted to answer.

"I ask the court to instruct the witness to answer the question," Rory said.

"May we approach the bench before you instruct, Your Honor?" Kathryn asked.

"I'm not fond of bench conferences, Counsel. What's so secret that you can't say it in open court?"

"It's a privacy issue."

Judge Franklin sighed audibly and said, "Fine. Approach the bench, Counsel. I'm curious to hear what's so supposedly private."

Rory turned to Sarah and said, "I'll go up by myself while you keep doing whatever incredibly important thing it is you're doing there on your computer."

Sarah handed him a slip of paper. "Here's my prediction of what the diary says. Don't open it until after you learn the answer, and we'll see if you really want to go on disparaging my research."

Chapter 29

Rory and Kathryn paused on their way up to the bench and watched as Mary Broom started to climb down from the witness box.

"Excuse me, Ms. Broom," the judge said. "What are you doing?"

"I'm coming over to join the conversation about my diary. I won't be able to hear from the witness box."

"Oh. I can understand your confusion. But that's not the way we do it. It's lawyers only."

"But it's my private diary," Broom said. "With my private thoughts."

"Yes, but you'll be represented in the discussion by very competent counsel."

Broom sighed deeply. "Alright. Shall I sit back down, then?"

"Yes, please."

When Rory and Kathryn reached the bench, the judge raised her eyebrows as if to say, "Wow, that was odd," and then said aloud, "What's this supposed privacy problem, Ms. Thistle?"

Kathryn turned to Rory. "May I have your assurance you will keep what I say strictly confidential?"

"Sure. Although I need to tell my associate." He gestured at Sarah.

"Fine, then. Your Honor, may we have this off the record?"

"Yes." She nodded to the court reporter, who had moved closer to the bench to be able to hear. "Corrie, for the moment, we'll be off the record." Corrie picked up her stenotype machine and moved out of earshot.

"Okay, then," Kathryn said. "The diary page contains references to the fact that Ms. Broom was pregnant at the time she wrote the entry about starting the script. If that is revealed in open court, it will cause a worldwide media frenzy. One that Ms. Broom, who has chosen to lead a relatively cloistered life, does not deserve."

"I wouldn't call filing this lawsuit cloistered," Rory said. "But what does any of this have to do with her memory of when she supposedly started to write a screenplay?"

Kathryn huffed herself up. "Well, Mr. Calburton, believe it or not, most women actually recall being pregnant. Ms. Broom remembered that she started the script on the day she learned she was pregnant. From a test. So she needed to look at the diary to confirm that her recollection of that date was correct."

Judge Franklin was sitting with her chin propped on nested hands, which caused her shoulder-length red hair to move forward and cover up most of her face. Rory thought it made her look like a sheepdog with a crooked nose.

"You know," the judge said, "I can understand why Ms. Broom wants to keep the information under wraps. It will obviously raise the question of whether she had a child, where the child is now if it was born, who the father is, and so forth."

"Thank you, Your Honor," Kathryn said.

"Don't thank me yet. Because on the other hand, Ms. Broom has filed a lawsuit and asked for the extraordinary remedy of blocking the wide release of a motion picture on which the defendant studio has already spent north of one hundred million dollars."

Kathryn, who could obviously see victory on the issue slipping away, said, "I don't think how much a defendant has spent ought to be weighed against a person's right to privacy, which the Supreme Court has ruled is protected by the Constitution."

"If only the Founding Fathers had had such salacious things to worry about when they were writing it," Judge Franklin said.

"I think she's lying," Rory said.

The judge had not removed her chin from her nested hands. She raised her eyebrows and said, "I think I need to take all of this under advisement and have my law clerk do some research on the legal issue involved. Ms. Thistle, please move on to a different area, and we'll return later to Mr. Calburton's request to further explore the diary entry."

"Your Honor," Rory said, "just to be clear, I don't want to explore the diary. I want to read it. Because I don't think it's her pregnancy Ms. Broom is trying to hide, but something that will show she's lying when she says she wrote the script for *Extorted*."

"We'll see, Mr. Calburton. In the meantime, please resume your questioning, Ms. Thistle."

On the way back to his table, Rory unfolded the note that Sarah had handed him. It contained one word: "Pregnant."

Chapter 30

"Thank you, Your Honor," Thistle said. "I'll move to a different area now, but I want to reserve the right to return to the diary when you've resolved that issue."

"Consider it reserved."

Kathryn looked to the witness, who had remained in the witness chair during the colloquy with the judge. "Ms. Broom, what medium did you use to write your script?"

"I typed it on my laptop computer."

"Where did you do that?"

"All kinds of places. At home, on airplanes, on movie sets. Just wherever and whenever I could find the time."

"Did you ever send the file to anyone else?"

"No."

"Why not?"

"I was worried that someone—even a friend—would find it too tempting and would forward it to someone else or reveal its existence."

"You don't trust your friends?"

"No, I do. Or at least some of them. But you see, if you're a movie star . . . well, you told me just to answer the question asked, so that's my answer."

"But what, Ms. Broom?"

"Well, I was about to say that fame is a funny thing, and that some people just can't resist talking about their famous friends. And the idea that a famous actress was writing a movie script might have been too much, even for those I trusted. So I kept it strictly to myself."

"When did you finish it?"

"Well, that depends what you mean by finish. Because I first did an extremely detailed outline, which I completed in only a few days."

"The outline that was introduced in evidence during the first phase of this preliminary injunction hearing, before Judge Cabraal?"

"Yes."

"How long did it take you to turn that outline into a full script?"

She paused and smiled, and Rory could have sworn she turned slightly and directed that smile, teeth still movie-star white, directly at the members of the press in the jury box.

"It took an embarrassingly long time because I wrote draft after draft and wasn't very happy with any of them."

"When did you finally complete the full script?"

"Now *that* I recall precisely, without any reference to my diary."

As she said it, she smiled over at Rory as if to say, "Take that!" and he found himself, despite the gibe, attracted to her. She would make a deadly effective witness if the case ever got in front of a jury.

"And what was that date that you recall so well?" Kathryn asked.

"It was Christmas Eve eleven years ago, and I recall it well because finishing up the script that evening and declaring it officially done was a kind of gift to myself. A last worldly thing, in a way, before moving on to something less material."

"Did you give yourself anything else for Christmas that year?"

"Yes, I gave myself permission to go to India and leave Hollywood behind." She looked away from Kathryn and glared across the courtroom at Rory as if he were the living embodiment of Hollywood.

Kathryn seemed not to notice and asked, "Did you print out a copy?"

"Yes."

"Do you still have it?"

"Yes."

"Where is it now?"

"In my bag."

"Would you get it out, please?"

Rory leaped to his feet. "I object and ask that this testimony be struck. And despite the court's earlier admonition, I object strenuously."

"Why am I not surprised?" Judge Franklin said.

"Your Honor," Rory said, "you may not be aware of how outrageous this is because you didn't do the earlier hearing and may not know the details."

"What details, Mr. Calburton?"

"We asked for copies of her supposed script during the limited discovery before the earlier hearing. We were told there was no copy, just the outline. If a copy has now magically appeared, counsel should have given that to us for authenticity testing long before this hearing got started. This is beyond outrageous."

Suddenly, Mary Broom chimed in. "I only found it yesterday."

Everyone looked at her as if she were an intruder. Witnesses weren't supposed to speak unless asked a question. Even her own lawyer just plowed on without acknowledging Broom's statement.

"You'll recall, Mr. Calburton," Kathryn said, "that I told you about it right after Ms. Broom found it, which was only yesterday. And I also told you I was delaying giving it to you until I could have it forensically tested by an expert. I'm happy to say I have two copies for you right now, plus one for the court. So there you go."

"There I do not go, Your Honor. Even if this is all true, which I doubt, we should have been given a copy of the script yesterday, when it was supposedly found. And at the very least well before court this morning."

"We can clear all of this up if I'm permitted to ask the witness a few questions before you rule on the objection," Kathryn said.

"Go ahead," Judge Franklin said. "But the explanation better be good, Ms. Thistle, because by springing this on us now, you have violated several local rules, not to mention been rather unprofessional toward opposing counsel."

Kathryn gave no indication of caring a whit about the judge's admonishment. She turned again to Mary Broom and said, "Would you take the script out of your bag, please?"

The witness reached into her bag and extracted a set of white pages more than an inch thick, bound at the spine with brass brads pushed through punched holes. "This is it."

"Thank you. Your Honor, may I approach the witness so that I can show the item to the court and to opposing counsel?"

"Yes."

Kathryn walked up to the witness, took the script from her and approached the clerk, who was sitting to the judge's right. "I'm handing the clerk a one-hundred-and-two-page typewritten document, which says, on the cover, 'Extorted, copyright Mary Broom.' This is the original that the witness found. I'd ask that this be marked as Plaintiff's Exhibit 1."

After the clerk had marked it and given the judge her copy, Kathryn walked over to Rory's table and handed him the original and two copies. Rory took the original from her and, while she stood there, spent almost five minutes examining it. Sarah stood up and read over his shoulder.

"Here you go," he said, handing the original back to Kathryn, who resumed her questioning even as she walked back to the lectern.

"Ms. Broom, where did you locate this?" she asked.

"I'm staying with Heather Prim now, and late last night we were having a drink after coming back from a late dinner. She asked me what I wanted to do with the box I had left with her when I moved to India. I had totally forgotten about it, so I said let's have a look."

"What did you find in it?"

"Well, it was an old banker's box. It contained mostly family photos, but there was also a manila folder in it that contained the script you're holding in your hand. I had forgotten about putting the original printout in that box."

"When did you tell me about it?"

"It was almost midnight last night."

"Right after you found it?"

"No, a couple of hours later. I wanted to read through it and confirm that it was in fact the script I wrote."

"Is it?"

"Yes. Every word. And it's the very copy I printed out on Christmas Eve, when I finished it. I signed it and dated it December twenty-fourth, on the last page, in blue ink."

"Did you ever create any other copies before I created copies for court today?"

"No, never scanned it or copied it in any way."

"Your Honor, I move that Exhibit 1 be admitted into evidence."

"I object," Rory said.

"Strenuously?" Judge Franklin asked, smiling.

"Even more than that, Your Honor. For all we know, the witness typed this out last week after she got her hands on a copy of the shooting script for the movie from friends in the industry. It shouldn't be admitted until I get a chance to cross-examine the witness, question

Ms. Prim, who supposedly had this document for years, and have it tested for age and authenticity by a questioned-document examiner."

Judge Franklin pursed her lips, tilted her head slightly and said, "You know, before ruling on any of that, the court would like the opportunity to examine the document with more care. Ms. Thistle, why don't you hand it up here, and let's resume in one hour."

Rory turned to Sarah and said, "How did you know she was pregnant?"

She glanced around the courtroom. "Too many ears in here. Let's go out in the hall and find a place where no one can hear us."

Chapter 31

They exited the courtroom and headed down to the very end of the hallway, which was empty of people.

"Okay, Sarah, how did you learn that Mary Broom was pregnant back then?"

"I not only figured that out, but I figured out who the father is."

"Who? And when was the child born?"

"Alex Toltec, and the kid was born fifteen years ago, on December twenty-fourth, which is a just-right date for the event."

"Why?"

"The average human pregnancy is two hundred eighty days. So if Mary Broom tested positive on March fifteenth fifteen years ago for being pregnant, and the test came up positive very early in her pregnancy—say ten days after conception—the child would have been born sometime around December fourteenth fifteen years ago, plus or minus a couple weeks in either direction. December twenty-fourth is in the ballpark."

"How soon after conception do those home tests work?"

"Ten days-ish."

"How did you figure out that they maybe had a kid?"

"Do you remember that I said I thought something was being hidden at the ashram, no tours anymore and stuff like that?"

"Yes."

"Well, I asked myself what kind of things people try to hide, and one thing on the list was an out-of-wedlock kid."

"Smart," Rory said.

Sarah beamed. "So I accessed the birth records for Los Angeles County for that general time period."

"How did you get access? I thought those records were blocked except to parents and the authorities."

"They are."

"And?"

"You know about the Dark Net, right?"

"Yeah. Legit stuff like private corporate networks and illicit stuff like porn, drugs and prostitution. What about it?"

"So I bought what I needed there, in terms of birth records."

Rory sighed. "I thought we had agreed that your PI days were over, and I probably don't want to know how you paid for whatever it is you bought."

"This had nothing to do with my PI days, and I paid in dollars—my own. I became interested in the whole thing in college, when it was all just getting started, so I know my way around."

"Let's cut to the chase. Was Alex listed as the father?"

"No, the father was listed as Red Cetlot. Do you see it?"

"No."

"Cetlot is Toltec backward, and Alexander backward is *Red*naxela."

"What's the kid's name?"

"Alma. The first two letters of each of their first names."

"Sounds at least quasi-persuasive."

"Get this, though. Her middle name is Ides."

"As in Ides of March . . ."

"Yes, the day Mary says she learned she was pregnant."

"This would all be a lot simpler if we could talk to Alex."

"Is there any word from the hospital?"

"I talked with one of the doctors this morning. Wouldn't tell me much 'cause I'm not a relative. I did worm out of him that Alex is still in a coma but quickly emerging from it and is expected to survive. Only question is whether there will be brain damage."

As they walked back toward the courtroom, Sarah said, "Hey, one more thing. When you cross-examine Mary Broom, see if you can find a way to ask her where she was having dinner the night that Joe was killed and what she was doing that afternoon."

"Why?"

"Because she had reason to want him dead, so where she was when he was killed is relevant."

"There are probably hundreds of people who had reason to want him dead."

"True. But none of those hundreds of people was suing this studio, with Joe Stanton standing in the way of a desire to be acknowledged as the author of *Extorted*."

"I really don't see it, Sarah. If Joe Stanton hadn't been pushing back against her lawsuit, someone else in the studio would have been opposing her. It's not like it was personal for him."

"Okay, okay. But just ask if you get the chance."

"I don't think I'm gonna do that. The judge will think I'm nuts."

"Well, if you won't do that, you should at least be able to make some hay out of the child thing."

"If I want to."

"Meaning?"

"If Alma was conceived on or near March fifteenth fifteen years ago, it means Alex was possibly in Mary's house when she supposedly started the script. Or right after. Which isn't such a good fact for us."

"Oh. I should have thought of that. My inexperience with trial work is showing."

"Well, my experience could be leading me astray. But we're in a pickle."

"Which is?"

"If I ask Mary about the child on cross, she might welcome it and reveal everything to prove that Alex had easy access to the outline of her script. In which case we probably lose the case—which turns what I thought was gonna be the first big victory of my partnership into defeat."

"And on the other hand?"

"If she wants to keep it secret, we could make settlement harder." He paused. "And we'll look like assholes for bringing a child into it."

Chapter 32

"All rise! This United States district court is again in session."

Judge Franklin was quickly back in her seat. "Ladies and gentlemen, I've done some research and reached some conclusions. I have three items to deal with. The script, the diary and Mr. Calburton's request to interrupt Ms. Thistle's direct examination of her witness by voir dire–ing the witness about the diary before he begins his own cross-examination. So let's deal with them one by one.

"First, Mr. Calburton, your request to engage in additional voir dire of Ms. Broom is denied. You can question her further about the diary when it's your turn for cross-examination."

"But, Your Honor—"

"Hang on, Mr. Calburton. I think you'll like the overall result when I get done."

"Okay."

She looked over to Kathryn. "Second, let's deal with the recently discovered script. Ms. Thistle, whatever circumstances led to the purported script being sprung on us at the last minute, I think it only fair that the defendant get to look at the script, and, if they wish, have an expert test it for authenticity, and all before you ask anyone any questions about it."

"Candidly," Kathryn said, "we don't trust them to have it in their possession. Movie studios have the technology to—"

"I don't propose they take it home with them, Counsel, like it was in a swag bag from a party. I will arrange to make it available here in the courthouse. One of my law clerks or some other member of the court's staff will be in attendance during the examination." She pointed to her law clerk, a young man who had been sitting on a single chair, stage left.

While Judge Franklin was speaking, Rory was only half listening, focusing again on her crooked nose and, upon hearing the swag-bag comment, wondering if the nose could help make her funny in stand-up. Was there maybe a clip of her doing stand-up on YouTube? He'd have to look.

"Mr. Calburton," the judge said, "do you have a view on the testing regimen?"

Rory shook himself out of his imaginings and walked to the lectern. "Uh, Your Honor, I'm sure it will be awkward for our experts to test here. They use sophisticated instruments and so forth."

"Okay. Well, with regard to your comment, let's do it this way. If your experts absolutely can't effectively examine the document here, we'll figure out some other way to do it. But let's start with it here."

"Okay."

Kathryn had appeared at the lectern, too, standing behind Rory. "Your Honor, may I be heard?" she asked.

"Yes, Counsel. Go ahead."

"With all due respect, I think it's inappropriate, at this time, to test the document, until I've completed my examination of Ms. Broom."

"Mr. Calburton, what do you think about that?"

"I think it will just delay things more, and we'll get super close to the wide release date of the film. I'm willing to take a chance that I'll want a second expert to take a look at it and have you say no."

"I agree with Mr. Calburton," Judge Franklin said. "We need to expedite this whole thing. My order with regard to the script will stand. My clerk will let both of you know who to contact about access to the script. In the meantime, I will keep it safely locked away in my chambers.

"And now let's deal with the issue of the diary," Judge Franklin said. "That seems to me a more difficult issue, since the diary is likely to contain private information irrelevant to the matter at hand in this case."

Rory smiled. "Whose relevance or irrelevance, if I may interrupt, Your Honor; we can't judge unless we see it."

"You're right, Counsel. And a solution is for the court to review it first, in a limited fashion. I propose to review, *in camera*, only the page before the page in question, the page itself and the page after. I can then decide whether to release those pages to the defendant to examine. Or whether I need to see more pages. What do you think about that, Ms. Thistle?"

"May I have a moment to consult with my client?"

"Of course."

Rory returned to counsel table, where Sarah was again hard at work on her computer. "What are you looking up this time?"

"How to take fingerprints from rocks."

"That can really be done?"

"Yes."

"Wow. What will they think of next?"

"What do you think Kathryn is going to do?"

Rory tilted back in the swivel chair and put his hands behind his head. "She ought to say okay, because if she doesn't, she's telling the judge she doesn't trust her. But take a look at what's happening." He pointed to the witness box, where Kathryn was standing, talking to her client, who was shaking her head vigorously back and forth, clearly saying, "No."

Seconds later, Kathryn was back at the lectern. "Your Honor, with all due respect, my client strongly objects to giving you or defendant access to anything in the diary other than a copy of the paragraph or line in which she makes reference to the date in question."

The judge paused for a moment and looked down at Kathryn. "I see. Well, the good thing about being a judge is that I get to listen to argument and then decide."

"It sounds as if you're about to rule against me."

"I am. I'm ordering your client to turn over copies of the relevant pages to the court by five p.m. today. I'll examine them myself, without anyone else present and, pending my decision, put them in my office safe, to which only I have the combination."

"Your Honor, will you stay your order until five p.m. tomorrow so that we may appeal it?"

"Seriously?"

"Yes."

Judge Franklin raised her eyebrows high. "You think it's an appealable order?"

"I do."

"You're going to ask the court of appeals to order me, a United States district judge, not to look at a document?"

"Yes."

"Well, Counsel, the court of appeals is, as I'm sure you know, right out in Pasadena, just a hop, skip and a jump up the freeway. This time of day, it's about a thirty-minute drive. I suggest you go back to your office, prepare whatever papers you need for an emergency interlocutory appeal and drive out there and visit with the clerk. I understand she's very friendly and helpful, and she can get the emergency appeal process started for you."

"That can take some time, Your Honor."

"You're right, Counsel. So you should probably call ahead and let them know you'll be getting your papers to them later today." She paused and smiled down at her. "And to make sure you have *plenty* of time to get it *all* done, I'll modify my order and make it effective by one p.m. tomorrow instead of five p.m. today."

"That still doesn't leave much time, Your Honor."

"Well, time comes to those who don't waste it. So I'm sure you'll have enough if you get busy."

Kathryn hesitated, as if she wanted to say something further, but then thought better of it. "Thank you, Your Honor."

"Mr. Calburton, do you have anything you want to add?"

Rory, applying once again his "no need to help opposing counsel dig a hole" philosophy, quickly said, "No, Your Honor."

"Very well then, we're adjourned until one o'clock tomorrow. You should be prepared to start your cross-examination then, Mr. Calburton."

Judge Franklin left the bench, and Rory watched as Mary Broom stepped down from the witness stand and followed Kathryn through the doors out into the hall. Then he and Sarah headed out. As they emerged from the doors, Mary Broom was standing in front of Kathryn and making a point with a stabbing finger. When she saw Rory, she turned and walked away. At that moment, several members of the media burst through the courtroom doors, cell phones extended and reporters' notebooks in hand, making a beeline for Broom. Just as quickly, three big guys in dark suits, with secret service–like earpieces in place, appeared seemingly out of nowhere and blocked their path.

"Ms. Broom is not giving interviews today, people," one of them said.

Kathryn turned to Rory. "My client would like us to talk seriously about entering into settlement talks in the very near future."

"Because of the diary-handover order?"

"That and other things."

"I thought you were going to the court of appeals."

"I'm considering it. But do you think the court of appeals will order this judge not to look at a document?"

"No. Maybe you'd have a shot if she'd told you to turn it over to us. But what's in it that's got your client so hot and bothered"—he gestured toward Mary Broom, talking on her cell phone behind her wall of security guys and looking regal even in that ordinary act—"that she doesn't even want a judge to see it?"

"Wouldn't you love to know? Anyway, are you open to settlement discussions?"

"Make us a reasonable demand, and not one that involves the studio financing Ms. Broom's movie. That was my position last week, and it still is."

"I will. As soon as I can give you the script that was actually submitted to the studio—the one with Alex Toltec's writing on it. We're still looking for that one, and once you see it our high demand will make more sense. I expect to have it very shortly."

Rory wondered if he should tell her he already had a copy of it.

Chapter 33

TUESDAY AFTERNOON
FEDERAL COURT—CIVIL DOCKET
Broom v. TheSun/TheMoon/TheStars

"All rise! This United States district court is now in session."

Judge Franklin was quickly in her chair. "Ladies and gentlemen, let's get a few preliminaries out of the way first."

Rory noted that Judge Franklin's hair was now parted on the left. Could the changes be some kind of mood indicator?

"Counsel," the judge said, "I need to let you know that I have a motion in a criminal matter to deal with briefly, so at some point I'll have to suspend this hearing for perhaps thirty minutes and then resume. As you know, federal judges are required to give priority to criminal cases."

The judge's clerk rose from his seat, went to the side of the bench and said something to her that Rory couldn't hear. The judge nodded, then resumed.

"First, Counsel, let me ask about the diary pages. Ms. Thistle, my clerk tells me that he called your office early this morning and was told that you did not appeal my order. Is that correct?"

"Yes, that's correct. Our research showed that Your Honor was correct about the difficulty of appealing that type of order. My apologies to the court for delaying the matter while we researched it."

"Fine."

Rory noticed that the judge did not, as judges usually did, say, "Apology accepted." When Franklin had been a mere lawyer, she'd had a reputation for holding a grudge. He could only hope it was still true.

"Ms. Thistle, do you have the copies of the relevant pages with you?" the judge asked. "The ones I want to examine before determining if Mr. Calburton should see them?"

"Yes, I do."

"Great. Could you please hand them to the clerk?"

Kathryn walked toward the clerk as the judge said, "Mr. Clerk, please mark those as the next exhibit in order."

The clerk handed them up to the judge. "Give me a moment to read these," she said.

Judge Franklin made something of a show of reading them, pursing her lips from time to time, stroking her chin, nodding her head and muttering something under her breath that Rory couldn't make out.

Finally, she looked up and said, "There's no reason Mr. Calburton shouldn't see these now. Please come up and get them from the clerk, sir."

"But, Your Honor," Kathryn said, "there needs to be some sort of court order protecting the confidentiality of this material."

"Fine. Mr. Calburton, you are not to show these pages to anyone else or discuss them with anyone else other than your co-counsel until further notice."

"What about my client?" Rory asked.

"Well, what about that, Ms. Thistle, can he show them to his client?"

"If it's limited to attorneys in the studio general counsel's office who are working on the case, okay. And assuming they're made aware of the confidentiality order."

"I'm okay with that for now," Rory said.

"Good," Judge Franklin said. "Ms. Thistle, please resume your direct examination of Ms. Broom."

The judge looked at Mary Broom, who was sitting at counsel table next to Kathryn, and said, "You may resume the stand, Ms. Broom."

As she walked to the stand, Rory noticed that Broom had exchanged the formfitting clothing of the day before for a long-sleeved black A-line dress that came below the knee. It had a high collar surrounded by fine white lace. Rory seemed to recall that she had been similarly dressed in some hit movie, although he couldn't immediately recall which one.

Once the witness had taken her seat, the judge said, "I want to remind you that you're still under oath."

"Yes, of course, Your Honor."

Kathryn walked to the lectern, asking her first question as she walked. "Ms. Broom, have you reviewed the shooting script for the released film *Extorted*?"

"Yes."

"Please tell the court your understanding of what a shooting script is."

"From my long experience in making films, it's the final version of a movie script that is given to the director, the actors and others as the way the movie is going to be. What the lines will be."

Rory laughed inwardly. When a witness led with a line like, "From my long experience in making films," it meant the testimony had been rehearsed. No humans spoke that way in normal conversation.

"Do shooting scripts ever get changed during production?"

"Yes, sometimes, but usually in small ways, unless some problem arises. An actor just can't deliver a line as scripted, despite numerous tries. Or the director thinks the scene just doesn't work as written. Or, more seriously, an actor dies in the middle of a film."

"What about changes made during principal photography?"

"Sure, studio execs watching the dailies can become unhappy and ask for reshoots or changes going forward."

Rory rose from his seat. "Your Honor, I object to this line of questioning. While this is all very interesting, it seems highly irrelevant to the issues at stake here."

"I'll move on," Kathryn said. "Ms. Broom, did you compare the shooting script to the released film?"

"Yes."

"How did you do that?"

"I took the shooting script with me to a screening of the film, and I compared it, word for word and line for line, to the lines spoken in the movie as I sat there with the script in my lap."

Rory made a mental note to ask her how she got into a prerelease screening and how she managed to read the script in what was presumably a darkened theater.

"Did you find the movie as shot similar to the script that you testified you wrote and printed out approximately ten years ago?"

"Objection," Rory said. "Compound. The witness didn't testify that she wrote and immediately printed what she'd written. She testified there was a long gap between those two actions. And I also object that the witness is not an expert in comparing scripts."

"Sustained," Judge Franklin said. "As to the compound objection."

"I'll break the question up, Your Honor," Kathryn said. "Ms. Broom, did you compare the script you printed out on Christmas Eve to the shooting script?"

"Yes."

"Did you find them to be substantially similar?"

"Objection," Rory said. "In fact, I object strenuously, with apologies to the court for adding an adverb."

"What's your exact objection, Mr. Calburton?"

"Whether two creative works are substantially similar is a question of law for the court to decide. It's the key *legal* question in this case. If the Christmas Eve script and the shooting script aren't substantially similar, there can't, as a matter of law, be an infringement, even if the studio somehow got access to the Christmas Eve script."

"I'll hear from Ms. Thistle before I rule on the objection."

Kathryn stood to respond. "It's true that the courts have adopted the phrase *substantially similar* as one test for infringement. But those words aren't in the copyright statute—they're not magic words. They're words courts have borrowed from the way people talk."

Judge Franklin smiled. "That's true, Ms. Thistle, but those are indeed the words that courts have come to focus on in determining whether there is or is not copyright infringement."

"But this witness *wrote* the Christmas Eve script and has also read the shooting script. So she should certainly be able to give her opinion as to whether there's substantial similarity between the two. It's only common sense."

"I'm going to sustain the objection," Judge Franklin said. "This witness may not give her opinion about substantial similarity. Note that I'm not deciding right now if substantial similarity is a question of law which is reserved to the court, or whether I will accept *expert* testimony on the subject. But I do know that this witness has not been qualified as an expert."

"May I be permitted to show that this witness is an expert on script comparison?" Kathryn asked.

"I object again," Rory said.

"What's your objection this time, Mr. Calburton?"

"The plaintiff shouldn't be able to put on an expert witness without giving us notice of who it is and permitting us to take the expert's deposition before they testify. Those are the rules."

"That's normally true," Judge Franklin said.

"If it's normally true—"

"But this is an extraordinary circumstance. We don't usually have hearings like this on preliminary injunction motions."

"Ms. Thistle had time to give us at least some notice," Rory said. "Instead she chose to give none."

"I'm going to permit Ms. Thistle to try to show that Ms. Broom is an expert on script comparison. Instead of taking her deposition, you can cross-examine her on the subject."

"Thank you, Your Honor," Rory said, although he was unhappy.

But the judge was not finished. "And after that, Mr. Calburton, I will decide if Ms. Broom can give expert opinion in her own case. Although I note that it's not unusual for parties to act as their own experts. It's just that when they do so, their testimony may be argued to lack believability."

"I reiterate my objection," Rory said. "No foundation has been laid for this witness's expertise in comparing scripts. She has, by her own account, written only five, and we've seen only one of them. The fact that she's an actress hardly makes her an expert on this."

Suddenly, Mary Broom spoke up. "I'm an actor, Mr. Calburton. We no longer use the sexist term *actress*."

Rory was trying to think of a sarcastic response when the judge took the issue out of his hands. "Ms. Broom," she said, "no one appreciates more than I do the need to rid our language of sexist terms. But, as I hope you can understand, witness comments during arguments about legal issues just complicate things."

"I apologize, Your Honor. I probably won't do it again."

Rory looked up to see if the judge's nose twitched at Broom's insertion of the unexpected "probably" in her apology, but he detected no motion.

Judge Franklin paused for a second and said, simply, "Thank you, Ms. Broom. Please go ahead with your questioning, Ms. Thistle."

With that, Rory listened as Kathryn elicited from Broom that she had gone to an elite college—Stanford—majored in comparative literature and spent a lot of time comparing the texts of authors like Charles Dickens and Victor Hugo. Wrapping up, she asked Broom, "What did that comparison involve?"

"Comparing themes and dramatic structures in one work versus the other and looking at how culture and language influenced those differences. Sometimes we actually made charts of the differences."

"What were you trying to judge, then, overall?"

"Whether two works were substantially similar."

Rory rolled his eyes. The witness had clearly picked up the phrase by listening to the objection he'd made. He wasn't about to let it pass.

"Objection," he said. "I move to strike the answer. It's an improper attempt by this lay witness to testify about the meaning of a legal term."

"It's not improper," Kathryn said. "If it takes an expert to use the phrase 'substantial similarity,' well, I've now more than qualified Ms. Broom as an expert who can give her opinion about that."

"Your Honor," Rory said, "if every comp-lit major was suddenly an expert on substantial similarity in copyright cases, then my undergrad major in biology should make me an expert on life on Mars."

The judge gave Rory a look and said, "I'm going to overrule your objection—for now. We'll see when we get further along how I'm going to rule when the issue resurfaces. I need to hear more."

"I'm going to move on," Kathryn said. "I've got some more questions, whose answers will lay an even firmer foundation for the witness's expertise." She turned to Mary Broom and asked, "How many movies have you appeared in?"

"Somewhere between fifty and a hundred. I've lost track. My former agent probably knows the exact number."

The judge interrupted. "I apologize. I've been told by my clerk that our criminal case motion is ready to be heard, so we'll need to take a break. I think this will take about thirty minutes. Why don't you come back then?"

As the judge left the bench, Sarah leaned over and said, "Why do you care so much whether Mary's an expert on scripts?"

"I don't want Mary Broom later presented to a jury as an expert on anything. And the time to shut her up is now."

Chapter 34

Once they were out of the courtroom, Sarah said, "I still don't understand why you don't want Broom to testify about this, jury or no jury. No one will care what she says. She's just an actress."

"Actor, you sexist pig."

"Fine, actor. But the judge isn't gonna give her testimony a lot of weight. In the end, Judge Franklin will make her own decision about whether the scripts are substantially similar."

"I don't want Mary Broom giving her opinion about it. Period."

"Why not? I mean, speaking bluntly, you almost have steam coming out of wherever, and you're beginning to look like an asshole about it. I don't think that last comment about Mars went down well with the judge."

"You don't understand, Sarah."

"What don't I understand?"

"First"—he raised his index finger—"if she's permitted to testify as to substantial similarity, we will have to go out and find and prepare our own expert on the subject. But second"—he held up two fingers—"and most important, this could go to trial. Usually, when a plaintiff loses the preliminary injunction, they figure they're gonna lose the trial, too, and they quickly settle or go away. But Kathryn Thistle is probably gonna take this one to trial before a jury. That's what she does."

"So?"

"So if the precedent is set here that Mary Broom can testify as to substantial similarity between the scripts, the odds are the judge is gonna let her testify the same way in front of a jury during a trial. She's a famous and very skilled actress. She'll have the jury eating out of her hand like a kitten licking up cream from a bowl."

"And we'll lose?"

"Yes."

"Well, I have bad news and good news, then," she said. "The bad news is that a few courts have permitted people to give expert testimony in their own cases. Although it's rare."

"And the good news?"

"I've used some sophisticated software to compare the two scripts, and I think you can use what I've developed to destroy her opinion that there's substantial similarity between the scripts. I'll send you the file."

"Great!"

"There's more bad news, too."

"Hit me with it."

"I'm bored out of my mind. And that's because I'm of minimum use just sitting next to you as some sort of human ornament. You can handle the courtroom stuff yourself on this one."

"Most new associates would be thrilled to get to sit in on a trial their second week on the job."

"I'm not—"

"I know, you're not most new associates."

"Right."

He thought about it for a moment. She was right. It gave him comfort to have her beside him, but, at least in this case, it served no function. "Okay, go and work on more relevant things."

"Like what?"

"Research further if she can be her own expert witness and write me a memo about it. I'd like it today, please. Also, shoot me a memo about what the expert document examiner you spoke with had to say. And call a few more experts and see if you can find someone with a more helpful opinion."

"Okay, boss. I'm on my way."

"Just one more thing, Sarah."

"What?"

"When you get back, draft the letter of resignation we discussed and put it in my desk drawer."

She looked crestfallen. "You were serious about that?"

"Every word."

"Alright, I'll do it."

Sarah left, and as she got into the elevator, she considered what she was actually prepared to do about the assignment she'd just been given. Maybe she'd talk to a couple more experts. That might be helpful. But she'd had her fill at the Supreme Court of writing memos. Maybe, though, there was something she could undertake that would be majorly useful to winning the case without running afoul of the truthfulness strictures Rory had put on her.

After Sarah left, Rory went down to the coffee shop on the building's first floor and had a cup of coffee and a raisin muffin. Then he went back to the courtroom, where the criminal matter was just finishing up.

As the lawyers in the other case left the courtroom, the judge said, "We're ready to resume the matter of *Broom v. TheSun/TheMoon/TheStars*. But I see Ms. Gold is missing. Mr. Calburton, do you want to call her and tell her we're ready to start?"

"No, Your Honor. She'll not be rejoining us today. She's working on another aspect of the case."

"Very well. Ms. Thistle, I believe you said you had some more testimony to elicit from this witness on direct. So let's resume, but try to keep it brief."

"Yes, Your Honor, I will."

"Please resume, Ms. Thistle."

"Ms. Broom," Kathryn said, "we were discussing, before the break, the number of movies you performed in. Do you recall that?"

"Yes."

"Did you discuss those scripts with anyone before performing them as an actor?"

"Oh yes. Before a movie was shot, I took those scripts apart—tried to see how the pieces fit together. Sometimes I did that with the director of the film and, often, with other actors in the film. And, of course, I read dozens, maybe hundreds of scripts for movies people wanted me to be in, where I declined the role."

"How many scripts would you estimate you have read, total, in your career?"

"Many hundreds."

"Alright, so while attending a screening of *Extorted*, you compared the script you wrote—what has been called here the Christmas Eve script—with the shooting script of the released movie?"

"Yes."

"Did you find any similarities?"

"Yes, many."

"What were they?"

"The overall plot. In each script, a president is being blackmailed about a homosexual affair he had in his youth. And in each, the blackmail is being carried out by a head of state of another country whom the president knew in his youth. And in each there's a plot to assassinate the guy."

"Objection, Your Honor," Rory said. "Ask that the answer be struck. The fact that two stories have the same general plot doesn't, as a matter of law, create substantial similarity between them precisely because you can't copyright ideas. Which is why movies with similar plots are often released in the same year. And which is why I continue to object to this witness being permitted to testify as an expert. She doesn't know what she's talking about."

"Mr. Calburton," the judge said, "I think—"

Mary Broom broke in. "I am certainly more of an expert on this topic than whatever know-nothing academic Mr. Calburton is planning to pull in here."

This time Judge Franklin's nose did twitch, and she glared over at the witness. "Ms. Broom," she said, speaking slowly and distinctly, "I don't think you understand. Your role here is to answer questions when they're asked of you by the lawyers or by me. It is not to speak out of turn."

"Like a schoolgirl?" Broom asked.

Another twitch. "Something like that. And for the same reasons. It's a rule that keeps both order and civility here, which we value. Perhaps things are different in your industry, and that's why you have twice now burst out with comments. Please don't do it again. If you do, I'll hold you in contempt and send you down to our lockup until you're ready to behave."

I bet, Rory thought, *no one's talked to her like that in decades.*

Broom paused for a few seconds, clearly trying to decide whether to fight back. Finally, she said, "I understand. I won't do it again."

Rory noticed she had not actually apologized.

"Mr. Calburton," Judge Franklin said. "Turning back to the matter at hand, your objection is overruled. Although plot similarity is not enough in and of itself to show substantial similarity, it can be one factor in that determination."

Kathryn resumed her questioning. "Ms. Broom, after you finished reading it, did you find the shooting script to be substantially similar to the Christmas Eve script that you wrote?"

"Yes."

"Objection. For the same reasons stated before. I move that the witness's final answer be stricken from the record."

"Sustained. The court reporter will strike the 'yes' answer of the witness."

"I have no further questions at this time," Kathryn said.

"Mr. Calburton, you may cross-examine the witness."

Rory walked to the lectern and began with a question he knew would draw objection. "Ms. Broom, when you compared the two scripts, did you anywhere find the same memorable lines in each of them?"

"Objection," Kathryn said. "'Memorable lines' is vague and ambiguous. I don't know what that means, and I'm sure the witness doesn't, either."

"The phrase does seem vague, Mr. Calburton," the judge said.

"Your Honor, as I'm sure the court knows, whether there are multiple identical lines or phrases in two creative works is one test used to see if there's been copying. If there are no identical or nearly identical lines, it's likely that only ideas were copied, and ideas aren't protected by copyright. So if you would allow the question, before you rule on the objection, maybe Ms. Broom can answer. I think she'll understand what I'm asking."

"Alright. Ms. Broom, if you can answer the question, go ahead."

Rory was counting on the witness trying to answer the question despite its ambiguity. Over the years, he'd learned that smart people hated to admit that they didn't know something. So instead of taking the cue from their lawyer that they were clueless about what was meant by a question, they went for it.

"I think I understand," Broom said. "Do you mean, Mr. Calburton, did I see any memorable phrases the equivalent of 'To be or not to be'—you know I once played Hamlet on the London stage—or 'You can't *handle* the truth!' in both scripts?"

"Yes, exactly. Did you find any such similarities between the two scripts? A Peter-Piper-picked-a-peck-of-pickled-peppers kind of identical line in both?"

She thought about it for a moment. "Not that I recall."

"So nothing at all memorable, phrase-wise, in one script that was also in the other?"

Kathryn tried again to get in the way. "Objection, Your Honor. Each of these scripts is over one hundred pages long. The witness can't possibly be expected to have done a careful comparison of the two scripts."

"Your Honor, I'm not asking the witness to do a careful comparison. I'm just asking her the simple question whether she remembers any special phrases that are repeated in both. If she does, great. If she doesn't, great."

"Overruled."

"Thank you," Rory said. "I'll ask the court reporter to read the question back."

The court reporter read:

"So nothing at all memorable, phrase-wise, in one script that was also in the other?"

"No," Mary Broom said.

"When you wrote the script, Ms. Broom, do you recall writing any lines of which you were particularly proud?"

"At this distance from the writing, I can't recall any."

"Do you recall writing any lines that you thought were particularly funny?"

"Again, at this distance, I don't recall any."

"Come on, Ms. Broom, writers always remember the funny lines they write. Are you sure you don't recall any?"

"Objection," Kathryn said. "Not a question in proper form and harassing the witness."

"Overruled."

"I, uh, really don't remember writing funny lines." She directed her megawatt actress smile at him. "Mostly I did drama, you know."

"Well, do you remember any particularly dramatic lines you wrote?"

"Uh, no, not that, either."

"Did you read the whole script when you rediscovered it?"

"Yes."

"How long did it take you?"

"I don't know. At least an hour, maybe longer."

"So in that whole time, Ms. Broom, you can't remember a single funny or dramatic line?"

"No."

He paused and then went for it.

"Ms. Broom, did you really write the script for *Extorted*?"

Rory knew as he was asking it that he was opening himself up for a tirade. Which was what he wanted. If he could get beneath the famous actress's skin—which was turning out to be rather thin—he might be able to get her to say what had really happened.

"You're damned right I did. And Alex stole it from me."

"Alex who?"

"Alex Toltec."

"Oh, you know him?"

"Yes."

"Well enough to call him Alex?"

She hesitated. "Everyone in Hollywood calls him Alex."

"Did you know him professionally?"

Kathryn no doubt realized that Broom's testimony was veering badly off course and tried to slow it down. "Objection. This is irrelevant and well beyond the scope of what I asked on direct."

Several seconds went by without a ruling. Rory looked up at Judge Franklin. He could have sworn that she wiggled her crooked nose. Finally, she said, "There's no jury here. Overruled."

"What was the question again?" Broom asked.

"Did you knew Alex Toltec professionally?"

Broom glared at him again, but didn't immediately speak. Rory sensed she was making a decision.

"Oh, what the hell," she said. "Of course I knew him. Professionally and otherwise. We were having an affair. That's how he got into my house and got access to the script."

Judge Franklin, focusing not on what the witness had just revealed but on the language she used to reveal it, said, "Ms. Broom, the court would appreciate it if you would avoid using swear words here, even mild ones."

"Sorry, Your Honor," Broom said.

Rory welcomed the brief interruption.

Broom's testimony, honest though it seemed, didn't help him because it explained how Alex could've gotten his hands on Broom's original script. Still, he smiled to himself—it at least did confirm that Dana had good sources.

And maybe it was better to get it all out on the table now, and worry later about how it all fit together. If it did.

Rory resumed his questioning. "Ms. Broom, did you give the script to Alex Toltec to read?"

"No."

"Did you see him reading it?"

"No."

"So how do you know he read it?"

"I talked to him about it, and I just assume, given how similar the shooting script is to my script, that he somehow read it and copied it."

"But you don't know how or when he did it?"

"No."

"Well, let me ask you this. In your sworn declaration, which you filed in the prior hearing, before Judge Cabraal, you didn't mention knowing Alex Toltec, let alone having an affair with him or his getting access to your script by personal contact with you."

"Objection," Kathryn said.

"I haven't even asked my question yet," Rory said.

"Overruled."

"So my question is, Ms. Broom, why didn't you mention your relationship with him in your declaration?"

Kathryn jumped to her feet. "Objection! Counsel knows full well that lawyers write declarations, not clients. The answer, if there is one, is protected by attorney-client privilege and attorney work product."

Judge Franklin sighed. "Sustained. You surely know, Mr. Calburton, that your question was, as posed, improper. Please move on."

Rory looked over at Broom. He could tell that she really wanted to answer his question. If he had to guess, and if she was like a lot of clients, she probably wanted to blame her lawyer for the omission.

"Okay. Ms. Broom, let me focus on a different area. Is your script original?"

"Objection," Kathryn said. "Calls for a legal conclusion. Original is a term of art under the copyright act."

"Your Honor," Rory said, "it's black letter law that if your writing isn't original, you can't get a copyright in it."

"I understand that, Mr. Calburton," the judge said. "But whether something is original is a legal conclusion that the court gets to make. And, in any case, the level of originality needed is incredibly minimal. A mouse walking across a keyboard would probably do the trick. The objection is sustained."

"I'll rephrase the question," Rory said. "Ms. Broom, are the ideas in the Christmas Eve script entirely your own?"

"Well, yes, although like all writers, I'm dependent on those creative people who came before me."

"Any particular ones you'd care to name?"

"No, I just mean in general."

"Ms. Broom, have you ever heard of the novel *Advise and Consent*?"

"No."

"If I were to represent to you that *Advise and Consent* was a 1959 best seller and, later, a 1962 movie, would that refresh your recollection?"

"No. I wasn't born in 1959, so you could hardly refresh my recollection about it, Mr. Calburton."

"What about if I were to represent to you that the plot of the novel involved a United States senator running for president who was being blackmailed because he was gay?"

"Objection," Kathryn said. "The witness has already said she has no knowledge of the novel."

"You may answer," the judge said.

"No, that doesn't refresh my recollection, either."

"Mr. Calburton," the judge asked, "are you planning to introduce that novel into evidence?"

"Not right now, Your Honor. I'll do it later, through our own expert, when we demonstrate that the basic plot of *Extorted* is not exactly startlingly new."

"Okay," Judge Franklin said.

"I have no further questions, Your Honor."

"Ms. Thistle, any redirect?"

"No, Your Honor."

"In that case, we're going to adjourn for the day. Due to the continuing demands of the criminal matter, we're unfortunately not going to be able to proceed further this week. So we'll resume with this matter next Monday at eight a.m. Have a nice rest of the week, everyone."

She rose and walked off the bench.

Chapter 35

Sarah had returned to the firm's offices, intending to do the research she'd been assigned. When she got there, she found in progress a coffee hour that the firm had organized for new associates—there were five others besides herself, and the fifth and final one, David Costameer, had arrived that very morning. Sarah stayed awhile, chatted with the others, quickly found a solution to her problem and went back to her office to make a phone call.

Shortly after that, she arranged for an Uber car to pick her up and take her down to the Palos Verdes Peninsula, a verdant idyll of lovely homes, horse paddocks and bridle paths that jutted out into the ocean. The drive took about an hour, and the house proved to be a large, vaguely Spanish two-story concoction with a red tile roof, stucco walls and a stunning view over the Pacific. A stone walkway wound its way through a cactus garden to the front door. Sarah assumed it had once been a green lawn but had been replanted in honor of the drought.

She rang the bell, heard it chime the first bars of Beethoven's Fifth, and was admitted by a maid in uniform, who showed her to a red-tiled courtyard surrounded on three sides by glass doors. The fourth side was open and faced the ocean view. The maid offered Sarah something to drink, which she declined.

Meanwhile, the lady of the house sat motionless in a throne-like wicker chair with a very high back, saying nothing. She was wearing a black-and-white polka-dot sundress with a flared skirt. Her face and neck were free of wrinkles but had clearly had a lot of work done to achieve the effect. The skin looked drawn back and tight, as if too firm a poke might break it open. The woman finally indicated with a hand gesture, still without introducing herself, that Sarah should take a seat in one of the low-backed wicker chairs that faced the throne.

"Well, I understand from your call that you're an attorney at Hal's law firm."

"Yes, I am. And I assume you're Gladys Stanton?"

"Yes, the widow Stanton, as I might have been called in a bygone era."

"Uh, yes, I guess so." Sarah thought of offering condolences, but instead said, "But I see you're not wearing black."

"But I am, but I am. The spots are black!" She gave a high-pitched titter.

"Well, times do change," Sarah said. "I saw you weeping at the funeral. Were those genuine tears?"

"An impertinent question in some ways, but since I tend to ask them myself at times, I will forgive you. And, yes, the tears were genuine, but I have tired of crying and have decided to move on."

"I see."

"Before we begin—Miss Gold, is it?—I'd appreciate seeing some ID, if you don't mind. One can't be too careful these days."

"Of course." Sarah dug in her purse and handed Gladys a business card and her driver's license.

Gladys glanced at the card and then peered at the license. "This is from Virginia."

"Yes. I just moved from there to take this new job. I've not had yet had time to get a California license."

"I see. Well, what can I do for you, Miss Gold?"

"As I said on the phone, Hal's defense team is a bit shorthanded at the moment, so another lawyer in the firm and I are helping out for a few days, and I have some questions you might be able to answer."

"What other lawyers in the firm are helping?"

"Right now, Rory Calburton."

"Oh, yes, I've met him. A bit down-market, I'd say."

"I'm sorry. I don't know what you mean."

"He went to one of those law schools named after some dead president."

"Well, most of our presidents are dead, you know," Sarah said, trying to put a Duchenne smile on her face without much success. "And in any case, I think Rory is quite a good lawyer."

"Do you now? That's good to know. But let's cut to the chase. What do you want to know?"

"Yes, we might as well cut to the chase. Do you think Hal Harold killed your husband?"

"No, not even for a second. Hal and Joe had been close friends for decades. Joe was fifteen years younger than Hal. Joe started out as a lawyer at The Harold Firm, and Hal was his mentor. It was Hal who suggested he'd be happier in-house at a studio and got him the job there."

"Well, if Hal didn't kill your husband, do you know who did?"

"No."

"What about Mary Broom?"

Sarah watched Gladys's reaction to her question carefully, but she didn't flinch. "Why would she want to kill him?"

"As general counsel of the studio, he was getting in the way of her getting credit for *Extorted*."

Gladys shrugged. "That makes no sense to me. Anyway, a pretty piece like that one has better ways to get rid of enemies than kill them."

Sarah decided not to pursue that comment and to refocus on Stanton.

"Did Joe have any enemies, Gladys?"

"Not a one that I know of. He was a sweet man."

"I see. Well, here's a different question: Did he know a lot of secrets?"

"What kind of secrets?"

"The kind that someone who's been general counsel of a studio for twenty-five years would know from being involved in a lot of claims of various kinds and settling a lot of disputes."

"I never thought about it that way, but, yes, I suppose he might have known a lot of secrets."

"What kind?"

She shrugged. "Who's sleeping with whom. Who's gay. Who's kinky. Who's got kids they don't acknowledge. Who lives rich but is actually on the verge of bankruptcy. Who drinks too much. The list goes on."

"Did he ever tell any of those secrets to you?"

Gladys smiled an enigmatic smile and asked, "Do you by any chance have a cigarette?"

"No. I don't smoke."

"Neither do I, but I used to, and your question suggested to me that it would best be answered if I could exhale a long, thin cloud of smoke while I did so."

Sarah paused for a second to think. Was Gladys a nutcase? Or someone well in control of herself who had seen too many movies? It was hard to tell.

"So," Sarah asked, "did Joe know any secrets that someone might have killed him to prevent being revealed?"

She paused a long time, as if a long line of secrets were running before her eyes, and, finally, said, "None that I can think of."

"I see. Do you think he knew that Mary Broom and Alex Toltec had a child together?"

"Did they?" She held her hand up as if holding a cigarette between her fingers and blew an imaginary stream of smoke.

"Apparently they did," Sarah said.

"Who says so, Ms. Gold?"

"I do."

"Well, that's a secret I never heard. But why would anyone kill someone to prevent a disclosure of parenthood? If that were the standard for murder, there would be lifeless bodies all over Hollywood every weekend."

"Well, I just thought I'd ask," Sarah said.

"Do you suspect me of killing Joe, by any chance, Miss Gold?"

"No, should I?"

"Well, some would think I had motives, you know. There were the affairs, and there's the fifteen-million-dollar insurance policy of which I'm the sole beneficiary. But do you think I need that?" She waved her hand around at the house that surrounded them. "All this is owned free and clear, and I inherited it all, along with the rest of a large, debt-free estate. More than enough to keep me in style on the French Riviera for the rest of my life. All the insurance policy will do is pay some estate taxes that will be due."

"What about the affairs?"

She gave a short, explosive exhale of breath. "We had an arrangement for years. My only condition was that he not take any of his bimbos to any truly important Hollywood events. Only *I* went to the Oscars."

"What about the Emmys?"

"He could take whomever he wanted to those."

"Were you aware that he was seeing Sylvie Virtin?"

"Yes, of course. He'd more or less settled down with her, which was good."

"Why good?"

"Men his age regularly drop dead of heart attacks if they gallivant around with someone too young and energetic. Sylvie was in her late forties."

It didn't pass Sarah by that Gladys had just referred to Sylvie in the past tense, but she let it pass. She had bigger fish to fry.

"I see," was all she said in response.

"How old are you, dear?"

"Thirty."

Gladys looked her up and down. "I would never have let Joseph near you." She chuckled. "Nope. Not. At. All."

"I wouldn't have chased after him, Gladys. I'm an old-fashioned girl about that kind of thing."

"Are you sure you don't want something to drink, Sarah?"

"Maybe I will have a Cocola."

"A what?"

"Oh sorry. I grew up in the South. That's the way they say it down there. I will have a *Coca-Cola*."

Gladys picked up a small silver bell from the table next to her and rang it. The maid appeared very quickly. "A Coke for Miss Gold, please. Ice or no ice, dear?"

"Ice, please."

The maid left to fetch it, and Sarah said, "You said he had 'more or less' settled down with Sylvie. Was there someone else?"

Gladys glanced around, pantomiming looking for eavesdroppers, and said, in a low, conspiratorial voice, "Well, there was Sylvie's twin sister, Carla."

"You mean Clara?"

"Yes, Clara."

"He had an affair with her, too?"

"Apparently so. Isn't that wicked? I mean, there's something just a tad perverse about that, even for Hollywood. They were identical, you know."

"Were?"

"Are still, I assume. The past tense was just a way of speaking. They are both very much alive, as far as I know."

The maid arrived with the Coke and placed it on the table beside Sarah. She picked it up and sipped at it, trying to make her next question seem as casual as possible.

"Do you know where Sylvie is now?"

Gladys pursed her lips and seemed to think hard about it. "Come to think of it, I haven't seen her since the unfortunate thing that happened to poor Joe."

"When did you see her last?"

"The morning of the day of the murder. She came out here that morning to complain about Carla. I mean Clara. Isn't that a hoot? The mistress coming to ask the wife how to lure back the husband?"

"Did you tell her how to get him back?"

"No. I had no ideas. She joked about killing him, though."

"In any particular way?"

"'I should strangle him,' that's what she said."

"Do you think she meant it?"

Gladys shrugged. "I rather doubt it. Joe was her pipeline to money, great parties and a certain kind of status. If she killed him, she'd have to know that would all go away. At almost fifty in this town, it's unlikely she would've sucked in anyone comparable. No pun intended of course. And I *know* she's not in his will. So her goal was to get him back, not to kill him."

"Was she here before or after Joe's murder?"

"I don't know, because no one seems to know exactly when during the day he was murdered. Or if they know, they aren't saying. I asked the police, but they wouldn't tell me."

"So the police have interviewed you?"

"Oh yes, several times."

"Here's a cleanup question I always like to ask people I'm interviewing," Sarah said. "Is there anything I haven't asked you about that you think is important in all of this?"

"Yes. You haven't asked me if Sylvie brought anything with her when she was out here."

"Did she?"

"Uh-huh." Gladys's face lit up. "She had a manila folder filled with papers. And she asked me if she could use my scanner to copy them onto a flash drive she'd brought along."

"Did she?"

"Yes."

"What happened to the papers?"

"I promised to shred them right away after she left. In my home shredder."

"And Sylvie trusted you to do that?"

"She did."

"Did you?"

"What do you think?"

Chapter 36

Sarah managed to get back to the law firm before Rory came to look for her. When he walked into her office, she was sitting at her desk, printing out the legal research memo he'd requested.

"Hi, Sarah, have you got that memo I asked for yet?"

"Sure do." She pointed to the printer on her desk, which was just starting to whirr with the noise of the pages slipping into the tray. When all five of them had printed out, she picked up the stack, stapled it and handed it to him. "Here ya go."

Rory stood there and skimmed it. "I'm impressed. I was beginning to think your only skill was skulking around houses and lying about visiting your mother."

"I cannot tell a lie about this one, boss. I didn't write that memo."

"Why is your name on it, then?"

"Look more closely."

He looked at the top of the first page. "Oh, it's to me from David Costameer. Who is he?"

"A new associate who arrived today. I kind of got him to research and write the memo."

"Maybe it's best I sit down while I ask the obvious question." He dropped heavily into one of the guest chairs. "Costameer wrote the memo while you did what, Sarah?"

"I went to visit Gladys Stanton down in Palos Verdes."

"Dear God. And she was willing to see you?"

"Yes, we had a nice chat, and I learned some things."

"Isn't that the kind of thing I told you to check with me about before you did it?"

"I thought that was about doing 'out of the ordinary' stuff in courtrooms."

"I suppose that is what I said, but . . . oh, never mind, tell me about your visit to Gladys."

She told him. After she'd finished, Rory said, "I'm far from pleased you went—on the edge of furious actually—but if I'd known you were going, I would have told you something that might have put you a bit more on your guard."

"You would simply have told me not to go. But putting that aside, what would you have told me?"

"Kathryn Thistle and Gladys are friends. Or so Kathryn told me."

"No shit. What do you think the import of that is?"

"I suspect that everything you told Gladys has now been reported to Kathryn."

"I didn't really tell her much."

"When a lawyer asks questions, the very questions he asks tell people a lot."

"I guess you're right."

"Do you have the letter of resignation I asked you for?"

"Not yet. If you're serious, I can do it right now if you want."

"I am serious, and I do want."

Rory watched as Sarah drafted the letter on her notebook, printed it out on her desktop printer, signed it and handed it to him. He took it and read it. "Perfect, it's just what I wanted."

"Are you going to send it to the managing partner right now? Because I went to see Gladys? That didn't involve any untruthfulness to you. And I told you right away who wrote the memo."

He stared at her for a moment, trying to imagine if she could really be controlled enough to be mentored, as Hal had suggested, or if it was hopeless. Finally, he said, "Yes, I'm seriously thinking about giving the letter to the managing partner, although I've not made up my mind for sure." He folded it, put it into his inside suit pocket and headed for the door.

"Wait, Rory. Can I appeal to you, like you were a court, to reverse your decision?"

"Like I just told you, I haven't made a final decision."

"But I think you have in your head. So I want to appeal what's in your head."

He laughed and thought about it for a moment. "Sure, hit me with your argument."

"Okay," she said. "First, all the things I've done have actually been helpful. I found out by going into Sylvie's house that there was a file. I found out by going to Virginia that Sylvie *is* missing."

"Yeah, but nothing you learned is key to anything, either in our copyright suit or in Hal's murder case."

"But I filled in a lot of details of what's going on with both cases. It will prove valuable in the long run. I'm sure of it."

Rory began to pace up and down in front of Sarah's desk. "Maybe, but you took extreme risks to get that information."

"Will you stop walking back and forth like that? Judges hearing a case don't pace up and down."

He stopped and said, "I gather you don't have any rebuttal to my point about risk."

"I do, actually. Yes, the first thing I did had risk to it. But the others didn't. There was nothing risky about my going to see Clara. Sure, I spoofed her as to why I was there, but it wasn't illegal or unethical.

With Gladys, there was nothing at all untoward. I told her who I was and why I was there. She didn't have to talk to me."

"Except you lied to Gladys by telling her that you're helping out Hal's case."

"Well, I do want to help him out. I'd think all members of this firm would want to help."

"Well, Sarah, as judges say, I'll take it under submission."

"I haven't persuaded you?"

"Not fully."

"I can maybe come up with other arguments."

Rory started to leave, but when he reached the doorway, Sarah said, "Rory, there's something you didn't ask me about my visit to Gladys."

He turned around. "What?"

"Whether she gave me the file that Sylvie brought out to her."

"Did she?"

"Uh-huh." She lifted it off her desk and held it up.

"She gave you the original?"

"Yes. Said she had no use for it."

Rory raised his eyebrows. "Really? Let me see it."

"No, it's got enough sets of fingerprints on it already. And we need to have it copied. No point in getting yours on there, too."

"What's in it?"

"Well, that's the disappointing thing. All that's there is the same script that you got from your cop friend. Except in this one the handwriting is in blue ink, so it's more of an original."

"But to go back to your original point, Sarah, we still don't know what else might be on that flash drive. If anything."

"No, we don't. For all we know, the script was the only item. But the whole matter was complicated enough that maybe it's got Joe Stanton's notes and other things of interest."

Rory turned to leave for the second time.

"Rory, don't forget your copy of the research memo before you go. You left it on my desk."

"Thanks," he said, taking it from her. "By the way, how did you get the new guy, David Costameer, to write your research memo for you?"

"Oh, I offered to give him my coffee mug that the Chief Justice had personally autographed."

"Is there really such an object?"

"Not exactly. One day, as a joke, all the clerks got together and traced the justices' signatures onto several dozen Supreme Court coffee mugs—the kind they sell in the gift shop. Then we clerks drank coffee from them all day."

"Did the justices notice?"

"Oh yes. And we told them the gift shop was selling them for forty-five dollars each. Several of them flipped out and stormed down to demand the mugs be taken off sale. In the end, each clerk kept one, and we gave one to each justice."

"And you gave David your coffee mug from that prank?"

"No, I gave him a copy of my coffee mug, of course. But please don't tell him it's a copy."

"Who thought up the prank?"

"Who do you think?"

Chapter 37

WEDNESDAY MORNING

In not all that many days, Rory had become accustomed, on waking, to seeing Dana's beautiful bare leg draped over his own naked calf. The last few mornings, when he had let his gaze wander upward, he had found Dana blissfully asleep. Today, though, she was wide awake and gazing at him.

"Good morning, Rory."

"Morning. I'm not used to finding you awake."

"I've been lying here, thinking."

"Thinking about what?"

"Thinking about whether I should tell you a secret I've learned. About Mary Broom. Something that might help out your case."

"I would prefer you did not, Dana. We agreed that we're not gonna exchange any information about the case. I've been scrupulous, I believe, in not telling you anything, even if it's public, and you haven't said a word to me about anything you know. Let's leave it that way."

"You don't watch me on our evening show?"

"No."

She pouted and said, "Darn. I look especially good on that."

"I'm sure you do."

"Well, I have a special report on at noon today. You should watch."

∗ ∗ ∗

Rory had a large-screen TV in his office. A few minutes before noon, he tuned it to TQEN. He had invited Sarah to watch with him.

At noon, Dana appeared and said, "We have a special report today on the ongoing lawsuit brought by famous actress Mary Broom against TheSun/TheMoon/TheStars."

The image then cut to a blown-up portrait of Mary Broom.

"Reliable sources tell us that, fifteen years ago, Mary Broom became pregnant and, nine months later, gave birth to a child—a daughter. The father was none other than Alex Toltec." As she said it, the portrait of Broom was replaced by a portrait of Alex Toltec sitting in a director's chair with his name stenciled in white across the chair back.

"That child would be about fourteen today. Her whereabouts are unknown, but TQEN is on the case, and we'll let you know when we find out where she is. If *you* know, e-mail us, text us or call us at 555-800-3456!"

"Shit," Sarah said. "When Judge Franklin finds out that you're shacked up with that . . . with Dana, she's going to think you told Dana about Broom's pregnancy. You're in deep trouble, even if you didn't."

"Deep trouble doesn't even begin to describe it," he said. "And it's definitely not true, by the way. I told her nothing."

He pointed the remote at the TV and clicked it off. "Fuck!" He scooped up the basketball and slammed it repeatedly against the wall, where it left large black marks. After the fourth slam, he let the ball fall to the floor and said, "Sarah, I need your help in figuring out what my options are."

"Well, let's list them."

"It's hard to see any good ones."

"Option number one is to go to the judge and tell her the situation. Which at least gets you out in front of the problem."

"I go to her and say what? 'Excuse me, Your Honor, I've been having sex with a TQEN reporter, and she's somehow found out about Mary Broom's pregnancy. I want you to know that I wasn't her source.'"

"Exactly."

"You realize I can't do that *ex parte*—I have to do it with Kathryn present. Presumably in chambers."

"How do you think she'll react?"

"She'd like to get rid of me and our whole law firm on this case. I assume she'll demand the judge haul in Dana to ask her who her source is, hoping Dana will say it was me, and then Kathryn will be rid of me."

"Maybe Dana will be willing to swear it wasn't you."

He thought about that for a moment. Dana wasn't likely to do that unless she had real feelings for him. He knew from their morning conversations that she wanted to leave entertainment news behind and become a real journalist. And he knew that real journalists wouldn't say anything about who their confidential sources were—or weren't—a code of honor he didn't think Dana cared about him enough to break, or at least not yet.

"I guess I'd be surprised if Dana were willing to say anything at all, one way or the other, about who her source was. And if the judge threatens her with contempt, she'll just see it as a great opportunity to jump up and down and scream about freedom of the press. Slimy outlets like TQEN don't get to talk about that very often."

Sarah walked over, picked the ball up off the floor and arced a shot toward the hoop. Swish. "Okay. Option two then. You tell the judge you think Dana sneaked a look at your iPad and saw the notes you left there."

"Sarah, could I see that ball for a minute?"

"Sure." She tossed it to him, and he turned it over in his hands several times, seeming to weigh it. "What are you doing?"

"Trying to see if it's tricked up in some way, like with a secret weight you somehow activate before you shoot it."

"Wow. You really are flipping out."

"No, no. Just checking."

"Okay, Rory. So what's wrong with option two: blame it on Dana's snooping?"

"It's not true, is what's wrong with it. And I don't plan to fix this problem by lying about it."

"Okay, although, as a great philosopher once said, small lies are the oil of social relations."

"Who was the philosopher?"

"Can't recall right now."

"Uh-huh. Well, can you think of any other options?"

Sarah picked up the basketball and said, "This way is really hard." She bounced the ball off a side wall. It caromed onto the other wall, dropped, hit the rim of the basket, wobbled there for a second and tumbled to the floor without going through.

"Rats," Sarah said. "I guess I'm not perfect."

"No kidding. Anyway, I was waiting for you to present other options."

"I think you should just overcome your scruples about blaming Dana for snooping. Even if it's not true, it has an aura of truthiness about it."

Rory scrunched up his face. "What the hell does that mean?"

"I'm kind of shocked you don't know it. It's a term coined by Colbert. It means something that feels true even though, factually, it might not be."

"That's ridiculous. And even if it feels true that Dana sneaked a look at my notes, saying that to the judge seems destined to ruin my relationship with Dana."

"Easy come, easy go."

"I haven't known Dana very long, but I really like her. She could even be the one, you know?"

"Well, there's always the third option."

"Which is?"

"Do nothing, and wait to see what happens. Kathryn may not be aware that you know Dana, so maybe nothing will happen, and life will go on."

"Yeah, right. That leaves the whole thing hanging over my head, waiting for Kathryn or the judge or someone close to the judge to find out about me and Dana."

"Stop seeing her for a while, then."

"All of your options seem to lead to my breaking up with Dana."

"Rory, may I speak candidly?"

"You actually need permission?"

"You created this problem for yourself. It's nuts for you, a lawyer involved in high-profile entertainment matters, to be dating someone whose stock-in-trade is digging up dirt about your clients."

He sighed. "Maybe so."

"Have you seen what she's been doing to Hal Harold every night?"

"No. I've avoided watching."

"Well, you should watch."

"As long as I'm not a source of information, why should it matter?"

"You know that guy I got to write the memo?"

"David?"

"Yes, him. Before I offered him the coffee mug, I tried to get him to do it by touting that he'd be working for one of the firm's young, up-and-coming partners, the future of the firm. And he ought to get to know you, and this was a great way to do it."

"I should make you into my agent."

"Do you know what he said?"

"No."

"He said, 'I've only been here for a day, but even so I've already heard he's shacked up with a tabloid TV reporter, the other partners are pissed and his days here are numbered.' Then he told me that rumor has it the executive committee is going to meet about you."

"What do you think I should do?"

"Stop seeing Dana."

"That will just make everyone think I did tell her the secret, and that I'm kicking her out because she went ahead and used it."

"I can't think of any other options."

"Please hand me the ball."

With the ball in hand, he took a deep breath and shot. It swished through. "Finally! That's a good omen for my plan."

"What are you going to do?"

"Something entirely different. Please call Judge Franklin's clerk and ask to set up a meeting with the judge in chambers. As soon as possible. Then call Kathryn's office and invite her."

"Don't the local rules say you have to notify Kathryn first and tell the court that it's a joint request or something like that?"

"Probably. But just do it the way I said, okay?"

"Yes, sir."

"Also, find a way to send me a clip of Dana announcing the pregnancy. Text it to me if you can."

"Okay."

"And one more thing, Sarah."

"What?"

"When we're in front of the judge, do not say anything. Nothing. Not one word."

***

Sarah proved prescient. Shortly after she left, a text arrived on Rory's phone:

Could you meet with us for a few minutes
in Conference Room B?

It didn't say who "us" was, but it came from Hwa Fung, who was the firm's managing partner. Originally from Shanghai—where the firm had established what it referred to as a toehold office to seek representation of directors and producers in the burgeoning Chinese film industry who wanted to do business in the United States—he had climbed rapidly up the hierarchy of The Harold Firm after his arrival in LA five years earlier. That had been particularly true as Hal gave up more and more management tasks and focused on schmoozing clients.

When Fung had formally taken over as managing partner two years before, he had given a speech to the assembled lawyers in which he described his management style as tough and bottom-line oriented. He had concluded by saying, "Just so you know, despite appearances to the contrary, I'm not at all a Fung guy." This had elicited groans from the audience but had certainly proved true in every respect. Yet Rory had to admit that the firm, which had been drifting prior to Fung's arrival, had prospered mightily since he'd taken over. Rory often thought he owed his Tesla to Fung.

When Rory entered Conference Room B, one of the firm's smaller conference rooms, there were seven chairs around the table. Six were occupied by the members of the executive committee: Mindie Sun, Joyce Mendlin, Dale Franklin, Roger Rosen, Julie Rutiz and Hwa Fung. The seventh chair was empty, and Fung waved Rory into it.

As he took his seat, Rory looked around and noted the half-eaten sandwiches and the mostly drained coffee, all on china monogrammed with The Harold Firm's initials and insignia, a herald in a golden tunic holding a long horn to his lips. They had clearly been there for quite a while. He hoped the entire meeting had not been devoted to him.

Hwa Fung spoke first. "We are concerned about you, Rory."

"About what?"

"About the company you're keeping."

"You're referring to Dana Barbour?"

"Yes. And to be direct about it, it looks very bad for the firm for you to be shacked up with her."

Fung's English was, as usual, perfect, right down to his colloquial metaphors.

"I'm not 'shacked up' with her, Hwa. We see each other from time to time, and, although I don't think it's any of the firm's business, yes, we even go to bed together."

"Every night for the last five nights, from what we understand," Julie Rutiz said.

"Well, and so what?" Rory responded.

Hwa picked it up again. "The 'so what' is that every day, before she goes home to you, she gets on TV and tapes a segment savaging Hal Harold, the founder of this firm. And our clients watch it on TQEN's seven o'clock show."

"Have they been calling you?" Rory asked.

"No, but they have been texting and e-mailing. I had twenty e-mails just today about it."

"Why do they care?" Rory asked.

"Isn't it obvious? They're afraid you're going to tell her some of the secrets this firm holds about our clients."

"I'm not, obviously. Just like I haven't told her anything about Hal. He makes his own bad weather without any help from me."

Hwa got up and walked to the window. He stood looking out, hands behind his back. "There needs to be a solution, Rory."

"What do you have in mind?"

"Leave her, or leave the firm."

"I'm not planning to leave either. I'm a partner now, so if you want me to leave the firm, you'll have to take a vote on it. At a meeting. I'll be attending with my lawyer, who will tell you guys how I'm legally protected from your demand in this situation."

Rory knew this to be a bluff, of course. He'd read the partnership papers carefully before he signed them. He could in fact be kicked out by a vote of a two-thirds majority of shares in the firm for, if he recalled the language correctly, "any reason or no reason."

Which didn't mean he would go without a fight, and he'd plan to leave with a large payout in exchange for signing a confidentiality agreement about the whole thing. He could use it to start his own firm. Then he had the odd thought that he'd want to take Sarah with him. If she'd go. And despite the fact that she had displayed, so far, all of the characteristics of a bad associate whose resignation letter he had in his suit pocket. Maybe he was attracted to her and didn't know it.

His reverie was interrupted by the ringing of the phone on the conference table. Mindie answered it. "It's Hal. He wants me to put it on the speakerphone."

She clicked the button, and Hal's voice boomed out. "What the hell are you guys doing? I just got this message from you, Hwa, passed on via Quentin, about expelling Rory? To help me? What the fuck?"

"We're trying to rid the firm of a large embarrassment," Mindie said. "Rory refuses to give up this Dana person, so we've told him we're going to vote to kick him out."

"Well, think again, guys. Not only is Rory my lawyer, but, no disrespect to a couple of you, he's the best litigator in the firm."

"We will outvote you, Hal," Mindie said.

"There are more of you than me, but I still own forty percent of this firm. So you can't get a two-thirds vote to kick Rory out, even if everyone else votes your way."

"Thank you, Hal," Rory said. "You won't regret your support here, and I'll always remember it." He pushed his chair back, stood up, turned around and walked out of the room, not bothering to look back or close the door.

As he left, he heard Fung saying, "This will not stand."

Chapter 38

Judge Franklin's chambers were not, Rory thought, anything to write home about. There was a big wooden desk, chipped along the edges; a high-backed leather chair in which the judge was sitting and three low, scoop-backed guest chairs, each one done in faded green fabric. There was only one photo on the desk, turned toward the judge, and no art on the walls.

"Welcome to my bare-bones chambers," Judge Franklin said, perhaps noting Rory's scan of the room. "As you can see, the General Services Administration has yet to find me appropriate furniture, although they've promised it's coming soon."

"What happened to the furniture of the judge who was in these chambers before you?" Kathryn asked.

Judge Franklin shrugged. "No one seems to know. The mystery of federal procurement."

"Wow," Sarah said. "Not at all like the Supreme . . . Well, never mind."

Rory shot her a stern glance.

"To what do I owe this visit?" Judge Franklin said.

"It's about this, Your Honor," Rory said, and propped his iPad up on the desk, facing the judge. He touched "Play," and they all sat and listened to Dana's noon report. Only the judge could see it, but all of them could hear it.

"I see," Judge Franklin said. "Somehow, that reporter got hold of information from the diary that I ordered kept secret for now."

"Yes," Rory said. "And I think either plaintiff herself or plaintiff's counsel are the ones who leaked it, intending to run down here and blame me. So I decided to beat them to the punch and tell you that I didn't do it. And I'm willing to say that under oath. But I'm willing to bet they did, as a way of trying to get me kicked off this case."

"Before we go down that path, Counsel, what do *you* think about this, Ms. Thistle?"

Kathryn smiled a broad smile. "Oh, he's half right. We did tell several reporters about it, including Dana Barbour. My client decided yesterday that it's not important to keep the diary secret, and we gave Dana Barbour a twenty-four-hour exclusive, which couldn't be released until noon today."

"Does that mean I get to see the whole diary now?" Rory asked.

"Yes, or at least the pages that are relevant to this lawsuit, which are very few, actually. Here they are." She handed him two pieces of paper and gave the judge a second copy.

"Are they now a part of the publicly available court record?" Rory asked.

"No. We request they be kept in confidence until Ms. Broom is ready to release them."

"That doesn't make a lot of sense if she's giving interviews to reporters about them," Judge Franklin said. "I'm not going to order that."

"What about the other diary pages?" Rory asked. "They probably contain information that'll be helpful to the defense."

"We have a solution for that," Kathryn said. "We'd like to give the entire diary—there are only seven volumes—to the court and ask Judge Franklin to review them and see if there is anything relevant to this case. We think there is not. I brought the entirety of the volume most at issue with me, to get started." She handed it to the judge.

Judge Franklin leaned back in her chair and laughed out loud uproariously. "Counsel, if you think I'm going to be turned into your paralegal, you are sadly mistaken."

"I'm sorry, Your Honor," Kathryn said. "I didn't mean that you needed personally to do it. I assumed you'd have one of your law clerks do it."

"You assumed wrong. But here's what I'm going to do," Judge Franklin said. "First, I'm giving this volume back to you, Ms. Thistle." She handed it back. "I'll keep the two pages you gave me initially, and I will look at those only."

"I demand to see all seven volumes," Rory said. "And I'm entitled to see them, since Ms. Thistle has opened the door on this whole thing. I'll happily read through them and reach my own conclusions about relevance."

"Hmm. Let me ask Ms. Thistle a question," Judge Franklin said. "Do you anticipate using any other pages from the diary in this case?"

"No."

"In no way?"

"In no way, Your Honor."

"Okay, then, Mr. Calburton. Given Ms. Thistle's answer, we're going to do it differently. If you want those volumes, you should serve a document request for them on Ms. Thistle's office. And if she doesn't want to give them to you, or you can't negotiate some compromise, you can go through the normal process under the rules, which involves filing the usual motion papers and then going to see the magistrate judge assigned to this case. *He* handles discovery disputes. Not me."

"That could take weeks, Your Honor," Rory said. "And the hearing might be over by then."

"Yes, it could take a long time. And, yes, it could be over. But you know what they say: the wheels of justice sometimes grind slowly."

Rory had to admit to himself that he admired the judge's solution. It saved all of them from delving into a diary that likely didn't have much material relevant to the case, and it saved having to keep all of it secret in some fashion. It also kept Kathryn from trying to use selected pages from it as a surprise, since she'd just forsworn doing that.

"Now that we're done with that, do you ladies and gentlemen have anything else to bring up?"

"Yes, Your Honor," Sarah said. "I'd like to ask Ms. Thistle why, after making such a big deal about keeping those diary pages secret, the need for secrecy has now evaporated."

"I'm not sure that's relevant, Ms. Gold," the judge said.

"Oh, I'll answer it, Your Honor," Kathryn said. "The diary has great commercial value. A lot of people will be interested in my client's intimate thoughts. And if this small piece of information comes out as a teaser, well, it does."

"You have a deal in place, right?" Rory said.

"Well, let me just say that we're in the process of negotiating an exclusive deal with a network to interview Ms. Broom about the diary and her life before and after she wrote it and to release selected pages of it before, during and after those interviews. And there will be a book, and maybe a movie."

The judge gave Kathryn what Rory interpreted as the evil eye. "So, Counsel, does this lawsuit with which you're tying up the court's valuable time play some role in all of this? Is the suit just about enhancing interest in these commercial endeavors?"

"Not in the least, Your Honor. My client wrote *Extorted*, and she wants both the credit for it and the profit she's due under the law. Because she's entitled to it."

* * *

Later, in the hallway, Rory looked at Sarah and said, "I thought I told you to stay silent."

"You did. But you were about to pass up an opportunity to learn something important."

"Perhaps so, but that was the last straw. I'm gonna give your resignation letter to the managing partner."

"Do what you have to do, Rory. But don't think for a moment that I'll go quietly. You coerced me to sign that letter."

"I'm not surprised, I suppose."

"Can we go back to the cause of all these bad vibes between us— you know, all that stuff you said to me about a come-to-Jesus meeting?"

"Yeah. What about it?"

"You need to have one with your friend Dana."

"Why?"

"Because fifty dollars says that when she told you to watch her special report, she knew full well that you already knew about the pregnancy, that you were bound to keep it secret and that people would assume you told her the secret. So she was screwing with your head."

"I can't believe she'd do that."

"Go ask her."

Chapter 39

Rory knew where TQEN's studios were, even though he'd never been there. The trades had been full of the news that they had moved only two weeks earlier to new digs in Century City's tallest building. He could walk there from the firm's Beverly Hills offices, which, after parking in his own building, was what he did.

He managed to talk his way past the security desk on the ground floor of TQEN's building. But once he got to TQEN's floor, getting in to see Dana proved another matter. The first barrier was a very buff-looking male receptionist, who wore a skintight black T-shirt with TQEN stitched on the right-hand sleeve in the show's trademark green and sported an equally green headset perched atop his jet-black curls. He looked Rory up and down after he identified himself and said, "Do you have an appointment with Ms. Barbour?" Rory could sense his doubts, probably based on the fact that although physically large, Rory wasn't toned enough to look good in a tight T-shirt and clearly didn't hail from celebworld.

"I don't have an appointment. But she knows me well, and I'm sure she'll see me if you just ring her up and tell her I'm here."

"I'm dreadfully sorry, Mr. Carbuncle, but—"

"It's Calburton."

"My apologies. Mr. Calburton. But in any case, I can't 'ring her up,' as you have so quaintly put it, unless you have an appointment, and by your own admission you don't."

"But I know her."

"If you understood, sir, how many people come in here claiming to know one of our on-air personalities, well, I could probably write a funny little book with their made-up stories."

"If I showed you that I have her personal cell number, would that help?"

"If you have her cell number, why don't you call her?"

"I did. It rang into voice mail. That's why I thought if I showed you that I have the number . . ."

"It would do no good, since I don't have her number to match it against. Nor do I have her personal e-mail address. So I'm afraid you're plumb out of luck. If you have a tip for her, here's a number to call." He slid open a drawer, pulled out a card and handed it to Rory. "The person who answers can tell you what our policies are about tips."

"I think I'll just sit in one of those green leather chairs over there and wait for her."

"You're certainly welcome to sit there, but I should tell you that our on-air personalities exit through a different elevator bank. To protect them from people like you."

"So if I want to kill someone at TQEN, I have to settle for you?"

"That's not very funny, sir, and if you repeat it, I'll have to summon security, and they will no doubt call the police."

"I was joking."

"It's not the kind of joke we appreciate, and I'll thank you in advance for not saying it again. Perhaps I should escort you out."

Rory looked at the man's biceps, which were so large that the guy had had to cut small notches in his T-shirt sleeves, and decided to leave. Then he heard a faint chirp and saw the receptionist cock his head, as if listening to someone talking in his earbud.

"Oh, alright," he said. "I'll send him up." He looked over at Rory. "Dana will see you. Around the corner to your right, there's an elevator with a gold door. I'll unlock it, and it will take you to twenty-seven. It's the only floor you'll be able to go to."

When he got off the elevator, Dana was waiting for him.

"How did the goon in the lobby let you know I was here?"

"There are a set of buttons under his desk, with each button matched to the name of one of our on-air personalities. If someone without an appointment arrives, he pushes the button for the person the guest desires to see. And then we can watch and hear what's going on through a small camera that's up in the corner of the lobby ceiling. If we want to see the person, we let the receptionist know."

"Clever."

"And helpful. Keeps out all kinds of folks. But why are you here? I thought we were meeting tonight at our usual place for dinner."

"I just came from Judge Franklin's chambers, where I learned you've entered into a deal with Mary Broom for rights to her story."

"Well, TQEN did the deal, not me personally. But maybe we should go to my office to talk, huh?"

Dana's office had green everything that could easily be made green—wall covering, leather desk chair and guest chairs—with everything else made of chrome and glass. It was otherwise plain, with the usual fifty-inch TV screen hung on one wall and many smaller screens perched on another. On the desk were a MacBook Air and a cluster of TV remotes.

"Where were we, Rory?"

"I was about to accuse you of knowing, when you told me to watch your noon report, that I already knew about Mary Broom's pregnancy."

"I didn't know for sure that you knew, and I tried to tell you what *I* knew. But you specifically refused to let me tell you anything at all. Remember?"

"If you suspected that I already knew, you should have insisted."

"I can't deal with that kind of emotional logic, Rory. A relationship like ours either has to have utter candor or it doesn't. And it has to have utter trust, too. It won't work unless it has both."

"Maybe that's impossible with us, given what we each do for a living."

"Well, if utter candor and utter trust aren't possible with us, what do you desire out of this relationship?"

"I don't know. But I feel like you're fucking with me."

"I am, remember?" She laughed. "I thought you liked it."

He laughed, too, and said, "I think we need to think this through, but maybe we need to take a break while we do that."

She sighed. "Okay, let's do that. How long is the break?"

"At least until I get this copyright injunction hearing out of the way. You guys seem to be all over that now, so it's going to be a continuing problem for us."

"I can see that, I guess."

"Dana, why are you guys so interested in that case? It doesn't seem to me to have the hot elements TQEN feasts on. Mary Broom has been gone from the public eye for ten years. And she certainly doesn't go to clubs and snort coke, if she ever did."

"Well, big boy, how does she look to you now that she's back?"

"Hot."

"Yeah. That's one reason we're interested. But we also think she's somehow connected to the murder of Joe Stanton. And we want to break that case open and scoop everyone else. It would take us from coverage of celebrity screwups and meltdowns to the truly big leagues."

"I still don't quite see the connection between my case and that."

"Well, now that we're taking a break, I can tell you something, right?"

Rory hesitated for a second. Did he really want to know more? Yeah, he did. "Sure, tell me."

"Alex Toltec got released from the hospital yesterday. He refused to go to rehab, and we got someone in to talk to him at his house."

"And?"

"We're not sure, but we think he's admitted that he read and copied an early version of Mary Broom's script for *Extorted,* and we're ready to put it on our air."

On one level, Rory wasn't surprised. The revelations about Mary Broom's affair with Alex had certainly hinted at Alex getting access to a script, but Rory had convinced himself that it was Mary who'd stolen Alex's ideas, not the other way around. His stomach turned over.

"Do you realize what that means for me, Dana? If it comes out, we'll lose the copyright case."

"That's why I'm telling you. I'm trying to be helpful despite your dumping me."

"I'm not dumping you."

"Well, it sure feels like it," she said.

"How certain are you about Alex copping to stealing the script?" Rory asked.

She tilted her head back and forth in that time-honored gesture that said not so sure and yet pretty sure. "Let me put it this way. We'll need some collaboration before we'll go with it on air. Or to talk to him when he's not taking painkillers."

"So TQEN is interested in this because Alex is a big-deal director of a big-deal film about to come out?"

"You've got it. And also because I think Alex, too, has something to do with Joe Stanton's murder. If I can link the two things up, it will be a giant coup for me."

"Why do you think they're linked?"

"Intuition."

"Well, putting your intuition aside, what do you think I should do with the actual information?"

"Whatever you want. I'm giving it to you as a parting gift. But if I were you, I'd settle your case while you're on top."

"I thought you liked to be on top."

"I'll take it any way I can get it."

Rory groaned. "I think all these double entendres mean we're not really over."

"I'll walk you to the elevator, Rory."

When they got there, he reached out to push the "Down" button, but she grabbed his wrist before he could touch it and said, "Do you think the problem we're having has to do, really, with your attraction to Sarah Gold?"

"I'm not attracted to Sarah."

"Are you sure?"

"Yes."

"Attractions run in two directions, Rory. Maybe she's attracted to you."

"I don't think so. And anyway, I don't think I could be in a relationship with anyone so volatile and, well, uncontrolled."

"I wonder if I should tell you this."

"What?"

She looked up and down the hallway. "I investigated Sarah a bit, too."

"Why?"

"Candidly, out of pique and jealousy. But around here, I don't need an excuse. I can investigate anything I want."

"Well, what did you find?"

"I think that there's a good chance Sarah was one of those people recruited right out of college by the CIA and that she still works for them."

Stunned, he instead turned to face Dana. "That's quite a thought," he said. "That would mean that Sarah was an agent while she was clerking for both the ninth circuit and the Supreme Court. Which would be a violation of separation of powers. One branch of government spying on another. That's shocking."

"You don't think they'd ever do that?"

He shrugged. "I take your point. It's not beyond belief in today's world. Was she with the agency while she was working at a bar in DC after college?"

"If you mean Another Bird in the Hand, my sources tell me that there was a pop-up place with that name that the CIA set up from time to time, when it served its purposes. And it wasn't a bar. It was a gentlemen's club."

"Sarah danced in a gentlemen's club? Really?"

"I didn't say that, and I don't know that."

"I suppose I ought to worry about what, if anything, she's currently doing for the CIA," Rory said. "And what the CIA's interest is in our firm and its clients, especially given that the CIA isn't supposed to do any domestic spying."

"Maybe she's no longer working for them," Dana said.

"I hope not. Anyway, I better go," Rory said.

"Give me a hug before you do. I don't know when we'll next see each other."

They held their hug, and Rory said, over her shoulder, "I read somewhere recently that a study showed that a hug only has emotional impact if it lasts for more than twenty seconds."

"Do you want me to count?"

"No, but we're almost there, I think."

When they broke way, he pushed the elevator button and said, "One more thing, Dana."

"What?"

"Please tell that little prick in the lobby that the next time I show up here, he should let me come up."

Chapter 40

On his walk back to The Harold Firm, Rory texted Sarah to please meet him in his office. She texted back to please come to hers. He reluctantly said okay. Then he called the acting GC.

When Rory showed up in Sarah's office, she was unrolling what looked like a long green carpet.

"What's that?" Rory asked.

"It's my new artificial putting green. Twelve feet long, and when you get the ball in the cup, it beeps and totes up your score. You can set it for multiple players and tell it each time who's shooting, and then it will keep tabs on your lifetime average."

"How does it know you've even taken the shot?"

"You're on your honor to tell it."

"But the green will be utterly flat. Not much of a challenge."

"You can put shims under it and give it slope here and there," Sarah said.

"I've never been very good at golf."

"That's great. I can beat you often, then."

Rory wondered if he should say it, and then he did. "Sarah, you won't be beating me at golf often, because you won't be here, remember?"

"Yeah, okay," she said. "I'm beginning to understand you're serious about that."

Rory decided to change the subject. "Sarah. I just broke up with Dana, and in the process she told me something that bears on our case. So we need to talk about it."

"I'm sorry to hear about the breakup."

"No, you're not. Now here's what she told me. Sit and listen."

When he'd finished telling her what Dana had said about Alex, Sarah said, "We need to talk to Alex, obviously, and see if what Dana told you is true."

"I'm not so sure that we want to talk to him. I might rather just settle the case now, and quickly, without knowing any more than I already know. Ethically, I think the less I know, the better."

"Right now it's just rumor, more or less?"

"Right. And I don't think the rules require me, in a settlement context, to disclose all the things I suspect, but only those things I know are true. And I might not even have to disclose those unless I'm directly asked about them."

"Do you have authority to settle?"

"I called the acting GC on the way back here, and he has given me lots of authority. And since the last thing we heard from Kathryn is that she wants to settle, too, we can grant her wish."

"What are you going to offer?"

"I'm not sure, but I may have to cave and offer a package in which Mary gets to direct a movie, which is something she wanted that I totally rejected a few days ago. I'll have to persuade the studio, though."

"What about cash?"

"I'm going to start really low, but I've already got authorization up to five hundred thousand dollars. If Kathryn has this on a forty percent contingency, that amount will float her boat, too."

"I still think we should talk to Alex first. It's not that I don't trust Dana—"

"Well, you don't."

"Okay, I don't. And who knows if she made the whole thing up just to punk you for dumping her?"

"I think it's going to end up being temporary."

"Whatever. She could be bitter."

Rory got up, put his hands behind his back and began to pace up and down.

"I don't want to talk to Alex," he said.

"You're stepping on my putting green, Rory. The instructions say that you should only walk on it with golf shoes."

"What, you're planning on stocking an array of golf shoes for your prospective opponents?" He shook his head. "Never mind. I'll buy you a new one if I damage it. Right now I've got this problem. And I need to solve it."

"I have an idea. How about I go to talk to Alex? I'll pretend it's unauthorized by you."

"Well, that won't be hard for you to pretend, will it?"

She smiled. "I could wear a disguise."

Before he could respond, his cell phone rang, and he answered it.

"Hi, Hal. What can I do for you? I'm sitting here with Sarah, and we're trying to get an urgent problem resolved, so I don't have a lot of time."

He listened, then touched the speaker button and put his cell down on Sarah's desk.

"Okay, Hal, we're on speaker. How did it go this afternoon?"

"Boring autopsy stuff. Nothing to worry about."

"Hope you're right."

"I'm glad Sarah's there. I can use her brain, too. I've also got a problem."

"What's going on?"

"I'm trying to remember, Rory," Hal said, "when you were at the DA's office, how much experience did you have?"

"I tried a couple dozen cases to verdict. All felonies."

"Good, good. What about you, Sarah? Do you have any experience with criminal law?"

"Not a bit," Sarah said. "Although when I was on the Supreme Court, we decided a lot of criminal cases."

Rory looked at her. "You know, Sarah, you weren't *on* the Supreme Court. You were just a law clerk there."

"I'm sorry. You're right. It's just a snotty way of speaking. I meant to say when I clerked *at* the court."

"Boys and girls, my problem is serious," Hal said. "So let's skip the nonsense between you. Which, by the way, means you two are attracted to one another."

"No, we're not!" They said it simultaneously.

"Anyway, what exactly is your problem?" Rory asked.

"I'm losing my defense lawyer. Quentin Zavallo told me after court today that he has discovered he has an ethical conflict in representing me in this murder trial. He won't tell me what it is, but he's withdrawing, as of tonight."

"What about someone else in his firm?" Sarah asked.

"I can hardly hear you guys," Hal said. "Can you get closer to the speaker and repeat what you just said, Sarah?"

Both of them leaned over the desk to talk directly into the phone. Rory reminded himself to use his new partner expense allotment for a better cell phone.

Meanwhile, Sarah was repeating herself. "I said what about someone else in Zavallo's firm?"

"Oh. Well, apparently Quentin believes the conflict—whatever it is—conflicts out all six lawyers in his firm."

"I can see that that's really disappointing," Rory said. "But there are hundreds, probably thousands, of criminal defense lawyers in Los Angeles. So ask the court for a brief delay in your preliminary hearing—I'm sure the DA will be delighted to agree to one—and find someone else."

"That's exactly what I don't want to do, Rory. Once I ask for a delay, it will inevitably lead to more delays. That's the way it works in the courts. As you well know. And meanwhile, I'll still be rotting here in this jail cell."

Sarah chimed in. "But you still have a right to a prelim within ten days of being incarcerated, so there shouldn't be too much of a delay."

"You're right, Sarah," Rory said. "But you've not been around the courts long enough to understand how it works. Once you yield even a little bit on your right to a hearing or a trial by a certain date, every-one—lawyers, judges, key witnesses—gets out their calendars, and all of a sudden whatever was going to happen tomorrow ends up happening next Easter."

"I see," Sarah said. "But, Mr. Harold, apart from not wanting to stay in jail any longer than necessary—absolutely understandable—is there any other reason you want the hearing now instead of delaying until your new lawyers can get prepared?"

"I think the DA isn't truly ready—they're already doing a bad job, so far as I can see—so that's a big advantage for me right now. And you're right: getting out of this jail cell sooner rather than later is a prime motivator."

"What can we do to help?" Rory asked. "Do you want us to help you look for a great criminal defense lawyer who can take this over quickly and do the hearing as scheduled? I know some people from my days in the DA's office who are now on the defense side and might be good."

"You can help by being my legal team."

"No," Rory said. "No. *Nyet. Non.*" He looked over at Sarah, who was grinning and nodding and giving him the thumbs-up sign.

"Look, I know you guys are in the middle of an important civil case. But Quentin has recommended a young guy with good experience who's ready, willing and able to take on my case on the current schedule. But I don't know the guy from Adam, whereas Quentin I've known all my life. So I figure you, Rory, can be the lead, Sarah can assist if she's got the time, and this guy can be your backup."

"Who is the guy that Zavallo recommended?" Sarah asked.

"His name is Otto Quesana."

"What's his background?" Rory asked.

"Apparently he's a young solo practitioner. A hotshot criminal defense lawyer, very successful—he's gotten a couple of unexpected acquittals."

"How well does Zavallo know him?" Sarah asked.

"Pretty well. Zavallo's been after him for some time to join their firm. He's even interviewed at the firm, and they were about to make him an offer. But they haven't pulled the trigger yet, so the guy doesn't have Zavallo's firm's conflict."

"Do you know anything else about him?" Rory asked.

"Frankly, if Quentin recommends him, that's enough for me. But I do know that his father, Oscar Quesana, has been a high-profile criminal defense lawyer in town for decades. But he's living in France now, and isn't interested in coming back."

"You want us to check young Quesana out?"

"No, I've already hired him. What I want you to do is work out how you guys and anyone else you need to call on in the firm can work together, with you as the lead, Rory. It should take only two days out of your life, and if I understand correctly, your civil case isn't restarting until next week."

"Is that an order?" Rory asked.

"Yes."

Rory sighed deeply. "Okeydokey. How do we get in touch with him?"

"I heard the sigh, Rory."

"I guess the speakerphone's working better suddenly, then."

"Yes. And he's on his way over there now."

"You do recall, Hal, that the other matter Sarah and I are handling is for one of the firm's largest clients?"

"Sure I do. But as I said, I don't think this will really interfere with that."

"Okay. Anything else?"

"No. Just call me back after you've met with Otto."

After the call ended, Rory looked at Sarah and said, "Why are you so enthusiastic about doing this?"

"It will be fun, and I don't know anything about criminal trials, at least on a practical level, so I'll learn something."

"This is, frankly, ridiculous. If this Otto guy is such a hotshot, Hal should just hire him to be the lead and authorize him to go out and hire whoever he needs. There are a zillion competent temp lawyers out there looking for work."

"Hal would have to pay for those. Probably not here, huh?"

Rory thought about it for a second. "Huh. That hadn't occurred to me. But it's still a bad idea all around."

"You need to lighten up, Rory. I'm sure it will be a blast."

The phone rang, and Rory picked it up and listened for a moment. "Okay," he said. "Give us about ten minutes, then send him up to my office."

"Who was that?"

"The receptionist. Quesana junior is on his way up to meet us."

"Well, what are we waiting for? Let's head over to your office."

"Where's the putter?"

"It's still in the box."

"Please get it out."

She did and handed it to him, along with a ball. Rory lined up his shot, tapped at it and watched the ball roll toward the cup but stop a foot before it got there.

"Well, Rory," Sarah said, "short, never in."

"What?"

"It's a golf saying. If you don't hit the ball hard enough, it'll never get there."

"Putting that aside, it stopped short because you already put in some of those shims to tilt the surface, right?"

She shook her head. "No. Maybe the floor's tilted slightly. But the good news is that the system's not set up yet to keep score, so we won't count that shot."

"I'm going to take another shot." Rory lined his shot up carefully and swung, hard. The ball careened down the green, hit the office's back wall and bounced back, coming to rest almost where it had started.

"Shit."

"Too hard's never in, either," Sarah said. "I'm afraid we're going to have to count that one, Mr. Calburton."

Chapter 41

Rory didn't know what he had been expecting—some big, brash guy with a fedora and a cigar?—but the man who walked into his office was of medium height and slim, with close-cropped dark hair and a small goatee. He was wearing what Rory took to be a thousand-dollar suit, at least one size too large.

He introduced himself almost diffidently. "Hi, I'm Otto Quesana. I know this is all a little awkward. But candidly, this is a bigger matter than I usually handle, and I'm happy for you to be the lead." He stuck out his hand to shake.

"I'm Rory Calburton." Rory shook Otto's proffered hand and said, "And this is my colleague Sarah Gold."

After Sarah and Otto shook hands, Otto looked at the guest chair and said, "May I sit down?"

"Of course," Rory said. "Would you like coffee or something?"

"No, no. I'm fine, thanks."

"So what can we do for you?" Rory asked. "Hal called, but I'm a little unclear about what's needed."

"Oh, gosh, what's needed, where I'm concerned, if you're to be the lead and I'm to back you up in court, is research backup and office space. I've been operating out of my father's old office in Venice, but as I told Mr. Harold, the lease on that is expiring next week, and I had been planning to take some time off, so I hadn't made other arrangements. And I let my secretary go, and so forth."

"We can find you an office," Rory said. "And supply some secretarial help, too. After all, Hal is our founding partner."

"You call him Hal?"

"I do. Sarah here calls him Mr. Harold."

Sarah rolled her eyes. "I think I'm about to change all that, now that he's an accused criminal."

Looking somewhat nonplussed by their banter, Otto said, "Uh, I think for now I'll continue to call him Mr. Harold."

"Suit yourself," Sarah said. She picked up the basketball and lobbed it toward the hoop. And missed. "Damn!"

"Don't mind her," Rory said. "She's kind of obsessed with improving her poor record with that ball. And now that you've seen what an odd place we are, welcome to the firm, even if not officially."

"Thank you."

"As far as associate assistance goes," Rory said, "Sarah here is a crackerjack researcher. She's the only associate available."

"That's good to hear. Sarah, since we're going to be working together, can I have a crack at shooting a basket?"

"Sure, but since you're sort of joining our firm, and we have a tradition here of betting on basketball shots, twenty bucks says you can't sink two baskets in a row." She picked up the ball and tossed it to him.

Otto sank two quick ones in a row without even getting up from his chair.

Rory broke into peals of laughter. "It looks, Ms. Gold, as if you've met your match. And you owe him twenty bucks."

"It's not that funny, Rory," Sarah said. "And I'm sorry, Otto, I don't have a twenty with me. I'll get it to you by the end of the day."

Why, Rory wondered, had he laughed so hard? Was it only because Sarah had gotten her comeuppance? Or because deep down he liked her spontaneity? Which was a crazy thought, because he was the one who wanted her gone.

Otto was looking at the two of them and no doubt wondering what was going on.

"I'm sure you're good for the twenty, Sarah. But what I really need right now is an update on the facts of the criminal case. The start of the preliminary hearing is only a day away. I told Mr. Harold that was not a great idea, that we needed more time to prepare. But . . ."

"But you take your clients and their wishes as you find them," Rory said.

"Yes, exactly. He wants what he wants. So now please tell me what you know about the case, Rory."

When they had finished, well over an hour later, Rory said, "A lot to absorb. I'm obviously going to have to spend a lot of time with Zavallo, too, getting briefed."

"Are you going to try to pin the blame on the others who had a motive?" Sarah asked.

"That's good on TV," Otto said, "but really hard to do in real life. Particularly in a preliminary hearing."

"Why?"

"Because the government just needs to show probable cause—that it looks as if Mr. Harold, based on the evidence, *could have* committed the murder. They don't have to prove it beyond a reasonable doubt like they will at trial. And they don't have to convince a jury, just a judge."

"May I ask a blunt question?" Sarah said.

"Sure."

"You said that this is a bigger matter than you usually handle. So if you usually handle small-potato cases, do you feel like you're really ready for this big potato?"

Seeming to take no offense at her question, he said, "Well, in criminal law, a potato is a potato, large or small. The core of a criminal trial is always the same. The government has the burden of proof—beyond a reasonable doubt at the trial—and it can't prove its case out of the defendant's mouth. He, or she, gets to remain silent. And the substantive law isn't usually vastly complicated, at least in a murder case. I hope that answers your question."

"I guess it does," Sarah said.

"And anyway, Rory is going to be the lead, right?"

"Yes," Rory said. "I will. And you'll have to excuse Sarah's question. She's something of a snot."

Sarah glared at him.

Otto ignored Rory's comment and said, "Do I seem weak to you, Sarah? Is that what's worrying you?"

"Well, no, I mean . . ."

"Look, I know I can come off that way, but as my mother used to say, I'm like an avocado."

"Meaning?"

"Soft on the outside, but with a very hard core. You'll see."

"Anyway, Otto," Rory said, "we'll get someone from support services to show you to a temp office."

After that had been accomplished and they were again alone, Rory looked at Sarah and said, "We still have our civil trial to worry about. Even though we don't have to be back in court until Monday, we can't just let the preparation for that drop."

"I understand. Please toss me the basketball."

He did, and she retreated to the far corner of the room, took a shot and sank it. Rory got up from his desk, moved to the corner, took the ball from her and took the shot. It wobbled on the rim and finally fell in.

"You're getting better, Mr. Calburton."

"Uh-huh." He looked down at her. "It's odd that we're so competitive."

She sat back down in one of the guest chairs. "Yes, but I'm competitive with just about everyone, actually. Probably why I don't like Dana, even though I don't want you for myself."

"Thank God."

She aimed a rather wicked smile at him. "Are you sure you wouldn't want me if I wanted you?"

Rory was tempted to ignore her question, which he took to be a tease, and just move on. In fact he knew that it could be dangerous to pursue her question. But since he'd always had to work to attract the women he really wanted, he was immensely curious. "Is that the way it works for you, Sarah? You can have anyone you want if you decide to want them?"

"It's more complicated than that, actually. We should go out for that drink we talked about, and I'll explain it to you, maybe in more detail than you want."

"You don't drink, remember?"

She smiled. "You'll drink. That will make it even more interesting. Now, what about that settlement we were discussing? If you can do that quickly, that would be a way to clear the civil case off our docket. And we could concentrate on the frankly much more interesting criminal trial."

"I already made Kathryn a settlement offer, and she hasn't countered it. So even though I'm prepared to go way up in our offer, if I now go back to her and up the ante, I'll be bidding against myself. In the great American way of bargaining, that's almost always a mistake."

"Almost always isn't always. And you yourself said that it's important to settle this soon, before Alex Toltec tells Kathryn he stole the script."

"*If* Alex really told Dana that, and *if* he really did steal it. He suffered a head injury in the crash and may not be in his right mind."

"I think we should go back to Kathryn and up our original offer, just to get this thing moving."

"I've never done that—bid against myself—and I'm not about to start."

"I took a negotiation course in law school, and its message was very much not to stand on ceremony with this kind of thing. To do what needs to be done and not worry about who's first on first."

He stared at the ceiling for a long moment. "You know, Sarah, I have no idea what that means as practical guidance in the real world. We might as well say—using a metaphor more in my experience—we shouldn't worry about whether we're going to make a first down. I mean, what the hell, of course you have to worry about that."

"I have an idea."

Rory lowered himself to the floor, lay on his back and said, "Hit me with your idea."

"What are you doing?"

"Well, I was about to say that I should probably lie down before I heard your idea."

"My ideas aren't all crazy."

"Like I said, tell me what it is."

"Okay. Why don't *I* go talk to Kathryn about settlement, pretending that I'm not authorized, that I'm offside?"

"The sports metaphors are getting to be a bit much," Rory said.

"In my negotiations course, they called it an authorized unauthorized approach. Usually done by someone junior."

"Fine. Why not? But your authority has to be constrained. So here it is: no more than one hundred thousand dollars cash, two movies to be directed by Mary Broom, combined budget of twenty million for the two, and she's to work for scale if she acts in them."

"How much is that?"

"For a movie with that budget, it's probably around three thousand dollars a week."

"That's not much for someone like her. I thought you said she could make more than that."

"Well, she's been living in an ashram, so it should be plenty. More than that would have to be negotiated by someone at the studio, so let's not go there. Those terms can be added later if necessary."

"Okay."

"And you are specifically to tell her that there's no deal 'til there's a signed deal, and if her client agrees to the basic terms, the preliminary injunction hearing has to be taken off the calendar for two weeks while we work on papering the details."

"Okay."

"Remember in *The Godfather* what Michael said to Fredo when he blew him off?"

"Sure. He said, 'I don't want to know you or what you do.'"

Rory got up. "Right. And if you screw it up, that will be my attitude about this little venture of yours."

"Got it, boss. I'm on my way. Hey, what are you going to do now?"

"I'm going to go see Quentin Zavallo and get debriefed on what's happened so far in the trial that I don't know about, what his plans were for the rest of the prelim and what the facts are. I may also try to worm out of him what his conflict is."

"Anything else?"

"Yeah. I'm going to go down to the jail to see our new client, Mr. Harold, and get him to tell me his story."

"Like how and when he cut his finger?"

"That and some other things."

"Ask him about Sylvie."

"Why?"

"I still think there's some connection between our copyright case and Joe Stanton's murder. And Sylvie is somehow the link."

Chapter 42

Quentin Zavallo's office was on the fourth floor of a low-rise building in Santa Monica. Its broad windows looked out over the ocean, which gleamed in the setting sun.

Rory's meeting with him had gone well. Quentin had greeted him like a long-lost friend, even though they'd only chatted briefly at the premiere. He'd given Rory all of his case notes, including his and his investigators' interviews with Hal and with potential witnesses, and invited him out onto his office balcony to smoke a cigar. Rory didn't smoke, but it had seemed polite to accept.

The balcony was clad in travertine marble and overlooked a bustling street scene in Santa Monica.

"So listen, Rory, I feel terrible to have put you into this very sour pickle," Quentin said. "The conflict that arose was quite sudden and unexpected. And quite distressing."

"Quentin, I looked into the ethics of this a bit, and it appears that your telling me what the conflict is would not, except in the most extraordinary circumstances, be unethical. And, indeed, the ethics rules appear even to permit me to keep the information you tell me from the client—from Hal."

Quentin slowly shook his head. "I've gotten advice from the state bar ethics hotline and from independent ethics counsel, and I cannot ethically tell you in the circumstances that confront me. Regrettable as that is." He took a long drag on his cigar and blew out a stream of smoke. "So let's dispense with that thought and discuss the case that I'm turning over to you. It will be a much more profitable discussion."

"Alright. I attended one morning of the trial, as you know. But I missed the testimony of the doctor who performed the autopsy."

"He said nothing of importance. Only that Joe Stanton was likely already unconscious from the blow to the head when he was strangled with a rope. And so whoever used the rope would not have had to be very strong to pull it tight and choke off his airway. There were no bruises on his hand of the type you'd expect if he had been trying to pull the rope off his neck."

"Did he have an opinion as to what caused the blow to the head?"

"Probably a hammer."

Rory winced. "Did he estimate the time of death?"

"Yes. Based on the report of the coroner's office personnel who examined the body at the studio, sometime between noon and four p.m."

"He wasn't able to narrow it down?"

"No, apparently the coroner's guys didn't get there until well into the evening—it was a busy day in LA, homicide-wise, so they were backed up. By the time they got there, the body was already cold, and they failed to measure the room temperature, for some reason. All in all, it made it harder to get a better estimate."

"To go back to the rope, did he have an opinion as to the type of rope used as a ligature?"

"The best he could say was that it was braided and probably made of plastic of some sort, since it left no fibers behind in the neck wound. He said a rope made of cotton or hemp would likely have left a fiber trace there."

"Was he asked if the suddenly discovered rope fragment that was on the floor was the murder ligature?"

"He was unable to say for certain. It was one of those 'could be the case' answers."

"What do you make of that piece of rope?"

"Well, obviously, they are going to try to link it to Hal," Quentin said.

Rory drew on his cigar, held the smoke briefly in his mouth, savored it and blew it out in a long stream. Now that he was a partner, he could afford to take up some affectations like that. Except that The Harold Firm forbade smoking anywhere on its premises, and his office had no balcony.

"Yes," he said, "I assume they'll try to link the rope fragment to Hal. But how?"

"We don't know," Quentin said. "And whatever the link is, they'll no doubt claim that they just now discovered it, so that they were unable to tell us earlier. *So sorry.*"

"Does Hal have any idea how they'll try to connect him to the rope?"

"None. He says he hasn't bought rope in years and doesn't have any in his house, his office or his car. And by the way, the police searched all those places and found nothing."

"Who's next up on their witness list?"

"The woman who did the DNA analysis and concluded Hal's blood matched the blood on the carpet."

"What's our point of attack there?"

"She didn't really try to age the blood spot. Because it's hard to do, if not impossible on any scientific standard that would be admitted into evidence. I have some notes on how to take that issue on. They're in that notebook I gave you."

"Okay. Anyone else?"

"Just the guy who will introduce the videotape of Hal driving off the lot, looking disheveled."

"What does Hal say about that?"

"He says he was on the lot having sex."

Rory raised his eyebrows. "Wow. That's unexpected. Who with?"

Quentin blew out several smoke rings before answering.

"With Sylvie Virtin."

"Seriously?"

"Yes, seriously. He says he was having sex with Sylvie Virtin in an empty room on a different floor from Joe's office. Apparently they were having a *petite affaire*. Hal's words."

Rory thought about it for a moment. "Remind me how old Sylvie is?"

"Late forties, I think."

"Well, Hal goes to the gym three times a week, so I guess . . ."

"I think it's possible, Rory."

"What time does he say this happened?"

"He says sometime between noon and two p.m."

"How did she get on and off the lot?"

"Hal says he doesn't know. She was there when he got there and still there when he left. And there's no tape from the main gate of her coming or going. So maybe she's the blurry person who went through the back gate."

Rory blew out another stream of smoke. "Well, at least she isn't married."

"Unless you think she's been married, for all intents and purposes even if not legally, to Joe Stanton."

"Or more recently, Peter Stanton."

Quentin laughed. "Yes, Stanton times two. And maybe that was involved here somehow. Although you would have thought one of the Stantons would have killed Hal or her, not the other way around."

"Sex distorts things in odd ways, I've found," Rory said.

"Oh, for sure it does. You know, Rory, if I look at all the murder cases I've defended over the last forty years, and putting aside stranger murders, I'd guess that more than half the killings, the ones where people knew each other, were due to sex. One way or another."

"Do you mind if we go inside?" Rory asked. "It's getting cold out here."

"No problem. We can't smoke inside, though." But then he winked.

They walked into the office and sat down around a small glass conference table. In the middle of the table was a Lucite cube with a knife inside it. "What's that?" Rory asked.

"A knife a client used to cut off her husband's balls—well, actually, ball. She only got one before he overcame her."

"Verdict for the defense?"

"Yep. I got the knife from the police when it was all over."

"They just took it out of the evidence room and gave it to you?"

"Not exactly."

"Okay. Well, quite the conversation piece," Rory said. "But back to Sylvie: Hal having had sex with Sylvie doesn't sound helpful to his defense. Because while it might explain his appearance as he left the lot, it doesn't provide him an alibi, and even if it could be twisted into one, it would require either Hal or Sylvie to testify. But he shouldn't, and she's missing. And if he testified without her doing so, too, he might not be believed."

"Quite right."

"Who else was on the studio lot that day?" Rory asked.

"So far the police have refused to tell us. They say they've investigated them all and none of them were remotely related to this crime, so that evidence isn't exculpatory of Hal, and they don't have to hand it over. And they've added a bizarre privacy argument about the list of names."

"That won't hold up," Rory said.

"Not for the trial, no. But for right now, you're probably not going to get the list."

"What about the bloodstain on the rug? How does Hal say it got there?"

"He says that about a week before the murder, he was in Joe's office discussing a case—the civil case you're involved in, in fact—when he cut himself on his lower arm somehow. Old skin is fragile, is the way he put it."

"And Peter was there?"

"According to Hal, yes, and even handed him a tissue to dab the blood up. Hal says it was a very small cut, more like a minor scrape. Which must, he says, have dripped a drop of blood, although he doesn't remember it doing so."

"Is there any trace of the bruise left?"

"No."

"What happened to the tissue with Hal's blood on it?"

"Hal says he thinks he dropped it in a wastebasket in Joe's office."

Rory drew heavily on his cigar until the tip grew red. Then he coughed. "I'm not used to this," he said, and put the cigar down on a large glass ashtray.

He coughed a few more times and, once he finally managed to stop, said, "So maybe Peter decided he wanted to kill his brother—"

"—and kept the tissue with Hal's blood on it and used it to try to frame him, by smearing some on the rug?"

Rory nodded.

"Hal doesn't know of any enmity between the brothers."

"Beyond the fact that they were both dating Sylvie."

"Hal says it was more like they were sharing her," Quentin said. "Or maybe she was sharing them. In any case, it was all in the open."

"I wonder if that's true."

"I don't know. But good luck using any of that in a preliminary hearing. Save it for a jury. This judge will never buy it as negating probable cause in a prelim. As she said, plan B only works on TV."

"Bottom-line it for me, Quentin."

He pursed his lips and looked out at the ocean. "Well, put it this way. Hal was at the studio around the time of the murder. On a Sunday when, most likely, not many other people were there. His blood is on the victim's rug, and he left looking like he was in a hurry. That's enough to win a prelim, given the low standard of proof. And if they need more, they'll link up Hal and the rope fragment. Somehow."

"So it's a loser," Rory said.

"Yes, unless you can pull something out of a hat. And we've looked in dozens of hats and found nothing."

"Bummer."

"Is there anything else I can help you with today?"

Rory sighed. "I don't think so, Quentin. Thanks for your time."

"Well, do be in touch if you need to know anything at all about our preliminary investigation."

"One more thing, Quentin, come to think of it."

"What's that?"

"Do you know who did kill Joe Stanton?"

"Good luck on the case, Rory." He held out his hand. "As I said, feel free to call on us about anything in our investigation before our conflict arose." He took Rory by the elbow, very gently showed him out and shut the door.

So, Rory said to himself as he got into his car, *someone Quentin Zavallo knows came to him and told Quentin that that person killed Joe Stanton, and told him in some way that made the statement privileged. So now Quentin's stuck. He can't represent that person, and he can't tell Hal. And I am left holding the losing bag. And I've sent crazy Sarah off to settle my civil case.*

***

On his way home, Rory used his car's hands-free feature to call his cop buddy, Lester, who picked up immediately.

"Hey, my friend, how are you?"

"I've been better," Rory said.

"Why?"

"Quentin Zavallo has developed some kind of conflict and has to drop out of representing Hal in his prelim."

"So a big delay, then? You looking for a rec on someone I think is good to defend?"

"I'm doing it."

"Whoa. Long time since you did crim law. Did you volunteer?"

"What do you think?"

"I see. Well, my condolences. That is one loser case, at least at the prelim stage. Because I suspect the DA is going to tie that rope fragment they found around Mr. Harold's neck."

"How?"

"I am actually not in the loop on that, believe it or not. But I can say this. You should push them hard on the insufficiency of the other evidence so they have to tell you about the rope, because you'll want to know about it sooner rather than later."

"Why don't they have to tell me now?"

"Oh, I think they do, but, you know how it is, they'll say they're still working on it or something. You used to do it yourself when you were on the side of truth, justice and the American way." He chuckled.

"Zavallo just told me he can't get a list from the DA as to who all was at the studio the Sunday Joe Stanton was murdered."

"I think you're entitled. I don't know why they won't give it to you. Privacy issues, maybe. But I can tell you that we checked out everyone on that list, and there's not even a whiff of suspicion about anyone on it. Mostly maintenance folks and a few producers who skipped going to the beach that day."

"So no names of potential interest."

"Just one."

"Who?"

"Mary Broom."

Rory pulled over to the side of the road even though there was no need to. "Say again?"

"Mary Broom was there."

"When did she come in, and when did she leave?"

"She came in about one p.m. and left about four thirty."

"Didn't they stop her and make her sign in and ask her where she was going?"

"She's famous, my friend. If they stopped her, it was probably only to ask for her autograph."

"What was she doing there?"

"I didn't interview her, and I haven't seen a report yet from the guy who did. So I don't know. But I do know that she's not an active suspect."

"Okay. Thanks, and please let me know if you learn anything important that you think you can share."

"I will, my friend, I will."

Rory sat for a moment without saying anything. He was most upset—if that was even the right word—that Sarah had somehow sensed Mary Broom's presence in the murder story. Or was Sarah once again out doing her own thing?

"Rory, are you still there?"

"Sorry. Yes. Just trying to take that in. Mary Broom being there is a surprise, to say the least."

"Well, murder cases are often full of surprises, but in the end most of them turn out to be meaningless."

"I guess. But you won't let them sandbag me, right? If anything really weird is about to come down, you'll give me a heads-up?"

"Of course. Which reminds me, speaking of heads, they caught the kids who were throwing rocks off roofs downtown, putting your head at risk."

"Who were they?"

"Four rich kids whose parents bought fancy condos in the new downtown, as they call it."

"So they weren't aiming at us?"

"They weren't aiming at anyone in particular."

"What's going to happen to them?"

"They're in juvie now, and probably nothing much will happen to them 'cause their parents are rich and connected. More's the pity."

Rory said good-bye and pulled back into the flow of traffic, happy to put the rock-throwing incident behind them but still wondering how the hell Sarah had figured out that they ought to be looking at Mary Broom as a person of interest in Joe Stanton's murder.

Chapter 43

THURSDAY
LOS ANGELES COUNTY SUPERIOR COURT—CRIMINAL
DIVISION
People v. Harold

"Let me be sure I understand, then, Mr. Zavallo," Judge Gilmore said. "You are withdrawing from this in-progress criminal case due to a just-discovered ethical conflict that you cannot overcome. Is that correct?"

"Yes, Your Honor," Zavallo said.

"And you, Mr. Calburton, are substituting in today?"

"Yes, Your Honor. My law firm is substituting in, and Ms. Sarah Gold of our firm, who is sitting to my right, will be assisting me. Mr. Otto Quesana will also be substituting in for the defendant." He gestured toward Otto.

"And you are prepared to proceed today?"

"Yes."

"Mr. Harold, is this all okay with you?"

"Yes, Your Honor."

"Mr. Harold, have you considered that being represented by attorneys from your own law firm—one of whom, I understand, found the body in this case—could present its own, if not actual ethical conflicts, at least difficulties?"

"Yes, Your Honor. I have considered that and have no problem with it. In fact, I welcome the representation."

"I ask, Mr. Harold, because, given the unusual circumstances here, you are certainly entitled to a continuance of the hearing either to give you time to find new counsel or to give the new counsel you've already chosen more time to get up to speed. Are you certain you want to waive your right to such a continuance? The court will gladly grant one."

"Your Honor, I want to go forward today," Hal said.

"Very well. If you were not an experienced attorney, I would probably insist on imposing a continuance on this matter without regard to your wishes. But since you are who you are, I'm satisfied that you are able to understand the risks involved and give your informed consent, and we will go forward today unless there are other objections."

"Thank you, Your Honor," Hal said.

"Mr. Trucker, given that Mr. Calburton found the body in this case, do you plan to call him as a witness?"

"Not in this prelim. Maybe in the trial. I don't see that as a problem here, and I have no objection to his substituting in as counsel in the prelim."

"And you understand, Mr. Trucker, that if you change your mind about that, I'm going to preclude you from calling Mr. Calburton as a witness here, and I might permit him to be counsel in a trial as well, even if you were to object?"

"Yes, I understand."

"Well, it's certainly unusual, but if you have no objection, Mr. Trucker, and both Mr. Calburton and the defendant himself are okay with it, I guess I won't stand in the way. Defendants are entitled to the counsel they desire, even if . . . well, never mind."

Rory thought about getting up to say that he might need some extra time to learn the case, then thought better of it.

"Let me make sure of one other thing," Judge Gilmore said. "Do you, Mr. Calburton, have all the information you need to pick up seamlessly from where we and Mr. Zavallo were at the end of the day yesterday?"

"Yes."

"And you've met with Mr. Zavallo and Mr. Harold about the case?"

"Yes."

"Very well, we'll go forward. Welcome to the case, lady and gentlemen. Mr. Calburton, the last time I recall seeing you in my court was when you were a young assistant DA, quite a few years ago. Welcome back."

"Thank you, Your Honor."

"And, Mr. Quesana, I don't believe you've appeared before me before, but I know your father well. Please give him my regards."

"Thank you, Your Honor," Otto said. "I will do that."

"Alright, Mr. Trucker, please call your first witness of the day."

"The People call Gabriella Chen."

An attractive woman in her midthirties took the stand and was sworn in.

"Good morning, Ms. Chen," Trucker said. "What is your profession?"

"I'm a technical analyst for the Los Angeles Police Department, assigned to the Hertzberg-Davis Forensic Science Center."

Trucker took her quickly through her training—bachelor's degree from UCLA in biochemistry, master's in biological sciences from Cal State Northridge and a certificate in DNA analysis from the Los Angeles Police Academy, plus seven years' experience and eight hundred DNA analyses of blood and tissue taken from crime scenes. Then he moved into the heart of the matter.

"What does DNA analysis involve?"

"Usually, I take DNA from a so-called reference blood sample drawn from a suspect, analyze the alleles from that DNA sample and compare them to the DNA taken from blood or tissue found at a crime scene."

"Have you done such an analysis in connection with the murder of Joseph Stanton?"

"Yes. I was given a blood sample identified as coming from the Stanton crime scene, marked as 'Crime Scene Exhibit 5,' and I compared its DNA to a reference sample taken from a suspect, which was labeled 'Reference Vial 2506Q.'"

"Did you form any opinions with regard to Exhibit 5 and Vial 2506Q?"

"Yes, I formed the opinion that the exhibit and the vial contained blood with matching DNA."

"Did you form any other opinion?"

"Yes. I formed the opinion that the blood from Exhibit 5 at the crime scene and the blood from Vial 2506Q came from the same individual."

"Did you form an opinion as to the statistical likelihood that both came from the same individual?"

"Yes, assuming the test is done correctly, and excluding identical twins, the chance of a match in this case is ninety-nine point nine nine nine nine nine nine nine nine nine percent, or what we call eleven nines of reliability."

"What is the chance that the crime scene sample and the sample taken from Mr. Harold did not come from the same individual?"

"Again, excluding identical twins, one in one hundred billion."

"Did you later learn the source of the reference sample in Vial 2506Q?"

"Yes, it came, according to the crime lab's records, from Mr. Hal Harold."

"Did anyone besides you verify that Exhibit 5 came from the Stanton crime scene and that Vial 2506Q was a reference sample taken from Mr. Harold?"

"Yes, two other analysts verified the source records and a supervisor as well."

"Thank you, Ms. Chen. I have no further questions."

As the last question was asked, Rory thought about the strategy being employed by the prosecution. The obvious weak spot in the prosecution's case was the relative age of the two samples. If Hal's blood had been put down on the carpet days or weeks before the murder, the DNA match became irrelevant. But instead of asking about the age of the blood spot, Trucker had left Hal's defense team to raise the issue—if they wanted to.

It was a clever strategy, because failure to prove the date that Hal's blood had found its way onto Joe's office rug didn't really get in the way of the prosecution's argument that it tended to show Hal was the killer. Why? Because people didn't normally shed their blood in other people's offices.

"Ms. Gold will cross-examine this witness," Rory said. They had agreed that Sarah, with her undergraduate science minor, would be best situated to take on the DNA witness, despite the fact that the only witness she'd ever examined was in a trial practice course in law school. Hal had blessed the decision. They had also agreed she'd go after the age of the blood on the rug.

Sarah walked to the lectern and said, as she approached it, "Good morning, Ms. Chen."

Rory noted that both the judge and Trucker appeared surprised that Sarah was going to cross-examine.

"Good morning, Ms. Gold," Ms. Chen said.

"Are you sure that the blood collected from the crime scene was human blood?"

"Yes. There's a special test for human blood, and all the samples I tested from the crime scene tested as definitely human."

"Focusing your attention on the blood you analyzed from Reference Vial 2506Q, do you know how old it was when you analyzed it?"

"Yes. According to the record made when the blood was drawn from Mr. Harold, it was approximately twenty-four hours old when I analyzed it."

"And that's because someone made a record of the time it was drawn and you read that record, right?"

"Yes."

"You have no other way to know the age of the reference sample, do you?"

"No."

"And it was in liquid form, right?"

"Yes."

"With a preservative in it?"

"Yes."

"Focusing your attention on Crime Scene Exhibit 5—the piece of carpet with Mr. Harold's blood on it—how long before you analyzed it had that blood left Mr. Harold's body?"

"At least one day before I analyzed it."

"And you know that because you know when it was collected from the crime scene and when you received it, right?"

"Yes. I know the date it was collected from the crime scene because the exhibit was labeled with its date of collection. And I know the date our lab received it, which was the day after its date of collection."

"So that was the day after the murder?"

"Yes."

"Now you said it was *at least* one day old when you analyzed it. Why can't you be more precise than that?"

Rory thought to himself that Sarah had just violated one of the cardinal rules of cross-examination. She had asked an open-ended question that would permit the witness to say anything she wanted to say.

Chen shifted in her chair and said, "I'm unable to be more precise because I don't know the exact hour when the bloodstain got onto the carpet."

Whew! Rory thought. The witness apparently wasn't preprogrammed to push some agenda for the prosecutor.

"And that's because you weren't there when it happened, right?" Sarah asked.

"Correct."

"And so far as you know, no one else from the LAPD or your lab was there when it happened, right?"

"Correct."

Don't, Rory silently willed Sarah, *ask her whether anyone else she knows about was present, because if she's sharp, she'll say Mr. Harold was there.* He breathed a sigh of relief when Sarah skipped asking that and instead asked a different question.

"Did you make any attempt at all to analyze the age of the blood on Exhibit 5?"

"Not initially."

"You mean not until someone asked you to do it?"

"Correct."

"Who asked you to do it?"

"Mr. Trucker."

"Did he call you up?"

"Yes."

"Did he say why he was asking you to do it?"

"Yes."

"What did he say?"

"Objection, hearsay," Trucker said.

"That's ridiculous, Your Honor," Sarah said. "Counsel is object-ing to this witness repeating what he himself said to her. The hearsay objection is designed to prevent witnesses from repeating statements made out of court that can't be cross-examined, so perhaps Mr. Trucker would prefer us to call Mr. Trucker himself to the stand so we can cross-examine him directly about what he said to Ms. Chen. Or he can put himself on the stand to contradict Ms. Chen. Either one of which seems to me a waste of this court's time."

Rory liked Sarah's response, which focused on helping out the court. She had good instincts.

"Well, Mr. Trucker, what's your response to that?" Judge Gilmore asked.

"Your Honor, what I may have said to the witness is subject to the investigatory privilege and would harm the public if revealed, since our investigation is ongoing."

The judge quirked her lips to the side. "If that's your only response, your objection is overruled. You've already charged Mr. Harold with murder and put on a witness here to bolster your charge. So even though you may still be investigating the crime, you can't invoke the investigatory privilege to deny Mr. Harold's attorneys the right to ask the witness what you said to her."

Judge Gilmore looked at the witness. "Please answer the question, Ms. Chen."

Chapter 44

"Let me repeat the question. Ms. Chen," Sarah said. "What did Mr. Trucker say to you about trying to judge the age of the blood spot that you matched by DNA to Mr. Harold?"

"He told me to do it, and I told him it was not easy to do, and he told me to make the best estimate I could consistent with good science."

"And so you made an estimate?"

"Yes."

"What was the basis of your estimate?"

"Freshly spilled blood starts out as red and then changes gradually to deeper and deeper shades of brown."

"What color does it ultimately arrive at?"

"Dark brown, almost black."

"So you just looked at the color of the blood spot on the piece of carpet and estimated its age?"

"Yes, using what I learned during prior training where I practiced estimating the age of the blood spots under laboratory conditions."

"When did you look at the Harold blood spot and make your estimate of how old it was?"

"Yesterday."

"Which was several days after your initial analysis of Crime Scene Exhibit 5, right?"

"Yes."

"You haven't done any actual scientific testing to determine the Harold blood spot's age, have you?"

"Yes. I made a by-eye estimate—I looked at the color and saw that it was a certain shade of brown and worked backward from that, counting days back and noting how I expected the color to change over time. I consider that to be scientific."

"Where did you learn to do that?"

"In school, when I learned to analyze blood. We were shown bloodstains of various ages on various surfaces, and then we practiced estimating their age in a blind test. The instructor knew the age of the samples, but we students did not."

"Were your personal test results always accurate?"

"No, but they were pretty good."

"Your Honor, I ask that the end of the witness's answer be struck as not responsive," Sarah said.

"Overruled. You opened yourself up for that answer, Counsel, by using the vague word 'accurate' in your question."

Sarah had indeed screwed up the question, Rory thought. She should have asked something along the lines of "And you made mistakes, didn't you?" As he listened, though, he heard Sarah trying to recover.

". . . and so how many times did you take the blind test, Ms. Chen?"

"The test had ten samples, and I was tested ten times."

"How many times did you get it wrong?"

"Only thirty times out of the one hundred samples."

"Was that a passing score?"

"Yes."

"Did you have the highest score in the class?"

"I don't know. I never learned the scores of the other students."

"Of the times you got it right, how many times were you just guessing?"

Chen paused and said, "I wasn't guessing on any of those. I was using my trained by-eye approach in each and every one."

"So you weren't guessing then on the ones you got wrong, either, correct?"

Chen hesitated again, clearly seeing what was coming. "No, I wasn't guessing on those."

"So you just got it flat wrong thirty percent of the time, despite your best efforts using your scientific by-eye test?"

"I guess you could put it that way."

Sarah grinned a full Duchenne smile. "I would put it that way," she said.

"Well, I—"

"There's no question pending," Sarah said. "Let me ask you this, though. What color was the carpet sample from Mr. Stanton's office on which you identified Mr. Harold's blood?"

"Dark brown."

"That made it harder to use your by-eye test for the brownness of the blood, didn't it?"

"Somewhat."

"When you did your training for the by-eye test, were the samples you evaluated laid down on some surface?"

"Yes."

"What was the surface?"

"We trained initially on a variety of surfaces, but the tests were on paper towels."

"White?"

"Off-white, I'd call it."

"But a shade of white?"

"Yes."

"I have no further questions, Your Honor."

Rory thought to himself that Sarah had, smartly, not asked the witness what day she estimated the blood got onto the rug. Should Trucker ask, Sarah had simply set herself up to be able to destroy the answer.

"Redirect, Mr. Trucker?" Judge Gilmore asked.

"Yes." He stood and asked, "Ms. Chen, using your by-eye test, did you make a scientific estimate of the date that Mr. Harold's blood was laid down on the rug sample, Crime Scene Exhibit 5?"

"Yes."

"And what was that scientific estimate?"

"The day of the murder."

"I have no further questions, Your Honor."

Judge Gilmore looked at Sarah. "Ms. Gold?"

"Yes. A couple. Ms. Chen, are you aware that in higher temperatures, the color of blood changes from red to brown more quickly?"

"Yes."

"Do you know the temperature of the room in which the murder occurred on the day of the murder?"

"No."

"Do you know the humidity of that room on that day?"

"No."

"Might high humidity in a room cause the color of blood to change to brown less quickly than in a very dry room?"

"It might."

"Do you know of any studies calculating the rate of color change based on either ambient temperature or humidity?"

"There may be such studies, but I've not looked at them."

"Ms. Chen, did you do any other tests on the blood sample other than the by-eye test that you've described?"

"No."

"Are you familiar with any other available tests?"

"There are a few under development, to my understanding."

"But you didn't use any of them, did you?"

"No."

"And that's because they haven't yet been proved scientifically reliable, isn't that right?"

"Objection," Trucker said. "The question is vague and ambiguous because the witness hasn't identified any particular tests under development. We're just talking about 'a few under development,' which could be almost anything anywhere in the world."

Rory understood that Trucker was trying to protect himself against being effectively barred from using any scientific test at trial because his witness was about to dis them all, without being specific, in the prelim.

"Overruled," Judge Gilmore said. "You may answer."

"Correct. They haven't been proved scientifically reliable. Yet."

Rory, had he been the questioner, would have skipped exploring what the witness meant by "yet." Asking that would give her too much leeway to try to figure out how to help out the prosecutor. He was pleased Sarah didn't take the bait, either.

"By the way, Ms. Chen," Sarah asked, "when you misjudged the date of those samples, how far off were you? A day, two days, three days?"

"I don't recall."

"I have no further questions, Your Honor," Sarah said. "But I do want to move to strike the witness's answer to Mr. Trucker's question—the answer in which she estimated the age of the bloodstain on the carpet as 'the day of the murder.'"

"And your grounds for that motion?"

"By her own admission, Ms. Chen was wrong thirty percent of the time over a hundred samples. And by her own admission, her so-called by-eye test might be affected by the temperature and humidity of the room in which the blood was laid down. But she doesn't even know the temperature or humidity of Mr. Stanton's office on the day of the murder."

"But she was right seventy percent of the time," Trucker muttered under his breath but loud enough so everyone could hear.

As if in response, but without acknowledging Trucker's comment directly, Sarah said, "And, Your Honor, if Ms. Chen's estimate was off by as little as twenty-four hours, it would move the date Mr. Harold's blood got on the rug to the day before the murder."

She paused to let what she had just said sink in. "And the day before was a day when Joseph Stanton was very much alive. Thus, Ms. Chen's testimony as to the date that Mr. Harold's blood was deposited on the rug is junk science, and California law is clear that junk science is not admissible."

Trucker was on his feet. "Your Honor, the fact that a scientific test is not one hundred percent reliable does not make it junk science. The trier of fact—that would be you in this preliminary hearing—can weigh the results of the test together with its possible error rate in the context of all of the facts. And in light of the standard of proof to be applied, which is only probable cause here, it is certainly admissible."

Without waiting to be invited to speak, Sarah said, "Junk is junk, whatever the standard of proof. And when a man is charged with murder, we shouldn't use slipshod methods to try to send him to prison for life. *Slipshod* originally described loose, ugly shoes; I don't think justice should be made to wear ill-fitting facts, let alone walk in them."

Judge Gilmore placed her hands on her chin. "Interesting metaphor, Counsel. I'll take the motion under consideration and rule after I've had a chance to do a spot of legal research on evidentiary standards for science evidence. Let's take a fifteen-minute break."

Rory turned to Hal and said, "I think we need to talk. Let's get the deputies to arrange a room for us so you can attend the meeting."

"Truth is, Rory, I need to use the bathroom. And they've got a special one back there for us prisoners. So you guys go talk. I really don't have much to contribute at this point except anger at being accused of something I didn't do and at rotting in jail while this farce goes forward. You can bring me up to date after the break."

Chapter 45

The three of them walked into the attorneys' lounge and took over a small area in a corner. There was no one else in the room.

"That was a great cross, Sarah," Otto said.

"Ditto that," Rory added.

"Thanks, guys. It felt good for my first time out. I went down a wrong path a few times, though. I need to learn not to ask open-ended questions."

"It takes a while," Rory said.

"So what's next, do you think?" Otto asked.

"Their witness list has only two more people on it," Rory said. "The first is a Detective Henry Masimo. He's going to lay the foundation about the security video that shows Hal leaving the studio, supposedly looking disheveled and so forth."

"Why aren't they putting on the guy from the studio in charge of the security system?" Otto asked.

"Don't know," Rory said. "But in this prelim it doesn't matter. We're not contesting the authenticity of the tape. The real issue is how to interpret what's on the tape, and the judge will have to do that for herself."

"Have you seen the tape yet?" Sarah asked.

"Yes," Rory said. "And it's pretty much as the prosecution contends. Hal looks as if he is fleeing something and is in a great hurry."

"Don't we have a way to explain away why Mr. Harold looks the way he looks on that tape?" Sarah asked.

"We do have a way," Rory said. "But, unfortunately, we'd either have to put Sylvie Virtin or Hal himself on the stand to explain. There's no way we're putting Hal on, and we don't know where Sylvie is—even if we wanted to put her on."

"Can I get us to think outside the box?" Sarah asked.

"Sure," Rory said. "Float above the box, and think any way you want."

"Well, why can't we put Mr. Harold on the witness stand? What's the downside?"

Otto spoke up. "The issue is, first and foremost, what's the upside? They've already put in evidence the fact that his blood was found in the victim's office. Once they add to that a tape showing he was nearby at the time of the murder, and everyone looks at it and concludes he was leaving the scene in a hurry, that's probably all they need to win this prelim."

"We can counter it," Sarah said. "By putting Mr. Harold on the stand and having him explain that his blood got there before the murder and the reason he was at the studio and needed to leave in a hurry."

"Yes," Otto said. "But if all he's got is a counter-explanation, it's not likely to sway the judge, because he'll be seen as having good reason to lie, and he has no evidence to corroborate his story. Sylvie's not around to corroborate the reason he was there. And I just read the transcript of Peter Stanton's testimony, and he's obviously not going to support the how-the-blood-got-on-the-rug story."

"Exactly right," Rory said. "Or, to put it another way, there's really no way we can win this prelim on the state of the evidence that's already gone in or is about to go in."

"You both have a really negative, bummer attitude," Sarah said.

"No, we both have a realistic bummer attitude," Rory said. "There's no upside whatsoever to putting Hal on the witness stand now. It won't win this prelim, and it will just give the prosecution an advance look at what Hal's going to say if he decides to testify later. Which will let them prepare better to cross-examine him at trial."

"It would be so much better to win here and not have a trial at all," Sarah said.

"If wishes were fishes, we'd all cast nets in the sea," Rory said.

Sarah smiled the smile of superior knowledge. "That's not the saying," she said.

Rory sighed. "What is it, smarty-pants?"

"If wishes were thrushes, beggars would eat birds."

"It doesn't have quite the same poetry about it," Otto said.

"Boys and girls, we need to get back to court," Rory said. "Otto, why don't you take this Detective Masimo on cross, and then we'll see who they put on next, if anyone."

"You're not crossing any witnesses yourself?" Sarah asked.

"No, I'm saving myself."

"Like I did for my husband?"

"I didn't know you had a husband."

"For about ten seconds, when I was married to Stanislaus Gold. Back when I was eighteen."

"Wow," Rory said. "I'd like to hear more about that poor man. When we're done with today, of course. For now, let's head back to court."

As they were walking out of the attorneys' lounge, Sarah's cell phone beeped. She looked down at it and said, "Huh. It's a text from Gladys Stanton. It says she'd like to see me again. And she wants to meet in person. She's asked if I can I drive out there this evening."

"Go ahead and go," Rory said. "Maybe she has some information that would help us. God knows we need it. And she's apparently a friend of Hal's, so maybe she's got something useful."

Chapter 46

"The People call Detective Henry Masimo as their next witness," Trucker said.

Masimo, a tall man who looked to be in his forties, took the stand. He was wearing a blue pin-striped suit that looked, in quality, to be somewhere north of Men's Warehouse, but well south of Saville Row. Once he was sworn in and had presented his background—twenty years with the LAPD, the last twelve of them as a detective, and six of those on robbery-homicide—Trucker asked his first substantive question.

"Detective, did you investigate who was present at the studios of TheSun/TheMoon/TheStars on the day of Joseph Stanton's murder?"

"Yes."

"How did you carry out that investigation?"

"I started by interviewing the guards who were at the studio's main entrance that day for their recollections."

"Anything else?"

"Yes, I examined and made copies of the logbooks the guards kept as to who came onto the studio lot that day. Certain people were required to present IDs, and their information was logged in."

"Were some people not required to present their IDs?"

"Right. Some people had drive-on passes, and the procedure there was that they would just flash them, and the guards would open the gate. They weren't required to stop and show ID and weren't usually logged in."

"Did you do anything else?"

"Yes. I reviewed certain security tapes from that day."

"All of them?"

"No. I reviewed only those that seemed relevant to me after I had interviewed each person on the entry log who entered the day of the murder between seven a.m. and midnight."

"Did you interview anyone who entered before seven a.m. the day of the murder?"

"No, because there were no names on the log for that time period."

"Did you prepare a list of who came and went that day who were logged in?"

"Yes, but it's a list of only those who entered, because I learned when I interviewed the guards that the guard gate does not keep a list of those leaving. You would have to look at the tapes to see that."

"Let me show you what has been marked as People's Exhibit 13, Detective." Trucker handed one copy to Rory, who gave it to Otto, and also walked one up to the clerk to give to the judge.

"Did you prepare People's Exhibit 13, Detective?"

"Yes."

"Based on your examination of the logbooks you reviewed?"

"Yes."

"Your Honor, the People offer Exhibit 13 in evidence. Mr. Calburton has seen the list and, to my understanding, will stipulate to its admission into evidence."

"That's correct, Your Honor," Rory said. "However, just to be clear, all we're stipulating to is that this is a list that Detective Masimo prepared based on the logs he reviewed. We are not stipulating that it is a fully accurate accounting of who came and went that day or a fully accurate accounting of what's on the logs."

"Understood, Counsel," Judge Gilmore said. "It will be received in evidence with that understanding."

"Detective, how many names are on the list?"

"Fifteen."

"Did you interview those individuals?"

"Yes, I interviewed each of them."

"Did any of them, to your understanding, have any connection to the victim, Mr. Stanton?"

"Only two."

"Objection, hearsay," Otto said. "Detective Masimo's statement that he interviewed multiple people and concluded that all but two had no connection to Mr. Stanton is an attempt to repeat what each one said to him. And since he wasn't asked to whom he spoke, the question is also vague and uncertain."

With no jury present, Rory probably wouldn't have bothered with the objection. A judge in a prelim wasn't likely to care very much about hearsay. Although he could certainly see what Otto was trying to do, which was to cast suspicion on all the nameless people that Masimo was preparing to forget about, any one of whom could have been the killer even if they had no preexisting relationship with Joe Stanton.

"Your Honor," Trucker said, "pursuant to California Evidence Code Section 872(b), in a preliminary hearing, a law enforcement officer is entitled to relate hearsay evidence without objection."

Judge Gilmore seemed to think about it for a second before saying, "I'm fully aware of the code section, Mr. Trucker. But I don't think that exception to the hearsay rule applies when the officer is testifying about his own conclusions based on multiple conversations with unnamed people. So I'm going to sustain the objection unless you want to break the question down and ask about each person he interviewed."

Rory was surprised that Trucker had not chosen the easier path to getting the objection overruled. And then he did.

"Well," Trucker said, "I'm not offering Detective Masimo's statement for the truth of what the people he interviewed said, but only to show the detective's state of mind as to why he didn't further investigate most of those on the list."

"Alright, the testimony is admitted for that limited purpose," Judge Gilmore said.

Trucker resumed. "Detective, did you further investigate those on the list whom you believed, based on what they told you, had no connection to the victim?"

"No, I only investigated the two who appeared to have a connection to Mr. Stanton."

"Why did you not investigate the others?"

"Upon interviewing them, I learned that all thirteen of them were there working on a construction project that was urgent enough that they were working on a Sunday. It was also a long way from the building in which the victim was found."

"Who were the two names on the list who appeared to you to have a connection to Mr. Stanton?"

"Mr. Harold and Ms. Sylvie Virtin."

"Didn't Sylvie Virtin have a pass?"

"One of the guards, a Mr. Singh, told me that she had forgotten her pass that day, so she had to stop and be logged in."

"Were you able to interview Mr. Harold?"

"No. His attorney objected to our interviewing him."

"Were you able to interview Ms. Virtin?"

"No, I wasn't able to locate her."

"Were you able to find any physical evidence of either Mr. Harold or Ms. Virtin having been present on the studio lot that day?"

"I reviewed a tape of Mr. Harold, which showed him coming onto the lot in his car at 11:00 a.m. and leaving at 3:20 p.m."

"Were you able to find a tape segment of Ms. Virtin coming onto the lot or leaving it?"

"No. No one was able to find one. It ought to be there, but it appears to be missing."

"Did you receive any explanation from anyone as to why?"

"No, no one could explain it."

"Do you know if they searched thoroughly for it?"

"I assume they did, but they had no luck."

"Your Honor, we'd like to screen the two tape segments of Mr. Harold for the court. Defense counsel has reviewed them."

"Any objection, Mr. Quesana?" the judge asked.

"Although I'm handling this witness, I think that's an issue that ought to be responded to by our chief defense counsel, Your Honor."

"Alright." She looked at Rory. "Mr. Calburton?"

Rory knew the judge was asking because the proper foundation hadn't been laid for the tape segments to be admitted—no one had testified where they came from. But since no jury was present, Rory decided not to care.

"No objection to their being shown, Your Honor," Rory said. "But we're certainly not agreeing that they can be admitted into evidence until a proper foundation is laid."

"Very well then, go ahead, Detective," Judge Gilmore said. She looked at her bailiff. "Bailiff, will you dim the lights, please?"

"The first clip is the entry clip," Trucker said.

The lights dimmed, a screen in the corner of the courtroom rolled down and a grainy black-and-white image flickered onto the screen. The first clip, which was only five or ten seconds long and had no audio, showed a dark-colored Mercedes drive up and slow down as it approached the guard booth. The guard leaned out of the booth, and the driver, clearly Hal Harold, said something to the guard. The guard nodded, the gate went up and the car passed through. Then the screen went black. A time clock running in the upper right-hand corner said 11:01 a.m. as the gate went up.

"The next clip is the exit clip," Trucker said.

The black-and-white image flickered on again and showed the same dark-colored Mercedes heading toward the guard booth, this time at a high speed, and coming to an abrupt halt at the gate. The driver could be seen pushing rapidly on the horn button in the middle of the steering wheel and waving frantically at the guard to raise the gate. The time clock in the corner showed 15:20 as the gate went up. As soon as the gate arm was high enough, the car accelerated rapidly away, fishtailing slightly as it left.

Chapter 47

Rory looked over at Hal, who was sitting there watching the clip, showing no visible emotion.

"That's it, Your Honor," Trucker said. "No further questions."

"Your witness, Mr. Quesana," the judge said.

Rory leaned over to Otto and said, "Hal doesn't look flushed to me in that tape. Maybe there's a way to nail that down."

Otto stood and said, "Detective, referring to the last film clip that we just saw, did you watch that by yourself or with a guard or guards from the guard booth?"

"The first time I watched it, they screened it for me, and we watched it together."

"Did any of the guards make any comment about the tape as you watched it?"

Rory held his breath. Otto was soliciting hearsay from the guards, with no idea what they might have said, and with no hearsay objection expected from Trucker if they said things that were damaging.

"No, they didn't say anything at all to me, either before or after. We just watched, and I left."

"So the guards didn't comment at all on the demeanor of the driver?"

"No."

"Or on his appearance?"

"No."

"Nothing at all?"

"Nothing."

Rory let out his breath.

"Detective, have you discussed those security film clips with anyone else known to you to be connected with this case?"

"Other than members of the DA's office or others who work for the LAPD?"

"Other than those."

"No."

"Has anyone in the DA's office ever told you that they thought Mr. Harold looked flushed in those tapes?"

"Objection," Trucker said. "Calls for hearsay."

"Well, Your Honor, I think the defense can take advantage of the hearsay exception to Section 872(b), too. But at this point, I'm only asking the question in order to understand Detective Masimo's state of mind as he undertook his investigation."

"The objection is overruled."

"Let me repeat the question, Detective. Has anyone in the DA's office ever told you that they thought Mr. Harold looked flushed in those tapes?"

"No."

"Disheveled?"

"No."

"Has anyone in the LAPD told you that he looks flushed or disheveled?"

"No."

"Do you think he looks flushed or disheveled in the clip?"

Rory thought to himself that he would never have asked that question. But at this point it only mattered what the judge thought.

"No," Masimo said.

Rory pushed a note in front of Hal. "Who said u looked flushed/disheveled in tapes?"

Hal wrote something and pushed it back. "Cop who interviewed me night of murder. Can't recall name."

Otto was continuing his questioning. "Detective, how long after the discovery of the victim's body did you examine the security clips that we just watched?"

"The next day. In the afternoon."

"Who gave you the clips to watch?"

"Well, first I watched them with the gate guards. They just dialed them up somehow. The ones we just watched were given to me by the studio security supervisor, a Mr. George Germaine."

"In what form did he give you the clips?"

"On a flash drive."

"Is it your understanding that he gave you the original flash drive on which the material was recorded?"

"No. My understanding was that he downloaded that material onto the flash drive from their master system."

"Was Mr. Germaine present when you watched the clips, either with the guards or later?"

"No, not at all. The guards simply called up and asked him to download those particular minutes."

"So you have no one way of knowing whether Mr. Germaine gave you everything that might be relevant?"

Masimo sat up a little and set his mouth in a straight line, as if he thought his investigatory integrity were being questioned. "What else would have been relevant?"

"Perhaps there was recorded material on the original taping system from earlier or later in the same approximate time period that showed Mr. Harold or Ms. Virtin?"

"That could be, but I'm not aware of it, and I'd be surprised."

Rory smiled to himself. A witness saying "I'd be surprised" was a rookie testimonial mistake, and it was a mistake that Otto took advantage of.

"Why would that have surprised you, Detective?"

"Well, because both the guards and Mr. Germaine were fully cooperative and seemed to have no trouble finding what I wanted."

"What did you tell the guards you wanted?"

"The recording of Mr. Harold coming and going from the studio the day of the murder. And that's what I heard the guards ask Mr. Germaine to look for when they called him."

"Did you ask anyone if Mr. Harold might have come in and out more than once that day?"

"No. I assumed it was understood that it was only once."

"Did you assume it was only once, Detective, because you had already concluded that Mr. Harold was the killer?"

"No. But the log showed him coming in only once."

"The log didn't show people leaving, did it?"

"No, as I said earlier, it didn't."

"Are you aware that the studio has a back gate?"

"Yes."

"Did you ask if they had tape of people coming and going through that gate?"

"Yes, but they said that the time clock on that security camera is broken. It's stuck at 12:01 a.m. So you can't tell for sure what day or time someone came in or out."

"Why didn't you look at that back-gate tape anyway, even if it didn't show time or date, to see if Mr. Harold—or anyone else of interest—appeared on it?"

"It cycles every twenty-four hours, so by the time I investigated it, it had cycled past the day of the murder."

"Did you ask anyone why it hadn't been fixed?"

"Yes, and they said it was because the live feed from that camera can be seen in the front guard booth, and its main purpose is to keep an eye on who is coming or going through the back gate. Which were in any case people who knew the keypad code, so they didn't have too much concern about them."

"Well, did you ask the guards if anyone on any shift had seen Mr. Harold—or anyone else of interest—coming through that back gate on the day of the murder?"

"No."

Don't ask him why he didn't ask, Rory thought. *Just let the "no" lie there.* It was better to have it seem like a stark bit of incompetence than to have it explained.

"I have no further questions," Otto said.

And so, Rory thought, it had been a good cross by Otto, but it had not accomplished much of anything except to show that the cops did only an average job of investigating. But eventually they'd bring in someone to lay a proper foundation for the tape that showed Hal looking desperate to get out of the studio, it would come into evidence and, along with the bloodstain, it would likely be enough to get Hal bound over for trial before a jury. They were effectively nowhere.

"Before you call your next witness, Mr. Trucker, I have a ruling on the defense motion to exclude the testimony of Ms. Chen," Judge Gilmore said. "The testimony, that is, with regard to the age of the bloodstain. I'll write this up more formally later, but I'm going to strike the portion of the testimony of Ms. Chen in which she estimated the age of the bloodstain by eye. In my written ruling, I'll attach the transcript from the court reporter and indicate exactly which lines of testimony I'm striking."

"Thank you, Your Honor," Trucker said. "I assume that your ruling is without prejudice to our attempting to reintroduce testimony of the age of the bloodstain at trial, using enhanced evidence."

"Yes, it is without prejudice to that. But, Mr. Trucker, although I'm not likely to be the trial judge, I think you may have difficulty persuading any of my brethren or sistren that the by-eye test is well-accepted science."

"I understand, Your Honor. We'll be working on that," Trucker said.

"May we have a moment, Your Honor?" Rory asked.

"Yes, of course."

Rory leaned over and motioned for the others, including Hal, to put their heads together. "Congrats on winning that, Sarah," he said. "But let's not get our hopes up. The blood is still there, and unless we can explain its presence—and, Hal, you're not going to testify, and I don't think Peter is going to change his mind—we're still sunk when it's put together with the tape clip."

"You mean I'm sunk," Hal said. "There's nothing 'we' about it."

"There's got to be something else," Sarah said.

"Let's hope their next witness isn't the something else," Otto said. "I don't recognize his name. Patrolman Luis Suarez? Who's he?"

"I think he's just an LAPD uniform who's going to clean up some foundational stuff," Rory said. "Because I've never heard of him. He's just one name on the long list of witnesses they gave us whom they might call. They keep adding and subtracting names. I think his was recently added."

Chapter 48

Luis Suarez looked pretty much like the stereotypical image of a young cop—tall, maybe six feet, buff, buzz cut. His uniform looked good on him. After being sworn in and taken through his brief career—graduate of the LAPD police academy three years earlier, a variety of assignments since then—he was ready for Trucker to ask his first substantive question.

"Officer, were you assigned to execute a search warrant at Mr. Harold's house yesterday morning?"

"Yes."

"Were you asked to search for anything in particular?"

"Yes."

"What was that?"

Rory leaned over to Hal and whispered, "Did you know about this?"

"No," Hal said.

Suarez was answering. ". . . all of the suits and sport jackets which were in his house."

"Where did you find them?"

"In the closet in the master bedroom. I also looked in the other closets in the house but found no additional suits or sport jackets there or anywhere else in the house."

"How many suits were there?"

"Twelve."

"How many sport jackets?"

"Six."

"What did you do with the suits and sport jackets?"

"I put each one in a plastic garment bag I'd brought with me and loaded all of them into a police van. Then I took them back to the station and turned them over to Detective Karen Small."

"What time did you hand them over to Detective Small?"

"About ten this morning."

"I have no further questions, Your Honor."

Sarah leaned over to Rory. "Is this the witness you were saving yourself for?"

"No, he's yours."

Sarah rose and said, "Officer, on whom did you serve the search warrant?"

"No one was home, so I left a copy of the search warrant on the entry hall table, and I also mailed a copy to the owner at the address."

"Were you aware that the owner, Mr. Harold, wasn't around to receive the warrant because he was in jail?"

"No."

"Did anyone tell you why the suits and sport jackets needed to be collected as part of the search?"

"No, I was just told to execute the search warrant."

"By whom?"

"By Detective Lester Lovejoy."

At first Rory thought he'd misheard the name.

"Didn't Detective Lovejoy say something about what it was all about?"

"No."

Clearly, Rory had heard the name right. It meant that Lester was fucking him over.

"Did he or anyone else tell you why the search hadn't been carried out earlier?"

"No."

"Were you asked to search for anything else beyond the suits and sport jackets?"

"No."

Sarah thought a moment and, realizing that Suarez really didn't know much and had to just be the setup witness for a witness yet to come, said, "No further questions."

"Mr. Trucker, do you have any redirect of this witness?" the judge asked.

"No, Your Honor."

"Do you have any further witnesses?"

"Yes, we do. The People recall Gabriella Chen."

Rory bolted to his feet. "Objection! This witness has already testified."

"Well, Mr. Calburton, so long as the People haven't rested their case, there would normally be no objection to the recall of a witness unless it's somehow duplicative or time wasting. But I will inquire. Mr. Trucker, why are you recalling this witness?"

"To present evidence about something that had not yet occurred the first time Ms. Chen testified."

"Alright," Judge Gilmore said. "I'll permit it. Ms. Chen, I'll remind you that you're still under oath."

Rory could think of no immediate response. He sat back down and waited to see what was about to be unloaded on them. He had a feeling that whatever it was would not be good.

"Ms. Chen, did you carry out an investigation related to this case earlier today?"

"Yes."

"What was the investigation?"

"I received from Detective Small multiple suits and sport jackets that I was informed came from Mr. Harold's house and belonged to him."

"Did you carry out any investigation with regard to those items?"

"Yes."

"What was that investigation?"

"I first used luminol to test the sleeves of each suit jacket and sport jacket for blood."

"Did you find any indication of blood on any of the sleeves?"

"No."

"Did you check any other parts of the clothing?"

"Yes, I used luminol to check the fronts and waist areas of the suits and sport jackets."

"Did you find any indication of blood in any of those areas?"

"No."

Rory looked at Sarah, and she looked back at him. Why would the prosecution put on a witness to say there was no blood on Hal's clothes? Something was going on, and it was probably going to be catastrophic.

"Did you do anything else with regard to those items?"

"Yes, I searched the pockets."

Oh shit, Rory thought. What could possibly be in a pocket that would relate to this case? The rope? No. Even assuming Hal had actually killed the guy, he would never have been dumb enough to leave the rope in a pocket. And besides, the hank of rope would have stuck out of an outside pocket or bulked up an inside pocket.

"Did you find anything in the pockets that appeared to you to be related to this case?" Trucker asked.

"Yes."

"What was that?"

"A receipt from AtoZHardware, dated two weeks ago, for a twenty-foot-long hank of three-eighths-inch polyethylene rope. It was six dollars and eighty-two cents."

"Objection, hearsay," Rory said. "Ask that the answer be struck. Ms. Chen is not a peace officer, and so the exception to the hearsay rule does not apply here."

"I'm going to sustain the objection and order that everything after 'A receipt from AtoZHardware' be struck from the record."

As the judge was ruling, Hal leaned over to Rory. "This is a fucking plant. I never bought any rope anywhere."

Trucker didn't look particularly set back by Rory's objection being sustained.

"Thank you, Your Honor," Trucker said. "We can get the content of the receipt into the record the long way instead. Ms. Chen, did you bring the receipt with you?"

"Yes."

"Could you produce it, please?"

Chen reached into the pocket of the blue blazer she was wearing and pulled out a plastic bag. A small piece of white paper, longer than it was wide, could be clearly seen inside. She placed it on the witness stand ledge in front of her.

"Your Honor," Trucker said, "before I question the witness about this receipt, I have a copy for the court and one for counsel." He strutted over to the clerk, handed him a copy to pass up to the judge and then tossed one on Rory's table. Rory read his body language as, "There you go. Case over."

"Can we, Mr. Trucker, have additional copies for my co-counsel and the defendant?" Rory asked.

Trucker smirked. "Sorry, that's all I've got. You'll have to share."

As Trucker returned to his table, Rory handed the copy of the receipt to Hal, who glanced at it and passed it on to Otto and Sarah.

"Ms. Chen," Trucker said, "could you read aloud what the receipt says?"

"Sure." She picked up the bag and read through the plastic. "It's dated two weeks ago today, and it says at the top, 'Receipt.' And below that, 'Poly Rope. One Unit. Twenty feet. Six dollars and eighty-two cents.' And then there are some numbers, 97360124, which I assume are like inventory numbers, and, finally, the name of the hardware store and its address."

"What is the address?"

"58256 Mountain Highway, Riverside, California."

"Your Honor," Rory said, staring at the copy of the receipt, which Sarah had returned to him, "I request that you order that no more questions be asked about this so-called receipt until the defense has a chance to examine it more carefully. This is the first we've ever heard of it, which is an outrage."

"I beg the court's leave to ask just a few more foundational questions," Trucker said.

"Very well, Mr. Trucker. Go ahead. But just a *few* more, please."

"Ms. Chen, when you extracted that receipt from the pocket of the blazer, were you wearing plastic gloves?" Trucker asked.

"Yes."

"And what did you do next?"

"Placed the receipt in this plastic bag."

"And has that paper inside the plastic been with you ever since you pulled it out of the pocket?"

"Yes."

"What did you next do with that piece of paper?"

"I took it back to our lab and tested it for blood with a chemical that doesn't damage paper. It was negative for blood."

"I have no further questions," Trucker said. "And I move that the receipt be admitted into evidence as People's Exhibit Fourteen. It's already marked, as are the copies."

"I object," Rory said. "I request the court to defer ruling on that request until I've had a chance to cross-examine the witness and demonstrate that this evidence has been intentionally withheld from the defense and should, as a result, not be admitted into evidence."

"I will defer my ruling," the judge said. "Your witness, Mr. Calburton."

Sarah leaned over to him. "Are you going to give yourself up for this one?" Sarah asked.

"Yes. I am."

Chapter 49

Rory rose and looked down at the few notes he had taken.

"Ms. Chen, did Detective Small tell you how long she had had the suits and sport jackets in her possession before she handed them over to you?"

"Yes. She said about thirty minutes and that she had not let them out of her sight."

"Did someone suggest to you that you should look in the pockets of the suits and sport jackets?"

"Yes, Detective Lovejoy did."

Rory went rigid. Lester again? His ears burned. He wondered if anyone would notice.

The questioning was continuing.

"Did he tell you why he thought you should look there?"

"No."

"Did anyone else tell you why?"

"No."

"Since you discovered the receipt, has anyone told you why they had concluded someone should search the pockets?"

"No, although I'd think it would be standard operating procedure."

"Do you normally search clothing as part of your job?" Rory asked.

"No."

"Your job is to do lab analysis of items brought to you, right?"

"Yes."

"Do you normally apply luminol to surfaces?"

"No."

"Why not?"

She hesitated, clearly looking for a way out. Not finding it, she said, "Normally, the luminol application would be done in the field, and material would be turned over to our lab only if there was a preliminary indication that there was blood on it. Then, when it got to our lab, we'd use a chemical assay specific to human blood to test it further."

"Luminol isn't specific to human blood, is it?"

"No, any creature's blood with hemoglobin will trigger it," she said.

"Did the receipt test positive for any other chemical or material?"

"Yes, it tested positive for a substance commonly associated with hair spray."

"Did you draw any inferences from that discovery?"

"Only that at some point the receipt was likely handled by someone who had hair spray on their hands."

"Could have been a man?"

"Yes."

"Could have been a woman?"

"Yes."

"Did you research the substance in question to see whether it was more likely to be used in women's hair spray than in men's?"

"No."

"Ms. Chen, did you test the receipt for fingerprints?"

"Yes, but we didn't find any."

"Do you distinguish between patent and latent prints?"

"Yes."

"Could you please provide definitions of those terms?"

"Patent are those you can easily see. For example, those that might come from blood on a finger. Latent are those that you can't see, where you have to use special powders or chemicals to detect them."

"Did you find any latent prints on the receipt?"

"No."

"What about partial prints, either patent or latent?"

"No partials of either type," she said.

"Not on either side?"

"No, not on either side."

"Did you find that unusual, Ms. Chen?"

"A bit, because normally receipts are handled with the hands, so unless someone was wearing gloves when they handled it, you'd expect a receipt to show at least partial latent prints."

"Can someone wipe prints completely off a surface?"

"Not exactly wipe them off. Fingerprints consist primarily of the natural oils and sweat that come from the sweat glands on your hands. Those oils cling to the friction ridges on your fingers and the lines on your palms and are then deposited on a surface, yielding patterns that we call fingerprints or palm prints."

"And that oil can be wiped off?"

"Not so much completely wiped off as smeared and moved around. So that while skin oils may still be there on the surface, ridge patterns from fingers or lines from palms are no longer able to be visualized, even using special chemicals."

"And there are, therefore, no fingerprints or palm prints?"

"Correct. We might say there are no latent prints, full or partial, that can be made visible. I should add, though, that every year, better techniques become available to help visualize prints. Prints that couldn't be seen fifty years ago are easily seen today."

"Do you know of any existing techniques that might make the prints on the receipt visible?"

"No."

"Okay. Now to go back to a situation where someone has wiped the surface, the skin oils are still there?"

"Probably. It depends on how much oil was deposited in the first place—how dry the person's hands were—and how absorbent the material used to wipe off the surface was."

"Would you agree, then, that someone probably tried to wipe this receipt clean of prints?" Rory asked.

"Objection," Trucker said. "Calls for speculation."

"Overruled."

Rory smiled to himself as he waited for the answer. He had, in effect, trapped the witness by inviting her to dive into her own expertise. And since she was no doubt fundamentally an honest person, she had forgotten whose side she was on, and let herself be maneuvered into a blind alley from which she was going to have difficulty escaping. But she tried.

"Well, that's one possibility. But it's also possible that whoever handled the receipt had really dry hands or handled it only by the corners."

Rory tore a piece of paper from his notebook and held it up, daintily, by one corner, his first finger and thumb barely touching it. "Like this, after the cashier handed the receipt to the customer?"

"I, uh, guess."

"Can you think of any other way the oils from the purchaser's hands might have failed to get on the receipt?"

"Perhaps it was dumped into the customer's bag without the customer's hands touching it."

"Wouldn't the receipt then have the prints of the clerk on it?"

"Possibly."

Rory again held up his notebook page with extreme daintiness, just barely hanging onto it by the corner. "Unless, of course, the clerk handled the receipt like this," he said.

"Objection," Trucker said. "That's not a question."

To that point, with the exception of his one objection, Trucker had been sitting in stony silence as the questioning of his witness went down a path he had probably not anticipated. Or at least that's how Rory interpreted it, since the witness had clearly not been prepared to answer the question of why there were no prints at all on the receipt.

Rory listened to the objection, sighed audibly and said, "I'll withdraw the question and ask it this way. So, Ms. Chen, if the clerk handled the receipt like this"—he held it up again by the corner—"there might be no prints from the clerk on the receipt, right?"

Trucker tried again. "Objection. Assumes facts not in evidence, namely, that there was a clerk who handled the receipt. Also, it's an incomplete hypothetical."

Desperate times yield desperate attempts at witness repair, Rory thought to himself.

"Overruled," the judge said.

"That's correct," Chen said.

"Ms. Chen, if someone tried to wipe the fingerprints off the receipt and didn't spend a lot of time at it and used something not so absorbent to wipe it clean, would there still be oil on the receipt even if it wasn't recognizable as a fingerprint?"

"Objection," Trucker said. "Incomplete hypothetical, vague and ambiguous and assumes facts not in evidence."

"Sustained," Judge Gilmore said.

"Let me try it this way," Rory said. "If someone tried to wipe fingerprints off a surface, but failed to wipe the skin oils completely off, would that skin oil still be detectable by a chemical test even if it didn't present a fingerprint?"

"Same objections," Trucker said.

"Overruled."

"I don't know," Chen said.

"Do you detect hair spray on a lot of samples you test?"

"It's not unusual. There's a lot of it in the environment, if you consider how many men and women use it, and it tends to persist on skin unless hands are washed thoroughly."

"If someone tried to wipe the hair spray chemical off, would it still be detectable by a scientific test?"

A puzzled look appeared on Chen's face, and as that look passed away, Rory thought he could almost see her decision take hold—a decision to be perfectly honest in her answer.

"Possibly," she said. "Because we would not be looking to discover a pattern, but just the residue of the chemical. And I assume it would be very hard to get rid of that entirely since these days we can detect quite small amounts of most chemicals using both assays and spectroscopic analysis."

"So whoever tried to wipe the prints off of this receipt might not have realized that they wouldn't be able to wipe off other chemicals on the receipt?"

Trucker stood up, clearly distressed. "Objection! Calls for speculation."

"Sustained," Judge Gilmore said, and gave Rory a look that he interpreted as saying, *You're being a bad boy, asking the witness to speculate about an unknown person's state of mind, but I get the point.*

"Did you test the receipt for the presence of DNA?" Rory asked.

"No."

"Why not?"

"That would take more time than I had before coming here to testify."

"Are you going to test it for DNA later?"

"I will have to discuss that with Mr. Trucker."

"I have no further questions for this witness," Rory said.

"Redirect, Mr. Trucker?"

Trucker stood and said, "Ms. Chen, in your experience, have you come upon people whose skin is so dry that when they touch things, they leave no latent prints?"

"Yes."

Rory could almost feel Trucker deciding whether to ask Chen if such people were common but then, not knowing the answer, shy away from asking it.

"Ms. Chen, is it possible that the chemical from hair spray came from you?"

"No. I don't use hair spray."

"From someone else in your lab?"

"I don't know."

"If you test the receipt for DNA, do you think you're likely to find any detectable DNA?"

"No."

"Why not?"

"It's easier to detect DNA on a nonporous surface like glass or plastic than on a porous surface like paper. And it's particularly difficult to detect DNA on paper that's been only briefly handled by someone. Unless they were sweating profusely at the time."

"Any other reasons it might be difficult on paper?"

"Yes. This receipt seemed printed on recycled paper, so it appears to present a very rough, porous surface."

"I have no further redirect," Trucker said.

"Mr. Calburton, do you have any recross?" the judge asked.

"One moment please, Your Honor, I need to consult with my client." He leaned down and whispered to Hal, "Do you ever use hair spray?" Hal shook his head.

"Just one question, Your Honor. Ms. Chen, did you request that one of the detectives working on this case find out if Mr. Harold uses hair spray?"

"No. Whether to ask about that is a decision for the detectives."

Rory did have some other things he wanted to know but, satisfied with Chen's last answer, decided that they could wait to be asked at trial. Which would be after their own experts had gotten their hands on the receipt and used DNA testing to see if there was any third-party DNA on the receipt or if there was any way to tell if the receipt had been wiped off.

"That's all I have, Your Honor," Rory said. "But I renew my objection to the receipt being received in evidence at this point."

"Mr. Trucker, do you plan any other witnesses who will address the receipt in any way?"

"No, Your Honor."

"Well, I'm going to overrule the objection and admit the receipt into evidence. Although I certainly understand the possibility, given all of the evidence adduced about it so far, that it was planted."

Bingo! Rory looked to the side and saw Hal, Sarah and Otto all smiling, while Trucker, across the way at his own table, looked like his favorite dog had just died.

"Mr. Trucker, do you have additional witnesses?" Judge Gilmore asked.

"No, Your Honor, I don't. The prosecution rests its case in this preliminary hearing."

"Mr. Calburton, are you planning to call any witnesses?"

"Yes, Your Honor. I am."

"This would be a good time to take a break, then. Please be back here in fifteen."

Rory turned to Sarah and said, "You might as well go and visit Gladys and see what she wants. I'm going to come back and beg the judge for the afternoon off so I can line up an expert to examine the receipt. I think she'll give it to me."

Chapter 50

Within minutes of the judge calling a break, Rory had left Hal and Otto behind and was outside the courthouse, heading for an empty bench on a patch of lawn devoid of people. He wanted to avoid being overheard if he lost his temper. He dialed the number as he walked, and it was answered on the second ring.

"Lester, what the hell are you guys doing?"

"I figured I might hear from you, Rory."

"And you are hearing from me. Where the hell did that receipt come from?"

"A tip line."

"Someone called you up and specifically tipped you to go look in Hal Harold's suit and sport jacket pockets?"

"Exactly."

"They didn't suggest you also look in his pants pockets or his shirt pockets, too? Or in his desk drawers? Or a thousand other places someone might leave a receipt?"

"Sometimes people know very specific things that other people don't."

"That is total crap. You and I both know this is a total setup."

"I don't know any such thing."

"Who called you with this supposed tip?"

"The tip line is anonymous, Rory."

"Oh, of course. Forgive me. I forgot. Well, when did the tip come in? You want me to believe it was this morning?"

"No, of course not. It came in two days after the murder, but it somehow got lost, and someone finally noticed it early this morning."

"Got lost? How the hell do you lose a tip?"

"The tips get logged in, and then each tip is written down on a piece of paper and given to everyone working on the team. Somehow the one about checking his pockets never got to the team."

"I should take you up to the top of the X2 and throw you off, Lester."

"You shouldn't threaten a police officer."

"I'm threatening you as a friend."

"I see."

"Seriously, I am enraged. First of all, I don't believe for one moment that that receipt was just found based on a lost tip."

"And second of all?"

"It's a plant, Lester. I mean, how does a receipt from a store, shoved into someone's pocket, end up with zero fingerprints on it, but hair spray chemicals instead?"

"Dry hands sometimes leave no prints, patent or latent. And I assume that's the case here."

"We're going to hire an expert to look for DNA on that piece of paper."

"What will you do if your expert finds Hal Harold's DNA there?"

"That won't happen."

"Well, that's for the trial, Rory. Because you are going to lose this prelim."

"We'll see," Rory said.

"Before you go, my friend, I need to let you know that you owe me a dinner."

"I don't know if I want to go to dinner with you ever again, Lester. But why?"

"Sylvie is dead."

He was taken aback. "Really? How do you know that?"

"We wanted to talk to her, and we called the number we had for her. In Chantilly, Virginia. A police officer answered, but wouldn't tell us anything. Later, through department-to-department official channels, we learned she'd been found dead."

"Cause of death?"

"They told us, but maybe I shouldn't tell you because it will get your lawyer brain working overtime."

"Tell me. I'm going to learn it eventually anyway."

"Okay. She was hit over the head with a blunt instrument and strangled with some sort of ligature. As for which was the actual cause of death, we'll have to wait for the coroner to tell us."

"Lester, do you think my brain really needs to work overtime to process that information and to conclude that the wrong person is in jail here in Los Angeles for Joe Stanton's murder?"

"I would but for the fact that Hal Harold's blood is in Joe Stanton's office, I've got a very nice film of him leaving in a hurry, and the receipt for a rope was in his pocket."

"What was his motive?"

"Don't know. Why don't you ask him?"

Rory was getting nowhere with Lester, but persuading the judge or the DA might be a different matter. There was also, of course, the identical-twin issue, but he decided to approach it indirectly. "Lester, how did they ID her?"

"I assume from a driver's license or whatever other ID they found on her. In fact, they asked if we could locate any fingerprints for her, because they couldn't find a match in the national fingerprint database or what they've got locally in Virginia. But the LAPD doesn't have any prints on her, either. Nor does the state."

"I've been out of law enforcement for a while, but I thought that by this time, with all the security concerns since 9/11, almost everyone has been fingerprinted."

"It's not much different from when you were a deputy DA. If you've never worked for the government, been in the military, been a teacher or health worker or worked for a corporation that requires prints, you're not likely to have been printed unless you've been arrested."

"Then how do you really know that Sylvie is dead if you can't match her prints?"

"I suppose we don't, but why would her ID be near the body if she's not Sylvie?"

Rory decided not to respond to that question. Instead, he said, "Will you try to find a relative and match her DNA?"

"We might do that if there's any doubt, but I don't see why there would be. And anyway, we sent them a photo of her we got from the studio, and they say it's her. But you keep pushing this. Is there something you know that I don't?"

Before Lester had screwed him about the receipt, Rory would have told him about Sylvie's identical twin sister. But he didn't think he was under any legal or ethical obligation to do so. If Lester already knew about Clara, great. If not, great.

"No," Rory said.

"Okay."

"Well, Lester, when you're one hundred percent sure it's Sylvie, let me know, and we'll settle up on the bet," Rory said. "As I recall, you will owe me five grand, and I'll owe you dinner."

"Will do," he said, and signed off.

Rory needed to find Sarah. He dialed her, and she picked up on the first ring. "Where are you?" he asked.

"In an Uber on the way to Gladys's house in Palos Verdes."

"Can the driver overhear you?"

"I assume so."

"Okay, well just say yes or no when I ask you some questions. Or say something that won't connect you to this trial. I'm calling because my friend on the police force, Lester Lovejoy, just told me that the local police in Chantilly found Sylvie Virtin dead at her house today."

"If it is really her."

"Exactly."

"Sarah, you can tell them apart, right?"

"Yes. I think so."

"How do you do it?"

"To tell you that, Rory, I'd need to say something well beyond yes or no."

"Okay, tell me later then."

"I can say this right now," she said. "I will need a picture." And then, in a whisper, "One that shows teeth."

"I'll see what I can do," he said.

"Hey, Rory, isn't the cop friend you just talked to the guy who was mentioned today in connection with that piece of paper?"

"The very one."

"And he's the guy you lunch with sometimes, right?"

"Also the very one."

"I guess he's just doing his job."

"That's one way to look at it, but not the only way. But hey, call me after you've spoken to the widow woman."

"Yes, boss. I should be there very soon."

Rory sat on the bench for a while and thought it through. If the dead woman was Sylvie, that might speak to a dispute with Clara, who had called Sylvie a bitch. But even if Sylvie were dead, it might or might not have anything to do with the death of Joe Stanton. Joe had known both women, but Rory'd found no evidence that either one had killed him. But then again, if the dead woman was Clara, that could well mean that whoever killed Clara also killed Joe, given the use of garroting in both cases. And who had easy physical access to both Joe and Clara without being labeled an intruder? Sylvie.

He concluded it was worth getting over his pique with Lester to find out exactly who was dead. Maybe that would allow him to puzzle it out better.

He called Lester and explained about Clara and Sylvie being identical twins and the need for a photo. When he was done, Lester said, "You weren't going to tell me, were you?"

"You promised to give me a heads-up about this kind of stuff. So can you blame me?"

"Maybe not. But, you know, I've got my own internal LAPD problems to think about before I disclose stuff to you on a back channel."

"Okay. That issue's not over for me, Lester, but what about a photo?"

"I will get it to you if I can. With teeth."

Rory sat on the bench for a few moments more, thinking, then headed back to the courtroom. When he got there, Judge Gilmore was standing to the side of the bench, chatting with her clerk. When she saw that everyone had returned, and that the sheriff's deputies had led Hal in, she climbed the steps to the bench and waited for the clerk to call the session to order.

Once that was done, Rory rose, intending to ask for the delay he needed to look for an expert to examine the receipt. "Your Honor—" he began, but the judge cut him off.

"Counsel, unfortunately a personal matter has arisen, which necessitates my delaying further testimony until tomorrow. We'll resume at ten a.m. tomorrow, Friday. Is there anything further we need to take up now before we adjourn for the day?"

"No, Your Honor," Trucker said.

"I'd like to arrange to talk with my client now," Rory said, "if the deputies could arrange that, please."

"Of course," Judge Gilmore said. "They'll find a secure room for you before they transport him back to the jail."

***

In the secure room, with two sheriff's deputies outside the door and Hal sitting across the table from him, handcuffed, Rory said, "Obviously, this doesn't look good."

"Obviously not. But that receipt was planted. I can't remember the last time I bought any rope. And I've never heard of AtoZHardware, let alone gone to Riverside to buy something there."

Rory handed him the copy of the receipt that Trucker had given him. "Have you got an alibi for the date and time this receipt says the rope was bought?"

Hal studied it. "Two weeks ago today, huh?" He paused. "I recall that day. I took it off because I wasn't feeling well. I stayed home and watched TV. Didn't even go out. I don't know how I can prove that, though, unless I show people my various canceled meetings for the day."

"That won't help a lot," Rory said. He thought for a moment. "You still live alone in a house, right? Not in an apartment building?"

"Right, no concierge or valet to say I didn't go out that day."

Rory pursed his lips. "I think we'll leave the alibi alone for now."

"Not credible?"

"More not provable, and I don't want you pinned down on it right now."

"Makes sense."

"Maybe later we can go in a different direction."

"Like what?"

"We'll check out whether anyone at the hardware store recalls someone else buying the rope. Or maybe there's security video showing it. But, to be frank, it's not likely we'll find either. A customer buying a hank of rope isn't exactly a memorable sale, and most stores don't keep their video that long."

Hal looked at him. "You do believe me, Rory, don't you?"

It was the first time Rory had ever seen Hal with a hangdog look. "Yes, Hal, I do. The problem we've got is that the rope receipt fits with the two other pieces of evidence they've got—the blood on the rug of the victim's office and your looking panicked when you drove off the lot that day."

"There are perfectly good explanations for those things."

"Yes, there are. But we'd have to find a way for those explanations to get admitted into evidence. The truly key one is how the blood got on the rug."

"Three people know how it got there."

"Right, but one, Peter Stanton, is prepared to lie about it. The second, Joe Stanton, is dead. And the third—you—are not going to testify."

"If I did testify—and I understand that would be against your advice—I'd explain that Peter's lying because he hates me."

"Why?"

"Because I had a fling with Sylvie."

Rory thought about telling him that Sylvie might be dead, too, but decided against it. Mostly because he wasn't sure exactly who was dead in Chantilly. It was unethical to lie to clients, but silence in the face of uncertainty wasn't exactly a lie. Or so he reasoned.

"Hal, that's ridiculous. Did you leave your lawyer brain at home? We'd have to put Peter on the stand, get him to deny he saw you bleed, then have you testify he's lying because he hates you and why. A long, detailed why, no doubt."

"Something like that."

"We'd be better off just putting you on the stand to say why you bled in Joe's office, and then let them put Peter on the stand to deny it happened. Which they'll do. And then I can cross-examine him and bring out his dislike for you."

"That should work."

"Not unless I can really tear Peter apart on the stand, and from my last experience with him, in the let's-send-Hal-back-to-jail hearing, he's a pretty cool customer."

"We'll still have to deal with why I looked the way I looked," Hal said. "And there's an explanation for that, too."

"What? That you were at the studio that afternoon not to kill Joe Stanton, but to have an affair with Sylvie, Joe's longtime paramour? And with Sylvie unavailable to back you up. Are you crazy?"

"I think it could work," Hal said.

"Maybe on a long shot in front of a jury. Not in a prelim where all the judge is looking for is to be persuaded that you *might* well have killed him."

"Again, I think it could work."

"I'm not going to let you testify in a preliminary hearing, Hal. No way. Because everything you say—which may turn out in retrospect to have been bad things to say—can be used against you in the trial."

"For example?"

"Suppose Sylvie reappears and denies that she was at the studio with you."

"She wouldn't lie."

"Dear God. For an experienced lawyer, you are naïve."

"I want to testify. I can persuade her."

"I say no."

"Rory, the law is quite clear that it's the defendant—that's me—who gets to decide whether to waive his Fifth Amendment rights and testify. It's not a tactical decision that gets made by his lawyer."

"You're right. And if you want to do that, and, like I said, make everything you say at the prelim, good or bad, admissible at the trial, I can't stop you. But I'm telling you it's stupid. And I'm telling you that even if you do testify, you're going to lose this prelim—the blood, your rapid exit from the studio and the receipt in your pocket are going to assure you'll be bound over for trial."

"Well, I guess you're saying the same thing Quentin Zavallo said. He didn't want me to testify either, and he didn't even know about the receipt."

"So take our advice."

"I'll think about it."

Chapter 51

THURSDAY AFTERNOON
CENTURY CITY
OFFICES OF THE HAROLD FIRM

When Rory walked into his office, the red light on his desk phone was blinking. He picked it up and was told that Alex Toltec was in the lobby and wanted to see him.

"Send him up," he said, and sat down behind his desk to wait.

A few minutes later, Alex, sitting in a wheelchair, was pushed into his office by an attendant. He was dressed in red flannel pajamas and had black felt slippers on his feet. His head was bandaged, and his left arm was in a sling. Famous for his girth, he now looked almost gaunt, with salt-and-pepper stubble on his face.

"Hi, Rory," Alex said as the attendant stationed the chair in front of Rory's desk and flipped the levers that anchored the chair in place. "I got a call from your associate, Sarah Gold," he said. "She left a message asking to meet with me. I thought it might be more efficient if I just came over here and saw you directly."

"That's perfect, Alex. And I must say it's very good to see you looking more or less okay."

Alex laughed. "Yes, well, to paraphrase Mark Twain, Internet reports of my death were exaggerated, although they almost weren't."

Rory considered staying behind his desk but, on second thought, concluded it would be rude and went around to shake Alex's hand. "I'm very glad those reports were exaggerated."

"So you could call me to testify in Broom versus the studio and say that I, and I alone, wrote the script for *Extorted*?"

Rory looked at the attendant. "I'm sorry, sir, but Mr. Toltec and I need to have a confidential conversation about a lawsuit. Would you mind going back down to the reception area? I can wheel Mr. Toltec down there when we're done."

"Of course," the man said.

Rory walked him out to the elevator, pushed the "Down" button and waited until he got in. The elevator was programmed to take him down to the reception floor or the lobby but not anywhere else.

When Rory got back to his office, he saw that Alex had picked up the minibasketball and was twirling it on his fingertips.

Rory ignored the basketball and said, "To pick up where we left off, your testifying in person would be great if you're feeling up to it. You can say exactly what you told me a couple of weeks ago and what you swore to in your declaration—that you're the sole author of the script and that Mary Broom had nothing to do with it."

"Well, there's the problem," Alex said. He arced the ball toward the hoop, and it swooshed through.

"Nice shot," Rory said.

"I played basketball in high school," Alex said. "Dweeby guys interested in making movies weren't of much interest to girls, but basketball stars were."

"So what's the problem?" Rory asked.

"I lied, is the problem."

The two of them looked at each other in silence for a moment.

"You mean Mary Broom wrote the script?"

"Not exactly."

Rory took a deep breath. "Okay, hit me with it."

"Well, it's complicated."

Rory knew that however complicated the explanation, his copyright case was probably over. Alex wouldn't have come to see him right out of the hospital if his lie had been a minor one. Rory felt like getting up, lifting the man out of his wheelchair and beating the shit out of him. Like he'd wanted to do to the guy who wrecked his knee in that long-ago football game. But he managed to put it aside, for the moment. "I'm a lawyer, Alex, I can deal with complicated. Please tell me what happened, in chronological order, if you can spin it out that way. It's easier for me to grapple with it if you don't just free-associate."

"Alright," Alex said. "Let me see if I can put it all in order."

"Good."

"Well, starting, I don't know, maybe sixteen or seventeen years ago, I was secretly dating Mary Broom. It was volatile. Sometimes we were on, sometimes we were off. Sometimes we fought."

"Was your relationship public?"

"Not really, and the tabloids, especially the TV tabloids, weren't quite the way they are now."

"Meaning?"

"If publicists fed them a steady stream of photos and stories, they didn't tend to investigate celebrities very much. It was before Paris Hilton and all of that."

"You were able to keep the affair pretty much below the radar, then?"

"Yes."

Alex had not, to that point, said anything about a child. Rory decided to let the interview go on without his mentioning it. It would be at least a minor test of Alex's current reliability—whether he was truly going to tell all or continue hiding things.

"How does this relate to the script?"

"Mary had written several screenplays. She asked me to read them. They were awful. Then she came up with an idea for a new one. The idea wasn't half-bad, so I worked with her on it."

"And she created the outline?"

"Yes. The one you saw. I have my own copy of it. Here it is." He handed Rory a sheaf of papers.

Rory paged through them and said, "It's got your handwriting on it."

"Right. They're my comments on the outline."

"There are a lot of them."

"Right you are again. The outline wasn't very good. It lacked, well, an arc and a lot of other key things. So my comments were designed to help her without just rewriting the thing myself."

"Did she redo it?"

"She made a half-hearted effort and actually produced a script. But then she got pregnant and ultimately stopped working on it."

"Pregnant with your child?"

"Yes."

Rory was pleased to hear Alex admit that, although the next question he intended to ask would perhaps tell if Alex was really going to be fully candid.

"I don't suppose it's truly relevant to the case, but just in case it is, where is your daughter now?"

"She's in India. She's fourteen. Her name is Alma. The last name on her birth certificate is Cetlot, but she uses Mary's last name, Broom. She was raised in the ashram that Mary lived in for the last ten years."

"But born here?"

"Yes."

"Does she know anything about this?"

"I don't really know, but I don't think so." He took out his wallet, extracted a photo and handed it to Rory. "This is her about a year ago."

Rory looked at it, and said, "Someday she'll be as gorgeous as her mother." He grinned. "Fortunately, Alex, she doesn't take after you."

Alex ignored the comment and said, "Well, Alma figures in this because, for many years, Mary wouldn't let me see her or even send me any photos. And I suppose it's one of the reasons I did what I did."

"Which was?"

"I asked her if I could rewrite the script. She said yes, she no longer cared about such worldly things. But as a sort of revenge, after I rewrote it, I left her name off of it and didn't mention her involvement to anyone."

"Including to me when I interviewed you."

"Correct."

"You realize, Alex, that I can't possibly make use of Mary's supposed agreement that you could rewrite the script."

"Why not?"

Rory sighed. "Because you don't have it in writing from her, and, given everything you've lied about so far, no one will believe you."

"Maybe she'll admit it happened."

"Maybe pigs will fly."

Alex looked at the floor, clearly abashed.

"Alex, let me ask you something else. How did you get the script into the studio and get it made into a film without anyone asking if you had any coauthors?"

"You don't really have to go through the whole formal script-submission process if you're well-known to the studio, which I was, since I'd done many films with them. There's no doubt all kinds of documentation about my deal as a writer-producer. Just no initial submission documentation."

"Didn't you think Mary would find out what you'd done?"

Alex shrugged. "Eventually, I figured she would, but she'd told me she no longer cared about worldly things, so I assumed she'd do nothing about it."

"But you miscalculated."

"So it seems."

Rory reached into his desk, pulled out a copy of the script that Lester had given him and handed it to Alex. "I got this from a thumb drive that the police, uh, found. And it's identical to a version Mary's lawyers just came up with. Do you recognize it?"

Alex paged through it for a few moments and said, "It looks like the script that Mary wrote before she went permanently to India, on which I had put some suggestions for changes—additional suggestions beyond what I'd put on the earlier outline. And long before I asked her permission to rewrite the whole thing."

"Her script is certainly quite different from the shooting script, but it seems pretty good to me."

"That's because you're a lawyer and not a writer, Rory."

"You know, you creatives can sometimes be really annoying."

"Live with it."

"Bottom line, then, you took this script and, after Mary left, improved it by rewriting parts of it and made it into what eventually became the shooting script."

"Yes," Alex said. "That's exactly what I did."

"If I take Mary at her word, why doesn't she have lots of drafts and lots of stuff on her computer showing the various drafts?"

Alex hung his head. "It's embarrassing. But before she went to India, she gave me her computer. Said she'd never need it again. I blanked it and then, just to be sure, took it to one of those places that drill holes in the hard drive to make whatever's on it completely unrecoverable."

Rory got up, picked the basketball off the floor, aimed carefully and watched as the ball spun briefly on the rim and then dropped to the floor. "Shit." He looked over at Alex. "You know, even if

Mary—against all odds—agrees that she gave you permission to rewrite the script and become a joint author, it's still going to cost you. Because as joint authors, you have to account to each other for any profits made from it."

"Sounds reasonable. And it's pretty much what Joe Stanton said when I told him all of this," Alex said.

"When was that?"

"Not too long after the suit was filed."

"So several weeks ago?"

"Yes."

All Joe had said to Rory was that he'd discovered some interesting things about the case. Was the discovery that Alex had admitted stealing the script? If so, why had Joe waited so long to even hint about it? Joe had talked to Rory about the case only two days before he died, and Alex had clearly talked to Joe long before that.

Instead of sharing all of that with Alex, Rory just said, "It's funny Joe didn't tell me what you told him. But then, you know, I was just the lawyer on the case."

"I didn't ask him to keep it from you."

"But he did, and, more importantly, you'd kept it from me first. You denied everything when I interviewed you, remember? And then I drafted a sworn declaration for you, saying you alone wrote the script. Do you remember signing that?"

"Yes. But Joe had asked me to keep it to myself until he could 'process it,' as he put it. So if I had told you at the time I signed the declaration, that wouldn't have been keeping it to myself."

Rory felt himself getting angry at the deceptions that had been visited upon him by both Joe and Alex. He hated being lied to. Well, maybe it was unfair to be angry at Joe. Who knew what Joe would have revealed if he hadn't been murdered. Or if Alex was, even now, really telling Rory the full story. Rory picked up the basketball again and slammed it against the wall, hard. They both watched it rebound and roll into the opposite wall.

"You're angry, Rory, which I get. But I'm trying to make amends."

"Maybe so, Alex, but I think you're still lying about something. I just don't know what."

"I'm not lying."

"Did Joe take notes of this supposed conversation you had with him?"

"It wasn't a 'supposed' conversation. But yes, and at the same time he made a copy of the version of the script that you just showed me."

"Did he tell you what he was planning to do about what you'd just told him? After he'd had time to 'process it,' of course, whatever the hell that meant."

"He just said he'd get back to me. That there was a big injunction hearing coming up soon, and that he didn't feel compelled to tell anyone else about it for the moment because he thought the studio would win the injunction hearing. And then the case could be settled on the cheap."

"He said that?"

"Yes. And ended by saying, 'Why break eggs?'"

Rory was by then boiling inside. Alex wasn't a studio employee, exactly, but close enough, and his lie was going to cost Rory a win on the case and turn it into an embarrassing loss. Because if he revealed what he had just learned to Kathryn and the court—which he was probably ethically required to do—the cost of settlement would skyrocket. Even though the studio was as much a victim of Alex's deception as was Mary Broom. Worse, even though the lies weren't his, in the eyes of the court, they might well stick to him.

"You're quiet," Alex said.

"Yes, just thinking. But here's my next question. Why did you come in here and tell me all of this?"

"When you get as close to death as I got in that crash, it makes you want to confess your sins. I know that sounds strange, or even stupid, but that's how it is."

"But your crash was long after you confessed your sins to Joe Stanton. So what motivated you to tell *him*?"

"I was just feeling guilty."

Rory had a sense he was being played, although he couldn't quite figure out how. He decided to take a shot at the real issue and see where it got him.

"Alex, did you kill Joe to silence him?"

"Say what?"

"I asked if you killed Joe."

"No. Why would I have wanted to kill him?"

"To keep him from exposing you in public as a fraud? As a man who stole his girlfriend's work?"

"If I'd been worried about that, why would I have told Joe anything at all? Or you, for that matter?"

"I'm trying to figure that out. But one possibility is that you didn't tell Joe anything. And he discovered the truth about your theft on his own and then confronted you with it two days before he died. And you killed him to shut him up. Or had someone else kill him."

Alex paused, took a deep breath and said, "Rory, I've now told you the whole truth."

"Will you testify in the copyright trial if I need you to?"

"I can't imagine why you'd want me to, but if you do, sure."

"How about the criminal trial?"

"I have absolutely nothing to do with that, so I don't know why you'd need me."

Rory's actual thought was that if he could manage to get Alex on the witness stand, he could have him declared a hostile witness and cross-examine him into confessing. A sort of *Perry Mason* dream.

Instead, he responded to Alex's question by saying, "Just tell me you'll cooperate in being a witness in the criminal trial if I want you to."

"To say what?"

"I'm not sure yet."

"It was really nice to see you, Rory. Can you have them send my attendant up?"

"Sure, but before you go, tell me about your accident."

"Mechanical failure, caused by my own clumsy efforts to maintenance the engine of my small plane. I screwed up the attachment of the oil filter somehow, and the engine just froze in midflight when it ran out of oil."

"You didn't try to commit suicide?"

Alex blinked. And then furrowed his forehead. "No, why would I want to?"

"To avoid acute professional embarrassment when Joe Stanton revealed what he'd found out about you and the script you stole."

A small smile passed across Alex's face. "Rory, I'm surprised that you don't know by now that it's almost impossible to embarrass to death anyone in the entertainment business. We just take whatever humiliating thing has happened to us to our agent and our publicist and try to figure out how to make hay from it."

Chapter 52

THURSDAY
PALOS VERDES ESTATES

Sarah took an Uber down to Palos Verdes to find out what Gladys wanted to say that required an in-person meeting. She was again admitted to the house by the maid and again led to the red-tiled courtyard. As before, Gladys was seated on her wicker throne. This time, though, she was clad in a red knit top and skirt that most sixtysomething women would likely have avoided. Sarah thought she didn't look half-bad in it.

After Sarah took a seat in one of the low wicker chairs that faced the throne, the maid, without being asked, place a Coke in front of her. Gladys was already drinking pale liquid from a tall, thin glass and said, "I recalled your preference for Coke. As for me, I'm drinking a Tom Collins." She laughed and raised her glass high as if in toast. "I know that's a bit of a throwback."

"I'm not familiar with it," Sarah said.

"It's basically gin," Gladys said. "But with sugar, lemon juice and carbonated water added. It's always served in one of these tall glasses. Sometimes I think I like the glass as much as the contents." She giggled.

"I see. Well, the glass is pretty, for sure."

"Would you like to join me, Sarah? We can have a collins out here for you in the blink of an eye." She giggled again.

"Uh, thanks, but I don't drink."

"Really? How can it be that a pretty girl like you doesn't drink?"

"My parents were very religious, and no alcohol was allowed in our house. I've left some of the things they taught me behind, but not that."

"You should try it sometime. It can grease the wheels, you know."

"The wheels of what?"

"Social interaction. Or overcoming inhibition. Or fear."

"I don't usually have a problem with those things. Sometimes I think I'd be better off with *more* inhibition."

"This feels almost like the start of a girl-to-girl talk, dear. Do you want to unburden yourself? I'm a good listener. Even better when I'm on my third one of these." She raised her glass again and giggled again.

"Not tonight," Sarah said. "Maybe we could just talk about why you wanted me to come and see you?"

"Yes, of course! And, truth be told, I've been drinking in part to have the courage to tell you what I want to tell you."

"I'm listening. What is it, Gladys?"

"I have something to show you." She picked up the little bell and rang it. The maid reappeared almost instantly. "Could you bring me the file that's on my desk, Julia?"

When they'd watched Julia slip away on her errand, Gladys said, "Before I show you what I'm going to show you, I should tell you that it really breaks my heart. But at least it will get Hal off of this ridiculous murder charge."

Julia returned with a manila file folder and handed it to Gladys, who opened it and extracted a single piece of paper. "This," she said, "is a summary of monies deposited into Joe's checking account over the last six weeks." She handed the sheet of paper to Sarah.

Sarah studied it. "It looks as if there are a series of deposits, each for fifty thousand dollars. Five of them."

"Yes, exactly."

"Did Joe have his own checking account?"

"Yes, we each had a separate account, plus a joint one for the house expenses."

"What are these deposits for, and why are you showing them to me?"

"Well, as you can imagine, since Joe died I've been going through his finances, with the help of our accountant. And I asked him the same thing, because funds from the real estate investments come into a different account, and the studio's salary to him is automatically deposited. These are check deposits."

"Have you figured it out?"

"Yep!" She took a big swig of her drink and handed Sarah another sheet of paper.

Sarah looked at it and said, "This is the back and front of a check for fifty thousand dollars from Alex Toltec to Joe, dated about ten days ago. Is this one of the deposits?"

"Yep! It sure is. I think Joe was extorting Alex about something, and Alex was paying him off."

"Do you know what about?"

"I think I do. You see, the night before he was killed, Joe turned to me in bed, right as we were about to go to sleep, and said, 'You're a friend of Mary Broom's lawyer, aren't you?' And I told him sure, that he already knew that."

"Excuse me," Sarah said. "This is a bit forward of me, I suppose, but were you and Joe still sleeping together? I mean with all the mistresses and so forth."

Gladys glared at her. "What an impertinent question. Of course we were. The mistresses were on the side. I was the main show, so to speak." She picked up her drink and took a large gulp, spilling a little down her chin.

Sarah watched as Gladys dabbed at her chin with a napkin, then said, "Okay. I'm really sorry. What else did Joe say to you about all of this that night? Or any other night?"

"He accused me of looking at a file on his desk about the litigation over *Extorted* right after the lawsuit started and then tipping off Kathryn Thistle about Alex's role in stealing the script."

"Did you?"

"No. I knew Mary Broom had accused him of it. But I knew nothing about it."

"Where is all this going, Gladys?"

"Those checks? I think Joe was blackmailing Alex, threatening to expose him as a script thief if he didn't pay him hush money."

"And so?"

"Can't you see it? It means it must be Alex who killed Joe. To cut off the payments but, more important, to make sure Joe never told anyone what he knew."

Sarah thought about it for a few seconds, turning over in her mind what Gladys had just said. "Well, it doesn't make a lot of sense to me, frankly. For one thing, why pay him and then kill him? Why not kill him right away?"

"Joe had told me they were about to win the preliminary injunction hearing and then they'd settle it on the cheap to avoid spending more legal fees on a trial. That made the timing perfect. Settlement would end the legal inquiry into who wrote the script. And then Alex, by killing Joe, could stop paying him."

"That doesn't make any sense, either. If the case went away, why would Alex have to keep paying Joe?"

"To keep Joe from telling the Hollywood press. Alex's real fear was the horrible publicity that would follow any disclosure."

"But why was Joe bothering to extort him? I thought Joe had all the money he needed."

Gladys stared at her for a moment and said, "Joe was into having power over other people. He got off on it. And this was even better, because it gave him a hold over an important director and would help to keep him in line."

"I thought Alex directed horror movies."

"Those make a ton of money, honey."

Gladys picked up the bell and rang it again. When Julia reappeared, Gladys held out her glass and said, "Refill, please?"

"Why does this exonerate Hal?" Sarah asked.

"Isn't it obvious? If Alex killed him, then Hal didn't. Have you ever heard of two people garroting someone to death?"

Sarah had the distinct feeling that she was being fed a line—a not very logical one at that—and she wanted to get out of there before Gladys got any drunker.

"Gladys, I'm glad you told me all these things. I think you're onto something, but I need to discuss it with Rory, and I need to get going. I have some other things I still need to take care of. But I have one final question."

"What is it, dear?"

"There's a lot of evidence to suggest Hal killed your husband. Why do you want to help him?"

"Hal is a dear friend. I cannot bring myself to believe he killed Joe. Now I think I've figured out that Alex did it, and I want to help Hal walk free. And nail the real killer. I did love my husband."

"Is Alex not a friend, too?"

Gladys shrugged. "He's neither a friend nor not a friend. And if he killed Joe, he's an enemy."

"Gladys, will you arrange for us to go to your bank and verify that the documents you just showed me are real?"

"Yes. I will call you tomorrow and give you the name of the bank contacts, and I will call them and tell them to expect your call."

"Are you willing to come to court and testify about what you've found, if you're needed?"

"Of course."

"May I take these papers with me?" Sarah asked.

"Yes, they are copies for you."

On the way back to the office, Sarah tried to puzzle it out. The best way to do it, she thought, was to eliminate suspects.

She started with Alex. Even assuming Joe was really blackmailing Alex, it made no sense to her that Alex would kill Joe to cut off the blackmail. As she had asked Gladys, why did he wait? Also, blackmailers usually needed money. Joe didn't. So she scratched Alex off her mental list.

What about Gladys herself? She had a sort-of motive, but if jealousy was a motive, why wait all these years? There didn't seem to have been any particular recent trigger. And there was no physical evidence at all pointing to her. So she scratched Gladys off her mental list, too.

That left Hal. Unfortunately, there was a lot of evidence pointing to him—he was on the scene at the right time, and his blood was in the room. And now the receipt for the rope was linked to him. But there was no known motive.

Perhaps Rory could figure it out.

Chapter 53

"Let's go down to the conference room," Rory said.

"Why?" Sarah asked. "Your office is perfectly comfortable, and I can shoot baskets."

"That's exactly why. I want to be far away from that thing. It's sapping my confidence."

"How about golf?"

"Like I said, let's hit the conference room."

After they got there and teed up some coffee, Rory briefed Sarah on his meeting with Alex and finished by saying, "Bottom line, he and Mary are coauthors of the script, and if he testifies at trial to what he told me, and Mary Broom confirms it—which she may not—we'll both win and lose."

"How do you mean?"

"Coauthors own an undivided interest in the copyright. They can each license to whomever they want so long as they don't make it exclusive. They just have to account to the other author for the profits and split them."

"So, let me get this straight, then," Sarah said. "Alex can license the script to TheSun/TheMoon/TheStars to make a movie, and Mary can't stop him, but he'll have to split his take with her?"

"Right, and she could license it to some other studio, too, and they can make another version of the same thing."

"Which isn't likely, right? That any other studio will want to do that?"

"Right."

"How will we lose, then?"

"There will be tremendous pressure on us, partly through the Writers Guild, to put her name on the credits and to renegotiate the overall deal so that it becomes a deal with both of them."

"I see. Messy, in other words."

"Right. Now tell me what you learned from Gladys."

"She claims Joe Stanton found out Alex wasn't the only author of the screenplay and was making Alex pay him hush money. Otherwise he'd out him as a fraud."

"How much?" Rory asked.

"According to the paperwork Gladys showed me, Alex had already paid two hundred fifty thousand dollars. Five payments of fifty grand over six weeks. What ended the payments was Joe's death."

"Why did she tell you now and not before?"

"She says she discovered it while going through Joe's bank account, and she wants to help Hal. Gladys thinks this shows he didn't do it."

Rory thought about it for a few seconds. "Did Joe ever tell Gladys that he was extorting Alex?"

"No, it's all supposition on her part."

Rory got up and began to pace around the conference table.

"Rory, what are you doing?"

"Thinking. I think better when I can move." After a few trips around the table, he said, "Somehow, none of this quite adds up, although I can't quite get it to add up in some other version of the facts."

"I can see one other thing that doesn't add up," Sarah said. "Why did Alex come to you and confess that, in effect, he stole the script? I mean, what motivated him? It doesn't benefit him at all as far as I can see."

"He claimed that being so close to death after the accident changed his views about things. Or something like that. But he told Joe the truth before his near-death experience, or so he claims."

Rory sat back down at the conference table and said, "The real question isn't whether Alex actually killed Joe. It's whether we can make it look like a real enough possibility that they'll let Hal go."

"There's also a second question, Rory."

"Yeah? What's that?"

"Can you pin the murder in the criminal case on Alex without Kathryn finding out that he copped to stealing the script?" she said. "Because once she finds out, her settlement number is going to go higher. A lot higher."

"It's worse than that, Sarah. I've got an obligation of truthfulness to the judge in the civil case. So I can't go back into that courtroom without formally revising the discovery we already answered, including Alex's apparently false declaration."

"So we're fucked," Sarah said.

"I thought you didn't use language like that."

"It's more like I save it for when it's really apt."

"Well, wait 'til you hear the other thing."

"What?"

"Right before you got here, Hal called from jail. He's decided, against my advice, to testify in his own defense."

"Why? I thought defendants never did that at the prelim stage."

"He's under the illusion that he'll be able to persuade the judge to let him go."

"So he's managed to get hold of hallucinogens."

"Apparently. I need to think," Rory said.

"So think."

"I don't think that well just sitting behind a desk."

She laughed. "You're not sitting. You're walking around the conference table, remember?"

"Oh, right. Sorry, kind of distracted."

"Where do you want to go? Do you want to take a walk around Century City? Go up to Franklin Canyon and hike a steep trail?"

"When I was in law school, there was a particular thing I did that helped me to think."

She raised her eyebrows. "What?"

He looked at her and grinned.

"Please don't tell me you go to strip clubs. Because I won't go."

"No, I go out to Magic Mountain, which is more or less right across the street from Chet, and when I get there I ride the X2."

"Which is what?"

"A roller coaster."

"I'm afraid of heights."

"Do you remember what you said to me about my sensitivity about where I went to law school?"

"Yes, I told you to get over it."

Chapter 54

They headed out of Century City in Rory's Tesla S to the nearest entrance to the 405 freeway. When they reached the red light at the entrance ramp, there were no cars ahead of them, and the freeway itself looked empty.

"Do you want to see how fast this thing will get to sixty, Sarah?"

"Boys and their toys. But sure, why not?"

"Does your cell phone have a stopwatch on it?"

"Of course."

"Get it out, set it up and tell me when you're ready."

A few seconds later, she said, "Ready!"

He stepped on the accelerator, and the acceleration pushed them both back in their seats.

"Sixty!" he shouted. "How long did that take?"

She peered at the phone. "Five point six seconds."

"Not bad. I've done it a little faster sometimes."

"You know, Rory, a Porsche 911 Turbo can do it in just under three."

"Maybe if we see one, we can issue a challenge."

"Well, don't put big money on it, because you'll lose."

The drive to Magic Mountain took about forty-five minutes. When they got there and pulled into the parking lot, Sarah looked at the forest of roller coasters and said, "Wow. How many are there?"

"It keeps changing, but I think around a dozen."

"Which one is the X2?"

"The one with the red tracks."

She stared at it. "Oh, my gosh. How high is it?"

"About two hundred feet, I think. Let's get in there. You can get a better look from inside."

When they reached the park gate, Rory pulled out a pass and showed it to the ticket taker.

"You have your own pass?"

"Uh-huh. It's an annual and entitles me to bring a guest."

"Did you really come here a lot during law school?"

"Yes, but the coaster I liked was an earlier, slower version called the X. The X2 got installed after I graduated."

"How often do you come now?"

"I try to come out here at least once a month, but as my friends have gotten older, it's harder and harder to get people to come with me."

"So I'm the latest victim?"

"No, you're the latest thrill seeker. I think you'll be hooked once you do it."

"Did you bring Dana here?"

"No, but I bet she'd be willing to come."

When they got to the X2, the line wasn't too bad.

"I'm glad the line's short," Sarah said. "That way I won't have to spend a lot of time contemplating this monster before I get on it." She peered up at the very top of the red metal tracks. "It looks, well, scary."

"It can be."

Sarah bit her lower lip. "I'm a person who likes to know what I'm getting into. But it's hard to tell from just looking at it exactly what tortures happen to you when you're on it. So tell me. And don't spare the details."

"It first climbs a pretty steep hill; takes about a minute. Then it drops into a fake dip, accelerates and then goes up a slight rise."

"What's fake about the dip?"

"It's not very steep. Its purpose is to speed up the car so it's already moving fast when it drops over the edge of a really steep hill."

"How steep is that one?"

"It wouldn't be inaccurate to call it straight up-and-down."

"Uh, how fast is it going when it drops over the edge there?"

"Not too fast. But by the time it reaches the bottom, it hits seventy-five miles per hour if things are going well."

"What if they're not?"

"Well, then you die." He laughed.

"That's not funny. Maybe I don't want to get on." She looked around. "Is there a way to exit this line?"

"I was just kidding. No one's ever died on the X2. But you can always chicken out, Sarah."

"No, no. I don't chicken out of things. But what happens when the car gets to the bottom of the straight-up-and-down hill? Will the ride be over?"

"No. You go into two raven turns, one backflip and a twisting front flip."

"I don't know what those are."

"They're all hard to describe. You just have to experience them."

By that time, they had advanced to the front of the line. They climbed into their seats, and attendants snapped bright-orange molded plastic restraints over their shoulders.

As the train started backing up, Sarah said, "Aren't we headed in the wrong direction?"

"No, we go up the big hill backward, so we can't really see exactly when we're going to drop over into the steep part. And your seat is independently hung on the car, so it can pivot three hundred sixty degrees at the same time we're going downhill."

As the train rumbled slowly up the long grade, she said, "I don't like this."

"Well, too late now. But, hey, there's good news."

"What?"

"The whole ride takes less than three minutes, so if you scream the whole way, you won't have been screaming long enough to damage your vocal cords."

"I haven't screamed at anything since my brother put a spider in my bed when I was ten."

Just then the train went down the first small dip. Sarah made a kind of mewling noise. When, seconds later, it plunged over the edge of the straight-up-and-down section, she began to scream. When they went into the twisting front flip, Rory put his hands to his ears. Sarah didn't stop screaming until the train rolled to a stop on the flat stretch of track from which it had started.

They lifted the orange restraints off their shoulders, and Sarah said, as she climbed out, "I need to go somewhere and sit down. And maybe have the first drink of my life."

Rory stayed put. "I want to ride it a couple more times," he said. "I really do need to think this through, and I get some of my best ideas here."

She gripped a railing with both hands, and Rory noticed that her beautiful green eyes had gone wide. "Won't you need to get in line again?"

"No. I come so often I've been granted what you might call special privileges. I can ride three times without getting back in the line. There's a coffee-and-pastry place over there." He pointed. "I'll meet you there in ten minutes."

He watched as she walked away and noticed that her legs were shaking. He ran over to her, put his arm around her shoulders and said, "Are you okay? I can ride the coaster later."

"No, no. I'll be fine."

He left her and walked back to the X2. Now, all by himself, with the aid of the thrill, he needed to figure out what to do about Hal and his crazy desire to testify.

Ten minutes later, Rory walked over to Sarah's table in the coffee place and sat down. "Are you feeling better now, Sarah?"

"Yes. Fully recovered."

"Good. And I've decided what to do about Hal."

"Which is?"

"I'm going to let him testify—well, there's really no *let him* about it, since it's his decision alone—but testify in the most minimal way I can get away with. Then I'm going to call Alex as a witness and try to trick him into confessing to the murder, or at least incriminating himself so badly that it will be clear to the judge that Hal didn't do it."

"Sounds like a plan. But how are you going to do it?"

"Damned if I know. But I've got all night to work on it."

"Rory?"

"Yes?"

"I want to go back on the X2 a few times."

"So you can scream some more?"

"No. I need to master it."

They rode it together six more times. When they disembarked from the last ride, the attendants gave them a round of applause and handed Sarah an X2 baseball cap.

Chapter 55

FRIDAY MORNING
CENTURY CITY
OFFICES OF THE HAROLD FIRM

When he'd returned from Magic Mountain Thursday night, Rory had called Otto and asked him to come into the office at six the next morning. When Rory got there, Otto was already sitting in one of the guest chairs, waiting.

"Hey, where's the basketball?" Otto said.

"In storage," Rory said. "It was sapping my self-confidence."

"Pity. I enjoyed that thing. Anyway, what's up?"

"What's up? Well, I have too much to do in this criminal case because Hal decided he wants to testify this morning." He rolled his eyes. "So I gotta prepare for that, plus get my closing argument together."

"He's testifying?"

"Yep. Tried to talk him out of it, but he won't budge."

"Good luck with that. How can I help?"

"You can help by taking a task in another case off my hands."

"Sure, as long as I don't have a conflict."

"I doubt you will. This is the copyright infringement case against our client studio, TheSun/TheMoon/TheStars." Rory debriefed him for about fifteen minutes, carefully avoiding telling Otto what Alex had told him about possible joint authorship.

"That's a lot to take in, but I think I get it. What do you want me to do, exactly?"

"I want you to go settle it with Kathryn Thistle."

"That's pretty odd."

"Yeah, it is. But I'll call her and tell her you're coming because I don't have time, and that we need to get this done quick. Tell her that's because the studio's about to name a new general counsel, replacing the acting, and my authority to settle this is from the acting. I don't know if the new guy—well, actually the new guy's a woman—is gonna be on board with offering anything to settle the case."

"How do you know they're about to name someone new?"

"Got a call yesterday from the studio head. He wanted to know my opinion of the woman in question. I doubt he really cares what I think. More a courtesy call to make me think I'm in the loop, because I'll have to work with her."

"So the reason to get this done quickly is real."

"Yep, it sure is."

Otto sat for a moment, seeming to think something through, then said, "I probably shouldn't say what I'm about to say."

"Why not, Otto? You're among friends. Say what you want to say—"

"Because, as you know, Mr. Zavallo has offered me a position in his firm. But after having spent some time with you and Sarah, I'm thinking maybe I'd rather try to talk you guys into starting a white-collar criminal defense practice and come here."

"In an entertainment litigation firm?"

"It's a growing area, Rory, and entertainers need criminal defense lawyers these days a lot more often than in the past."

"True. But why are you hesitant to say what's on your mind?"

"Because I want to say that you must think I was born yesterday. And that might . . ."

Rory laughed. "What, piss me off? Well, you just said it. So elaborate."

"You must be sending me to negotiate with Kathryn Thistle because you've learned something that threatens your case. I need to know what it is. Because, strange as it may seem, hiding something from her, even though I don't know what it is I'm hiding, is going to make me uncomfortable. Is that crazy?"

"No, not crazy at all. And you're as smart as Quentin says you are."

"And whatever it is that's going to make your case worse must be about to break publicly, and that's why you want to get it done quickly."

"You're more or less right, so I might as well tell you this much. I'm gonna go into court today and try to pin the murder on the director of the film, Alex Toltec. Once I do that, it will blow the civil case wide open, I'm sure."

"Why?"

Rory shrugged. "I can't say exactly how. I just know it will. And it will up Kathryn's settlement ask."

Rory considered also telling Otto the rest of it—that Alex had copped to coauthoring the script—but he decided not to. After all, Alex could well be lying about the whole thing. Plus, if Judge Crooked Nose, as he'd come to think of her, somehow got involved in the settlement talks, Otto couldn't be uncomfortable withholding information he didn't know.

"Okay, I'll do it," Otto said. "But only if I can tell Kathryn about the criminal stuff. If I have to."

"Agreed. I've prepared a couple of settlement sheets setting out the various levels of your authority, and who you have to call if you need to go higher. The sheet has the acting GC's cell number on it." Rory handed him a manila folder.

"Anything else?"

"Yes, one thing. I suspect Mary Broom is going to sue some other people, too, once she finishes with us, like the distributor, for starters."

"Didn't she have to add them in when she brought this suit?"

"Not necessarily. In any case, as part of the agreement, please put in that if Mary gets money from anyone else in connection with who wrote or promoted *Extorted*, that will get deducted from whatever the studio has to pay."

"Consider it done."

"Good. I'll be in court, so I won't be able to get texts or calls or e-mails. But there'll be breaks, I'm sure, and I'll check in with you then."

After Otto left, Rory called Kathryn and left her a voice mail about who was coming to settle the case and why it was urgent to get it done. He hoped she wouldn't call him back.

Then he swung by Sarah's office—he had asked her to get there early, too—and they headed downtown to meet with Hal.

Chapter 56

FRIDAY MORNING
LOS ANGELES COUNTY SUPERIOR COURT—CRIMINAL
DIVISION
People v. Harold

Rory had arranged for the sheriff's department to bring Hal to court a little early, and they met for thirty minutes in one of the small rooms, with two sheriff's deputies outside the door. After a lot of argument back and forth, the strategy they had finally agreed on was simple: Rory would ask Hal some very straightforward questions, and Hal would try his best not to give elaborate answers. Rory's hope was that by limiting Hal's direct testimony, he wouldn't open Hal up to too robust a cross-examination by Trucker. Maybe it would work; maybe it wouldn't. It would all depend on how tightly Judge Gilmore held cross-examiners to the topics testified about specifically during direct.

As his parting remark, Rory said to Hal, "No speeches, no snotty remarks, no long explanations. Just answer the questions I ask you as simply as you can. Remember not to give ammo to Trucker to attack your entire relationship with Joe Stanton when he cross-examines you."

"Got it," Hal said.

"Oh, and one more thing. They're obviously going to bring up Peter Stanton. Please answer only exactly what you're asked. No snotty remarks about his women, his failing garage business, or his fancy cars—I know you liked to ride in them—or anything else about the guy. Nada. Nothing. If they want any background on him, they've got to put him on the stand. Where I can cross him."

"Got that, too."

Judge Gilmore took the bench promptly at eight. She looked down at them and asked, "Is everybody ready to proceed?"

"Yes, Your Honor," Trucker said.

"Yes, Your Honor," Rory echoed.

"Good. Mr. Calburton, you indicated yesterday that you might have witnesses for the defense. Do you?"

"Yes. The defense calls Hal Harold."

There was a slight rustle in the courtroom at the surprise Rory had just delivered.

"Alright," Judge Gilmore said. "Before you take the witness stand, Mr. Harold, I need to assure myself that your decision to testify is entirely voluntary. So let me ask you a few questions."

Hal looked up at her. "Of course."

"Mr. Harold, I know this seems a bit odd to ask, considering that you are an experienced lawyer, but are you aware that under the Fifth Amendment you have an absolute right not to testify and to remain silent during this preliminary hearing?"

"Yes, Your Honor, I'm very aware of that."

"Good. Are you also aware that the prosecution in this case, should the matter go to trial, may contend that you have, by testifying here, waived your right to refuse to testify in the trial?"

"Yes."

"Mr. Trucker, have you entered into any agreement with the defense that you will not so argue at the trial, if there is one?"

"No, Your Honor. And we will indeed contend that Mr. Harold has waived the right not to testify at trial."

She turned again toward Hal. "Mr. Harold, are you also aware that, even if you cannot be compelled to testify, what you say here today may be used by the prosecution against you? That they may be able, whether you testify or not, to read what you say today to the jury at a trial and may also use it during opening statements and closing arguments?"

"Yes, Your Honor, I'm aware of that," Hal said. "And anyway, how could they compel me to testify? The rack?"

Judge Gilmore smiled. "Not yet."

Everyone laughed.

"Continuing," the judge said, "and that if you do choose to testify at a trial, the prosecution may be able to cross-examine you with your testimony today?"

"I'm aware of that risk, too, Your Honor."

"Mr. Trucker, have you reached any agreement at all with the defense as to the use you will seek to make of Mr. Harold's testimony today at a later trial, if there is one?"

"None, Your Honor," Trucker said.

She swept her gaze across all the lawyers. "Alright, I'm satisfied Mr. Harold understands the risks. By the way, I'm not saying today how I might rule, if there is a trial and if I am the trial judge, on the questions I've just asked. I'm just making sure Mr. Harold is aware of the risks."

The attorneys all nodded in apparent agreement.

"One more thing," the judge said. "Mr. Harold, the decision as to whether to waive your Fifth Amendment rights is yours and yours alone. It's not a decision to be made by your attorneys. Is this your decision alone after consulting with your attorneys?"

"Yes, Your Honor," Hal said.

"Very good, then. Please take the witness stand."

Hal walked up to the witness stand with an almost jaunty step.

Rory consulted his notes and asked, "Mr. Harold, on the day Joe Stanton was murdered, were you in his office at TheSun/TheMoon/TheStars?"

"Objection," Trucker said. "We don't know if Mr. Harold knows what day the murder was, and the question is therefore ambiguous."

"Overruled. You can cover that in cross if you want to, although since Mr. Harold has sat through this entire hearing, it would be a bit odd if he didn't know the date."

"No, I was not in Joe's office that day," Hal said.

"Not at any time that day, from sunup to sundown?"

"No, not at any time."

"Were you at the studio of TheSun/TheMoon/TheStars on the day Joe Stanton was killed?"

"Yes."

"What were you doing there?"

"I was having a sexual tryst with Sylvie Virtin."

"Who is she?"

"She was, at the time, Joe Stanton's longtime assistant."

"Where was your tryst with her?"

"In Building 6, on the third floor, in—this is embarrassing—a storage room."

"How far is Building 6 from the Executive Office Structure?"

"About a ten-minute walk."

"What time did you arrive at the studio?"

"About eleven in the morning."

"What time did you leave?"

"About a quarter past three."

"Did you go directly to Building 6 when you arrived at the studio?"

"Yes."

"During the time you were on the studio lot, did you go in any building or structure other than Building 6?"

"No."

"Did you leave Building 6 at any time between the time you arrived at the studio and the time you left?"

"No. Except to walk to my car and drive off the studio lot."

That was obviously a long time for a tryst in a storeroom, but Rory and Hal had decided to let it alone and let Trucker try to deal with it on cross.

"Did you see the film clip shown here that depicts you driving off the lot?"

"Yes."

"Did you notice that you were leaning on the horn?"

"Yes."

"And waving your arms in a way to suggest that the gate needed to go up right away?"

"Yes."

"Were you in a hurry?"

"Yes."

"Why?"

"Well, this is, again, embarrassing, but I had to pee. I had kinda forgotten to do that before I left Building 6. There's a gas station about a block from the studio, on the same side of the street, so I wanted to get there pronto."

"Why was it so urgent?"

"I'm seventy-five."

There was laughter in the courtroom.

"Did you hear the testimony here about the receipt that was allegedly found in a pocket of one of your suits?"

"Yes."

"Did you purchase the item—a hank of rope—indicated on that receipt?"

"No."

"Did anyone purchase it on your behalf?"

"No."

"Had you ever before seen that receipt other than the day you saw it here in court?"

"No."

"Did you know it was in one of your suit pockets?"

"No."

"When was the last time you were in Riverside?"

"It was about five years ago."

"Why were you there?"

"I was accepting an award from the Riverside County Entertainment Law Bar Association."

"Have you ever been to AtoZHardware in Riverside?"

"No."

"Have you ever been to any hardware store in Riverside?"

"No."

Now they had to get to Hal's testimony about the blood evidence— in some ways the hardest thing to explain away.

"Mr. Harold, did you hear the testimony that blood matched to your DNA profile was found in Joe Stanton's office shortly after his murder?"

"Yes."

"Do you know how it got there?"

"Yes."

"Please tell the court how it got there."

Hal looked over to Judge Gilmore. "About a week before the murder, I was in Joe's office discussing a case that had been filed against the studio for copyright infringement. Somehow, I cut my arm. I'm not sure how, exactly. But old skin is fragile. I must have bumped something or rubbed against something sharp or rough."

"What was the size of the cut?" Rory asked.

"Not large. More like a scrape. And when I noticed it, someone handed me a tissue. I dabbed the blood up and dropped the tissue in a wastebasket."

Rory and Hal had decided that Hal would not volunteer who had handed him the tissue. Trucker could probe into it if he wanted to. And, of course, everyone in the room who had attended the "back-to-jail" hearing, as Hal called it, would be aware that Hal contended Peter Stanton had handed him the tissue. But if Hal didn't bring that up specifically on direct, Trucker might fear to ask him about it on cross, because he'd get a bad answer that he'd have no way to counter with Peter Stanton missing.

"When did you notice the cut?"

"Right before I was ready to leave."

"Do you know how your blood got on the rug?"

"No, the cut must have still been bleeding slightly when I walked out, and it dripped."

"Objection," Trucker said. "Since the witness clearly doesn't know how his blood got on the rug—we contend it came from the day he murdered Mr. Stanton—his answer is speculative. I ask that the answer be struck from the record."

"Overruled. I suspect cross-examination is soon upon us, and you can take your shot at it then, Mr. Trucker."

Sarah shoved a note at Rory. "Aren't you going to ask if he killed him?"

He looked briefly at Sarah, who'd not been present for his prep session with Hal, and shook his head.

Her question was a logical one. Should he ask Hal point-blank if he had killed Joe Stanton and let him strenuously deny it? After talking with Hal about the risk of not asking at all, he decided to wait. Because if he asked the question, it would open up Hal's entire relationship with Joe Stanton as fair game for questioning. In particular, it might permit Trucker to ask Hal about his possible motives to kill Stanton. As it stood, Rory's questions had touched on Hal's relationship with Joe Stanton only once.

"I have no further questions, Your Honor," Rory said. If Trucker wanted to ask Hal on cross if he had killed Joe, he could go ahead and do it on his own ticket. If he did, Hal had a response waiting that Rory might have had difficulty getting into evidence on direct.

"Your witness, Mr. Trucker," the judge said.

Chapter 57

Although he and Trucker had overlapped at the DA's office when Rory was first starting out, Rory had never seen Trucker cross-examine anyone, and he was curious to see his technique.

Rory himself regarded cross-examination as an almost physical exercise. If direct testimony was a stone wall, cross was like looking for the cracks and crevices in that wall and trying to wedge your fingers into them so you could pull and tear and rip pieces of rock out until the wall crumbled into dust. That was when things were going well, of course. Sometimes the wall stood strong, and you just ended up with bruised and bloody fingers.

His and Hal's intent, in creating such a minimalist direct examination, had been to leave a wall with very few cracks in it.

Trucker stood up at his table. "Good morning, Mr. Harold."

"Good morning . . . Mr. Trucker." Hal delivered Trucker's name precisely as he would've said "asshole." Rory looked up at the judge and saw her smiling. She'd heard it, too.

Trucker frowned. The manner in which Hal said his name had apparently not escaped his notice, either. Then he recovered and said,

"You said, sir, that you were having a tryst with Sylvie Virtin on the day of Mr. Stanton's murder, is that correct?"

"Yes."

"What did you mean by 'tryst'?"

"We had sex."

"Despite your age difference?"

Rory could have objected that that was not a proper question, but he let it go. Hal could take care of himself.

"Mr. Trucker, the old are not without an interest in sex, as you'll find out as you age. And, since you're being nosey about it, I take Viagra."

It was a great answer, and Rory made a mental note to try to get some old people on the jury if the case went to trial.

"I'm not being nosey, Mr. Harold," Trucker said. "I'm just probing the truthfulness of your statements." He paused and asked, "How long did this sexual tryst last?"

Hal shrugged. "Sylvie had not arrived when I first got there. So I busied myself reading a book I brought along."

"Do you recall the name of the book?"

"No, I don't."

"Do you know where she was?"

"No. Sylvie was always way late for things, so I just assumed she was running late. I never asked her where she had been."

"Do you recall how late she was?"

"About an hour, I think."

"You earlier testified that you arrived at the studio about eleven, is that correct?"

"Yes."

"So that would mean that Ms. Virtin arrived to get together with you at about noon, is that right?"

"Close enough."

"And you testified that you left about three fifteen. Is that also correct?"

"Yes."

"So that's a three-hour-and-fifteen-minute"—he used his crooked fingers to put air quotes around the word—"tryst?"

"Yes."

"Did you use more than one Viagra?"

There was laughter. Rory thought of objecting that he was harassing the witness, but decided to let it go.

"No, just one."

"Isn't that a long time for a tryst for a seventy-five-year-old man?"

"Actually, my birthday was just a few days ago, so I was seventy-four."

Hal hadn't actually answered the question, and Rory waited to see if Trucker would follow up and repeat it.

"Mr. Harold, do you want this court to believe that you, a then-seventy-four-year-old man, had sex for over three hours?"

"Well, I didn't, Mr. Trucker. To put your perfervid imaginings aside, there was a lot of talk before, during and after. Senior sex involves less sheet tearing."

There was again laughter in the courtroom. The problem Trucker was having, of course, was that he had assumed Hal would be reluctant to tell him the sexual details. But Rory and Hal had agreed that Hal would go as far into descriptions of intimacy as Trucker wanted to go. And since Sylvie was missing, there was little risk of being contradicted. Rory would have preferred, though, that Hal avoid the fancy word. Jurors might see parading his large vocabulary as snotty and dislike him.

"Did you and Ms. Virtin leave at the same time?" Trucker asked.

"No. She left quite a bit earlier."

"Do you know where she was going when she left?"

"No."

"What did you do after she left?"

"I went to the men's room to clean up and then went back to reading my book for a while."

"Wasn't there a more comfortable place available to read?"

"You don't get it, Mr. Trucker. The affair was secret. So I didn't want to emerge onto the studio lot at the same time as Ms. Virtin, because someone might have seen us there around the same time and put two and two together. By staying there to read, I avoided the risk."

Rory understood that what Trucker was trying to do overall was suggest to the judge that there was plenty of time for Hal to walk over to the EOS and kill Joe. But he thought Hal was doing a pretty good job of defending against that idea without any help.

"You still don't recall what book it was?"

"No."

Rory thought the pursuit of that question was pointless. Even if you assumed Hal was lying about not recalling the name of the book, what difference did it make?

"Are you sure you don't recall?"

Before Hal could answer, Judge Gilmore interrupted and said, "I can't see why the title of the book matters, Mr. Trucker. Can you move on?"

"Of course, Your Honor." He turned back to Hal. "So, Mr. Harold, your testimony is that after Ms. Virtin left, you just lay there and read a book?"

Trucker had tried to put a note of incredulity into the question. How much more credible it would have been, his tone of voice seemed to suggest, for Hal to admit that he next walked over to the EOS and murdered Joe Stanton.

Did Trucker know before Hal's testimony that Sylvie and Joe had been lovers? Apparently not.

"No, actually, I started to read the book," Hal said. "But then I fell asleep for quite a while."

"Mr. Harold, you said this tryst was in a storeroom on the third floor of Building 6, is that correct?"

"Yes."

"Had you used that storeroom for sex before?"

"Yes, but only with Ms. Virtin."

"When did that begin, the sexual relationship with her?"

"Objection, irrelevant," Rory said.

"Overruled."

"Maybe a couple months earlier," Hal said. "We first got together in a hotel at a conference we were both attending about entertainment litigation."

Trucker looked surprised. "Why would Ms. Virtin, who was an assistant and not a lawyer, attend such a conference?"

Hal shrugged. "Joe Stanton sent her, so I don't really know. He never said."

"Was he there, too?"

"Yes."

Rory could tell from Trucker's body language—he stood up straighter after hearing that answer—that he thought he'd finally found a crack he could pull apart.

Trucker stood there for a few seconds, clearly trying to figure out where to go with it.

Trucker's problem was that he probably didn't know as much as Rory did—thanks to Sarah's trip to Virginia—about the Stanton-Sylvie-Clara relationship. If he had, he might have been able to get to the really juicy theory: That Hal killed Joe either at the jilted Sylvie's suggestion or to get rid of a rival. Or both.

Sarah had been sitting quietly beside him, saying nothing and passing no notes, which was unusual for her. But he felt her stiffen slightly as the questioning headed toward Joe's relationship with Sylvie.

Trucker asked his next question. "Did Joe Stanton know that you had shacked up in a hotel room with his assistant?"

Rory didn't himself know the answer to that.

"I don't know," Hal said. "If he did, he never mentioned it to me."

"Do you know if Sylvie told him?"

"I don't."

"Did you ever tell him?"

"No."

"Were you worried that someone would think the relationship was improper?"

"No. She didn't work for me or for my law firm, and she was hardly an inn . . . a child."

"You started to use a word other than 'child,' sir. What was it?"

"No, I just stumbled in my speech, which I do on occasion." He smiled at Trucker. "Old, you know?"

"Who located the storage room as a trysting place?"

"Sylvie did."

"Do you know how she found it?"

"No."

"Do you know if she had ever used it with others?"

"No."

"Was there a key to the room?"

"Yes, and she gave me a copy."

"Do you know how she acquired the key?"

"No."

Rory liked all the "no" answers. Unless a witness could be shown to be lying, the answer "no" was hard to get your fingers into.

"So, Mr. Harold, was this trysting place set up like a hotel room? Bed, dresser and so forth?"

"No, it had an air mattress, sheets and a blanket." He laughed. "Bathroom was down the hall."

"Were there sheets kept there?"

"No, Sylvie brought them each time and took them away with her."

"But weren't the sheets left there so you could read your book while lying on them?"

"Oh sorry, no. There was a chair in the room, too. I sat in the chair to read the book. And I've now remembered what the book was."

"Which was it?"

"*All Quiet on the Western Front.* One of the great novels about World War I. I can lend it to you if you want."

Rory wished Hal had not offered to lend it. It sounded a bit too cheeky for something as serious as a murder case. He'd have to counsel Hal against doing that with a jury present.

"Where did you park your car when you went to Building 6?"

"In front of the building next door. It was Sunday, and there was almost no one there."

"Did you go out at all during the time you were there?"

"Just to go back to my car and drive off the lot."

"Did you see the security video that showed you honking your horn and making crazed arm motions to get the gate up quickly?"

"Yes, but I'd not agree that the motions were crazed. Just urgent."

"And your explanation is that you needed to pee and wanted to get to the gas station down the block?" Trucker's voice dripped with incredulity.

"That's right."

"Why didn't you just use the bathroom in Building 6 before you went to your car?"

"Mr. Trucker, do you really want me to go into the issue of geriatric male urinary issues?"

"What I really want is a true explanation of why you didn't go while in Building 6 and instead made up this peculiar excuse."

Rory thought of objecting, but, once again, passed on it.

"Well, Mr. Trucker, here's the truth. Sometimes, at my age, you don't have to go and then, all of a sudden, minutes later, you do. So when I left the building, I didn't. And as I reached the gate, I did. And the gas station was by that time a lot closer, with no stairs or elevator to overcome."

"Did you actually use the facility at the gas station?"

"Yes."

"So if they have a security video, it would show you pulling in on that day?"

"I have no idea if it would or wouldn't, since I don't know if they have one or where it is or what it photographs. Or how long they keep the footage."

Rory had checked, and the good news was that the station kept the images for only seventy-two hours. He assumed Trucker had learned that, too, so he seemed unlikely to pursue it.

Trucker bent down to look at his notes. As he did so, Rory realized that no one had come into the courtroom to tell him they had located Alex Toltec, who was to be his last and only other witness—if he could be found to be subpoenaed. And if the judge would enforce a subpoena issued on such short notice. He was about to ask the judge for a brief break so he could make the needed calls when she helped him out.

"Mr. Trucker, are you close to being done?" she asked.

"I still have a little ways to go, Your Honor."

"Well, in that case, I need to attend to my own needs." She smiled. "So let's take a ten-minute break. But I mean just ten. Please be back in your seats by then."

Chapter 58

Out in the hall, Rory spent most of the ten-minute break on the phone, trying to find out if the process server had found Alex Toltec to serve a subpoena on him. The answer was no. Sarah just stood there, watching him make the calls, saying nothing.

When he hung up, she said, "Rory, I've got a problem."

"What?"

"An old filling in a tooth came out at breakfast this morning. It took some of the tooth with it, and the part that's left now hurts, big-time." She put her hand to her cheek near the jawline and pressed on it, as if that might make the pain go away.

"No wonder you've been so quiet. Does it hurt a lot?"

"Yes."

"Is there any way you can just suck it up until tomorrow?"

"I don't think so. I might end up having to leave in the middle of things if I go back into court. It's getting worse and worse."

"Alright. Do you have a dentist?"

"No."

"I'll text you right now the name of the office I use. They're in Century City. If you use my name and tell them it's a true emergency, they'll probably see you, and if not they'll recommend someone who will."

"Thanks. As soon as I get that from you, I'm going to Uber out there. I'll try to get back here as soon as I can."

"Check with me first before you come back, because I'm going to try to get this thing delayed if I can. I've also got a PI out looking for Alex. Maybe they'll find him in the next half hour."

"You could have used me for that." She grinned and then winced and stopped grinning because it obviously hurt just to smile.

"Not on your life."

Sarah left, and Rory walked back into the courtroom. Hal was already back on the witness stand. Rory resumed his seat, and the judge and Trucker followed shortly thereafter.

"Let's resume," Judge Gilmore said. "Mr. Harold, I'd remind you that you're still under oath."

"Yes, Your Honor, I understand."

"Mr. Harold, let's talk about the blood on the rug," Trucker said. "You testified that it occurred when you were in Joe Stanton's office. I think you said you were there about a week before the murder, is that correct?"

"Yes. To the best of my recollection."

"Alright, and you said you cut yourself in a way you didn't notice, and you think it dripped on the rug as you left. Is that also correct?"

"Yes."

"Is that a problem you have often?"

"Which problem?"

"Cutting yourself and not noticing."

"I don't know that I'd say often, but it has happened a few times over the past year. My skin gets dry and almost cracked." He pushed up his suit sleeve, unbuttoned his shirt and rolled up his sleeve. "Would you like to look?"

"I don't think that's necessary. At least not right now."

Rory was surprised Trucker hadn't taken up the offer. He would have photographed the arm and taken the photos to an expert dermatologist to evaluate.

"Mr. Harold, have you accidentally cut yourself since the day of the murder?"

"Not that I recall."

"Have you ever consulted a doctor about this problem?"

Hal pursed his lips. "Not specifically. I think at my last physical, which was almost a year ago, my doctor noticed that my skin was dry, but to anticipate your next question, I don't know if he marked it in his chart."

Rory made a mental note to himself to remind Hal not to anticipate questions. He should know it could get you in trouble.

"Did he prescribe anything to help with the problem?"

"No. He just suggested that I could stop swimming every day, since chlorinated pool water dries out your skin."

Rory groaned inwardly. Hal should have just said no.

Rory could see it coming.

"You swim every day?"

"Yes."

"So you have a strong upper body?"

"I suppose."

Rory saw the light blink on in Hal's eyes.

"Strong enough, you suppose, to garrote someone?"

"Objection!" Rory said. "Calls for speculation. Who knows how much strength that takes?" And by saying that, Rory had done something he usually avoided doing—trying to telegraph the answer to his witness via his objection.

"Overruled," the judge said and raised her eyebrows at Rory. Had she punished him for what he did by overruling his objection? Maybe.

Hal tried to recover. "Well, I don't know how much strength that would take, but, in truth, my upper body is quite weak these days. The reason I swim is to try to keep it from going further downhill."

Trucker looked at his notes.

"Mr. Harold, were there any witnesses to this alleged bleeding episode?"

"Yes, Joe Stanton and Peter Stanton."

"And Joe is dead, right?"

"Yes."

"Were you in court when Mr. Peter Stanton testified, saying he didn't witness that bleeding episode?"

"Yes."

"Do you remember specifically that he said—"

Rory was on his feet before the question could be completed. "Objection! The question calls for rank hearsay. If Mr. Trucker wants to explore what Mr. Peter Stanton said or didn't say, he can call him as a witness."

"Unfortunately, Your Honor, Mr. Stanton is out of the country and not expected to return for several weeks."

Judge Gilmore shrugged. "Well, I have no power to order him back here, so that's unfortunate, but it is what it is. The objection is sustained."

Trucker made one heroic try to get what he wanted. "Your Honor, the hearsay rule says you can't admit into evidence something someone supposedly said out of court. And, as you well know, the big reason for that rule is that the person who allegedly said it isn't in court to be cross-examined about it."

"Yes," the judge said. "I think I'm aware of the rule. What's your argument?"

He took a deep breath. "The testimony by Mr. Stanton ought to be admitted because his statement was *in* court, in fact in this very court, and it *was* cross-examined by, in fact, the defendant's own lawyer at the time."

He paused. "I therefore request to read into the record in this proceeding Mr. Stanton's sworn testimony about the fact that he doesn't recall the bleeding incident."

The judge looked at Rory. "Mr. Calburton, what do you have to say to that?"

"I say that the cross-examination in that case was for a very different purpose—to keep Mr. Harold from being sent back to jail because of a visit he made to Mr. Peter Stanton's house. Most of the testimony focused on that. I was in court that day, and I know that Mr. Zavallo was not focused on trying to show that Mr. Peter Stanton was lying about what happened or didn't happen in Mr. Joe Stanton's office that day. So the cross was aimed in another direction entirely."

"I think I'm going to add to my original ruling," the judge said. "And rule that the transcript cannot be admitted in the face of the hearsay objection. Rulings in preliminary hearings are rarely appealed successfully, but I think that should I let that evidence in and decide there is probable cause here that Mr. Harold murdered Mr. Joe Stanton, it will invite an appeal."

Rory started to say something about not deciding the probable cause issue itself until all the evidence was in, but the judge cut him off. "Don't get in a twit, Mr. Calburton, about what I just said. I have absolutely not made up my mind on the issue of probable cause. I have plenty of evidence to permit me to rule one way or the other, but I need to weigh all of it together. All I'm saying is that there's no need to complicate it with this."

Rory took a deep breath—he had won the key issue on Stanton's testimony not coming in—and just said, "Thank you, Your Honor."

"Please give me a moment," Trucker said.

Rory could see Trucker was trying to decide whether to ask Hal anything further. If the judge wouldn't let him use any of Peter Stanton's testimony to cross-examine Hal, Trucker might still gamble on asking Hal point-blank if he had killed Joe. There seemed to Rory nothing whatever to be gained from that for the People, though, because Hal would just deny it flat out.

Apparently Trucker agreed, because he said, "No further questions, Your Honor."

"Any redirect, Mr. Calburton?"

Rory saw nothing he could improve on by asking more questions, and several things he could accidentally damage by trying to improve Hal's answers, so he just said, "No." The stone wall of the direct exam had held up pretty well to Trucker's attempt to tear it down.

"Mr. Harold, you may step down," the judge said. "Do you have any other witnesses to call, Mr. Calburton?"

"Just one, Your Honor, Mr. Alex Toltec. But the process server is having trouble finding him right now."

"Is he evading service of your subpoena?"

"Probably, but I don't know for sure. But he's a key defense witness, and I would beg the court's indulgence in delaying this hearing until late this afternoon so that we may continue our efforts to find and serve him."

"Do you have any objection, Mr. Trucker?"

"No."

"Alright, I'll do you one better, Mr. Calburton. We'll resume on Monday morning. And I'll enforce the subpoena if you find Mr. Toltec, even though there may not be enough notice for him to appear under the local rules. Indeed, this is important enough that I'll issue a bench warrant for him and have the US Marshal go look for him."

"Thank you, Your Honor."

"Well, don't thank me until we find out where he's hiding out. Because if he's not found by Monday morning, we're going to have final argument on Monday morning and close this proceeding. We're adjourned until Monday morning at eight."

Chapter 59

Rory's dentist—a Dr. Tara Behzadi—proved willing to see Sarah on short notice. She took an Uber to the office, took care of a couple of things she'd intended to do but hadn't gotten done, picked up a few items she needed and then walked to Dr. Behzadi's office, which was only a few blocks away on a low floor of a Century City high-rise. It was very contemporary in decor. The waiting area featured chrome and leather chairs and polished marble tables. Best of all, the tables were filled with gossipy magazines like *People*, *Us Weekly* and *Vanity Fair*, plus a sampling of their British counterparts. Sarah didn't subscribe to any of them or even read them online, but she always enjoyed perusing them when she was in a doctor's office. She managed to page through *People* and *Us Weekly* and was just starting on *Vanity Fair* when she was called in to see Dr. Behzadi. She had spotted two items of interest in the magazine and took it with her into the exam room.

As she expected, after poking and prodding and taking an X-ray, Dr. Behzadi told her she'd need a root canal. She treated the tooth to reduce the pain, gave her a prescription for an antibiotic to combat the infection and suggested Sarah see her receptionist for an immediate referral to an endodontist.

When she was done, Sarah said to her, "Can I take this *Vanity Fair* with me? I can return it tomorrow."

"Something in there piques your interest?"

"Oh no. I was just surprised by something I saw in it."

"A celeb who's gotten fat?"

"No, no. Just a picture of, uh, an old friend looking not her best."

"Show me the cover?" Sarah did, and Dr. Behzadi said, "Oh that's quite an old one. No need to bring it back. It was a pleasure to meet you. Do schedule the appointment with the root canal specialist on your way out."

"I think I'd like to do that a bit later, if that's okay. I need to check some things on my calendar and make sure this trial gets over as scheduled."

"Sure, but don't wait too long, Ms. Gold, because if you let the problem fester, the procedure to fix it will be a lot less pleasant."

"The procedure will be pleasant?"

Dr. Behzadi laughed. "Well, not exactly pleasant, I suppose. But if you wait too long, it might turn out be a good deal more *un*pleasant."

"Thanks. I'll be sure to schedule it."

Sarah tossed the magazine into her purse and left as fast as she could without running.

Once outside the building, she dialed Gladys and said, "Gladys, I wonder if I might come down and see you today?"

"When?"

"Right now."

"What about?"

"I just found a picture that I think will nail Alex for killing Joe. But I need to have you look at it and confirm that I'm seeing what I think I'm seeing."

"This isn't a very convenient time. All my help has the day off."

Sarah laughed. "I can fix my own Coke."

"Are you sure it's got to be today?"

"Yes. It's got to be now because I think the judge is close to rul-ing that Hal can be bound over for trial. Once that decision's made, it's going to be hard to roll back. But if we can get this picture into evidence in the afternoon session, maybe we can put an end to the idea that Hal did it."

"Can't we do it on the phone? You could just fax or e-mail me the picture."

"It's on glossy paper, and I'm afraid the detail I need won't come through."

"Alright, fine. But I don't have a lot of time to spend with you."

"That's okay. Thank you, and I'm on my way. See you shortly."

Chapter 60

On her way to Palos Verdes, Sarah called Rory. He picked up immediately. "Hey, are you on a break from the trial?"

"No, I'm back at the office. The judge has given me until Monday morning at eight a.m. to get Alex in here. If we can't produce him by then, the testimony phase of the hearing will be over, and she's going to move directly into closing arguments. And we'll lose. At least I think we will, unless I can get Alex in here and get him—somehow—to incriminate himself."

"I hope we can find him," Sarah said.

"The PI thinks he knows where he is, and the judge agreed to issue the subpoena on an emergency basis and make it so he has to come in in the morning if we can find him. Or even have the US marshal go look for him."

"I see."

"How did your session with the dentist go? Are you still there?"

"No, I'm finished. She reduced my pain a lot. But I have to have a root canal when this trial is over."

"Ugh."

"Yes, exactly. I may have to wait until the civil trial hearing is over, too, I guess. Almost forgot about that."

"Well, I'm hoping we can settle that. I think Otto is making progress. But one way or another, we'll find a way to get your tooth treated promptly. Anyway, where are you, Sarah? Are you on your way back to the office?"

"No. To be *truthful*, I'm in an Uber, on my way to see Gladys again."

"What? Why?"

"I think I've found something that will get Hal out of jail."

"What?"

"It's too complicated right now. When I see you—I should be back in just a couple of hours—you can tell me about the settlement progress, and I can tell you about the get-out-of-jail-free card."

"Well, I think you should tell the Uber driver to turn around and come right back because—"

Sarah terminated the call without waiting for Rory to finish his thought just as the car pulled up in front of Gladys's house. Her cell rang, immediately, but it wasn't Rory. She took the call and asked the caller to hold for a moment.

"Do you mind," she said to the driver, "if I sit here for a few moments and take this phone call?"

"No, that's fine, lady."

When she'd finished with the call, she set her phone to record, thanked the driver (after giving him a large tip), got out of the car, and walked up to the front door. She pushed the bell button, but no one came. After a few moments, she pushed it again, and still no one came. Finally, she rapped hard on it, and, after another long wait, Gladys finally opened it.

"Well," she said. "If it isn't the fairy princess of The Harold Firm."

"It's nice to see you, too, Gladys. Are you going to invite me in?"

"Of course. It's still warm enough to sit in the courtyard. Please follow me back." And then she said, over her shoulder, "If I hadn't known you were coming, I'd never have known you were here. The doorbell's broken. Got to get it fixed."

They reached the courtyard, and Gladys pointed to one of the low chairs. "Take a seat." Then she sat down herself on her high wicker throne.

Sarah glanced at the table in front of her chair and saw that a tall, frosted Tom Collins glass had already been set out on it. "Gladys, I don't drink, remember?"

"Oh, I remember. That glass is filled with Coke, not gin. With the maid gone, I just couldn't find the glasses for soft drinks. Hope you don't mind."

"Not at all," Sarah said, and took a sip. It was indeed Coke. "It's cold. Thanks."

"Well, I'm glad you like it that way, dear." She giggled. "I'll just continue drinking my good old Tom Collins." She pointed at the identical glass sitting on her own table.

"Gladys, I want to talk to you about a picture in *Vanity Fair* from a few months ago," Sarah said. She took the magazine out of her purse and started to open it to a premarked page.

"A picture of whom?" Gladys asked.

"Of Alex."

"Ah, I see. Why?"

"I think it may help prove him guilty."

"I'm very anxious to see that, obviously," Gladys said. "But I'm afraid I have to ask you to wait to show it to me. I have a call scheduled with my accountant in just a couple of minutes."

"I can wait."

"Okay. I'm going to take it in another room and then come back. Sorry about the bad timing. On the other hand, you did come without an appointment, dear." She raised her eyebrows and smiled a crooked smile that Sarah read as adding, "you impudent piece of snot."

"How long do you think you'll be?"

"I hope no longer than half an hour. If you need something to read, please feel free to take a book." She pointed to a bookshelf across the room.

"Thanks, perhaps I will."

Gladys got up and disappeared through the small door behind the throne.

Sarah went to examine the books in the bookcase. She looked to see if there were any telltale signs of missing dust in front of a book, but saw none. Finally, after rejecting the idea of going to inspect the rest of the house—what she intended to accomplish with Gladys was too important to risk screwing it up by snooping—she pulled a book of Keats's poetry off the shelf and went back to the low chair to read. Keats was one of her favorites, and she was soon lost in it. While she read, she made it a point to empty her glass of Coke.

When Gladys reappeared, she was carrying a large purse slung over her shoulder. She reseated herself and said, "I'm so sorry. I didn't realize that would take forty-five minutes. My deepest apologies. On the other hand . . ."

Sarah finished the thought for her. "I came without an appointment."

"Exactly. So, what picture do you want to show me that you think will nail Alex? As if the record of his extortion payments to Joe weren't enough."

Sarah pulled the *Vanity Fair* out of her purse and opened it to the page she had marked, which was part of the magazine's Oscar coverage, featuring hundreds of tiny pictures of celebs and their friends attending after-parties. She placed it on a table in front of Gladys and said, "Please take a look at this."

"I'm looking at it, Sarah. And I've been to lots of Oscar parties, so I know what it is. What in particular do you want me to look at?"

Sarah pointed to a picture in the upper-right corner of the right-hand page. "Do you see this picture of Alex Toltec?" she asked.

"Yes, what about it?"

"If you look closely, you can see he's chatting with a woman—she's identified in the caption as Marilee McCandless. I guess she's an actress. But right behind them, looking over his shoulder, is an unidentified big guy. Do you see him?"

"Yes, but I don't know him."

"I believe that's Mitch Crunk."

"Who is he?" Gladys asked.

"Well, rumor has it he's a hit man." Sarah tried to keep a neutral face as she said it, because, in truth, she had no idea who the guy was.

"I'm sure I don't know him," Gladys said.

"Well, okay, I guess I've struck out, then. I figured since you know Alex, you might know some of his friends, too, and might be able to confirm that that is in fact Mr. Crunk."

"You think I know a hit man?"

"Apparently not, but from some other evidence I've gathered, I think Alex may have hired Crunk to kill Joe."

Gladys raised her eyebrows. "Really?"

"Yes, really. But I can't go into court and suggest that unless I'm sure that's Crunk, and so far I can't find anyone to confirm the identity of the man in the photo. You were my last hope."

"Sorry to disappoint."

"Hey," Sarah said, "before I go, could I trouble you for another Coke? Just the can will be okay."

"Certainly. I'll be right back with it." Gladys disappeared again through the small door.

While she was gone, Sarah reached out, picked up Gladys's glass by the bottom edge and drank down the very small amount that was left in it. It was the first alcohol she'd ever drunk, and it burned as it went down. She then swapped her glass for Gladys's, put hers down on

Gladys's table and put Gladys's glass down on her own table. She realized her hands were shaking.

Gladys came back into the room and handed her a Coke can.

"Wow, that *is* icy cold. I think I'll just drink it from the can. Reminds me of my law school days."

"You can just take it with you as you depart," Gladys said. "I've got work to do."

It was now or never, Sarah thought, and prayed her hands wouldn't continue shaking.

She picked up the glass from her table—her hand remained steady—and said, "Gladys, this might sound odd, but do you mind if I take this with me? I promise to return it to you. I really love these old, 1950s-style cocktail glasses—I'm a bit of a collector—and I want to see if I can find an exact match. Do you recall where you got them?"

Gladys stared intently at the glass. "You swapped our glasses," she said.

"No, I didn't."

Gladys narrowed her eyes, paused a moment, and said, "Of course you did."

"Why would I do that?"

"I don't know why. But the glass I was using had a very small chip out of the thick bottom, on the side. That glass is now on your table. So you for sure switched them."

"I didn't switch them, but if you'd rather I took the other one, I certainly can," Sarah said.

Gladys's face lit up as it hit her. "You bitch. You're trying to grab that glass so you can get my DNA off of it."

"That's crazy. Why would I want your DNA?"

"You think I killed Joe, and you're planning to try to match it to the third blood spot in his office. Or maybe the skin oils on the receipt. I read about all of that in the *LA Times*."

"Why would I think that?"

Gladys reached out and raked through the pages in the *Vanity Fair*, still open on the table, until she came to the other picture Sarah had found: a shot of Joe and Sylvie posing with an actor who was holding her Oscar statuette. Gladys stabbed at it. "This is the real reason you came. You saw that picture, and you remembered my unfortunate, loose-lipped comment to you that Joe could take anyone he wanted to the Emmys, but only I got to go to the Academy Awards."

As Gladys spoke, Sarah cursed herself for employing that particular *Vanity Fair* as a ruse to meet with Gladys. The instant she'd seen the cover, of course Gladys must have recognized it.

"I do recall your saying that, but so what?" Sarah said.

"Well, your little brain probably put it together that I was angry at Joe for having broken his promise, and that I killed him to get even."

Sarah decided to take a stab at it. "Did you?"

She smiled a half smile. "Of course not. I paid someone else to do it. Just like I paid the same someone else to off the twin sluts. Although I wish the guy had used a different method on them. It looks suspicious that he garroted both Joe and them." She laughed. "Apparently it's part of his brand."

They are both dead? Sarah was shocked to her core. But she managed to hide it and keep the focus on what she had come for. "You killed him just for taking Sylvie to the Oscars?"

"No, it was simply the last straw. I allowed him his rut, but when he did both of them and began not coming home for weeks at a time, it was too much. I began to feel like a widow. Then came the Oscars, and I concluded it was best to be one."

"You've just admitted your guilt to me."

"And I assume you're recording this conversation and transmitting it."

"Yes, I am."

"Well, dear, you may well have recorded it, but nothing has transmitted, because this patio has zero bars of cell service right now."

"It had four bars a few minutes ago. I checked."

"That's because I have a repeater that enhances the signal. I turned it off right after I left the patio. Go ahead and look."

Sarah took her cell phone out of her purse and looked. She was right. It showed no bars. She put it back in her purse.

"Alright," Sarah said. "So it hasn't transmitted, but I still have the recording, I'm sure, and you were dumb enough to admit what you did." She started to get up.

Gladys reached into her purse and came up with a large black handgun. She pointed it at Sarah. "I am not stupid. Sit back down."

"If you kill me, you'll never get the blood out of here. And you'll get caught for my murder, at least, if not Joe's."

"I don't plan to kill you right here unless I have to. I was gone for forty-five minutes just now, arranging some things. And not with my accountant. My man will be here shortly, and he'll decide what to do with you. And if I have to shoot you before he gets here, well, so be it. He'll get a good cleanup crew in here, I'm sure."

When Sarah had stopped briefly by the office on her way to the dentist's office, she had picked up her pistol and put it in her purse. Just to be safe. But as soon as she reached for her purse, Gladys would shoot her.

"Sarah, take your cell phone back out of your purse and give it to me."

Sarah couldn't believe her luck. Apparently, Gladys hadn't considered that she might have her own handgun. Every once in a while, the assumption that beautiful blondes were stupid and helpless proved a blessing.

She'd get only one shot, though, and it would have to hit Gladys's gun or the arm or hand holding it.

"I said give me the phone."

"Sure," Sarah said. And as she said it, she reached into her purse, grabbed the gun and released the safety. She swung it up, aimed, fired and missed. The slug went harmlessly into a wall to Gladys's right. In the twinkling of an eye, Gladys leaped from her chair, raised her right leg and kicked the gun out of Sarah's hand. It skittered across the floor and came to a stop on the other side of the room.

"You're not such a good shot, Sarah." She smiled the half smile again. "I wish my kickboxing instructor could have seen that. He might stop saying I'm getting too old and slow to do it."

"What now?" Sarah asked.

"I'd really enjoy killing you, you know. But it would make such a mess. I think I'll wait for my man and just hold this gun on you while we wait. But don't move, because I will shoot you. And enjoy it."

"We could bargain," Sarah said.

"You don't have much to bargain with, I don't think."

"We could bargain about risk. Because if I go missing, people are going to look for me. And I took an Uber here. So the records will trace me here, and you'll be questioned. And Rory knows I came here. And who knows, maybe you could get arrested."

"So?"

"They would swab your DNA, and then they'd have something to compare against for the DNA in the skin oils on that receipt. Or did you have your man go get the rope?"

"No, he wouldn't buy it himself. I had to do it, but I got enough for the girls in Virginia, too, so I only had to go to Riverside once."

"So if you let me go, I can give you my phone, and you can erase the tape. And I give you my word I won't rat you out. I will swear on it, and oaths sworn to God are serious to me."

"You must be kidding."

As she thought about what to say next, Sarah saw Rory emerge from the small door behind the wicker throne. By force of will, she went on talking to Gladys and hoped her face didn't betray her.

"I'm not kidding. There's much less risk in taking my proposal than in killing me. I'm a former Supreme Court law clerk. My disappearance is going to be investigated for weeks. You can't possibly escape scrutiny."

Rory, she realized, had a logistical problem. The wicker throne was high enough that he couldn't easily reach Gladys and her gun over the top, and if he came around the side of the chair, even if he was fast, there was still a risk he'd end up with a bullet in him from the big black gun.

"They can scrutinize me all they want, because—"

Which were the last words she spoke as Rory bent low at the knees, gripped the top of the chair back with one hand and the seat bottom with the other, lifted the whole thing off the ground and whipped it sideways in a single motion. Gladys was tossed out of the chair like she'd been flung from the head of a lacrosse stick. Sarah heard Gladys's head crack as it hit the wall and watched her fall to the ground, limp.

"Grab the guns," Sarah yelled. "I'll call 911 on the house phone."

As they sat and waited for the ambulance and the police, with Sarah's gun trained on the unmoving form of Gladys, Sarah asked, "Why the hell did you come out here?"

"Truth is, I mainly came out to vent my fury after you hung up on me and once again went off on an unauthorized adventure. I was planning to drive you back to the office and give your letter of resignation to Hwa Fung, the managing partner."

"And when you got here?"

"I rang the bell, but it apparently doesn't work, and nobody seemed to hear my knock. So I walked around to the side of the house and still couldn't rouse anybody. I thought you might be in trouble, and I let myself in the kitchen door, which was unlocked. And, well, I overheard what was going on, and you saw what happened after that."

* * *

Minutes later, the ambulance and the police arrived. They watched as the EMTs worked on Gladys, put a cervical collar on her, loaded her onto a gurney and slid her into the back of the ambulance.

"Will she survive?" Rory asked one of the EMTs as she was closing the back door of the ambulance.

"You never know about these head injuries," she said. "We'll see."

After that, a police detective from the Palos Verdes police force, Detective Gloria Rivas, interviewed each of them, separately, for almost an hour. She took Rory's statement first, then Sarah's, using the kitchen as an interview room. She recorded both of their interviews.

When Sarah finished, she found Rory waiting for her outside. "Hey, thanks for waiting around for me. I thought maybe I was such a bad girl again that you'd have left for the office without me."

"No, I decided to wait for you. Get in, and we'll drive back together."

Once they were underway, Sarah said, "Thank you for rescuing me. I take back what I said about football players lacking grace."

"You're welcome, although it wasn't so much grace as brute strength. I was a linebacker, you know."

"Hey, good news. The cops separated us so quickly I didn't have time to tell you. I've got a recording on my cell phone that will set Hal free. I don't know if you heard the whole thing, but Gladys confessed and admitted that she had the twins killed, too."

"I only heard part of what she said, so that's great, and I'm sure Hal will appreciate it. But candidly—and I know that this is a hell of an awkward time to say it, because you're probably still in shock, like me—I just don't think you've got much of a future at our firm."

"Why not?"

He looked over at her. "Because you can't stop yourself from doing this shit."

"I think maybe I can. Like if I ride the X2 enough."

"I don't think the coasters are gonna do it, Sarah."

She sighed. "So what, then?"

"We go back to the office, you debrief me on all that went on here at Gladys's, and then I give your resignation letter to Hwa Fung. I assume you're an honorable person and you'll keep our deal and resign. But you'll have a month before you actually have to leave."

"But I have an appeal pending with you, Rory."

Rory paused for a few seconds. "Oh right. Well, I forgot to tell you, your appeal was denied. You still have to go, and I'm still sending in your resignation letter."

"Maybe you won't need to send it."

"What do you mean?"

She shrugged. "Nothing. It was just nervous chatter on my part."

Rory's cell phone rang through his car's Bluetooth, and he pushed the "Speaker" button.

"Hey, it's Otto."

"Hi," Rory said. "I've got the speaker on. Sarah's here, too. We've had quite an adventure today, which we'll tell you about later. But what's going on?"

"I've been negotiating with Kathryn Thistle for hours, both in person and on the phone. We've gone through several rounds of demand and offer. They've put a demand on the table now that I think the studio should take."

"Hit me with it."

"Okay. Mary Broom gets three hundred thousand dollars in cash."

"That's good. Within my authority and lower than I expected. Good work."

"Mary gets half of whatever Alex got for writing the script and directing the movie. If she can get Alex to pay her that himself, great. But if not, the studio will pay her."

Rory paused, thinking about it. "Okay," he said, "I can probably sell that to the studio, so long as Alex agrees to pay, and given his confession, I don't see how he can say no. If the studio has to pay her, that's a much harder sell."

"There's more."

Rory sighed. "Go ahead."

"Mary gets half of what Alex was going to get on the back end—percentage of first-dollar ticket sales and all of that complicated stuff. The details to be worked out after they see Alex's original deal. Again, if Alex will agree to split his share, the studio doesn't have to pay."

"Hmm," Rory said. "This is getting more and more expensive for our client, potentially, but go on."

Sarah chimed in. "What about writing credit?"

"She gets credit as cowriter," Otto said. "All existing prints of the film to be changed to reflect that before release."

"That might have to come a little later," Rory said. "I don't know how long it would take, technically, to make that change."

Otto didn't say anything for a while.

"You still there, Otto?" Rory asked.

"Yes. You probably won't like this part much."

"I already don't like some of the earlier parts. What is it?"

"The studio finances a movie for Mary—"

Rory cut him off and growled, "We're not doing that."

"Hear me out, please. It's better than you think."

"Okay. Tell me. I'm listening."

"The studio puts up five million dollars for the film—that's down from their starting demand of twenty million. So it will be a small movie. But if Mary can raise more from other sources—which she probably can—then the budget will be higher. But the good news is the studio doesn't have to distribute the film or market it."

Rory thought about it for a moment. "Well," he said, "if she writes the film and directs it, which is what she wanted last time around, I suppose that's five million down the drain. But maybe the studio will go for it. It'll be a tax write-off for them and better than spending endless money on the litigation."

"Maybe it's not down the drain, Rory. The deal is that *Alex* will direct and Mary will act in it for scale and, of course, a share of the profits, if any. Details to be worked out. Nothing was said about who will write it."

Rory didn't respond.

"Rory?"

"Yeah?"

"What do you think?"

"I think I first need to tell you what you don't know yet." And he proceeded to fill Otto in on what Alex had told him about who supposedly really wrote the script.

After Rory was done talking, there was a long silence on the other end of the line. Finally, Otto said, "So you lied to me."

"Well, it's more like I just didn't tell you everything. For your own good, of course."

"You realize, Rory, that I will probably never trust you again."

"Maybe someday you will. But it was information I felt I had to keep from you. Anyway, do you think Kathryn and Mary knew Alex's version of the story while you were negotiating with them?"

"They didn't say anything, but thinking about it, now that you've told me the truth, I'd guess they did. Otherwise, they wouldn't have been so confident Alex would give Mary half of his share or agree to direct for, by their telling, not much in the way of a fee or a share."

Rory waited a moment, then said, "Well, whatever, I can probably sell it to the studio. Much as I hate to do that, because I'll have to tell the studio about Alex's lies. And no matter how I spin it, I'll look bad, too. But I suppose I'll survive."

"Kathryn wants an answer by tomorrow morning at nine."

"I'll see what I can do, although it might take longer. These deadlines are never real, by the way. Thanks for your hard, good work on this, Otto."

"You're welcome. I think."

Rory terminated the call.

"Now what?" Sarah asked.

He shrugged. "Now I eat crow with the client."

"But it's not your fault."

"It's always your fault if you lose. That's just the way it works. What do *you* think I should do?"

"Settle it. Alex's lies give you no choice."

"You're probably right."

"See. I give good advice. You should keep me around."

"No. It's over, Sarah."

"You know, my lying to you was no different than your lying to Otto."

"It's different. I didn't put the firm at risk. So, like I said, it's over."

Chapter 61

By the time Rory got back to the firm's office building, the adrenaline from the day's events had totally drained away, and he wondered if he'd be able even to make it to his office without collapsing. After he took care of a couple of things, he'd go home and crash. But before he did that, he was going to submit Sarah's resignation letter. On that, there was no going back.

When Rory walked into his office, he found Hwa Fung sitting behind his desk. Hwa made no move to relinquish the chair. As usual, he was impeccably dressed in a blue pin-striped suit, crisp white shirt and a red patterned tie. Hwa waved him to one of the guest chairs.

"Hwa, isn't this my office? Why are you sitting in my desk chair?"

"Yes, it is your office. Please sit down, and I'll explain."

"I'm kind of tired. Won't this wait?"

"No. Please take a seat."

Rory flopped into one of the guest chairs. "Is this about my having to settle the copyright case because Alex Toltec lied to me?"

Hwa gave him a quizzical look. "I don't know about that. What I do know about is this." He held up a single sheet of paper.

"What's that?"

"It's Sarah Gold's letter of resignation, which she sent to me by e-mail earlier today."

"She resigned?"

"Yes, she did. And I am very upset about it. We moved heaven and earth to get her."

Rory put his head in his hands. "This must be a bad dream. Can I wake up and come back later?"

"Well, good dream or bad, we need to undo this, Rory."

Rory stood up. "Wait. Do you know the whole story?"

"I think so. I called her after I got this—caught her in a car on the way somewhere—and got the entire story."

"Alright, what story did she tell you?"

"That she'd undertaken some initiatives of which you didn't approve."

"Initiatives?"

"That's the word she used, and given the details she described, I think it fits."

Rory took a deep breath. "Did she tell you about breaking into a house and searching it?"

"She did, and I'd agree that's the one thing that was inappropriate and could have put the firm at risk. And she's remorseful about it."

"Hwa, it may be true that the other things she did weren't illegal, but one of them—what she calls spoofing someone—is at least on the edge of unethical. And another one—talking to a potential witness in a case—may be ethically okay, but it wasn't cleared with me, and it's hard to run a case if associates can go off and do whatever they want whenever they want."

Rory started to look for the basketball, with a mind to heave it against the wall, but then remembered he'd taken it away.

"Are you looking for something?"

"No. Just walking around because I'm so pissed off about this whole thing."

"Sarah recognizes the problems of being a runaway associate. And says she will not do it again."

"She's said that before."

"She's even going to turn in her PI license."

"What about the gun?"

"What gun?"

"Ha! She didn't tell you about that, huh? She has a concealed-carry permit."

Hwa paused, clearly thinking about it. "Well, I don't think we have a firm policy about bringing a gun in here. But if it's lawful, and we have no policy, then until we have one, I guess it's fine."

Rory rolled his eyes. "God."

"God what?"

"God, this is ridiculous."

"Well, Rory, the bottom line is that I have persuaded her to stay, but she'll only stay if you agree to it."

"I see." Rory paused. "And if I don't?"

"I will be unhappy with you. And I plan to run this place for many years, so it will be a long and likely shared unhappiness."

"Did she tell you about her illness?"

"The ICD? Yes. Our HR department is looking into whether some intensive group therapy for that can be covered under our health plan. It looks good for that."

Rory sighed. "But it is entirely up to me as to whether she stays or goes?"

"Yes, but I'd appreciate it if you would do me the courtesy of meeting with her before you decide."

"Alright, but before I do that, I need to understand why you want to keep her."

"Certainly. One, we are understaffed. You, for example, need two associates to assist you with a heavy caseload. One is in Africa for the next several months. If Sarah goes, you won't have any assistance."

"What's reason number two?"

"Two, we issued a press release about acquiring her. She was among the most sought-after associates nationwide. If she goes, some story that makes us look bad, whether true or not, will end up in *American Lawyer* and that popular lawyer-gossip website."

"Above the Law."

"Yes, that one. And those stories will make it more difficult for us to attract new high-caliber associates in the future."

Rory looked at him. "Is there a third reason?"

"Yes. We think you are the best young litigator in this firm. And we think you and Sarah, with your different talents, will make a great duo. Who will win many cases and bring us more great clients. That's why we paired you."

"Why not pair her with someone else? There are lots of other great litigating partners in the firm."

"We always pair partners with new associates for a minimum of two years. We've never broken the pair, and we're not about to do so now."

"I see." Although he really didn't and began to think about how to get her paired with someone else. He couldn't immediately think of who else would want her.

"Please have your meeting with Sarah soon and let me know what you want to do."

"I will need a little time before I set up that meeting," Rory said. "A few days to think on this."

Hwa nodded. "I understand. And one other thing. Please keep the firm's interests in mind as you go about making your decision. I know you can do that, just as you did when you decided to stop seeing that reporter."

"Dana."

"Yes."

Rory thought of telling him that the executive committee's pressure on that issue had had nothing to do with it, but decided to skip it. "May I have my chair back now?"

"Of course." Hwa got up, came around the front of the desk and gestured at the just-vacated chair. "There it is."

"Thanks."

"You know, Rory, desk chairs are highly overvalued. They give you a false, and not very useful, sense of power over those who come to see you."

"Do you have a suggestion for a different arrangement?"

"There are many cultural traditions you could tap into. Perhaps Sarah will have ideas."

Chapter 62

FIVE DAYS LATER—LATE AFTERNOON
CENTURY CITY
OFFICES OF THE HAROLD FIRM

Sarah walked into Rory's office, still beautiful, but dressed down in blue jeans just this side of ratty and an old green sweatshirt.

"Slumming today?" Rory asked from behind his desk.

"You didn't hear, Mr. Calburton? It's a casual day, declared by Mr. Harold in celebration of the murder case against him being dismissed. And there are cookies and champagne on every floor."

"I did hear," he said, loosening his tie. "I just forgot. But I didn't know about the cookies and champagne."

"How about the private event he's sponsoring at the House of Blues tonight? Are you going?"

"No, I don't think so."

She shrugged.

"What do you hear about Gladys and all that?" Rory asked. "I haven't read the papers or listened to the news in almost a week. And I expected the cops or the DA to call me, but they haven't."

"I heard that Gladys is expected to survive and make a full recovery. The DA is going to charge her with murder one, three counts, and maybe ask for the death penalty, although there's some question about whether she can be tried here for murders in another state, even if she plotted them here."

"Who's representing her?"

Sarah smiled a broad smile. "Quentin Zavallo."

Rory thought about it for a moment. "Oh, so maybe that was his conflict. Gladys could've hired him to talk about a legal problem and then blurted out that she killed Joe."

"Would that actually create a conflict for him?"

Rory shrugged. "I'm not an expert on legal ethics, but I suppose it could. Or at least make him uncomfortable with continuing to represent Hal."

After that exchange, Sarah stood there for a moment, saying nothing, while Rory sat—despite Hwa's comment—behind his desk, also awkwardly quiet. Finally, Sarah sat down in one of the guest chairs, peered up at him and said, "You look glum, Rory."

"I've been thinking about things."

Her eyes sparkled. "Riding the X2 while you thought?"

"No, I went to Taos and spent three nights in an Indian sweat lodge, trying to find myself."

"Seriously?"

He laughed. "No, I've had it with sweating, after all of those years playing football. I was right here in LA, thinking."

"So you were thinking about . . . what?"

"You know very well what. Whether you stay or go."

"I know." She paused. "I do want to stay, if that makes any difference."

"It does, some. And it's about me, too, of course. Because if I decide you should go, I'm planning to go, too. We'll both land on our feet somewhere else, no doubt. But our 'pairing,' as Hwa Fung calls it, will be over."

Sarah bit her lower lip, looked at him and said, "Rory, I want you to know that I'm very sorry for the things I did that caused you discomfort."

Rory narrowed his eyes. "That sounds a little like what people in the dependency recovery community call making amends. Are you telling me you're an alcoholic or a drug addict?"

Sarah laughed. "No! Not at all. Whatever gave you that idea?"

"From talking to my cop friend, Lester."

"Who said what?"

"He said some cops and some people in the military, too, get off on the thrill of doing dangerous things. It's a small percentage, but among that group, psychologists sometimes refer to them—or they refer to themselves—as non-using addicts."

She looked puzzled. "Non-using?"

"Meaning that addicts and these folks share an addiction to risk-taking thrills. Except that these people don't actually drink or take drugs. Or at least they don't right now."

"'Right now' meaning you think I used to drink or do drugs?"

Rory smiled. "During—"

"—the two-year gap."

"Yep."

"Well, that's nonsense. I told you the truth about that gig at the Bird. Plus I don't drink or do drugs, and I never have."

"Okay, okay."

Rory stared at her for a few moments—she was right that anger, or at least great emotion, made that easier—until the silence drove Sarah to speak. "So what are you going to do?"

"I'm inclined to let you stay and see if we can become the great legal pair that Hwa seems to think we'll be."

She smiled. "Did you ever read that old comic strip *Pogo*?"

"Never even heard of it."

"Well, Pogo used to say, 'The future lies ahead.'"

Rory laughed. "So true."

"But you said you were *inclined* to let me stay. Inclined must mean you've not fully decided. What's holding you back?"

"Well, my first idea was to impose some conditions on you. But I don't think that's gonna work. So I want to know what conditions you're gonna impose on yourself, Ms. Gold."

"Oh. Well, I guess that makes sense."

"So?"

"Well, here's what I'm going to do. I've joined an ICD group, and I'm going to go at least once a week."

He raised his eyebrows. "Even though that may not be your true diagnosis."

"I think it is, but if you can find me a group for non-using addicts, maybe I'll go to that, too."

Rory pursed his lips, considering. "What else do you have in mind?"

"That we meet once a week and go over our ideas for the cases we're working on. And I will tell you all of my ideas, crazy and otherwise."

"And?"

"And you agree to give them serious consideration, but if you say no, I will not do them."

"Which will be the hard part for you."

"Yes, but if my ideas get seriously discussed and . . . I'm searching for the right word . . . *respected*, I think is right, then I think I can decide not to do them."

"That makes sense."

"But, Rory, I hope some of my ideas that may seem crazy to you at first will turn out to be things you can embrace."

He closed his eyes, lowered his head and was quiet for a moment. Finally, he looked up and said, "Okay, Sarah, it's a deal."

She jumped up and clapped her hands. "Thank you! And now, Mr. Calburton, in celebration, I think you should take me out for a drink."

"This will be one of those drinking sessions you proposed where I drink and you don't?"

"Precisely."

"Where do you have in mind?"

"Ever been to a Mexican bar and restaurant in the Valley called Casa Vega?"

"No."

"I propose we go there. It opened in 1956. You'll like it, I think."

He paused. "Uh, why do you think I'll like it there?"

She grinned. "Because it's very dark inside, so you won't be able to see me all that well, and you'll have an easier time looking directly at me."

Rory sighed. "That's not fair, but we can talk about that issue, I suppose. Shall we take my car, then?"

"No, let's take mine."

"You bought a car? Great. What kind?"

"A Lamborghini."

Rory whistled. "Wow. Where'd you get the bread for that?"

"From the bonus Mr. Harold gave me for nailing Gladys and getting him out of jail."

ACKNOWLEDGMENTS

I want to thank my former editor, Kjersti Egerdahl, for encouraging me to start a new series that goes beyond the adventures of Robert Tarza and Jenna James in *Death on a High Floor* and its sequels and then so effectively seeing it through the key part of the edit process. And I owe a big thank-you to my agent, Erica Silverman, for guiding me through the process of bringing *Write to Die*, the first book of the new series, to fruition. And my thanks also to my new editor, Jacque BenZekry, for seeing the book through to completion with brio and enthusiasm. And my thanks as well to the rest of the talented editorial group at Thomas & Mercer, including most especially Gracie Doyle and Sarah Shaw. I must also mention and thank Alan Turkus, who "green-lighted" the book, and the production crew, including most especially the project manager, Jessica Tribble. Although the production crew often works in relative obscurity, I know how much talent and hard work it takes to change a completed manuscript into an easy-to-read Kindle book, a great-looking and feeling print book and a wonderful "listen to" Audible book.

Of course, when you hand in a manuscript, it awaits many kind and competent hands to help transform it from what is always a somewhat raw form (despite how much the author thinks it's done!) to a finished product. For the transformation of this manuscript, I owe a huge debt of gratitude to my developmental editor, David Downing, who did a superb job of encouraging me to rework certain plot points, deepen the characters and their relationships and eliminate the unnecessary. I also owe many thanks to my copy editor, Dara Kaye, who did such a great job on my last novel, *Paris Ransom*, and also copyedited this new one to terrific effect. She has once again done a yeoperson's work in improving and smoothing the prose, finding and correcting errors and inconsistencies both small and large, suggesting small but important changes and also dealing authoritatively with the thing that drives many authors (including me) somewhat crazy—complying with the ever-evolving dictates of the style manuals. And my thanks as well to Katherine Richards, my excellent proofreader, for finding not only the inevitable typos, dropped quotes and missing (or overabundant) punctuation but also for spotting several outright mistakes that no one else (especially not me!) had called out. Any errors that may remain are, of course, my own.

In this, my fourth novel, I have come once again to understand what a gift it is to have friends and colleagues willing to read early drafts and provide comments and critiques, as well as to be able to call on experts for their advice—while any errors, of course, are very much my own.

Those generous people include Roger Toll, Marty Beech, Stan Goldman, Maxine Nunes, Roger Chittum, Nadine Eisenkolb, Brinton Rowdybush, Michael and Genie Haines, Nona Dhawan, Joel Davison, Mary Lane Leslie, Melanie and Doug Chancellor, Wendy Joseph, Dale Franklin and Barbara Wong, Ray Fisher, Mindie Sun, Deanna Wilcox, Tom and Juanita Ringer, Prucia Buscell, Bob and Carolyn Denham,

Sam and Mi Ahn, Daniel Wershow, Diana Wright, Bob Stock, Harold (Hal) Kwalwasser, Amy Huggins, Drew Pinsky, Dana Barbeau, Jessica Kaye, Hwa Kho, Linda and John Brown, Marielena Frances and Ruben Benitez, Lori and Tom Stromberg, Roger Rosen, Joyce Mendlin, Wendy Perkins and my son, Joe Rosenberg, whose comments on the arc and pacing of the story proved, as always, extremely helpful. As did those of my wife, Sally Anne, who read and commented on every draft chapter as it emerged from the "typewriter." And although I sometimes grumbled at her suggestions, they almost always proved right.

ABOUT THE AUTHOR

Charles Rosenberg, a practicing lawyer, has put his legal background to acclaimed use in his bestselling legal thrillers, *Death on a High Floor* and *Long Knives*. He is also the author of *Paris Ransom*, a heist mystery set in the French court system. He has also been asked to consult on scripts for the television shows *Boston Legal, L.A. Law, The Practice* and *The Paper Chase*. During the O.J. Simpson criminal and civil trials, he was one of two on-air analysts for E! Entertainment Television's live coverage of the trials. A graduate of Antioch College and Harvard Law School, Rosenberg has had a long career as a partner in several large law firms and as an adjunct law professor. He is currently a partner in a small firm in the Los Angeles area, where he lives with his wife.